Praise for Haywood Smith

"Praise for the sharp-eyed portrait of a Southern suburb in a turbulent political era . . . is both touching and fresh. Smith . . . jumps the Mason-Dixon line with an achingly real portrait of a middle-aged single mom who longs for a bridge from the family she never had to the one disappearing before her very eyes. It's easy to root for these Dixie belles."

—*Publishers Weekly* on *Wife-in-Law*

"A rousing paean to newly empowered middle-aged women everywhere, Smith's zesty read-in-one-sitting romp promises to delight loyal fans and gain new ones."

—*Booklist* on *Waking Up in Dixie*

"Smith engagingly reconstructs the rise and fall of Betsy and Kat's friendship as it weathers nearly all of life's toughest storms. Smith . . . once again proves herself a devoted champion of middle-aged women who confront and overcome devastating domestic situations."

—*Booklist* on *Wife-in-Law*

"As usual, Smith deftly evokes strong women becoming stronger as they face heartbreak and loss."

—*Richmond Times-Dispatch* on *Wife-in-Law*

"[S]mith gives readers a lovely comedy with poise."

—*Publishers Weekly* on *Ladies of the Lake*

"Smith shakes up the midlife marriage renewal subgenre with [an] emotionally complex tale."

—*Publishers Weekly on Waking Up in Dixie*

"Smith's fizzy exploration of enduring friendship and family signals more changes ahead for Georgia, her family, and the red hat matrons. Fans of the series will enjoy and look forward to the next."

—*Publishers Weekly on Wedding Belles*

"This is a wonderful story filled with love, laughter, and a family . . . this book is a winner."

—*Night Owl Romance on Ladies of the Lake*

"Haywood Smith's brilliant new novel *Wedding Belles* hits all the right notes because of its authentic Southern voice but will satisfy readers everywhere because of its heartfelt message for mothers, daughters, and yes, even mothers-in-law. Smith is hilarious and wise. It's perfect for book clubs."

—Dorothea Benton Frank on *Wedding Belles*

"A joyous, joyful ode."   —*Booklist on The Red Hat Club*

"I absolutely loved this book and can't wait to share it."

—Cassandra King *on Wedding Belles*

"Haywood Smith knows what the readers want, and doesn't hold back."   —*A Romance Review on Ladies of the Lake*

Also by Haywood Smith

Waking Up in Dixie

Ladies of the Lake

Wedding Belles

The Red Hat Club Rides Again

The Red Hat Club

Queen Bee of Mimosa Branch

Haywood Smith

Wife-in-Law

St. Martin's Griffin 🐾 New York

WIFE-IN-LAW. Copyright © 2011 by Haywood Smith. All rights reserved. Printed in the United States of America. For information, address St. Martin's Press, 175 Fifth Avenue, New York, N.Y. 10010.

www.stmartins.com

The Library of Congress has cataloged the hardcover edition as follows:

Smith, Haywood, 1949–
    Wife-in-law / Haywood Smith.—1st ed.
        p. cm.
    ISBN 978-0-312-60977-1
    1. Marriage—Fiction. 2. Female friendship—Fiction. 3. Triangles
(Interpersonal relations)—Fiction. I. Title.
    PS3569.M53728W54 2011
    813'.54—dc22

                                                            2011019513

ISBN 978-1-250-01389-7 (trade paperback)

First St. Martin's Griffin Edition: September 2012

10 9 8 7 6 5 4 3 2 1

This book is dedicated to my sister Elise, who has always been Christ's hands and heart in my life.

Acknowledgments

Though I briefly lived across the street from my ex-husband and his new wife, whom we both knew years ago from church, that is the extent of any similarities to real life and the contents of this book. All the characters and events in this novel are entirely fictional and do not bear any resemblance to actual events or real people, including my ex-husband (who is gentle and talented) and his second wife (who is a warm, Christian woman). I remain grateful to have them in my life.

First, I'd like to thank all my readers who e-mailed me at haywood100@aol.com to tell me they liked my books. I print out and respond to every one, and when I'm discouraged, I get out those letters to cheer myself up. Works every time. God bless you for the encouragement.

Special thanks, as always, go to my wonderful editor, Jennifer Enderlin, who pulls the best out of me, even when I'm recovering from surgery. Thanks also to my agent, Mel Berger, to whom I am deeply grateful, despite the wretched contract clause. And I deeply appreciate the support from my faithful friends in Georgia Romance Writers, my new friends and fellow Christian authors in the WORD chapter of American Christian Fiction Writers, and the great folks at the Atlanta Writers Club and the Atlanta branch of Pen Women, committed writers and talented souls, all.

Extra-special gratitude goes to my longtime friend Magistrate Court Judge Bill Brogdon for information about the court systems, and for being such a wonderful gentleman that he restores my faith in the male gender. Thanks too to his wife, brilliant Julie, who always "gets it."

When it came to writing this book, I needed a lot of help figuring out how to be accurate about what happens in Sandy Springs, Georgia, when somebody dies under suspicious circumstances. So I owe a debt of gratitude to Erica Hosley of the Sandy Springs Police Department for information about false alarms. And thanks so much for help and information from Gail Picard of the Fulton County Superior Court, April Champion of the Fulton County Criminal Courts, and Jennifer Bagwell, senior attorney with the Hall County District Attorney's Office. And special thanks to Sgt. Lindstrom, detective with the Sandy Springs Police Department, for generously taking so much time to answer my questions. If I made any mistakes about procedure, they are mine and mine alone.

Thanks to my friend Anna DeStefano, a wonderful writer and a great driver and traveling companion who carted me to St. Simons Island for the Scribblers' Retreat Writers' Conference after one of my surgeries last fall.

Acknowledgments

To my usual support group, I must name you, because I'd never be able to do this without your friendship: "Miss Debbie" McGeorge, my pal and my grandchildren's favorite librarian; to Doug, my friend and a reader par excellence who keeps me up with what's good on the bookshelves these days. Thanks go to all my friends in John and Sharon Summers' Small Group Bible Study, mighty prayer warriors who've been there for me through the storms of life; to all my single friends in Wade and Mary Ash's SPLASH Small Group Bible Study (I need all the help I can get) at Blackshear Place Baptist, my amazing church in Oakwood, Georgia. You haven't heard a sermon till you've heard Brother Jeff preach. Every time I do, I leave renewed, thinking, "You know, God, between You and me, we might just be able to do this thing." Thanks to Brother Scott and Brother Dave for offering help and support to our congregation. And a special dose of gratitude and admiration for my friend and brother in Christ Ken Miller, who has used his strength to help me when my arthritis keeps me from doing what needs to be done at home.

Personal thanks and good wishes go to my longtime friend and bridge partner, Roslyn Carlyle, one of the smartest, funniest women I know. Aren't we lucky that heaven's just a breath away?

And thanks to my wonderful roommate, Sandi Grimsley, for being a prayer partner and a shoulder to cry on. Thanks for the friendship—and the rent. God bless you.

And to my next-door neighbor, Celia Dasher, thanks for being such a wonderful neighbor over the past thirty-nine years, and for feeding the cats and the fish when Sandi and I are away.

Thanks to my instructors, Dr. Guerty, Dr. Warwick, Dr.

Acknowledgments

Shields, and Dr. Nicklas, for the wonderful teaching and encouragement. I love Gainesville State College, and if I live long enough, I might just graduate. Special thanks to Carolyn Swindle and her colleagues with the disabilities office; couldn't do it without you.

And last but not least, thanks to God that I have a job I can do in a recliner, with a ten-foot commute and a dress code of pajamas. It's hard work writing funny stories about deadly serious women's issues, but I love it. I'm now working on *Out of Warranty* for 2012, a book that sends up the health insurance industry, the medical profession, and falling apart ten years before Medicare. As always, I hope it makes you laugh a lot, cry a little, and feel great in the end.

Wife-in-Law

One

Somebody once asked me how I pick my friends, and I just laughed, because God usually does the picking for me, and believe me, He has a wicked sense of humor. So when it came to my best friend in the world, never in a million years would I have chosen Kat Ellis. And never in a trillion years would I have ever imagined that we'd both end up married to the same man—or that one of us would kill him.

Los Angeles, California. July, three years ago

The drive from my daughter's house in Fullerton to the L.A. airport was like a tour of Rachel Carson's *Silent Spring*. Smog bathed "paradise" in pollution, while the huge refineries we passed just belched out even more, along with the endless, suicidal traffic that filled the freeway twenty-four/seven.

Wonderful jobs had brought my elder daughter Amelia and her husband Sonny to Tinseltown, but my poor little granddaughters . . . How they could escape getting emphysema before kindergarten was beyond me. But being the good mother-in-law that I am, I'd held my peace all week and not insisted that Sonny move the family to a nontoxic environment. I waited till I kissed him and the children good-bye, then announced that I'd be sending them all respirators, as soon as I could find some in toddler sizes.

I wasn't kidding, but Sonny just laughed. Sigh.

Now, on the way to LAX for my flight back to Atlanta, Amelia turned her eyes from the insanity on the freeway to shoot a brief frown of concern my way. "Mama, are you okay?"

"I'm fine, honey." As fine as a dumped housewife could be. At least Greg paid my alimony and health insurance on time, thanks be to God. "How about you?"

All week, Amelia'd been holding something back, shooting me sad looks when she thought I couldn't see her, but we'd both been so busy with Macy, three, and Madison, one, that we hadn't had much time to talk in private. But Amelia never could keep a secret, so I wasn't surprised when she'd announced that Sonny would be keeping the kids while just the two of us went to the airport. "You've seemed so preoccupied all week," I prodded.

She scowled at the traffic ahead. "I . . . I'm fine, Mama, really."

"Really?" I nudged. "Everything okay with you and Sonny?"

She nodded rapidly, eyes ahead. "Fine. Fine."

Right in front of us, a flame-bedecked lowrider—bass throbbing—started to "hop" at sixty miles an hour, and I slammed my foot to the floorboard at the same instant Amelia, along with all the other drivers in the vicinity, braked to give him wide berth.

Heart racing, I gasped out, "People are crazy in this town."

Amelia grinned. "Yep. That's one of the things I like best about it."

She'd always been the artistic one in the family—flamboyant, dramatic, marching to a different drummer from the other suburban kids back in our Atlanta suburb, Sandy Springs. Then she'd aced prestigious Parsons School of Design and started doing costume work for Broadway, so I'd reconciled myself that she wouldn't be coming home. Her current success designing and coordinating wardrobes for TV and movies was a dream come true, but was it too much to ask for my grandbabies to be able to *breathe*?

I bit back the question before it escaped, saying instead, "Is everything okay with work? Really?"

There was a recession, after all. It cost a fortune to live in L.A. And even though Sonny was one of the most sought-after young cinematographers in town, they weren't making movies at the rate they used to. Plus, bargain-basement reality series were slowly eating up time slots on TV.

"I already told you, Mama, we're fine financially," Amelia said with a hint of annoyance, stomping the brakes to avoid hitting a car that cut right in front of her, which set off a series of screeches behind us. I flinched, waiting for the crunch of metal that never came, but Amelia just kept right on with our conversation. "Business is great. Did you think I was lying when I told you?"

"No, honey. Of course not," I said, breathless from the close call, "but obviously something's bothering you." I knew it wasn't the kids. Both Amelia and Sonny were calm, adoring parents who rolled with the punches. "If it's not Sonny and it's not work, what is it?"

A pinch of pain flashed across her strong profile.

"I'm your mother, honey. You know you can tell me anything." She risked letting go of the steering wheel with her right hand long enough to grip my left one briefly. "I know, Mama. I know."

Just then, some idiot on his cell phone in a Land Rover with DRECTER plates swerved over on us, so we had to swerve over on somebody else, setting off another chain reaction that prompted my sweet, precious Southern daughter to blare her horn and let loose a stream of profanity that would scorch the paint off an army tank.

"Amelia Harcourt Wilson," I gasped out in shock, "wash your mouth out with soap!"

"Sorry," she said without conviction.

Like an EEG settling down after a petit mal seizure, the traffic around us smoothed back to its steady pace as if nothing had ever happened, but I was still floored by Amelia's language. "I hope you don't talk that way in front of my precious grandbabies!"

Amelia chuckled. "Only when I'm alone, Mama." She signaled for the turn into LAX.

"Alone? What am I, chopped liver?" Jolted back into mother mode, I jabbed a finger her way. "This place is corrupting you."

My daughter responded with her favorite phrase from adolescence: "Oh, Mama, lighten up." She headed into short-term parking. "Nobody can drive in this traffic without cussing sometimes.

It's legally required. Anyway, a little private profanity is good for the soul."

"Yours wasn't private," I reminded her.

"Sorry," she repeated, then scanned the crowded rows of parked cars for an open space. "Don't you ever cuss?"

"Only when I'm alone. *Really* alone."

I'd cussed a *lot* when her father ran off with his secretary two years before, but it hadn't helped. Only time and therapy had helped. And a shipload of antidepressants and antianxiety drugs.

Good old drugs. They'd definitely gotten me over the hump. I planned to wean myself off them, but not just yet.

Amelia spotted an empty space and pulled in. She turned off the ignition and paused as if she was going to say something, then changed her mind and opened the door with a too bright, "Well, here we are. I'll get your luggage."

"You don't have to go in with me, honey," I said for the third time. "I promise, I can manage."

"Mama, we went over this. I want to be with you till the last minute. We only see each other once a year." Avoiding eye contact, she gathered my things and led the way into the terminal. After I'd checked my bag, she kept glancing around the concourse, anxious, as if she was looking for something. "Are you hungry, Mama?" she asked. "Why don't we find someplace to eat?"

At the airport, paying three prices for everything? "We just finished that lovely breakfast you made," I reminded her.

There was that look again. I stopped short. "Amelia, I wish you'd just come out and tell me what's bothering you."

"Mama, I . . . Not here. It's so public."

Good Lord. What on earth was it?

All kinds of dire possibilities flooded my brain. My heart dropped to my bladder and bounced. "Oh, God. You're not sick, are you? Or the children? Or Sonny?"

"No, no," she hastened to assure me. "Please don't faint." She hustled me to a nearby bank of worn chairs. "It's nothing like that. Here. Sit." Leaving the seat between us empty, she sat too. "Mama, I didn't mean to upset you. I'm so sorry. We're fine."

"Thank God." I pressed my hand to my racing heart. "You scared the life out of me."

She shot me that pained look of pity for the fortieth time.

I'd had enough of this pussyfooting around. "Then what is it? Spit it out, before I have a heart attack."

Her eyes filled with tears. "It's Daddy." She pressed her left fist to her chin as if to block what she was saying. "He and Kat are getting married."

Oh, *that*.

"Duh!" No surprises there. "I figured they would. Your daddy never could take care of himself."

Poor Kat. Desperately lonely after Zach died of ALS, she'd been a perfect target when Greg had come back to Atlanta looking for somebody to nursemaid him. Thanks to therapy, I'd known better than to encourage him when he came sniffing around, but Kat . . .

"Mama," Amelia protested, "she's your best friend! I can't believe she'd even *date* Daddy, much less marry him!"

"Oh, honey, it's okay." Why did everybody want me to be mad

at Kat, anyway? She'd had nothing to do with the breakup of my marriage.

Frankly, I felt sorry for her. Lord knows, she'd seen what Greg had done to me, and I'd warned her that he would probably just do it again, but she'd simply stopped calling me. Word on the grapevine was, Greg had told her I was just jealous. And frigid. And a prescription-drug addict. All bald-faced lies, and Kat knew it, but Greg was so charming, he could make you believe your mother was a monkey.

Kat also knew how selfish he was—and I'd done my share of making him that way—but she'd been so lonely since Zach died that I guess she'd convinced herself Greg had really turned over a new leaf.

Who knows? Maybe he had. For Kat's sake, I hoped so. I only knew I didn't want to be his mother anymore. Taking care of my own kept me plenty busy.

But how could I explain all this to Amelia without saying anything bad about her father? She still wouldn't speak to him or let him see the girls, even though he'd moved his mistress to L.A. after our breakup, ostensibly to be near Amelia and her family. As it turned out, the mistress thing hadn't worked for him either. Women our daughter's age don't wait on men the way I'd always waited on Greg.

I collected my wits. "Honey, listen to me about your daddy." Careful. He was still her father. "As Aunt Emma used to say, 'That train has left the station.'" I shot her a wry smile. "After it ran over me about six times." I'd tried desperately to save our marriage at first, but one person can't do it alone, so I'd finally seen our relationship for what it really was—and wasn't—and let go. "I've moved on, and so has your dad. I really hope he and Kat will be happy together," I said with absolute conviction.

Let *her* take care of him. At least the girls wouldn't have to worry about him anymore.

A delicious thought occurred to me, one I planned to act on as soon as I got home.

Amelia scooted into the seat beside me for a big bear hug. "Oh, Mama, you are too good. Daddy didn't deserve you."

I stroked her hair, meeting her grief with calm. "Your daddy deserves to be loved for who he really is." I'd loved him for rescuing me and making me respectable. I'd loved our life, and all the things he'd given us. But that was just as selfish as he had been in the end.

Amelia started to cry. "I hate what he did to you, to all of us. And now this. I hate *him*."

"Well, you can hate him if you want to," I soothed, quoting another of Aunt Emmaline's wise sayings, "but it won't change anything, sweetie. It'll just make you miserable, and I don't want you to be miserable."

"I can't help it," she said, her voice tight. "It's awful. Awful."

"It's all going to be okay, honey," I promised. "You love Kat and her kids, and that's fine with me. Maybe your daddy can be happy with them. I hope so." God, it was good to be *over* Greg at last.

Catching a glimpse of the clock, I gave Amelia a parting squeeze, then stood. "I'll call you after I get home, and we can talk some more. But for now, I need to head for security if I'm going to make my flight."

Amelia wiped her eyes as she stood, the weight of the world on her shoulders. "I just hate this. Hate it all."

Poor kid. Smiling, I lifted her chin with a wry, "Lighten up, kiddo. Look at the bright side. When you come home to visit, you'll just have to cross the street to see your daddy."

Oh, man. How was *that* going to play out?

Maybe I'd get lucky, and they'd move.

The past. Sandy Springs, just outside of Atlanta. June 1974

It rained the morning that providence brought Kat Gober and me together, leaving the air heavy and humid, rich with the smell of wet lumber and exposed red clay from the construction all around us in Eden Lake Estates (which had no lake, and only the inklings of a swim/tennis club, so far). Sandy Springs was the hinterlands of Atlanta, beyond even the new, barely used Perimeter Highway. But our first house was as close to town as my up-and-coming accountant husband could afford, so I'd made up my mind to be the best housewife and the best neighbor in the subdivision.

All my life, I'd dreamed of having a home of my own, and now, at last, my dream had come true, complete with stylish harvest-gold appliances, shag carpeting in the den, and an elegant avocado-green powder room. All I needed were some neighbors.

A month ago, a SOLD sign had gone up at the house across the cul-de-sac, and I'd found out from the sales office when the buyers—a couple our age—would be moving in. Grateful for our very first neighbors, I'd spent the day before their arrival cooking a meal to welcome them, all from scratch: my famous devil's food cake with seven-minute icing, a nice pot of pole beans (peeled down both sides, lest anyone, God forbid, get a string), and three dozen ears of fresh stewed corn. I'd left frying the chicken till that morning, so it would be perfectly room temperature when I delivered it under a new red and white kitchen towel that would serve as a welcome gift.

As soon as I kissed Greg off to work at Arthur Andersen Accounting and cleaned up after breakfast, I put on a kettle of water for iced tea and started frying, grateful to God Almighty for air-conditioning, my favorite thing about our new house.

Aunt Emmaline had always said that air-conditioning destroyed the sense of community in the South, and she may have been right, but to me, it was well worth the sacrifice.

I used up five pounds of flour and four fryers before I was done. Then I cleaned my kitchen till it sparkled, taking great satisfaction in the ritual.

After the chaos and grime of growing up with Mama, the order and newness of my own home made me so happy, every single day, that I couldn't imagine considering cleaning it a chore. I loved the fresh aroma of Pine-Sol and the shine of the new appliances and fresh, cheerful vinyl and Formica, and the pattern the vacuum left on my soft, carpeted floors. Never mind that Greg accused me of making up the bed when he went to the bathroom in the middle of the night; I loved my all-brick, colonial basement ranch with a passion I would never feel for a mere man.

Once the house was spotless, I bathed, then freshened my perfect blond flip and makeup. Appearances mean so much. I'd once read in one of Mama's old *Ladies' Home Journals* that if a man ever saw you looking less than your best, he'd never forget it, so I always got up well before Greg to put on my face and fix my hair. I have no eyes, au naturel.

Next, since I only had one chance to make a good first impression, I decided to wear a black A-line skirt I'd copied from *Ladies' Home Journal*, with matching sandals and a cute little fitted white blouse with a Peter Pan collar that looked just like a real John Meyer. And pearls, of course (only cultured, but I'd never tell).

Not too dressy, not too casual. Wouldn't want to put the new people off.

Then I sat in one of my new flame-stitched wingback chairs by one of the full-length windows in the living room to wait and watch for the movers. I'd finished the current issues of *Good Housekeeping* and *Southern Living*, cover to cover, before I heard the rumble of a truck and looked across the cul-de-sac to see a battered U-Haul pull into the opposite driveway, followed by a Volkswagen Vanagon with dealer tags and a big peace sign on the bumper. To my dismay, a herd of hippies erupted with a halfhearted cheer in a cloud of smoke from the van, then set about unloading the sorriest collection of garage-sale rejects I'd ever seen (and believe me, I'd seen plenty growing up).

But hope springs eternal, so I told myself they were probably just a bunch of Gypsy movers, and the real neighbors would arrive eventually. Then a frizzy-headed, petite, skinny redheaded girl in bell-bottom hip-riders and a halter top started directing the men where to take the furniture, so I had to wonder. A man's paisley necktie circled her forehead à la Jimi Hendrix, and her commands easily reached me across the cul-de-sac, her cracker accent as broad as the Chattahoochee, and just as red.

The princess phone beside me rang, causing me to jump. "Hello?"

"Did they come yet?" Mama demanded.

"I'm not sure." I had no intention of telling her that hippies had invaded the neighborhood. She'd get too much satisfaction from it. "The movers are unloading now."

"And?" Mama insisted. Never mind that she hadn't set foot outside her house since Daddy left when I was five. She lived vicariously through me. "What kind of furniture do they have? You can tell a lot about people by their furniture, you know."

Why I couldn't just lie to my mother, I have no idea, but she had an uncanny ability to see right through me, so half-truth was the best I could ever get away with. "It looks . . . ordinary," I reported. And old. And battered.

"That doesn't tell me anything," she fussed, picking up on my hesitation. "What kind of ordinary? Williamsburg? Mediterranean? Traditional? French provincial?" Mama might be crazy, but she was still intelligent and reveled vicariously in the minor mysteries of my life. "Don't tell me it's contemporary," she said. "I can't stand contemporary people."

"It's eclectic," I offered. "A mix. Not everybody decorates in a particular style." God knew Mama didn't, but she was the first to criticize the rooms in the decorating magazines she insisted I pass on to her. She was always telling me about recipes from *Southern Living* too, but she hadn't been able to get to the stove since I thank-God-and-hallelujah married up, moved out, and gave her the extra microwave we'd gotten from one of the partners at Greg's firm.

"You're no help," Mama grumbled. "Take pictures, so I can see for myself."

"Mama, I have no intention of sneaking pictures of my new neighbors' furniture from behind my drapes to satisfy your curiosity." Maybe it was the threat of hippies, but I got so annoyed, I blurted out the unspeakable. "If you want to see what they have, come over and look for yourself."

She could, if she would just take her meds like she was supposed to. But no. She said they made her feel "flat," whatever that was. To me, it sounded like her paralyzing phobias had become her friends, better friends to her than she would ever let me be.

After a wounded pause, Mama accused, "That was cruel, Betsy. I was just being curious. You had no cause to be so cruel. I didn't bring you up to be so mean to your mother."

She didn't bring me up, period. I'd had to take care of *her*.

"I'm sorry," I apologized, as I always, always did, no matter who was wrong. "I just think it would be very rude to take pictures of their stuff. They're the only neighbors we have. I want to start out on the right foot."

"I still don't see why you and Greg bought the very first house in that subdivision," Mama harped. "That was very risky, you know."

"Which was why we got such a good deal," I responded on cue. The only thing my husband hated worse than taking chances was spending more than he had to.

Across the street, the redhead continued to direct the movers, then planted a peck on the cheek of a particularly scruffy man wearing shirtless overalls that exposed a huge tattoo on his upper arm (!), his dark hair pulled back into a ponytail that was almost as long as his scraggly brown beard. Please, no.

"Mama, I think I see them driving up now," I lied, surprised that I sounded so convincing. "Gotta go take them the meal I made and introduce myself."

"What'd you fix?" Mama demanded. No matter how often we talked, she never let me go when I asked her to.

"Fried chicken, pole beans, stewed corn, and a devil's food cake with seven-minute icing," I rattled off, glad for the diversion.

"Sounds yummy." A pregnant pause followed.

I rolled my eyes. "I made enough for all of us. I'll be over by four to bring you some." It would take me half an hour to get down to Mama's ratty little house on Rhomboid Avenue, off Defoors Ferry near Howell Mill, and I needed to be home with supper ready and Greg's martini made when he walked in at six.

Mama's mood lightened. "Good. That's a good girl." I'd always done the cooking, even when I was little. "And don't forget my magazines."

"Okay," I said. We had a deal: she got my old magazines as long as I could take out the ones she'd read, along with one other thing. "Go ahead and pick something out for me, but remember, jewelry doesn't count. It has to be at least as big as a shoe box." Last time, she'd tried to get away with a broken plastic necklace and earrings, which didn't qualify.

"I don't know why I ever let you badger me into this arrangement," she muttered.

Because I'd threatened to quit coming to see her if she didn't, and meant it. Frankly, though, it only gave me the illusion that I was making a difference. The truth was, as long as she had a phone, Mama kept right on squandering her disability check on "treasures" from catalogues and the want ads, so the *stuff* that clogged all but the narrow pathways through her house never really diminished, no matter what she gave me to throw away.

"It's *my* life, not yours," she whined for the jillionth time. "*My* things. What harm does it do you? Or anybody?" she went on, according to script. "I don't know why you insist on torturing me this way, but I'll pick something out." I heard what sounded like a minor avalanche beside her chair as she hung up with a parting, "Torture."

I closed my eyes, holding the phone to my chest in exasperation, then heard a commotion outside. The movers were pulling away, crammed into the cab of the truck, leaving the ZZ Top guy with his tattooed arm around the skinny redhead as they waved their helpers off with thanks.

There goes the neighborhood.

Greg would *die* when he found out. He'd been hoping for another Young Republican to play tennis with, as soon as the club was available.

Oh, well. Might as well make the best of it. I headed for the kitchen to load up the tray with food, topping the containers off with red plastic plates and cups, and a bread basket filled with red and white checkered paper napkins wrapped around sets of plastic cutlery and tied with white curling ribbon. The effect was festive and perfect.

Even hippies had to eat, and I certainly didn't want to get on their bad side.

By the time I reached their front door with the heavy tray, they'd gone inside, but the Vanagon was still there. I rang the bell several times and waited before I finally heard some muffled cursing from inside, then laughter, followed by approaching footsteps and the redhead's hollered, "Git decent. We've got company."

The door flew open to reveal her flushed and tying her halter top. "Sorry," she said, "my old man's an animal." She caught the aroma of the food and zeroed in on it, wide-eyed. A harsh, sweetish, acrid odor wafted out from behind her. "Wow. You a caterer, or somethin'?"

"No." I did my best to look friendly, which wasn't easy in light of the smell from the house, one I recognized as the stink of burning hemp twine. I was so naïve, I didn't even know what it was. "Actually, I'm your new neighbor Betsy Callison from across the street. I figured you wouldn't be set up to cook today, so I brought y'all some food to welcome you to the neighborhood."

"Wow. Great." She studied me with intense, light brown eyes, as if I were some kind of alien. "I'm Kat Gober. My old man's Zach." She grinned, her pale red lashes visible for an instant. "We been together five years now, since I was sixteen. Met at a love-in at Piedmont Park."

Together? Oh, Lord. This was supposed to be a respectable neighborhood.

This woman needed a marriage license almost as much as she needed some mascara.

I was so nonplussed, I forgot to hand her the tray.

"Come on in." Kat motioned me inside, hungrily eyeing the tray. "What a feast."

I felt myself blush and extended the food her way. "Just plain old Southern country cooking."

Kat shoved aside some boxes on the scarred dining room table. "Here. You can just set it down here." She glanced, frowning, toward the kitchen. "God knows where the dishes are."

I smiled and pointed to the eating supplies. "Oh, I brought everything." As I set the pitcher of tea on the table, a loud belch behind me drew my attention to the bearded man, who stopped short in the hallway and stared at me in amazement.

"Damn," he breathed out, sending those acrid, sweetish fumes my way as he rubbed his eyes. "Am I trippin', or is Betty freakin' Crocker in our dining room?" His cultured Southern accent didn't fit his coarse comment.

"Mind your manners, Zach," Kat scolded. "This is our new neighbor, Betsy . . . sorry, I didn't catch—"

"Betsy Freakin' Callison," I said, smooth as my smile, "of Greg and Betsy Callison, your only freakin' neighbors in the subdivision. So far."

Zach grinned with a definite spark of intelligence. "I like you," he said, extending a callused hand with grease under its nails. "Glad to meet ya." He followed the flick of my eyes to his nails, then hastily withdrew his hand. "Sorry. I'm a plumber. It's hard to get 'em clean."

Embarrassed that he'd noticed my reaction, I shifted to the food. "I hope y'all like fried chicken and stewed corn and pole beans."

"Do we ever." Zach eyed the cake keeper with alacrity. "And cake."

"It's devil's food with seven-minute icing," I couldn't resist bragging. "My specialty."

Zach plopped down into a chair, untying a set of utensils. "Man, oh man." He grabbed a paper plate, then pulled back the checkered dishtowel and helped himself to a chicken leg. "Maybe you could teach Kat to cook," he said as he heaped on a pile of pole beans with the slotted spoon. "She doesn't even make coffee."

"I kin make vegetable soup," Kat defended, clearly feeling at a disadvantage.

Zach guffawed through a mouthful of chicken. "Only if somebody dies or *seriously* screws up." He waggled the half-consumed chicken leg my way. "You ever see her making vegetable soup, head for the hills, 'cause there's a funeral or a tongue-lashin' in it for somebody."

Kat shifted uncomfortably. "Hush up, Zach. We just met this woman. She don't care why I make soup."

I felt sorry for the girl, married to such a mannerless man who looked like a hobo and told their secrets to strangers. Or not married to him. Or whatever.

"Well, I guess I'll just head home," I told them. "I have to go visit my mother and take her some supper."

Kat brightened with interest. "Your mama live nearby?"

I knotted up inside the way I always did when anyone asked about Mama, but didn't let my expression show it. "Down in town."

Kat eyed my clothes. "Buckhead, I bet."

I just smiled, a master at avoiding awkward questions. "Y'all use the tray and the dishes as long as you need, but the dishtowel is a housewarming present." I started edging toward the door. "Don't get up," I said with more than a hint of sarcasm as Zach shoveled in the food I'd made. "I know you must be tired. I'll just let myself out."

Kat followed me, suddenly shy. "Thanks so much for the food and all. Maybe we'll see each other around on the weekends."

"I'm sure we will," I said with a warm smile and a wave goodbye, silently dismissing the couple as potential friends.

The other four houses on the cul-de-sac were almost finished. Surely somebody with whom Greg and I had more in common would move in soon. Kat and Zach just weren't our kind of people.

But God, as He so often does, had other plans.

Two

Thanks to Atlanta's ever-present road construction and traffic, I was almost an hour late getting to Mama's that afternoon. If I didn't do a fast turnaround, I'd end up stuck in rush hour. I parked on the crumbling pavement in front of Mama's tiny house and unloaded the food. When I got to the chain-link gate to her tiny yard, her next-door neighbor appeared on the other side to let me in, hoe in hand.

"Afternoon." He went back to weeding the tomatoes Mama let him plant all the way around the inside of her fence.

The guy hardly ever spoke. Mama said that gardening was his only escape from taking care of his wife, who was dying long and hard of Alzheimer's. But Mama's motives weren't completely altruistic: she loved home-grown tomatoes, and his were prizewinners. His own little yard was crammed with gorgeous vegetables, which he also shared with her.

I noted that some of the tomatoes were almost ripe. "How do you get them to ripen so early?" I asked him.

He beamed. "Plant 'em early, in March," he said. "I cut the bottoms out of gallon jugs and cover them. On warm days, I take off the jug tops. Only way to get tomatoes in June this far north."

It was the most he'd ever said to me in fifteen years. "You're a real wonder-worker in the garden."

He hesitated, frowning, as if he owed me a compliment in response. "Your mama's lucky to have you lookin' out after her." His face flushed with embarrassment.

"Thanks."

He went back to his hoeing, so I headed inside with the food.

I didn't bring up our brief conversation because Mama would analyze it to death, and I didn't want to talk about the man behind his back.

"Hey, Mama!" I called over the blare of *The Match Game*, carrying the food down the narrow path to her TV tray.

"Hey, yourself." She didn't turn down the TV. She never did. "What'd you bring?"

"Fried chicken, pole beans, stewed corn, and devil's food cake." I set the containers on her tray. "What did you pick out for me to take?"

"For heaven's sake, Betsy, you just got here," she deflected. "Can't that wait? I haven't even eaten."

I stood in the small space in front of her recliner, my nose twitching at ancient dust and decaying paper. "Mama, pick something. Now," I said over the TV, "or I'm taking this food home with me and not coming back for a week." We both knew it wasn't an empty threat.

Mama went canny. "How did I raise such a cruel child?" she repeated in cultured Southern tones. Despite her arthritis, she rose gracefully from her recliner and pulled a middle-sized box from atop the heap of stuff beside the TV. It was a miracle she could move at all, since her only exercise was going from the bathroom to the refrigerator and the sink and the microwave, then back to her chair. How she kept her figure was beyond me.

Still, Mama was a striking older woman—beautiful even, if she'd just take some care with her hairstyle or makeup, but she refused to let me make her over with just as much vehemence as she refused to let me clean her house. Ironically, she kept herself squeaky clean.

She thrust the box at me. "You want this so bad? Take it. It's pieces of me."

It wasn't pieces of Mama; it was pieces of soap—five pounds of the dying slivers of a jillion colors and textures—and they hadn't been there when I moved out to get married two years before. Right after I left, she'd piled the one shower-bath full of junk, so she must have been washing from the sink, which couldn't account for all that soap. Lord knows where it had come from. I shuddered to think.

"Good job, Mama. Good job," I encouraged, still grasping at the illusion that behavior modification might work with total insanity.

I leaned over and gave her a hug and a kiss on the cheek. "I can't stay, or I won't get home in time to have Greg's martini ready." I gripped the box of slivers hard against me, in case she tried to take it back. "I'll see you Friday."

"Go on, then," she grumbled, waving me away. "Leave me alone here. See if I care."

Why that kind of talk still got under my skin, I couldn't tell you, but it did. Was it too much to hope for at least a little gratitude?

Mentally ill. She's sick, not deliberately trying to drive me crazy too. "See you Friday, Mama."

Thanks to her delays, I barely had time to get home and set the table, warm up dinner, and have Greg's martini made before he drove into the garage. Glass in hand, I exhaled a cleansing breath, then put on my best Total Woman smile.

The door from the garage opened and Greg shot me a smug look. "That's my girl." Kissing me on the cheek, he took the martini. After a hefty slug, he headed for the den with his *New York Times* (expensive, but deductible).

"Hard day at work?" I asked lightly.

He paused just inside the den, but didn't turn around. "Crazy."

Normally, I gave him time alone to detox from work, but I'd learned to read the nuances of his posture and inflection, and there was definitely something wrong. So I broke with protocol and followed him into the den, where I found him behind the financial section in his tasteful wingback leather recliner. "Want to talk about it?" I asked.

"Not till after dinner," he said through the paper. "I need to unwind first. With another martini." His eyes never leaving the news, he shifted the paper to his left hand, then slugged what was left of the first drink and extended the glass my way.

Must have been a *very* bad day. Whatever that meant. I had no idea what kind of problems he faced at work. Greg never talked about them. He said it just made him feel worse to rehash the negative.

"Martini, coming up," I said. After I delivered that, I retreated to the kitchen. Though Greg often said that a man's home was his castle, a woman's kitchen is *her* domain, so I always found confidence there. Keeping an eye on the martini by his chair, I waited till it was almost gone before transferring the corn and beans into serving dishes.

Greg loved my fried chicken and pole beans and stewed corn, so surely dinner would cheer him up. I poured his sweet tea and my plain, then lit the candles and said, "Supper's ready."

Looking gorgeously rumpled with his collar open and his tie loosened, Greg took his place, rolling up the sleeves of his pinpoint oxford button-down. Finally, he looked at me. "So, what's the story with the new neighbors?"

Uh-oh. Not a topic to cheer him up. "Why don't we eat first?" I deflected.

A brittle gleam reflected in his dark eyes. "Why? What's wrong with the neighbors?"

When my husband looked at me that way, avoidance only made him angry, so there was nothing to do but spit it out. "They're hippies."

He frowned in disbelief. "Hippies can't afford to live in Sandy Springs. And anyway, why would they want to?"

"Beats me."

Fork poised, Greg voiced the very thought that occurred to me in that instant. "What if they're drug dealers?"

"But this is the suburbs," I protested, still firm in the belief that our location protected us from such awful things. The South has always lagged behind the social cutting edge—maybe because we're weaned on the Bible and the importance of our heritage—so the "tune in, turn on" movement was pretty much limited to the go-gos down on Tenth Street.

Greg took a bite of chicken and mulled on that.

"You'd think drug dealers would want to blend in," I went on, "but those two are gonna stick out like a sore thumb out here," I said. "He looks like that hairy guy from ZZ Top." We in the South knew all about ZZ Top long before the rest of the country caught on. "And he has *tattoos*." I took a bite of corn.

"What's *she* like?" Greg asked, assuming there was a she. In our world, single people didn't buy houses in the burbs.

"She looks like a kid. Frizzy red hair, no makeup, freckles." I leaned closer to confide, "I don't think they're even married. She said they'd been 'together' since they met at a love-in at Piedmont Park when she was sixteen."

Greg's proper Presbyterian genes got in a wad. "I'm gonna kill the developer. And those agents in the sales office. We have covenants to keep out riffraff."

Like me?

I sighed. "I checked the covenants. There isn't a 'no hippies' clause. Or 'no tattoos.' And not a word about having bad furniture."

"Damn." Greg slammed his tea to the table with such force, it sloshed onto my white cutwork cloth. "Just damn." Glaring into the middle distance, he shoved in a mouthful of beans and chewed with excessive force. When he finished, his eyes narrowed. "Well, there's certainly a restriction about doing anything illegal. One of my clients is a captain with APD. I'll have a word with him. Get him to check them out."

"Great." Greg was one of the most connected men I'd ever met, so I gladly entrusted the matter into his capable hands. "But in the meantime," I cautioned, "it's our Christian duty to be nice to them. They might not be drug dealers, and they are our only neighbors."

"I don't suppose he plays tennis," Greg said.

"I doubt it. He's a plumber. And his beard would definitely get in the way."

"Just damn." Greg fell silent, focusing on his food for the rest of the meal, with only an occasional burp of profanity between bites.

Maybe dessert would help a little. He loved my devil's food cake. So did I, which was why I'd gained fifteen pounds since we married, but Greg said it only made me more voluptuous.

I waited to pick up his plate till he laid his silverware across it, the signal he was done. "Would you like some coffee? I made your favorite for dessert."

He lightened up a little. "Tea's fine."

Sure enough, a big slab of my moist, sweet confection did the trick, and he came out of his funk.

I cleared the rest of the table while he ate it. Greg had never touched a dirty dish, a matter of pride with me. "Why don't you go stretch out and watch some TV after you finish?" I suggested over my shoulder as I started loading the dishwasher. When I got no response, I turned to find him frowning again.

"Honey, come sit down," he said gently. He never called me honey unless it was something awful. "There's something I need to tell you."

My heart contracted to the size of a walnut. Oh, God. Was I going to lose my house? Had they fired him? Was that what had happened at work?

I don't remember sitting down, but I did.

Greg took my hand in his and said, "I had a hell of a day till I opened my mail this afternoon and found out I passed my CPA," he said as if he was telling me he had cancer, instead of reaching one of his most important goals.

Thank God, thank God! He hadn't lost his job. But why wasn't he bursting with his usual pride of accomplishment?

"So they're promoting me, two years early," he told me with a look of pity.

"Oh, honey, that's amazing." I gave his lips a congratulatory buss. "I'm so proud of you. *Nobody* passes their CPA the first time. You worked so hard for this."

He took a leveling breath, then said, "The bad news is, they want me in Chicago tomorrow." Tomorrow? For how long? "A new client, and a big one, but the account's such a mess that our guy up there just quit and walked out, so we fired him."

But this was a promotion for Greg. If anybody could slay this dragon, he could, and what a coup that would be. "You'll be able to handle it," I said. "I know you will."

He glanced to the floor. "It will definitely make me or break me." His gaze met mine. "The trouble is, I'd thought we'd have at least another year before this happened, time for you to make some friends, so you wouldn't be all alone out here. I don't like leaving you in this situation." He scowled. "Especially with those *hippies* across the street."

"Honey, don't you worry about me for one instant." There would be other neighbors soon enough. "I'll be fine. At least four of the houses on our street are almost finished, and lots more all around us. I'm sure they'll sell quickly. More people will move in before we know it."

I paused, then ventured, "How long will you have to be gone?"

"Normally, I'd get two weekends a month off," he said, "but the mess they've got up there . . . it might be longer than that. I'll just have to see."

How would I fill my time without a husband to care for? Greg was adamant that no wife of his would work. "I can do some charity work, meet some people there. Take bridge lessons," I told myself and him. "Get more active at church. Learn needlepoint," I said with forced cheer. "I'll be fine."

And I'd make sure his weekends home were memorable. My innards did a flip just thinking about it.

Grateful, he cupped the side of my head in his palm, stroking my temple with his thumb. "You're such a trouper. I know you can manage. God knows, you managed worse than this growing up." For the first time in quite a while, he really *saw* me. "I'm just sorry that you have to." His expression sharpened. "First thing tomorrow morning, I'm calling the alarm people and having one put in. Top-of-the-line."

I still marveled that a man like Greg cared so much about someone like me. "Goodness. I'll be safe as a bank."

"Safer," he said. He rose, giving me a kiss on the cheek. "I think I will watch a little TV. The Braves are on."

And once again, all was right with the world. Except for those hippies.

The next day, I drove Greg to the airport and kissed him off, then came straight home so the workmen could install the alarm, complete with battery backup and a direct connection to the police and fire departments, plus smoke and carbon monoxide detectors, and a panic button by my bed. Having it made me feel secure.

It felt a little odd to be alone in our king-sized bed that first night, but I was worn out from cleaning up after the workmen, so I didn't even make it through Johnny Carson's opening joke before I fell asleep. It was almost midnight when the phone rang beside the bed.

I fumbled for the receiver, then said a groggy, "Hullo."

"Hey," Greg answered. "Sorry. Did I wake you up? I forget, it's an hour earlier here." His voice sounded weary.

I rolled over in the dark. "Can't think of anybody I'd rather have wake me up. How was day one in Chicago?"

"Worse than I thought," he confessed. "Turns out the client's trusted comptroller has been embezzling for years through dozens, maybe hundreds, of dummy accounts. It'll take me fourteen hours a day to track them all down and assess the loss before the close of the business year. Then I have to devise a more secure set of bookkeeping protocols to reduce the risk of having it happen again."

I was touched that he'd finally confided in me about his work. "Wow. Sounds like a job for Superman. Good thing they've got you to take care of it."

"Thanks. That's nice to hear," he said, then yawned. "Whew. I'm beat. Did they get the alarm in?"

"Yep. The code's 19481952," I told him, "the years we were born. I put yours first because it came first."

"Good idea." He yawned again. I could picture him in his hotel room, tie loose, eyes drooping, and I missed him.

"Did they test it out?" he asked.

"Did they ever," I said, remembering the earsplitting racket it made. "You never heard such noise. The hippies probably thought it was a tornado alert."

"Good." He yawned again. "Oh, speaking of the hippies, that police captain said he checked them out, and we don't have anything to worry about."

"How could he be so sure, so fast?" I asked, skeptical.

"Don't know, but the guy was adamant. He did say he'd have a patrol car come by to check our house as often as they can, though, just in case. So I guess that's it."

"Okay, then." I still had my misgivings, but caught myself starting to nod off in the pause that followed.

"Guess I'd better go," Greg said. "Want to get into the office by six."

"Be sure you eat well, honey," I told him. "You have to keep up your strength."

"I won't be able to find cooking as good as yours," he said, "but I'll make sure to eat."

"Sweet dreams," I told him, just the way I always did when he was there beside me.

"Sweet dreams." He hung up, and I went back to sleep, safe in the confines of the alarm system.

Greg called every night at first, but we quickly ran out of things to tell each other. Apparently, he couldn't discuss anything else about the client. He was working a killer schedule, and I was keeping busy with the house. Not a lot to talk about there.

So we lapsed into talking only every few days, which was okay with me, because I knew he was putting in long hours instead of hanging around Chicago alone with nothing to do with his evenings.

I managed fine the first week, but by Tuesday of the second, I'd run out of things to do. I'd scrubbed my poor house to smithereens, ironed everything I could get my hands on, including the sheets, and discovered that churches and charities don't usually do much in the summer, so service work was out till fall. My freezer was full of home-cooked food, and there was not so much as a single weed or shred of crabgrass in my lawn or flower beds.

I read, of course. I'd always loved to read, but after the third or fourth book, I started having this nagging feeling that I should be *doing* something. For the first time in my entire life, I didn't have anybody to take care of, and it didn't feel good, I can tell you.

I'd always been the doer. I had no idea how to be a be-er.

I actually considered going over to Mama's and cleaning, no matter what she said, but she'd probably have a nervous breakdown, for real, so I didn't.

As for the hippies, criminals or not, I wasn't inclined to make any further overtures. They hadn't even returned my dishes, much less called to thank me or come to visit, so all was quiet on their side of the street. I hadn't even seen them since Greg left, but I knew they weren't out of town. The Vanagon was gone at intervals—I sometimes heard its beetley retreat—but the only other sign of life from their place was charcoal smoke and the smell of barbecued chicken from behind it on Sunday afternoon. I wasn't jealous. Their backyard got the full force of the afternoon sun, so it must have been hot as blue blazes back there.

At sixes and sevens on Tuesday afternoon, I decided, late, to drive down to my favorite fabric shop in Atlanta for some material to make drapes for the guest bedroom, the last bare window in the house. For supper I stopped by Henri's Bakery for a sandwich and a French apple tart, so the sun was low and blazing by the time I reached our subdivision. "It's a scorcher," the weatherman on WQXI blared cheerfully. "Ninety-one degrees, with eighty-three percent humidity. Three-day forecast, the heat continues, with no relief in sight except for the occasional afternoon or evening shower." Shower? They were gully-washers. "Lows in the high seventies. Better grab that pitcher of tea and head for the pool. And now, back to our Golden Oldie Hour with 'Good Vibrations' from the Beach Boys!"

Psychedelic music filled the car as I reached our cul-de-sac and turned in to see what looked for all the world like a funeral tent in the hippies' front yard, shaded from the sun by their house. Underneath it sat some chairs, with a little blue boat about four feet long, so small that the motionless arms and legs of the person inside it were hanging over the edges.

I slowed. Dear Lord. Please tell me that's not some dead *body* they're going to bury in their front yard. Surely that was illegal.

To my relief, the body reared up and hollered in Kat's unmistakable accent, "I *said*, bring me some more ice, 'fore it all melts. I'm dyin', here!"

I couldn't help myself; I pulled up alongside her and rolled down the window to ask, "Are you okay? Do I need to call for help?"

Kat sat up, clearly embarrassed. "Oh, Lord, no. I'm just hot."

On closer inspection, I saw that the boat was really a boat-shaped kiddy pool, and the hose was running into it, setting up a steady overflow that watered their thirsty new sod.

Kat tucked her feet back into the water with a wry smile. "I never had a house before. We always rented. I remembered to pay the water bill and the *mortgage*," she said, elongating the last word, "but I completely *fergot* about the power. So when the builder's line got turned off, we didn't have any juice."

She was so calm about it, and so *honest*. I certainly wouldn't have told anybody if I'd done something that dumb, much less somebody I barely knew. Who lived across the street.

Kat went on. "It's a hunnerd and ninety-seven inside, so we borrowed this tent from a friend of ours, just till we get hooked back up." She turned toward the house to bellow, "Zach! If you melted in there, please tell me! Otherwise, bring me some more *ice*!"

She said the word like "aaahs."

I spotted a couple of deflated air mattresses by one of the chairs. "How long will it take to get your power back?" I asked. Surely they weren't planning to sleep out there, with all the bugs and the heat.

"Not till tomorrow."

Zach erupted from the front door with a heavy cooler, his tattooed biceps bulging as he brought it down the front stairs. "You want *aaahs*," he mocked good-naturedly, "you've got *aaahs*." He tipped it over the boat and dumped in at least three bags' worth, sending a small tsunami over the gunnels.

Kat shrieked with delight. "Aaaaggh! That feels fabulous!"

Zach laughed. "Well, enjoy it, 'cause that's the last of it." Then he turned and granted me a smile from the depths of that nasty beard. "Hey there, Betsy Freakin' Callison."

"Hey." Suddenly, I was all too conscious of the fact that I'd been gawking at their misfortune. Without any conscious participation on my part, I heard my voice say, "It's too hot and buggy for y'all to sleep out here. You'll get eaten alive. Why don't you stay with me? I've got plenty of room, and plenty of air-conditioning."

I did *not* just ask a couple of unmarried hippies to spend the night under my roof! When my husband was away!

Kat jumped up out of the water with a shriek of joy. "Would we ever! Just give us time to get changed, and we'll be right over."

Dear Lord. There was no taking it back now.

Zach nodded in gratitude. At least I think it was gratitude. Hard to tell with all that hair.

I hoped he was at least planning to put on a shirt under his overalls. I shuddered to think what else might or might not be under there.

Kat splished toward her door, then turned to point at me and say, "Now, *that* is what I call a good neighbor."

Suddenly queasy, I waved my fingers, then rolled up the power window and backed up, then headed for my garage.

Please don't let anything bad happen, I prayed in general. And please don't call tonight, I prayed in Greg's direction. When he found out, he was going to have a *fit*.

Three

Kicking myself for what I'd done, I tucked away the fabric in the sewing station I'd set up in the closet of the third bedroom. Then I went to the guest room and put a drop of vanilla on the light bulb before turning back the seersucker coverlets and crisp white sheets on the beds. I was plumping the pillows when the doorbell rang.

A shard of adrenaline went through me. *Why* had I done this?

I did my best to compose myself on the way to the door. I opened it to find Kat wearing an almost-normal sundress, her wet hair pulled back into a low ponytail, and Zach in clean jeans and a T-shirt that was only slightly damp with sweat from the walk over.

"God bless you fer this," Kat gushed as I motioned them inside. She inhaled a huge breath of cool air. "Oh, man, does that feel good."

Smiling, Zach scanned my living room. "I swear. Betty Freakin' Crocker."

Kat elbowed him, hard, in the side. "Shut up, Zach. This woman rescued us from spendin' the night in a furnace with a million mosquitoes. Don't make fun of her just because she's a better housekeeper than I am." She looked over my perfect parlor. "This is beautiful. Did you have a decorator?"

Not a polite question, but I knew she meant well. "No, I did the whole house myself." I stepped toward the hallway. "Let me show you to your room."

As they followed, Kat took everything in with wide-eyed approval. "Wow. This is gorgeous. You really got a knack."

When we reached the guest room, they exchanged a brief glance on seeing the twin beds, but didn't comment, and I didn't offer to push them together. The last thing I wanted was to hear them humping through the wall.

"Have y'all had supper?" I asked, hoping they had.

Zach's eyes lit up. "Actually, we were so hot, we didn't feel like eating." As if on cue, his stomach growled loudly. "But now that we're cool, I could use a little something. But don't go to a lot of trouble."

What did I have on hand? Pork chops in the fridge, and butter peas in the freezer. I could make a salad to go with it. "Do y'all eat pork?"

"Oh, yes," Zach said eagerly.

"Great. Y'all just relax, then." I pointed to the little color TV on the dresser. "Watch some TV if you'd like. I'll have supper ready in half an hour." I started for the kitchen, preoccupied with ordering my tasks.

Kat followed. "Please let me help."

Remembering what Zach had said about her cooking, I knew her "help" would only complicate matters, but it would be rude to say no, so I accepted. "Sure. Come on."

I heard the Braves game coming from the guest room as we entered my eat-in kitchen with French doors onto the back deck.

"Ho-lee crap!" Kat said in awe. "This looks like a magazine." She peered at the gleaming surfaces. "How do you keep it so clean?"

I responded with a massive understatement. "I like things clean." I got the butane grill lighter and headed for the deck. "Just let me light the grill, and we can start cooking."

"A gas grill," Kat admired, following me to the door, but staying inside the cool as I braved the heat. "I swear, this place is perfect."

I couldn't help feeling proud to hear it. Back inside, I headed for the refrigerator to take out the meat and salad things, then start the butter peas cooking. "I know you're tired from all that heat. Why don't you just sit down and keep me company while I throw things together?"

I could see Kat was relieved. "Thanks." She pulled out a chair to face me and sat. "My luck, I'd probably make a mess or break somethin', anyway."

Maybe it was her transparency, but I heard myself confide, "I had to learn to cook when I was little. My mother was too sick to do it. I started making recipes from the paper when I was only eight."

Sympathy clouded Kat's features. "Wow. Is yer mama okay now?"

"Managing," I said, wondering why I was telling her. "I still bring her food."

"In Atlanta."

"Yeah. Off Defoors." Too much, I'd told too much. I didn't even know this woman. "How about you? Is your mother living?"

Kat shrugged. "Beats me. She drank a lot, and it made her mean. Then she took off when I was twelve. Daddy did everything after that, but it broke his heart. He'd cussed liquor so long because of Mama, but after she left, he took to drink too. I tried to help him, but it never worked. Finally it got so bad, I took off and headed for Tenth Street."

I'd been tempted a thousand times to leave Mama, but never had the courage to do it on my own. "How did you manage?"

Kat grinned. "I met Zach the first day. The rest is history."

Minus a little thing called a wedding. I put a couple of strips of bacon into the boiling butter peas, then washed my hands and got out the cutting board to make the salad. "Do you like green peppers in your salad?"

She colored, her glance shifting to the side. "Well . . . I like them, but they don't like me, if you git my drift."

"That's okay. I'll leave them out." I reached for my little food diary and opened it to *K* for Kat, then wrote her name, with "no green peppers" underneath.

"What's that?" Kat asked, alert.

"A list of what everybody does and doesn't like to eat, so I won't ever serve them the wrong things."

Kat's expression was a mixture of awe and *this woman doesn't have enough to do.*

"Anything else y'all don't like?" I asked her, pen poised.

"Onions, actually." She leaned forward to confide, "They make me fart like a biker at a bean-eatin' contest."

I couldn't help laughing. She was crass, but frankly funny.

I couldn't imagine being so honest. Didn't she know that people could use that to hurt her? "Okay. No onions for you." I wrote them down, then skipped to the middle of the page and wrote Zach's name. "What about Zach?"

"Zach'll eat anything," Kat said. "Even *snails.*" The last came with a shudder. "But me . . . no insects. Not that you'd serve 'em, of course," she qualified. "And I cain't stand guts of any form. No chitlins or liver or brains or anything, no matter what kinda animal it comes from. I'd probably be glad to git 'em if I was starvin' to death, but otherwise, *n-o.*" She smiled. "That's about it fer me."

"I'm the same way about liver and all," I said as I recorded the guts part, though I'd never thought of it in such crass terms. That done, I put the book back alongside *The Joy of Cooking,* then went to wash my hands.

"You think that book up all by yourself?" Kat asked.

I finished my handwashing ritual by drying thoroughly with a fresh white towel, then using some unscented lotion. I washed them so often, they chapped if I didn't.

"One of my home ec teachers told me about it," I said. "She was really a great teacher."

Kat's eyes narrowed. "I bet you were real good at school, weren't you? All organized and everything."

Too much. Too many personal questions, too soon. I turned it around with, "How about you? Did you like school?"

"Yep." That was a surprise. "I love readin'," she told me, "but I was a lot better in math. I was takin' calculus before I quit tenth grade, but that was that."

The idea of Kat taking calculus in tenth grade seemed like a total oxymoron, but it made me realize I'd definitely made some hasty judgments because of her accent and bad grammar. "Did you ever miss school? Regret dropping out?"

"Oh, I got my GED soon as I hooked up with Zach," she said, matter-of-fact. "He insisted."

Good for Zach.

"I'm startin' college in the fall," she said with pride. "Got me a scholarship to Oglethorpe."

Wonders never ceased.

"What about Zach?" I prodded.

She glanced back toward the sound of the Braves game, then told me in a confidential tone, "This is supposed to be a deep, dark secret, but seein' as we're neighbors, I'm gonna trust you." She shot another glance at the hallway door to make sure Zach wasn't coming, then said, "Don't let on, but he's got his MBA. From *Hah*-vahd." She mimed locking her lips.

I was properly shocked, but that explained his cultured accent.

Then she dropped another little surprise. "Went to work for one of them huge Fortune Five Hundred military-industrial companies, but they used him for a slave and tried to kill his soul. So he finally just dropped out." She straightened, her features clearing as she draped one arm over the chair. "Never looked back," she said with pride. "Plumbin' suits him a lot better. He gits to help people who need him, and he says at least he can be honest shovelin' the shit fer real. Plus, no pressure." She grinned. " 'Cept water pressure, of course."

Harvard?

"I knew that would set you back on your heels," Kat said with glee.

"What would?" Zach asked, his question preceding him into the kitchen.

Kat went scarlet. "Just girl talk. Never you mind." She pointed to the plate of pork chops. "Why don't you grill them chops fer Betsy?" She looked to me. "He's great with the grill. If he wasn't, we'd both starve."

I handed Zach the plate with new respect, but couldn't resist cautioning, "They're better if they're not too well done. Well, they do need to be *done*, but not dry."

He grinned, carefully keeping the food away from his beard. "Done, but not dry, comin' up."

While he was doing that, I finished the salads, then hesitated before setting the table. They'd probably feel bad if they knew I'd already eaten, so I decided to set myself a place too. Once everything was done, I put the salads and the bowl of butter peas on the table, then lit the candles.

"Candles?" Kat protested mildly. "You don't have to use up yer good candles fer us. We're just grateful to be here."

" 'Treat royalty like friends and friends like royalty,' " I quoted, snapping the lighter off. "I love making things special."

Kat peered at me in assessment. "Bless yer heart. Nobody ever made things special fer you, did they?"

In one brief conversation, she'd gotten closer to the truth than any of my other so-called friends. "I just like to do things for people," I blustered. "Strictly selfish. Makes me feel good."

Fortunately, Zach arrived with the pork chops, and the conversation shifted to eating. During supper, I steered the topic to the development, and we shared what we'd heard or seen about potential buyers and the beginnings of the swim/tennis club. Both Zach and Kat turned out to be quite witty, and we all laughed a lot. By the end of the meal, something amazing had happened: I felt quite at home with these weirdos.

So when I turned off my bedside light to watch the eleven o'clock news, I did so without a shred of fear. I didn't even care if my guests were fornicating on the other side of the wall. After getting to know them, it didn't matter so much. After all, their relationship was their business, really, and Christians aren't supposed to judge.

I couldn't wait to tell Greg what had happened. Now that I knew all about the neighbors, he couldn't get mad at me for rescuing them from the heat.

The trouble was, I only *thought* I knew them. Turns out, transparent Kat wasn't really that transparent, and Zach had deeper, darker secrets to hide, ones that didn't blow up (literally) till later.

Four

The past. Sandy Springs. June 1974, the day after the hippies spent the night

Y ou *what?*" Greg hollered so loud, I had to pull the receiver away from my ear. "Good Lord, Elizabeth," he scolded, "have you lost your mind?"

That stung, in light of Mama's mental illness, which I prayed daily wasn't hereditary. "Calm down, honey," I soothed. "I couldn't very well just drive right past them when they were camping out in the hundred-degree heat under a *funeral parlor* tent in their front yard. It wouldn't be Christian. The mosquitoes would have eaten them alive."

"And probably gotten high in the process," Greg snapped. "Honestly, Betsy, this makes me wonder how I can leave you alone. Letting those people into our house was absolutely reckless."

"Well, I had my panic button," I defended. "And anyway, it

was fine." I explained everything I'd learned, finishing with, "So you see, the police chief was right. We don't have anything to worry about. They're really very nice. A college student and an Ivy League–educated plumber." A thought occurred to me. "Heck, he might even play tennis, after all. I should have asked."

"No you shouldn't," Greg bit out. "He shouldn't have even been there in the first place, much less talking to you."

"But honey, it all worked out fine," I coaxed.

"Lucky for you," he said. "What if it hadn't? The police would have had to break in to find your body."

I could tell he was really shaken. Greg was so protective of me, he didn't even like my going to my old neighborhood alone—in broad daylight—to see Mama. "Honey," I said, "I didn't mean to upset you. I'm so sorry." How could I make it up to him? "I invited them on impulse. I promise I'll never ask anybody to spend the night again without talking it over with you first."

That seemed to mollify him. "Good. And stay away from that Zach guy, okay? He's still a hippie. He might slip you drugs, then ask you to do a threesome or something."

"I promise you, he's harmless." I was flattered by my husband's jealousy, but Zach didn't seem to be the underhanded type, and he definitely wasn't a swinger. In my old neighborhood, I could tell by the time I was twelve who was and who wasn't a swinger, which was why I'd been so drawn to Greg when we met. I'd liked that he was older, already settled with a great job, and so protective of me.

"I mean it, Betsy. Keep your distance from that guy," he repeated.

He was just worried about me. It had been reckless, inviting them over without knowing anything about them. "Okay," I conceded, "I'll steer clear of Zach. But is it okay if I have Kat over, by herself? She doesn't know how to cook, and it would be fun to teach her."

Greg hesitated, then said with reservation, "Okay. As long as she's alone. But make sure she doesn't put anything into the food. Those hippies try to turn people on all the time." As if he knew, which he didn't. So far, the closest my husband had gotten to a hippie was when we drove within three blocks of Tenth Street to see the opera at the Fox. Still, it was sweet of him to worry about me.

"I'll keep an eye on her."

"Okay. And keep an eye on things across the street. If you see anybody suspicious over there, write down their license numbers."

Oh, really. "What if I can't see them?" I asked.

"Use the binoculars in the top drawer of my dresser."

I rolled my eyes. "Okay. But only because it'll make you feel better."

A pregnant pause followed, then Greg said, "I almost hate to bring this up now, but there's been a change of plan. The client's board wants me to give a report on our progress at their regular meeting Monday, which means I'll have to work all weekend to put it together."

So he wouldn't be able to come home on schedule. My heart sank, but I resolved to remain upbeat. He couldn't help it, after all, and he'd warned me this might happen. "I'm sorry, honey. I'd planned a special celebration, but it'll keep. When will you be able to come, or do you know?"

"Oh, the weekend after, absolutely. And I'll get to stay till Wednesday this time, so I can turn in my paperwork and bring the office up to speed."

"That's fabulous." That would give me five whole days with plenty to do, and my husband back in my bed. I hadn't realized how horny I was till I thought about it. "I can't wait to see you."

"You sure are a wonderful corporate wife," he complimented, his voice warm.

I smiled, missing him intensely. "You sure are a wonderful corporate husband."

"I love you," he said, the first time in quite a while. The fact that he didn't say it often made it even more precious.

"It sure feels good to hear that," I mooned. "I love you too."

"Bye. I'll call tomorrow." The line went dead.

I lay back in the muted light of the TV, happy that I was married to a man as good as Greg. And happy that I'd gotten past telling him about the hippies. "Dodged a bullet there," I said aloud.

But I'd be alone this weekend. And bored.

Maybe it was time to start teaching Kat to cook.

Wide awake, I got out of bed and headed for my cookbooks to find some simple recipes to start with.

Greg's warning resurfaced on the way to the kitchen: *But make sure she doesn't put anything into the food.*

I mean, really.

Somehow, I had to figure out a way for Greg to meet Zach and

Kat on level ground. I knew he'd like them, if he just gave them half a chance. Especially if Zach played a decent game of tennis. The courts were coming right along.

Maybe Zach could braid his beard to play.

Three years ago, home from L.A. to Hartsfield Airport, Atlanta

I always hate coming home from a trip. I hate good-byes. And returning to reality.

Normally, Kat would have taken me to the airport and picked me up, but ever since Greg had started filling her head with lies about me, I hadn't felt comfortable asking. My younger daughter Emma had up and moved to Alaska when her father refused to support her after she finally graduated two years behind her class, and Mama was useless, of course. I wasn't close enough to anybody else to ask, so I'd driven myself and parked in the cheapest long-term lot I could find, miles from the airport.

My flight landed in Atlanta on time, but we were stuck on the blazing tarmac forty minutes, waiting for a gate. Once we finally deplaned, I went to baggage claim, where it took another forty minutes for my suitcase to come up. Then I wrangled my luggage out into the afternoon heat to get to the long-term parking shuttle. Fifteen minutes later, I got out at my white Infiniti SUV and popped open the back for the shuttle driver to load my suitcase and carry-on. "Thank you so much." I tipped him five as he closed the hatch. "I really appreciate that."

"Thank *you*, ma'am."

I always overtip. It's a compulsion.

The metal roof overhead radiated heat like an oven as I walked to the driver's door and opened it to a blast of stale heat.

I cranked up the car and set the air to high on recirculate. Mama always insisted I should roll down the windows as soon as I got in, to let out the worst of the heat, but on days like this, that was like opening the door of a blast furnace, so I didn't. Till I had to give the cashier my ticket at the gate.

"That'll be a hundred and forty dollars, please," she said cheerfully. "Would you like a cold drink?" As if it would make up for the outrageous rates they all charged.

May as well. I handed her my Visa. "Diet Coke, please." I usually avoided canned drinks but one drink wouldn't kill me, and I was still parched from the long flight.

She handed me the cold can and the receipt to sign. "Thank you for using Park N Pad."

I scribbled my name and handed back the receipt, anxious to get the window back up, then drove away.

Once I'd navigated the maze to the connector, I settled back for the slow, congested ride up to the I-75 cutoff and the Howell Mill exit to see Mama, consoling myself that at least I wasn't coming home to Rhomboid Avenue. I loved my house, even if it was across the street from my ex and my future wife-in-law.

I remembered the delicious idea that had occurred to me when I heard about the wedding, and brightened. Might as well have a little fun with the situation.

Buoyed, I called Mama with my cell to see if she'd eaten.

"Hey, Mama. I'm back. Amelia and Sonny and the girls send their love."

"I've practically starved to death since you went off and left me," she complained. "That Meals-On-Wheels crap is inedible. All I can stomach is the milk. Who eats plain baloney on trash bread?" she said for the hundredth time. "Who in their right mind eats baloney, period?"

I overlooked the irony of the "right mind" comment, and reminded myself that this was her way of saying she'd missed me. "I missed you too, Mama," I said. "How about I bring you Varsity for supper?"

She cheered right up. "Oh, now, that would be wonderful. I'll have two regular burgers, a chili dog, and fries and rings," she rattled off, as if I didn't know the drill. "And a brownie. And a Big Orange. Not an orange frosty, a plain Big Orange." The same thing she'd always ordered for as long as I could remember.

"Comin' up." I was feeling so mellow, I didn't even ask her to pick something out for me to take home. She wouldn't do it, anyway. "See you in thirty or so. Bye."

I flipped the phone closed, then got off the freeway just before the North Avenue overpass, then drove to Atlanta's favorite melting pot and went in to pick up the food. Watching the red-capped servers put two orders of rings into the box, I remembered what Kat had told me about onions that long-ago time they'd spent the night, and chuckled. One nice thing about going back to my empty house: I could eat all the onions I wanted, then "pass wind" at will, and nobody would ever know.

The past. Sandy Springs. July 1, 1974

The cooking lessons turned out to be a disaster. I couldn't tell if Kat just wasn't interested in learning, or she had some kind of disconnect when it came to the whole process.

She laughed a lot when her efforts went awry, but she was clearly embarrassed.

Two weeks into our sessions at my house—after a particularly frustrating morning of trying to make biscuits—I took her tray and mine out of the oven. They didn't even look like the same food group.

Kat braced her dough-stuck hands on the island and sighed. "This is hopeless. Yours come out floatin' and melt-in-yer-mouth, and mine come out like hockey pucks. With freckles." She sighed heavily, then ventured, "I swear, Betsy, I 'preciate you tryin', more than I can say. But this ain't gonna work. Maybe it's my aura or somethin'." She leveled a frank gaze at me. "Truth is, I got school comin' up, so maybe this idn't the exact right time fer me to start cookin', anyhow. Way I see it, cookin's kinda like sewin'. Once people find out you know how, they 'spect you to do it, don't you know?"

So she didn't really want to learn. "Oh. I'm sorry," I said. "I didn't mean to press."

Kat reacted to my disappointment. "Now, don't go gittin' yer feelins hurt," she cautioned. "You've been a real good friend, doin' this fer me, and I'll never fergit it. I'm *lucky* to have a friend like you, right across the street 'n' all. I just think we need to find somethin' else to do together, maybe."

Well, if she really didn't want to cook . . . Different strokes for different folks. I looked at Kat's biscuits and laughed out loud. "Maybe you ought to stick to vegetable soup, after all."

She sagged with relief. "Thanks. Yer the best. I knew you'd understand." Happy, she went to scrub the last of the overworked dough from her hands.

"C'mon, then." I put some of my hot, fluffy biscuits on a plate and headed for the butter and jam on the table. "Bring our tea. We can figure out what you'd like to do while we eat."

Kat brought over our iced teas and sat, her expression intense. "Whut I'd really like is fer you to take me to museums and teach me about culture. Most of the other students at Oglethorpe probly know about all that stuff, but we didn't have any museums where I come from back in Kentucky, so I never learned any of that stuff."

"I learned all that from books," I confessed. Georgia State wasn't big on the fine arts when I was there. "But it would be fun to see the museum collections." I could find out everything about the local museums from the reference department at the library. "Which one would you like to go to first?"

"That High Museum, downtown," she said. "Way I figure it, best to start with the biggest, then work our way down."

"Sounds like a good plan," I told her. "Maybe they have guides who can tell us about the paintings."

"Perfect." Kat glowed.

Regardless of the differences between our politics and lifestyle choices, Kat and I both came from humble backgrounds, and we both wanted more out of life. It was as good a basis as any for a friendship.

Five

Worn out from the long flight from L.A., I left Mama's in time to get home before dark.

I always hate coming home to a stale, stuffy house after a trip, especially to find my ex-husband's car parked across the street in my widowed best friend's driveway. Especially when he's cheerfully cutting the grass in the ninety-degree heat, something he never did at my house, regardless of the temperature.

He actually had the nerve to wave at me as I turned into my driveway.

What a hypocrite.

I just ignored him and kept right on going.

If Greg was willing to go to those lengths to impress Kat, she must not be sleeping with him yet. Not that I cared if she did, except for the fact that she might catch something from him.

Perversely, I wondered if my presence would be there with them when they finally did get down and dirty.

An evil smile overtook me as I wondered if Kat liked it quick, with no foreplay. I had, because Greg was the only man I'd ever slept with, but that didn't apply to Kat.

I wondered if Zach's presence would be in bed with them too.

Served Greg right, if it was.

I pulled into the garage, then closed the door behind me and got out to the smell of hot, oily metal from the car. Lugging my suitcases out of the trunk, it occurred to me that it might be fun to ask Greg to come do it for me. But I decided it would be even more fun to ask him to cut *my* grass—in front of Kat. See how long this Mr. Fixit façade lasted when I asked him to do something nice for me, for a change.

Entering my house, I was greeted by two weeks' worth of hot, stale air.

"Whoa." My personal thermostat shot to boiling, so I made straight for the AC control and adjusted it from eighty to sixty-eight. While I waited for things to cool down, I gulped two bottles of cold spring water, then went to freshen up. After much blotting, I renewed my undereye concealer, lipstick, and mascara. No need for blush in this weather. I was red as the beefsteak tomatoes in my vegetable patch.

Looking human again, I gulped down another cold water, then headed across the street in the sweltering dusk.

I hadn't reached the sidewalk at Kat's before she came out to see what was up. I waved to her and called over the lawn mower, "Congratulations!"

Seeing Kat, Greg pulled out the earplugs to his iPod and followed her line of sight to me. Immediately, his features congealed.

Good. He ought to be wary. I knew the sordid truth about his desertion, things I hadn't even told Kat because they were too humiliating. Clearly, Greg hadn't shared them with her either. He always had been able to erase unpleasant realities from his mind, especially when they got between him and what he wanted.

Not that it was my business to tell Kat the gruesome details. She knew what he'd done to me, but still wanted him anyway. Maybe Greg's flexible memory was contagious.

I passed him with a friendly wave and greeted Kat with a cheery, "Hey."

"Hey." She watched with suspicion as I climbed the stairs.

Boy, had he brainwashed her. I smiled. "Amelia tells me you two are going to get married."

Defensive, Kat started up with, "Now, Betsy. We've been through all this already. Greg's gotten right with God. He's not the same man he was."

"And glory hallelujah, thank God for it," I said as sincerely as I could manage. I waved again to Greg, who abandoned the lawn mower in concern and headed our way. "I think I'll wait till Greg gets here to tell y'all both what I came over to tell you."

Kat's suspicion deepened. "Are you sure that's necessary?"

It hurt to see she didn't trust me anymore. She'd find out the hard way about the man he really was. But that was her problem, not mine. I was just glad he had somebody to look after him, so the girls wouldn't have to worry about him.

Panting from the heat, Greg wiped his face with a spotless

linen handkerchief as he approached. In spite of his sweat-soaked T-shirt, he draped a possessive arm across Kat's shoulders. "So. What brings you here, Betsy?"

I looked at them both, amazed at how peaceful I felt. "I've just come to congratulate Greg and wish you both the best."

Their mouths almost dropped open.

"I mean it." I turned to Kat. "Kat, honey, I hope you have every good and gracious thing together." Not that I believed they would, but I could hope. "You deserve it."

Greg tightened his arm around Kat, unconvinced, but she pulled free of him and hugged me gingerly. "Thanks, Betsy. That means a lot to me."

God bless her. She'd need it.

Heck, maybe Greg really *had* changed. That would be even better. Kat would be happy, and Greg might cut my grass sometimes. Lord knows, Kat was welcome to him. After what he'd done to me, I certainly didn't want him anymore.

Now for the fun part.

I leaned toward Kat in earnest. "Would you like for me to walk him down the aisle and give him away with my blessing?" I asked. "Because I'd be delighted to, really."

The look on their faces was worth a million.

"It would make things so much easier on the kids," I said, "don't you think?"

Greg frowned in disapproving confusion. Kat pursed her lips, nostrils flaring, and bit out, "I don't think so."

Boy, was it good to be over my ex. "Okay. Whatever you want." I started for home, leaving them frozen in consternation. "But if you change your mind, just let me know." I stopped at the edge of the porch. "Oh, and Greg, while you've got the lawn mower out, would you mind doing my yard too? My lawn mower's on the fritz." True.

He scowled. "Sorry, but Kat's is about all I can handle."

I pretended to be disappointed. "Oh. The thing is, I can't find anybody to come fix mine. They all want me to bring it to them, and there's no way I can get it into my trunk." I used my best poor-pitiful-me face. "But if you can't, you can't. I was just thinking about the neighbors. Don't want my yard to be the sore spot on the block."

Kat elbowed him. "Greg, do it," she whispered sharply. "She needs help."

Greg did what Greg did best: he balked. "Sorry. No can do." He grabbed Kat by the elbow and dragged her into the house, leaving the lawn mower sputtering in the yard.

Suppressing a smile, I turned and went home without looking back.

Once there, I went straight for the snacks and the white zinfandel, then sat eating chips and salsa, sipping my wine and thanking God that I didn't have to take care of anybody but myself for the moment.

After I unpacked and went to bed, I said my prayers for the girls and my grandchildren, then added, "And God, please help Greg be the man Kat deserves. She's already so hurt from losing Zach." My spoiling had helped make Greg the selfish jerk he was, but Kat didn't deserve to be taken advantage of. Greg's lingering hostility to me kept me from believing his sudden conversion. He was simply doing whatever it took to get Kat to take care of him. "Please, God, protect her."

Leaving it on God's doorstep, I rolled over and went to sleep, then ruined everything by having an erotic dream about my ex at four in the morning. I was so mad when I woke up, I wanted to call his cell phone and cuss him out. Only good sense kept me from doing it.

After all, it wouldn't do to tell *him*. He'd gloat forever.

Why had I let him into my dreams? Was just seeing him enough to trigger it? Lord, I hoped not.

Lying there in the dark, I wondered how I was going to manage, day in and day out, with Greg across the street.

How can you move on with your ex married to your best friend across the cul-de-sac? But Greg was a creature of habit who hated change, so I knew better than to hope he'd move away once they were married. The flat real estate market aside, Kat's home would be way too convenient and familiar for him, doggone it.

Speaking of dogs, he'd have some adjusting to do with her feckless menagerie. I let out an evil chuckle.

And Kat's horrendous housekeeping. That wasn't going to sit well with my marine.

I smiled in the darkness. Maybe if Kat was lucky, Greg would get tired of the mess and clean it up himself. Now, there was a picture.

One thing was sure: things were about to change at Kat's. I just hoped it would be for the better.

On that happy thought, I rolled over and went back to sleep.

. . .

In spite of my continued efforts to be friendly, Kat still froze me out. By the time her kids started decorating her house for the wedding, Amelia—who'd refused to have any part of her father's remarriage—was begging me to come see her in California, so I wouldn't be there when it happened. On the other hand, Emma, who'd been flown down for the wedding, argued that it was fine if I stayed home during the ceremony—as long as I didn't peek out the windows while the wedding was taking place on Kat's front porch.

Personally, I didn't see what all the fuss was about. I'd meant it when I said I hoped my ex and my wife-in-law would be happy. I just wished they'd do it somewhere else.

Six

April 1, 1957. Rhomboid Avenue, Atlanta

Daddy was packing, but I didn't believe he was really leaving. Mama had said he was, but it was April Fools' Day. So I didn't cry when she'd told me over breakfast that he was leaving us for another family, and I couldn't talk to him about it, not one word, or he'd get mad and never come see me again. Or even call. But it had to be a joke.

I knew my father loved me, and he would never leave me with crazy Mama. Even if he did find another family without a crazy mother like mine, he'd take me with him. So I sat on the big bed and swung my feet back and forth while he packed, waiting for him to say "April Fools!"

Mama was in her chair in the living room, watching her soap operas, as usual, another reason not to believe Daddy was really leaving. If he really, truly *was* going, Mama would be hysterical. I mean, how would she live? She never went out anymore, not even to take care of the roses she used to love when I was little.

Where would she get money for food, and who would bring the groceries without Daddy? Who would take me to the bus stop and pick me up on rainy days?

No, he couldn't really be leaving.

But when he scanned the room with tears in his eyes, then latched the big, beat-up suitcase he'd found in all the stuff Mama piled into our little house, I stopped swinging my legs.

His tears came faster, flooding his cheeks as he looked at me as if his heart would break. Then he hugged me, drawing me into his lap on the bed. "If there was any other way to do this," he whispered, his words shaking, "my darling girl, I would find it. I tried, spent everything I had to try to keep you, but the judge was a throwback to the Middle Ages."

Throwback? What was that?

Daddy sure wasn't acting like this was a joke. My blood congealed inside me, prickling everywhere there was life. "Keep me?"

Daddy's body quaked, holding me tight. "I thought sure they'd let me take you when they saw how sick Mama is, but they didn't. So now it's too late. Your mother signed the divorce papers, and the judge said you have to live with her."

I loved my mama, but her sickness had made me dream of escape with my father ever since I was old enough to realize that other people didn't live like we did.

"Now, the only way I can make the payments is to take the job in Saudi Arabia." He broke down and sobbed.

I didn't know exactly where Saudi Arabia was, but I knew it was very far away.

Divorce.

This couldn't be real. Daddy couldn't go off and leave me with Mama.

Cold. My hands and feet were so cold.

I grabbed on to Daddy with all my might. "You can't leave!" My voice came out high and shrill as a two-year-old having a tantrum. "Take me with you! I'll do anything, just don't leave me here with *her*! Please, God, no!"

Daddy pried himself from my grasp and stood. "I have no choice." He wiped his eyes with his shirtsleeve, suddenly looking like an old man.

"Betsy," Mama shouted over the blaring TV, "let your father leave in peace. Remember what I told you."

That he'd never call or visit if I tried to talk to him about it.

Grief and fear battled inside me, but in the end, fear of never seeing him again kept me silent. He was really going, saving himself, going to a normal family. And leaving me behind as a human sacrifice to Mama's never-ending needs and craziness. I sat there, crushed by the horror of being responsible for Mama. It weighed so heavy, I could barely breathe.

"There's a good girl, now," Daddy soothed. He reached into his pocket and handed me a business card that said "Family and Children's Services" with some woman's name and number at the bottom. Daddy's voice dropped to a tight whisper. "Hide this from your mother. If she doesn't take care of you, call this lady, and they'll get in touch with me."

He kissed the top of my head, then started working his way through the narrow path to the front door. "I'll write you," he called without looking back.

Too devastated to cry, I just sat there on my parents' bed as I heard the front door open, then slam.

This couldn't be happening. It had to be a nightmare, and I would wake up, and everything would be the same. Daddy would just be traveling on business. He was a very good salesman, so he traveled a lot.

I closed my eyes, hard, and willed it to be a dream. But I didn't wake up. My parents' room was just the way it always was, crammed with junk on Mama's side, and clean on Daddy's.

Crazy, how little of the piles and piles of *things* in our house had been his.

Hate exploded inside me, aimed at the idiot judge who'd refused to let me go with my daddy, and at my mother's sickness that had driven the one person I truly loved from my life. I started screaming from the bottom of hell and couldn't stop.

Mama appeared at the door to her room. "Good Lord, Betsy, you'll raise the dead. Shut up, before someone calls the police."

"I hope they do call the police," I shouted through my rage and grief. "And I hope they put you in jail, so I can go with Daddy!"

I expected her to scream right back at me, but instead, she came in and pulled me to my feet against her, gently rocking me back and forth despite my stiffness in her arms. "Oh, honey, I'm so sorry," she said with her cheek against the top of my head. "I didn't want to get divorced, but your daddy couldn't handle my sickness anymore. I couldn't let you go. You're all I have left in the world. You're my daughter, and I'm your mother. Nothing should take a daughter from her mother."

Torn asunder, I felt like some ancient old hag, dried up and empty, with the weight of the world on my shoulders. Of course Mama couldn't let me go. She needed me to take care of her.

But I was just a little girl. Mama was supposed to take care of me, not the other way around.

In that moment, I hated both my parents for what they'd done and vowed that I would never hurt my children the way Mama and Daddy had hurt me.

Even so, I missed my father so much, I could hardly get out of bed in the morning. At first, I raced to the mailbox every day when I got home from school, praying for a letter from him, but I never got a single one.

I made up all kinds of dramatic excuses in my mind for why he hadn't written, but as the months passed into years, I gradually accepted the fact that he'd abandoned me.

He was gone, but every Christmas and Thanksgiving after that, the dark bitterness of his absence hovered at the edge of my vision like a ghost. I never got over losing him.

And the more dependent on me my mother became, the more I resented Daddy for escaping, at my expense. I came to hate him as much as I longed for him.

So I never trusted my heart to anyone again, until my own children were born. The love I felt for my girls helped me understand why my mother couldn't give me up, even for my own good. Thanks to that, I stopped hating her, at least.

And I vowed to be the best wife and mother who ever breathed, so my husband would never, ever have cause to leave me.

Seven

When Kat came over for coffee, I was reading the paper and fuming.

She greeted me with, "Lord, you look like thunder and lightnin'. What's got yer panties in a wad?"

I showed her the headline: WILBUR MILLS DRUNK ON BOSTON STAGE WITH STRIPPER FANNE FOX. "Can you believe that idiot?" I fumed. "Chairman of the House Ways and Means Committee, and first he's caught speeding with that *stripper* in his car, and now, just a few weeks later, he's on stage with her, drunk as a skunk. No wonder this country's going to hell in a handbasket, with idiots like that in Congress."

He was a Democrat, of course.

Kat poured herself some coffee. "I thought it was pretty funny, myself."

She would.

"Just like the Kennedys and Marilyn Monroe," I grumbled. "And LBJ and his hookers, using the Secret Service as pimps. I mean, really. Why can't Democrats keep it in their pants?"

"I told you," Kat retorted, "those were just rumors about JFK and Marilyn Monroe."

How somebody as practical and flat-footed as Kat could still believe the myth of Camelot was beyond me, but we'd been round and round about this, so I didn't beat a dead horse.

"Well, there's no denying this stuff about the stripper and Mills," I told her. "There were plenty of witnesses. The man's married, for God's sake." I slammed the paper to the table in outrage. "It's bad enough the Democrats spend our tax money like it's water. Why can't they keep it in their pants?"

"I dunno," Kat said. "Maybe for the same reason the Republicans keep lying and selling the taxpayers down the river to special interest groups."

She had me there. With friends like Richard Nixon, conservatives didn't need any enemies, and Gerald Ford was the current national joke. "Why do you think their wives put up with it?" I asked. "I'd be out of there."

Never mind that going home to Mama wasn't an option. How could those women let their husbands shame them that way?

"You wouldn't give Greg a second chance if he had an affair?" Kat asked in genuine amazement.

"Not if I caught him cheating on me, then he did it again, in public." I took a sip of coffee, glad the conversation had shifted away from politics. "Fool me once, shame on you. Fool me twice, shame on me."

She shook her head. "Monogamy may have worked when people only lived to thirty-five, but in this day and age, it's absurd to expect it. That's why Zach and I don't want to get married. We're in the relationship because we want to be, not because we have to be."

Pure BS, perpetrated on women by men who didn't have the guts to commit, but I'd already made my feelings clear to Kat on that subject too. "What if you picked up the paper and it was Zach on the front page with his mistress?"

Kat wasn't ruffled. "I'd deal with it. But I wouldn't throw away a good relationship because he did something stupid. When all's said and done, he'd come to his senses."

I tucked my chin. "I hope you haven't told him that. It's giving him permission."

She slowly shook her head. "No it's not. It's being real." She let out a low chuckle. "But he's not going anywhere. I give the best head in the nation."

"Head?" It seems impossibly ignorant that a married woman like me didn't know what "head" meant in sexual terms, but I didn't. Whenever I'd asked Mama about sex, she'd said it was far too private to discuss with anybody but your husband, and that was that. So I'd learned about it from prudish manuals, not by talking to anybody my own age. With family secrets like mine, close friends had always been too risky.

"You know, *head*," Kat said, then mimed what she was talking about.

"Oh. Sure. Of course." I was appalled that she'd talk so openly about something so private. But at least she hadn't made fun of me for being so ignorant.

"You know what they say," Kat said with a sly grin, clearly enjoying my discomfort. "You can't keep 'em if you don't eat 'em."

"Oh, gross," I sputtered. "*Way* too personal."

Kat laughed, but she wasn't laughing *at* me. "Honey, it's just sex, a perfectly natural biological process. People shouldn't be so uptight about it."

"When you look up 'uptight' in the dictionary," I shot back, "you'll find my picture, so kindly tread lightly, here."

There was no intimidating Kat. "Mark my words," she advised. "You want to send Greg to nirvana, try it sometime."

That would shock him, for sure. He'd always taken the lead. When I considered springing something like that on him, I shocked myself, with a surprising response from my female parts.

No way would I ever tell Kat, though, if I did try it. Or anybody.

"What's your favorite position?" she prodded.

For us, there was only the one. "I don't know." Maybe I ought to take advantage of her more worldly experience. "What's yours?"

"I like to be on top, and ride him till his back arches like McDonald's."

Good grief. But it might be fun to try a little variety.

"Zach likes that?"

Kat helped herself to a powdered doughnut. "Loves it. But I save it for special occasions."

I couldn't believe we were talking about our sex lives. Or Kat was, anyway.

She eyed me askance with mischief. "I've got a book you need to read. Great stuff. It's called the *Kama Sutra*, from India." She chuckled. "It's an illustrated sex manual. It'll do wonders for your marriage."

I considered, then decided that looking at a book in private would be a lot less embarrassing than talking about my love life with Kat. "Okay. But do me a favor, please. Please don't tell anybody about it, even Zach. Or about this conversation. I'd die of embarrassment."

Kat patted my arm. "Don't worry. My lips are sealed. Best friends never rat each other out, especially to their husbands."

Best friends?

Nobody had ever used those words to apply to me, and my eyes welled in gratitude and astonishment. "Thanks," I stammered. "And your secrets will be safe with me. That's what I do best, keeping secrets." Kat's heart was as big as the moon, and I liked the idea of finally having a *best* friend at last.

She looked at me with such compassion, I almost lost control and cried. "Don't worry, Bets," she said with absolute sincerity. "I'm safe. You can trust me with your secrets."

"Okay." After all those years of keeping people at a distance, trusting Kat was one of the hardest things I ever did, but I never regretted it.

As for the *Kama Sutra*, Greg enjoyed my experiments immensely, but eventually grew suspicious and asked me where I was getting all my ideas.

I just smiled.

Let him wonder. Keeping a few secrets from your husband can be very, very sexy.

Eight

The second Tuesday in October, 1976. Eden Lake Court

Nineteen seventy-six was one of those good news/bad news years on Eden Lake Court. The good news was, Kat and I had become best friends. In the past two years, she'd looked out for me like nobody had since Daddy left me to fend for myself. She never questioned my helping my mother, but always took my side when Mama acted up. Kat always noticed whenever I was down, and cheered me up with funny stories from her life. She could even tell when I was getting sick, before I could (she said I "had that coming-down look"), and always brought me flowers (mostly from my own garden, but I didn't mind). It's the thought that counts, and she didn't have any flowers in her own yard.

We shopped together, did projects together. And we went to every chick flick that came to town. So, in the past two years, we'd been good company for each other, in spite of our opposite ideas about most everything, especially politics.

The bad news was, 1976 was our first major election as friends, and a sorry election it was.

Of all the Georgians in the history of my native state, why the good Lord and the devil made a pact to run Jimmy Carter, of all people, as our first and only presidential candidate was beyond me.

I'm not saying he wasn't a good man. I truly believed he was—committed to his ideals and Christian faith, and his marriage vows, which counts for something. But his platform and politics were pure pie-in-the-sky. He'd won the governor's seat by painting himself as a fiscal and political reformer, promising to clean up the excess and corruption that had pervaded Georgia politics since Reconstruction. But all Carter did, once elected, was shuffle departments and rename them, which didn't accomplish much besides infuriating the powers that be (including our Antichrist of a political boss, Tom Murphy). The most notorious example was the renamed state trade delegation, which couldn't even get anybody overseas to take their calls, much less see them, till they went back to being the Georgia Trade Commission—with a whopping big stationery bill, paid for by we the people. Multiply that times twenty, and you get the picture. So much for fiscal reform.

Not that I don't give the man credit for trying. But it's like what Teddy Roosevelt said about trying to reform the Department of the Navy: it was like boxing with a feather bed; when it was over, he was worn out, but the feather bed was in the same shape it was when he started.

So there Carter was, running for president, promising to fix things nobody could fix. All the transplants in the neighborhood and at church thought I'd be thrilled to support a native son for president, but I set them straight, making sure to compliment his morals.

I tried to set Kat straight too, but she refused to listen. Seems Carter met Zach at some state function several years ago and asked if he was married, and Zach told him he and Kat had been together for two years. Carter clapped him on the back and said a good woman was hard to find. Then, last June when Zach was in New York on business (I guess plumbers have conventions too), he ran into Carter and his entourage in a hotel lobby, and Carter not only remembered his name (hard to forget Zach and all that hair), but asked how Kat was doing.

After that, it was all over but the shouting. The day Zach got home, he staked Carter signs every two feet along the sidewalk in front of their house, then bumper-stickered the Vanagon to smithereens. The next thing you know, Kat was volunteering full-time at Carter's campaign office downtown.

Forget issues—most notably, who was going to *pay* for all these programs he was promising. (We, the people.) But Kat and Zach, like most Americans, had been seduced by image, and there was no talking to them about the bottom line.

Meanwhile, I was left having to support *Gerald Ford*, of all people, a national joke with the face of a Gila monster, who'd pardoned Tricky Dicky (don't get me started on him!). Worse still, the party had picked Bob Dole for his running mate, who made a pressure-treated two-by-four look like the life of the party. Most recently, Ford had embarrassed us further by publicly declaring that the Poles were free and unoppressed. How ignorant can you get?

I mean, what kind of choice was a man like that? Definitely *not* the person I wanted with his finger on the red button in the war room.

For the second time (Watergate being the first) I'd seriously considered canceling my membership to the Republican Party. But Greg—a die-hard fiscal reactionary—asked me not to, for business reasons, and my fellow party members played the Armageddon card (spendthrift Democrat policies), so I sucked it up and stayed on board.

So, as president of the Young Republican Women, I agreed to host a makeover brunch at nine on the first Tuesday in October for fifty prospective members, with a drawing for three complete makeovers. I'd invited Kat, who needed a makeover more than anybody I'd ever known, but she'd turned me down, horrified that I'd thought she might consider fraternizing with so many Republicans.

That morning dawned clear as a bell, with a crisp, seductive little breeze that cheered up everybody, including me. By nine, the refreshment committee had set up the buffet, and the hairdresser and makeup artist were ready to make over the three lucky women who won the door-prize drawing.

People didn't really start arriving till twenty minutes later, which was to be expected, and they all made straight for the buffet. I stationed Sarah McGuire at the front door while I checked to make sure the homemade goodies were replenished. Sure enough, we were running low on my special spiced cider. I was adding some brown sugar and lemon to a fresh pot of apple juice on the stove when Sarah came up behind me and tugged at the sleeve of my Sunday dress. "Betsy, I don't know how to tell you this," she said in an urgent whisper, "but some scary-looking bums are out there picketing your house. They're yelling at the guests and blocking their way."

What? "How did they get past security at the subdivision gate?" Alicia shrugged. "I have no idea."

"Here." I threw some nutmeg into the pot, then jerked off my apron and handed Alicia the ladle. "Stir. I'll take care of this."

On the way to the front door, I saw that everyone had gathered at the windows, craning their necks and buzzing.

I got to the front porch and saw Kat, along with about thirty disreputable-looking hippies chanting "Vote for Carter, vote for change!" as they picketed on the sidewalk in front of my house. Whenever one of my guests approached, the picketers deliberately blocked their way, so the sidewalk was stacking up with a frustrated traffic jam of women in their best tea party attire.

I could not believe my best friend would do this to me. When I glared at her, Kat shot me a mischievous grin. "Down with Republican corruption," she hollered. One side of her placard read GERALD FORD SUPPORTS CRIME, and the other, FORD WOULD PARDON HITLER.

The other placards bore similar Democrat hysteria, interspersed with Carter signs.

"Shame," the picketers shouted to our approaching guests as they tried to come up the driveway. "Vote for Carter! Vote for change! Nixon was a criminal, and Ford pardoned him!"

"Tommy," Kat called to one of the men over their chanting. "Where's the media?"

The media! Spare me.

"I called the paper and the TV," he shouted back. "They were supposed to be here, but some guy got his legs caught in a ditch cave-in downtown, so they're all down there covering that."

"Bummer," another man weighed in as Kat made a face.

Furious, I forced myself to conceal the anger and betrayal I felt as I hurried down the driveway as fast as my three-inch heels would allow. When I came alongside Kat, I said, "Kat, honey, I know we don't see eye-to-eye on politics, and I'll be the first to defend your right to free speech. But you and your people can't go intimidating my guests. Or blocking their access to the house. So could you please just ask your people to back off?"

Kat shot me a confrontational glare and kept right on marching as if I were just some annoying stranger, which hurt my feelings even more.

I tried one more time to get her to listen to reason. "Nobody's saying y'all can't picket. You just need to leave my guests alone."

Without even looking at me, she returned fire with, "Oh, really? The way you and these reactionary so-called pro-lifers leave women alone when they're trying to git a perfectly legal abortion?" Whoa. "'Scuse, me, but what's sauce fer the goose is sauce fer the gander." Her features congealed. "We're only doin' what we have to do to save this country from four more years of those criminals in Washington."

"Oh, please," I said. "Like the Democrats didn't have any criminals in Washington?"

Kat scowled at me and picked up her pace.

This was ridiculous. "Kat, honey," I bit out, "I'm asking this as a favor, friend to friend: have your people leave my people alone. I don't want any trouble here."

Her only response was to hold up her sign and holler, "Vote for the people, not the fat cats! God save democracy!"

"I've told you a million times," I snapped, "America is a democratic *republic, not* a democracy. Pure democracy is tyranny of the masses. It didn't work for the Greeks, and it won't work here."

She just smiled at me in challenge, then yelled to her cronies, "Sit-in for democracy!" In a blink, they broke ranks and sprinted for my front walk and the garage doors. Propelled by adrenaline, I ran after them, heels and all, and barely managed to get to the front porch before they formed a human blockade, then lay down, making it impossible for my guests to get in without climbing through my three-foot-tall azaleas.

Buzzing with outrage, my guests surged up the driveway, then congregated on the other side of the demonstrators.

Oh, Lord. What was I supposed to do now?

Kat and her thugs were trespassing, but if I called the cops, they'd arrest her along with the others. Even after what she'd just done to me, I didn't want that.

At the forefront of the waiting guests, several members of my thrift shop committee from church stopped in consternation, looking to me as if I could wave my magic wand and make this go away.

Think! There had to be some way to deal with this diplomatically.

The last thing I wanted was to have my best friend hauled off to jail. No matter how betrayed I felt over what she'd done to me, I refused to stoop to her level.

Then it occurred to me that Kat might want me to call the cops, so she could get some publicity. But friends don't have friends arrested, in my book, even if they are rabid Democrats with no respect for private property.

I had to think of something.

Then it came to me, like a ray of sunshine on a stormy day.

"Ladies," I called to my blockaded guests, "if y'all could please bear with me, I'll be right back and deal with this."

I raced inside to my dressing room and the bathroom, grabbing what I needed, then I headed for the kitchen. "I need this," I told Sarah as I untied the cutwork apron she was wearing, then put it on and dropped what I'd collected into its deep pockets.

I motioned to the stylist and makeup artist. "Could you two please bring some of your things and follow me?"

They exchanged curious glances, then nodded. The stylist grabbed his comb and scissors, and the makeup artist gathered a few brushes and her tackle box full of cosmetics.

Back on the front porch with them in tow, I smiled and raised my voice to declare, "As you ladies know, we are giving away some free makeovers today, thanks to two of Buckhead's finest cosmeticians, Stephen Manus for Salon Divine, and Kelly Cooper from You, You, You on East Paces Ferry."

A smattering of applause prompted the cosmeticians to take a bow.

I went on. "As it turns out, we have quite a few uninvited

guests." A murmur went up among the women. "Never let it be said that the party of Lincoln lacks manners," I went on. "So I am now extending the makeovers to include our protesters."

A confused murmur passed among the lie-ins.

I bent over to tell them, "Anybody who wants to participate, please remain lying on the ground. We will take this as a sign that you want to have a makeover. If you don't want one, simply get up and go back to the sidewalk."

Amused chuckles and applause spread through my side of the confrontation.

Kat tucked her chin in consternation.

I straightened, waiting for a response. When none of the picketers got up, I summoned my courage and initiated Plan A. "Well, it looks like you all want to participate. This is going to be fun."

Pulling my battery-powered hair clippers from my apron pocket, I stepped over behind the head of the hairiest of the lot, a tall, fat man with tattoos and long, frizzy hair, plus a huge multicolored beard. "You, sir, are our first lucky 'Dress for Success' makeover winner!" I flicked on the clippers, then grabbed his beard and managed to cut off two-thirds of it just below the chin before he jerked away from me and shot to his feet.

"Bitch, you cut my beard!" he hollered.

Cheers erupted from my guests, inside and out.

"Nobody gets away with that," he bellowed, drawing back a fist.

The onlookers gasped, but before he could hit me, Kat leaped up and hung on his cocked arm to stop him. "No, Moose! Don't. This is a nonviolent protest. Peace, man. Peace!"

Meanwhile, the braver of my guests came out onto the porch to back me up.

Furious, Moose stroked the scraggly remaining tress of his beard. "I'll sue you for doing this to me!" he shouted, towering over me.

"But we're not finished," I said cheerfully. "I'm sure you'll love it when we're all done." I looked to the stylist. "I'm thinking crew cut. What do you say?"

Stephen blanched, eyes wide.

Then a skinny male protester with a ponytail jumped up and pointed at me. "That's assault and battery," he accused. "I was a law student. That's assault and battery."

I knew all about assault and battery from growing up in my old neighborhood. "Actually," I said sweetly, "assault is a threat of harm or violence." I scanned my watching guests. "We have plenty of witnesses, here. Were any threats of harm or violence made?"

"No!" they responded as one.

Defensive, the ex-law student stuck out his chin. "Well, you can't cut somebody's hair without their permission!" He waggled his finger. "That's battery, and battery is a felony."

He didn't scare me. "But I had tacit permission, which *is* permission, by default," I responded, undaunted.

"That's garbage," another of the prone protesters said from behind the hand shielding his long moustache from potential attack.

"No, it's a tacit agreement," I said, eliciting more applause from the onlookers. I stepped over to stand behind the head of another longhair. "Once again, anybody who doesn't want a makeover *must* go to the sidewalk. Failure to do so will constitute your permission for a makeover, complete with shave and haircut."

"This is pure crap!" Moose thundered. "I'm gittin' outta here and callin' the cops."

"Feel free to use my phone," I told him sweetly as he stomped toward Kat's house, "but be sure to mention that you and your friends are criminally trespassing and assaulted my guests."

"You're not getting rid of us this easily," the ex-law student said, flopping back down beside the others, who stayed put.

I turned to ask them, "Anyone else like to leave? 'Cause if you don't, you're all going to get a shave and a haircut."

"Betsy, stop it," Kat said from her spot on the ground, "before things get out of hand."

"You stop it," I told her, the first hint of anger creeping into my voice. "You're supposed to be my best friend. No best friend would embarrass me like this. Why would you do such a thing?"

"You know I'm an activist. It's a matter of principle," she shot back, "not personal."

"Well, it feels pretty personal to me," I retorted. "I'm against smoking pot on principle, but you don't see me calling the cops, do you, when these bozos start toking at your house, in plain sight?"

A shocked murmur went up from the onlookers.

Kat turned beet red. "I cain't believe you'd bring that up in front of all these people."

At least I hadn't included her in my accusation. I motioned to the twenty women on the other side of the human blockade. "And I can't believe you would keep all these people from coming to my party. It's typical of you liberals. You want your freedom, but don't want anybody else to have theirs."

Applause and approval from my guests.

Suddenly I became aware that Kat and I had become the main attraction, so I forced myself to calm down and get back on plan.

I smiled and turned the clippers back on. "Okay. Since our first makeover winner decided to leave, I'll choose somebody else." I did a quickstep to the next protester and, catching him by surprise, grabbed a hank of his greasy bangs, then managed to buzz a strip from forehead to crown before his shock wore off and he escaped.

Cussing a blue streak, he told his cronies I was crazy, and he was leaving, and they should leave too, before I struck again. Apparently, the rest of the men decided the game wasn't fun anymore. I mean, principles were one thing, but hair was another, and anybody who tells you men aren't vain doesn't know what they're talking about.

"I didn't sign on for this," one of them complained as he got up and collected his placard.

"Me neither," said the one with the moustache. The rest of the men got up and headed for Kat's too, leaving her with only a handful of women.

Immediately, my waiting guests shot the gaps and headed inside, congratulating me on their way.

"All right," Kat said to me as she got up. "You win this one, but I'm not through."

"Bring those people back onto my property," I said firmly, "and I will have you all arrested."

"Why didn't you do it in the first place?" she challenged.

"Because I thought you were my friend." Turning my back, I shepherded the last of my guests inside, then closed the door behind me.

I had trusted her, let her into my heart, told her my secrets—well, some of them—and she'd betrayed me . . . for *political principles*. My stomach roiled.

Sissy Adams, sitting in one of the wingback chairs, looked out the front window. "The last of the protesters are going across the street," she announced. "Thank goodness." She turned back to tell me, beaming, "This was the most exciting thing that's happened to me since high school. Where can I sign up to join?"

Sarah waved the membership forms. "I have the sign-ups right here. Everyone who joins is eligible for the makeover drawing. Who'd like one?"

Hands went up everywhere as conversation swelled.

Sarah started distributing the forms. "When everyone's finished filling them out, we'll draw three for the makeovers."

"Just as long as Betsy doesn't do them," a girl on my ALTA team (Atlanta Lawn Tennis Association) called out.

Laughter evaporated the lingering tension, and the party went on as planned. Forty of the fifty-three guests present signed up as Republican Women, making the event a smashing success.

All was well until thirty minutes later, when we were all sipping tea and watching Stephen give the first makeover winner, drab Helen Foster, a cute shag haircut.

At the sound of cars and voices from the street, Sissy looked out and said, "Uh-oh," immediately diverting everyone's attention.

I went to the window and saw that a Fulton County sheriff's car had pulled up in front of Kat's, and two deputies were standing on her front walk surrounded by gesturing protesters, all talking at once and pointing to my house, while Kat looked on from her front porch, doing nothing to stop it.

My stomach ricocheted off my diaphragm. *They* had called the cops on *me!*

That tore it. I'd been Kat's friend, and this was how she repaid me.

A subdued buzz swelled behind me as my guests started getting up to see what was going on. "Hold that thought," Helen told Stephen as she joined them, still in her plastic cover.

While the policemen were taking notes and trying to maintain order, the WSB-TV van pulled up behind the squad car, and a reporter and a cameraman started setting up on the sidewalk.

A low moan escaped me. "Looks like I didn't dodge that bullet, after all."

Cindy Ashe came up and put her arm around my shoulder. "Don't you worry, sweetie. If they try to make trouble, my husband"—an up-and-coming trial lawyer downtown—"will take care of this for you. Don't you worry one little bit." She looked to the others. "We'll tell them what really happened, won't we?"

Affirmation surrounded me.

Across the street, the camera cranked up as the reporter started interviewing the guy I'd skunk-striped.

Sarah wrung her hands. "Everyone, why don't we go back to the makeover?" She did her best to shepherd the girls back to their rented chairs, but the real show was outside.

We all watched as the reporter tried to interview the deputies, then followed them up to my driveway, where the policemen motioned them back onto public property.

Poised, the cameraman kept shooting while the deputies came up and rang the bell.

Just damn. Kat had set me up, and now the law was at *my* doorstep!

Nine

The deputies looked truly apologetic. "I'm sorry to disturb you ladies," the shorter one said, "but we'd like to speak to"—he glanced at his notepad—"Miz Betsy Callison, please."

This could *not* be happening. I'd never even gotten a traffic ticket, and here was the law on my doorstep.

Act as if, act as if, act as if. My heart beating so hard I could hear my pulse, I answered with a composure I did not feel. "I am she."

"Miz Callison," the deputy said, "two men across the street claim you cut their hair without their permission." His partner grinned with approval. "Is this true?"

"No," I told them. "They, and all the others over there, were trespassing on my property and preventing my guests from entering."

"In a very threatening way," Cindy piped up from beside me.

One of her friends said, "I want to press charges! They blocked my way in a very menacing fashion."

The policemen looked to the others, who had gathered behind me. "Is this true?"

They all started talking at once in affirmation.

The policeman raised his hands. "Whoa, whoa, whoa." He looked to me. "Is it all right if we come inside and take statements?"

I stepped back. "Please do." I turned around. "Could everybody please just sit down? The deputies want to take your statements."

Immediately, they obeyed, the gleam of righteous anger in their eyes as they sat, straight-backed, waiting for a chance to weigh in.

Alicia appeared with two plates piled high. She batted her eyelashes at the taller deputy, who was practically salivating. "Would you two gentlemen like a little something to eat while you're working?"

The younger deputy reached out, but his partner smacked his arm with the notebook, saying, "Thank you so much, ma'am, but we're on duty, here."

"Maybe later," his disappointed partner whispered behind the older man's back. "After we're done."

"Absolutely," Alicia murmured with a seductive look.

"Jack," the older deputy ordered him, "you interview Miz Callison. When you're done, you can help me with the others."

Jack cast a long look at the retreating food, then turned to me and opened his notepad, pen poised. "All right, Miz Callison. Could you please explain to the best of your ability what happened here?"

I did. When I got to the part about cutting the beard and hair, he laughed out loud, earning a scowl from his partner, then apologized and finished taking my statement. When we were done, he shook his head and murmured, "Boy, are the guys back down at the station gonna love this."

Once everyone was finished, the older partner came to me with, "This is pretty complicated, ma'am. I'm gonna have to call in and get some clarification about the legalities. Could you please wait here? I'll be right back." He pointed to Jack. "Stay."

We watched him exit. "He doesn't like you much," I asked Jack, "does he?"

"That's putting it mildly," Jack confided.

"Maybe this will help," Alicia said, handing him the plate of food and a tall iced tea.

Jack beamed. "I do believe it will." One eye on the door, the deputy started gobbling it down like a famine victim.

"Show's over," Alicia announced, leading Helen Foster back to the makeover chair. "Stephen, could you please finish Helen's haircut?"

"Absolutely," he said with relief, but nobody paid attention when he resumed. We were all waiting for the deputy to come back.

Cindy gave me a sidelong hug. "Don't you worry, honey. I already called Forrest, and my daddy." A lawyer too, I assumed. "If they try anything, we're ready for them."

"Thanks. That makes me feel much better," I lied.

An approaching siren broke the silence as Stephen finished Helen's hair, almost drowning out his "And voilà," as he fluffed the flattering shag.

The doorbell rang, and Jack jumped up and stashed the remaining crumbs of his food as Alicia opened the door and let the older deputy in.

Hands gripped in my lap, I said a fervent prayer that this would all go away.

The older deputy walked over to Jack and whispered something, then Jack left.

He then approached me with a sheepish, "Miz Callison, much as it pains me to have to do this, I'm gonna have to ask you to come downtown with me. Since charges have been filed on both sides, we're gonna have to take everybody in and let a judge sort this out."

My guests erupted in protest.

Arrested? I was being *arrested*?

"Normally," the deputy said, "we'd take everybody down and book them, then wait for the judge to set bail. But because of the . . ."—I swear, he almost smiled—"unusual circumstances here, one of our Superior Court judges has agreed to hear the charges immediately."

A smug look on her face, Cindy clutched my shoulders. "Do not say a word till Forrest gets there. No small talk, no nothing. Not one word, except, 'I want to see my lawyer.' I'll call him, then be right behind you in my car." She gave me a peck on the cheek. "See you in court, sweetie." She smiled in reassurance. "Trust me, this is going to go away."

Alicia spoke for the rest of my supporters. "We're coming too. We're witnesses."

I motioned to her as I rose. "Please call Greg and tell him

what's happened, first," I asked. Not that he could do anything from Chicago. "His number is beside my bed."

Alicia nodded. "Don't worry, honey. I'll get him."

He was going to kill me for this. Especially if the firm's name got dragged into it.

Fighting back tears, I faced the deputy. "Are you going to handcuff me?"

Sympathy softened his features. "No, ma'am. As long as you cooperate, that won't be necessary."

Thank God. "I'll cooperate."

"I really am sorry about this." He took my arm. "If you'll just come with me . . ."

Feeling like I was living a Fellini movie, I went outside to find cameras from not only WSB, but WAGA and WXIA aimed my way.

Across the street on her porch, Kat jumped up in dismay as the protesters cheered my arrest. But their cheers stopped abruptly when three more patrol cars and a paddy wagon, sirens fading, ran the stop sign at the corner and headed their way. The cameras did a one-eighty to record their arrival.

Jack hollered for everyone to remain where they were, but one of the protesters booked it for the hills. The cameras captured Jack's pursuit and apprehension of the runner. Meanwhile, six patrolmen corralled the rest of the demonstrators, then herded them into the paddy wagon amid protests of "pig" and "fascist."

Halfway down the driveway by then, I halted abruptly in fear. "Are you going to put me in there with *them*?" Heaven only knew what would happen, if he did.

"No, ma'am," the deputy assured me. "You'll be with Jack and me."

Another small blessing in the midst of chaos. "Thank you so much."

Meanwhile, a significant number of my guests made for their cars to follow. "Remember," Cindy called as I was escorted into the backseat of the squad car, "don't say anything till Forrest gets there!"

I turned my head to escape the blinding glare of the cameras as the patrol car inched through the confusion for what seemed like ten minutes. Then, at last, we left them behind.

Dear heaven. My arrest was going to be on the nightly news.

I prayed that UFOs would buzz the White House, or anything of similar newsworthiness that would bump my story to oblivion, where it belonged.

Obeying Cindy's instructions, I didn't say a word all the way downtown. Sirens blaring, the paddy wagon caught up with us and followed the rest of the way to the Georgia Superior Court building, where a crowd of reporters waited.

"Maybe we ought to take her to a secure entrance," Jack suggested.

His partner nodded. "For once, a good idea."

So while the media cannibalized the protesters, we went around back where I was able to get out, unobserved, at a secure parking area, then make it to the courtroom unmolested by the media.

The bench was empty when we entered from a back hallway. "Ma'am, if you'll please just sit right here," Jack told me, indicating a chair beside the far table facing the bench.

"Thank you." I sat, my legs still trembling.

One of the two bailiffs, a heavyset black man, came up and offered a gentle, "May I get you some water, ma'am?"

I realized my mouth was dry as dust. "Thank you. Please."

Everyone was being so nice.

I wondered if they'd be that nice if I were black, or looked like Kat and her friends.

Speak of the devil, the doors to the courtroom burst open as the deputies led in the protesters, followed by a huge crowd of reporters and spectators.

I'd expected the reporters, but the others . . . Where had *they* come from? I watched the seats fill to capacity with a smattering of hippies and a jillion executive types clad in expensive professional attire. More than a few in suits waved to me or gave me the thumbs-up.

What was going on? All I'd done was use a blunt object to cut part of a beard and one swipe of hair from the trespassers on my property, after I'd given them plenty of time to leave.

Embarrassment sent heat surging up from my chest, setting my ears aflame. *Please, Lord, let something earthshaking happen somewhere else, right this minute—with no loss of life or property, of course. Anything, to take the attention off me. All I did was cut some trespassers' hair and beard!*

Cindy's husband, an impeccably dressed, good-looking guy with a thick mane of dark hair, strode into the courtroom and made a beeline for me. When he extended his hand to shake mine, I noted his starched French cuffs and real gold cuff links. "Hi, Betsy. You probably don't remember me, but I'm Cindy's husband, Forrest. We met at the last fund-raiser."

I didn't know how cold my hands were till I shook his warm one. "Of course I remember you. Thank you so much for coming. This whole thing is so crazy."

He nodded, grasping my upper arm with his free hand in reassurance. "Don't worry. Cindy filled me in. This shouldn't take long." He gave me a conspiratorial wink. "Remember, at times like this, it's not what you know, but who you know."

Whatever that meant.

"Thank you so much for coming," I told him, my voice shaky. "I'll be happy to pay you—"

He raised a staying hand. "Don't even think of it. What are friends for?"

Another blessing, and not a small one. "I *really* appreciate that." The knot in my chest eased a smidgen. Greg wouldn't be quite so mad if this didn't cost us anything.

A tingle in my back prompted me to turn around and look at the protesters sitting in the first four rows across the aisle. My focus settled immediately on Kat, who gazed at me, her face distraught. "I'm sorry," she mouthed. "So sorry."

Tears welled in my eyes. Part of me wanted to forgive her on the spot, but the rest of me, wounded and angry, shouted silently, *Why didn't you think about the consequences before you did this to me?*

Then my inner guilt accused, *You chose to cut their hair. Why didn't you think about the consequences before you did that?*

I should have. This was just as much my fault as it was hers. I should have just called the cops.

Closing my eyes, I turned away from Kat. She'd already been

arrested a dozen times for protesting. I didn't even know where the jail *was*.

The kind bailiff joined his counterpart at the front of the courtroom. "All rise for the Honorable Tiberius Blount, judge of the Superior Court of Georgia."

As we all stood, a wave of dismay went through the opposition.

"Judge Blount," I whispered softly. "Where have I heard of him before?"

"Probably in the paper," my lawyer whispered back, out of the corner of his mouth. He leaned close to my ear. "Crazy as a bedbug, but a rabid right-winger. He's Cindy's second cousin, once removed. Thinks she hung the moon."

Relief flooded through me. At long last, the good ol' boy network was working in my favor.

Happily, the judge didn't *look* crazy. A medium-sized, balding man with reading glasses, he sat down and scowled at something on his desk.

"You may be seated," the bailiff announced.

We sat. After a long pause, during which I deduced that the judge was reading something, he looked up. "Are all the parties involved present?"

Jack and his partner stood. "They are, Your Honor."

"Thank you. You may be seated." Cindy's cousin started reading again. As the silence lengthened, a murmur arose in the spectators, prompting him to bang his gavel.

"Order in the court," the bailiff scolded.

After what seemed like an hour, the judge looked up at last. "I see that Mrs. Callison has an attorney present to represent her. Am I correct?"

My lawyer rose. "You are, Your Honor."

"Long time no see, Forrest," the judge said, then told me, "Good choice."

Then he looked to the protesters. "Do any of you wish to have an attorney present to represent you? Under the law, that is your right. I can delay these proceedings while you acquire representation, if you so desire."

Kat stood. "Yer Honor, may we please talk this over among ourselves fer a minute?"

He waved a hand in dismissal. "Be my guest, as long as you maintain order and respect."

"Thank you, Yer Honor." Kat turned to the demonstrators. "Does anybody have a lawyer they'd like to call? Please raise yer hand if you do." After subdued discussion they fell silent, and no hands went up. When she was sure everybody had had time to consider, Kat asked, "Does anybody wanta be represented by a public defender? Please raise yer hand if you want a public defender." That prompted several snorts of derision from her cohorts, but once again, there were no takers.

"Okay, then," she said. "Would any of you like to represent yerselves?"

All of them raised their hands, including Kat.

She turned to face the judge. "As you kin see, Yer Honor, it's unanimous. We want to act pro se in this matter."

The judge glared at her. "That is your right, little lady."

Kat reddened in outrage at his dismissive form of address, but he didn't seem to notice.

Forrest whispered in my ear, "The only thing old Ti hates worse than hippies is people who act pro se. Puts a real burden on the judge."

The judge went on. "But are you sure you and your . . . hippie friends," he said with obvious disapproval, "understand the seriousness of such a decision? Are you *competent* to make such a choice, little girl?"

That tore it with Kat. Her accent was wide open when she shot back, "Just because I look like this and talk like this, does *not* mean I am *ignerent*, sir, or my friends. This ain't the first time we've been to court fer protestin' the corrupt Republican administration, and it won't be the last."

Oh, Kat.

The gavel came down. "Watch your tongue, missy, or I'll hold you in contempt."

The ex-law student jumped up. "We hold *you* in contempt. This trial is a farce."

Reporters scribbled away furiously as the judge aimed his gavel at the offender. "Bailiff, take that man into custody." He banged his desk, then narrowed his eyes at the shocked protester. "I hereby fine you three thousand dollars and sentence you to thirty days in jail for contempt." He waved his gavel. "Take him away."

Three thousand dollars? Could he *do* that?

Kat and her buddies watched in resentful silence as the bailiff carried out the judge's order.

Judge Blount smoothed the front of his robe, then said, "Very well. Be it so noted that the protesters in question have chosen to act in their own behalf."

After consulting his notes again, he said, "According to these statements, the protesters in the first four rows, here, obstructed Mrs. Betsy Callison's invited guests from entering her property for a makeover party, despite Mrs. Callison's repeated peaceful requests that they stop assaulting and obstructing her guests." No guessing which way the wind blew with him. "Then said protesters trespassed onto Mrs. Callison's private property, where they lay down and obstructed access to Mrs. Callison's home, despite Mrs. Callison's repeated peaceful requests that they leave." Reporters scribbled away as he shuffled the notes.

The judge went on. "When the trespassers refused to go back to the sidewalk, Mrs. Callison announced that they were eligible for free makeovers, along with her other guests." A low buzz among the onlookers elicited no rebuke from the bench. The judge just raised his voice. "Mrs. Callison then made it clear that by remaining on her property, the protesters were agreeing to participate in the makeovers, which included a shave and a haircut."

Chuckles erupted from the gallery, but the judge didn't seem to mind.

He peered over his readers at Kat. "Have I got that right so far?"

After a brief, murmured conference across the aisle, Kat rose. "That is correct, Your Honor."

The judge nodded. "Then, after repeated clarifications of the terms, Mrs. Callison chose a makeover winner among the protesters and, using electric clippers, *not* scissors," he emphasized, "proceeded to begin shaving"—he looked back to his notes—"one Julius Rabinowitz"—more chuckles—"who then got up and threatened Mrs. Callison with violence, only to be stopped by one Kat Rutledge, who lives across the street from Mrs. Callison, and is her best friend."

Julius shot to his feet. "She cut my beard! That's a felony!"

The judge practically crawled over his desk. "Do not *dare* to lecture this court on the law, sir! I, and I alone, will decide if a crime has been committed here! Now sit down and shut up, unless you want to join your loudmouth friend!"

Wisely, Julius sat down.

The judge pointed to the guy I'd skunked. "You, sir, with the blessed beginnings of a crew cut. Please stand."

His hand protectively over his bald patch, the guy stood.

"State your name for the court."

The guy looked down, barely managing a thready, "Ken Stilson."

"Do you still wish to prefer charges against Mrs. Callison?" Judge Blount asked in a warning tone.

The guy glanced from me to the judge, and back again, then bent his head and mumbled something that prompted a hissed reaction among the ranks.

"Speak up, young man," the judge ordered. "I'm not a psychic."

"No, sir," the guy repeated loudly. "I do not."

"You do not *what?*" the judge demanded.

"I do not wish to prefer charges." The guy sat abruptly and slunk down.

Judge Blount smiled. "Be it so noted, that Ken Stilson has dropped the charges against Mrs. Callison." He aimed his gavel at Julius. "And you, sir. Stand up." Julius slowly rose. "After further consideration," the judge said, "do you still wish to prefer charges against Mrs. Callison?"

Julius shot a pained glance to Kat, but remained mute.

"Speak up, sir," the judge insisted. "Have you reconsidered bringing charges against the law-abiding citizen on whose property you were criminally trespassing?"

So much for a fair trial.

Julius bent to whisper in Kat's ear. Kat nodded, then rose to address the court. "Yer Honor, you told Mr. Rabinowitz to remain silent on threat of contempt."

"Smart-ass hippies," the judge muttered, then said, "He has the court's permission to speak when directly addressed by the bench."

"I am still preferring charges against Mrs. Callison," Julius said, defiant.

Kat briefly closed her eyes in dread.

The judge turned to me. "And you, Mrs, Callison," he said kindly, "do you wish to prefer charges against these . . . *hippie* trespassers?"

Forrest put a staying hand on my forearm as he rose. But his "Yes, Your Honor" was drowned out by my firm "No, Your Honor," as I stood beside him.

"Counsel," the judge warned Forrest. "Consult with your client." He looked behind me. "I see a Mrs. Louise Taylor, one of Mrs.

Callison's guests, listed as bringing charges for assault. Mrs. Taylor, you wish to prefer charges." It was a statement, not a question.

Cindy's friend started to rise behind me, but I turned and shook my head no. She looked from the judge to me in confusion.

"No," I said in a desperate whisper. "Please don't."

She shrugged, then did as I asked. "No, Your Honor. On further consideration, I have decided to drop the charges."

The judge was not amused. "Very well. Be it so noted." He frowned down at me. "You are certain, Mrs. Callison, that you do not wish to press charges?"

"No charges, Your Honor. Kat's my best friend," I explained. "No matter what she did, I can't have her put in jail."

Pencils scribbled harder as a buzz of sympathy passed through the onlookers.

Across the aisle, the trespassers looked at me in shame—all but Julius/Moose, who was still loaded for bear, maybe because his sissy first name had been revealed in public, and I do mean public.

Kat had a furious sotto voce argument with him, but he clearly refused to budge.

"Betsy," Forrest whispered in a patronizing tone, "I know you care about your friend, but she and the others broke the law. It won't look good if you don't press charges."

"I appreciate your advice, Forrest," I told him. "Really, I do. But this isn't a matter of legalities. Kat's the only true friend I've ever had. I can't have her arrested."

"All right, then," he said. "But the others . . . surely you don't want to support such lawlessness."

My whole body ached from the humiliation of Kat's betrayal and the insult of having my private business hung out on public display. "I just want this to be over." I gripped his forearm with a desperate, "Please. I want it to be over."

He sighed in disagreement, but addressed the judge. "Your Honor, against counsel's advice, my client does not wish to press charges."

The judge studied me with a mixture of admiration and disappointment. "While I admire the loyalty of your decision," he said, "I cannot approve its wisdom. Nevertheless, be it so noted that Mrs. Callison has declined to press charges against the criminal trespassers."

He glared across the aisle and banged his gavel. "Will all the parties please rise and face the court for my decision?"

I could barely stand, shaking at the prospect of actually being thrown in jail.

"In the matter of Mr. Julius Rabinowitz's charges of simple battery against Mrs. Betsy Callison, the court hereby dismisses the charges and warns Mr. Rabinowitz that if he ever comes before this bench again, his previous disrespect for this court and the law of the land will weigh heavily against him." Scowling, the judge banged his gavel one last time. "Court is dismissed. You are all free to go, though the majority of you shouldn't be."

"All rise," the bailiff ordered with a grin as the judge flounced out.

Cheers and applause broke out among the onlookers as the reporters rushed forward to get statements.

Ignoring their clamor, I shook Forrest's hand. "Thank you so much. And please thank Cindy for me. I was scared to death."

Cindy rushed forward to give me a hug. "I told you this would work out," she said with a wink. She gave Forrest a peck. "Good job, Counselor. You're the best."

He circled her waist for a sidelong hug. "See why I love her? I didn't do a thing, but she compliments me." He let go of Cindy and nudged her my way. "Let me take care of the press. Hon, why don't you get Betsy some lunch at the club? Give things time to settle down. Then you can take her home."

"Sure thing." Cindy stepped over and put her arm around my shoulders. "Come on. I'm buying you a nice lunch. And wine. Plenty of wine."

"Sounds like a plan." Maybe it would bring back the circulation in my extremities.

"Okay. Out we go," Forrest said to me. At least Forrest would get some good publicity out of this.

He led me into the hall, where glaring TV lights kicked on, almost obscuring the mob of reporters who barraged me with questions.

Clearly, the UFOs hadn't materialized, and the Berlin Wall was still standing.

Forrest stepped between me and the reporters, looking gorgeous as he lifted a hand for a perfect photo op. A battery of flashes went off.

Cindy drew me aside while the attention was on him.

"Ladies and gentlemen of the press," Forrest said without so much as a blink. The press fell silent, microphones thrust forward as my lawyer declared, "Fortunately for Mrs. Callison, Judge Blount saw through the spurious charges brought against her by the criminal trespassers who assaulted her guests and committed obstruction. Only my client's loyalty to her friend, however misplaced that loyalty might be, spared the perpetrators from the punishment they so richly deserved."

Maybe my loyalty to Kat was misplaced, but I couldn't help caring about her, or grieving for what had happened.

"Come on, honey," Cindy murmured, pulling me toward the elevators. "Forrest can handle this. Let's get some food in you, then I'll take you home."

I nodded in gratitude. "I may never go outside again."

When we were safely in her car and on our way, I humiliated myself further by bursting into tears.

Cindy patted my arm. "Don't cry, honey. It's all over now."

"No it's not," I wailed. "It's all over the *network news* and the front page of the paper! I won't be able to show my face in this town. Greg is gonna kill me for embarrassing him like this."

"Aw, sweetie, don't cry," she told me. "You're a hero. You forgave those who despitefully used you. That's nothing to be ashamed of."

Brokenhearted, I put my face into my hands and sobbed out, "I can't believe Kat did that to me. I finally trust somebody, and this is what I get!"

"Good riddance to bad rubbish," Cindy fumed. She patted me again. "She didn't deserve you. You can have any friend you want. *I'll* be your best friend, if you want."

Curling in the seat, I turned away from her and wept for what Kat's misplaced principles had cost us. "It'll never be the same."

Her eyes on the road, Cindy reached across me and opened the glove compartment, then grabbed a wad of Varsity napkins and proffered them. "Here you go, honey. Dry those tears. We're almost at the club, and you don't want anybody knowing how much those awful people upset you."

She had a point. With a broken exhale, I wiped the mascara from under my eyes, then put on some fresh lipstick.

"That's my girl," she said as we turned off Piedmont into the club. "Never let the bastards see you cry." She pulled into the porte cochere, where the cute valets opened our doors. Cindy came alongside me as we entered. "Nothing some wine and chicken salad can't cure."

I wasn't sure, but didn't contradict her.

Fortunately, I was able to keep the chicken salad down while Cindy small-talked about anything but the day's debacle, God love her. But after two glasses of wine, I was semicomatose when we got back in the car and headed north.

By the time we got to Roswell Road, I lay my head back against the seat and fell asleep. I didn't wake up till we got to my driveway and Cindy said, "I cannot believe that bitch has the nerve to be there!"

Kat sat huddled on the edge of my front porch with her soup pot, her eyes swollen to slits from crying.

"You wait here," Cindy said as she pulled up to my front walk. "I'll take care of this."

"No!" I grabbed her arm before she could get out. "I appreciate it, Cindy, really I do, but I can handle this just fine." I got out, then leaned back inside before closing the door. "She's my friend." The only real friend I'd ever had. "One stupid mistake doesn't erase that. I can see she's sorry."

Cindy looked at me with a new respect. "You make me wish you really were my best friend. That kind of loyalty and grace is hard to come by."

Spoken by a woman who'd probably never known what it meant to be really lonely, to have a shameful secret to hide.

I managed a sad smile. "Please don't let the others be mad at Kat. I should have just called the police. It's my fault as much as hers that this whole thing blew up into a federal case."

Cindy nodded. "I wish *you* were running for president."

I laughed, cleansed by it. "Honey, I am too smart to ever do that. Talk about a no-win job. Spare me." I shut the door and watched, waving, as she backed out.

Then I turned and faced the music. Kat stood, tears running from her swollen eyes, the big pot in her hands. "Betsy, I am so sorry. Please forgive me." Seeing her, the anger all ran out of me. "I figured you'd call the police and we'd get some publicity, that's all," she sobbed out. "I never meant for it to end up like this." She proffered the pot. "I made you some soup."

I took the pot, then gave her a sidelong hug. "Thanks, honey."

"I'm so sorry."

I drew her close. "I know, sweetie. I know." Resentment is such a heavy burden to carry, and I was glad to feel it lighten. "Let's just forget it, okay? We both did something stupid, but it's over."

I wanted it all to go away.

I got the key from under the mat and unlocked the front door. Inside, the house was clean to perfection, the food cleared and the rented chairs gone, bless the refreshment committee's hearts. I drew Kat in. "Come on. Let's put some cold teabags on those eyes. It wouldn't do for Zach to come home and find you like this."

"Zach doesn't give a rat's ass what I look like," she fretted, "or he'd never have taken up with me in the first place."

I stroked her frizzy hair. "Zach thinks you're beautiful, and so do I. If you'd just fix up a little, so would the rest of the world."

"I'm *not* letting you make me over," she grumped.

I laughed. "You don't have to. I love you anyway."

Kat started sobbing afresh. "I don't deserve you. I don't know why you're even speaking to me."

Guilt must be satisfied, so I hauled off and whacked her on the butt. "You want punishment, is that it?"

Kat straightened in disbelief.

I whacked her again. "Is this what it takes to get you to let this go? 'Cause that suits me fine." I tried to spank her again, but she dodged it.

"Quit that!" Kat scolded with a blessed hint of her old spunk.

"Make me." I slipped in a quick whack.

Kat bowed up. "I cannot believe you'd resort to violence."

I managed a quick hit from the side. "And I can't believe you would orchestrate something like what happened today." I got in another lick. "I thought you were my friend."

Indignant, Kat retreated out of range. "I *am* your friend. It was stupid. I already apologized."

"What about *Julius*?" I goaded. "Is he going to sue me, huh? Is he?"

Kat settled down a bit. "Well, actually, no. There was an outstanding warrant on him for parole violation, so the cops were waiting when he came out. He's on his way to finish his term in Florida."

"For what?" I asked. "Murder?" Maybe he *would* have killed me if Kat hadn't intervened.

"No." She laughed in spite of herself. "For impersonating an officer, then beating the real officer up when he found Moose in the motel shagging the guy's wife."

I let out a low whistle. "Not a smart move."

"Moose isn't very bright," Kat admitted.

"You mean *Julius*?"

Kat laughed, the tension cleared. "Boy, when his real name gets around in prison, and it will, Moose is dead meat."

"Serves him right." I pulled some cold family-sized teabags from the fridge. "Here. Sit down." When she did, I handed her the cold teabags. "These are left over from the party. Put them on your eyes."

Kat leaned back her head and obliged. After a few seconds, her breath caught. "I'm so sorry."

"Stop it. Apology accepted. All I ask is that we never, ever let politics come between us again. Agreed?"

"Okay." She sighed. "No more politics on Eden Lake Court."

"All right, then." I turned on the stove. "While I'm heating up the soup, we're gonna watch a funny movie. I went to the film

112

rental place down on Spring Street and got a projector and rented three. You pick."

"No, you," she said.

Exasperated, I grabbed the one on top. "Okay. *Young Franken-stein*, it is."

Kat hiccupped a chuckle. "Perfect. Nothing like a little insanity to help get over the insanity."

"Amen, sister."

We ate our soup and laughed away the evening, and never talked about politics again.

Till Ronald Reagan ran against Carter four years later.

Ten

July 15, 1984. Piedmont Hospital Medical complex, Atlanta, Georgia

Kat had always insisted she and Zach didn't want any children. They had dogs, instead—huge crazy Labs who whipped around neurotically in circles, and fat golden retrievers that exploded hair all over their house when they so much as breathed. And at least six cats. I wasn't sure, because they always ran away whenever I came near them. Since earth-mother Kat didn't believe in using chemicals on her pets, their whole place was probably riddled with fleas. Yuck.

Ironic, that her hyperorganic self wouldn't use flea powder, but she secretly smoked, puffing out tar and nicotine into the environment, along with whatever pollutants Zach contributed with his pot-smoking. I smelled the strong odor of cigarettes on Kat from time to time, yet—despite some heavy hinting on my part—she never acknowledged it, so I finally gave up and ignored it too.

As for babies, I had wanted one ever since we'd bought the house. Greg had other ideas though, insisting that we shouldn't start a family till he finished traveling, so I wouldn't have to manage a baby on my own.

Frankly, I'd learned to manage just fine without him ninety-nine percent of the time, but he wouldn't budge about getting pregnant, so I dutifully took my pills.

I didn't know it at the time, but he'd agreed to do ten years on the road instead of the mandatory five, in exchange for early partnership. But did he tell me? *No.* All I heard was that he was doing so well, the company kept extending his time as a flying auditor.

He could have told me. I never argued about his work.

But when he called in May of 1984 to tell me that he'd be coming home for good on June twenty-second, I quit the pill and planned a stem-winder of a welcome-home weekend. Six weeks and a missed period after we celebrated his return, I sat in Dr. A. C. Richardson's office with my urine sample double-bagged and wrapped in my purse. I'd picked Dr. Richardson because he was supposed to be the best in town. As instructed, I hadn't had anything to drink since dinner, then collected the sample first thing, a most unsanitary process.

I sat there on needles and pins, trying to concentrate on the ancient copy of *Family Circle* I'd gotten from the basket in the waiting room.

Imagine my surprise when Kat walked in.

I put down the magazine. "Well, hey. You didn't mention coming here." Usually, we told each other everything—except the smoking, of course.

What was she doing there? Kat hated doctors. She used chiropractors and those whacky homeopaths instead.

Something must be really wrong.

She seemed as surprised as I was to see me there too. "You didn't tell me either." She sat several seats away, a dead giveaway that something wasn't Kosher.

"Are you okay?" I asked, worried.

She glanced toward the ceiling, her signal that she was about to tell a lie, then said, "I'm fine. Just a checkup." Her eyes narrowed toward me. "What about you?"

Besides Greg, she was the first person I'd tell if the pregnancy test was positive, but I didn't want to say anything till I was sure. So it was my turn to lie. "The same. Checkup."

The skeptical look in her eye told me she wasn't any more convinced than I was.

The door to the back office opened and a nurse said, "Mrs. Callison? We're ready for you now."

I rose and asked Kat, "Want to have lunch after? My treat."

She glanced aside, clearly uncomfortable, but answered, "Sure. If you don't mind waiting."

"Not at all." I'd get the truth out of her then.

After I turned in my specimen and got into the stirrups, Dr. Richardson examined me, then said, "We'll have the test results in two hours or so. If it's positive, I want to see you regularly. Since you're over thirty"—by just two years—"you qualify as a high-risk patient. But don't let that term worry you. You're healthy, and clearly, your reproductive system is working fine, so I don't anticipate any complications. It's just better to be safe than sorry, so we'll be doing a few extra sonograms, and maybe an additional test, just to be sure."

"What kind of complications?" I asked, worried for the first time.

He patted my shoulder. "As I said, I don't anticipate your having any, so put that out of your mind. If anything happens, I'll let you know and we can deal with it then."

Easy for him to say.

He smiled his kind smile. "We don't even know yet whether you're pregnant."

"I've never missed a period in my life," I told him for the second time.

"We'll call you as soon as we get the results," he said, then left me to dress and check out.

After I'd done that, I sat in the waiting room, waiting for Kat.

Twenty minutes passed before she came out, flushed and upset under her forced smile. "Hey. Where do you want to eat?"

"I'm in the mood for a real lady lunch," I told her. "How about the tearoom in Vinings?"

The service was slow, but I loved the ambiance and the food.

Kat brightened. "Ooo, yes. Suddenly, chicken salad and buttermilk pie sound really good to me."

Or their chocolate chess pie. *Yum.*

We walked to the parking garage together, our progress punctuated by strained silence. For the first time since we'd become friends, I felt a barrier between us, which was disturbing, because nothing before that had ever interfered, not even sending the police to my house that time. We differed on politics, abortion, nutrition, housekeeping, medicine, the ERA, religion, pacifism, and legal marriage, but we were still best friends.

"Let me drive you to your car," I said when we got to my secondhand Volvo.

"That's okay. Mine's just down the row. See you there." She seemed anxious to get away, another signal that something was wrong.

"Okay. See you there."

Twenty minutes later, we parked side by side at the tearoom, then headed inside, both of us carrying our lunchbox-sized cell phones, but neither of us commenting about it. Inside, we got a window table despite the crowd of women who were already there. After the waitress took our orders and brought us our iced tea, we lapsed into pregnant silence till I couldn't stand it anymore. "Kat, what's wrong? I'm your best friend. Please tell me. Why were you seeing Dr. Richardson?" One of his specialties was female cancer surgery.

Kat exhaled long and slowly, her eyes on the flowered tablecloth. "I . . . it was just a test. I didn't want to say anything till the results came back. No sense troubling trouble."

"Oh, my God," I said, the air suddenly squeezed out of me. "Did you find a lump?"

Kat looked at me with pleading eyes. "Please, Betsy. Can we just drop this? I'm asking you, as a friend."

"Okay. Sure." It must be something terrible.

Usually we chattered all through lunch, but this time, both of us made stilted small talk for the next half hour, wondering what was keeping our food.

"Sorry for the delay," our waitress explained when we asked, "but we ran out of mayonnaise, so the cook had to send for some, and the closest grocery store's way down at Northside Parkway. Shouldn't be much longer."

Of all times for us to be tied up waiting.

Almost thirty minutes later, the waitress appeared with our chicken salad plates. "So sorry she had to make the chicken salad."

We ate in strained silence, not saying anything till we dove into our desserts.

There's nothing like sweets to break the tension. "Oh, man," I rhapsodized as I savored that first, perfect bite of chocolate chess pie. Why is it that the point always tastes best? "For some reason, this is ten times better than usual. I wonder if they changed the recipe."

"I don't know," Kat said, "but mine's so good, it'll make you slap your mama."

Relaxing at last, we fell back into our usual easy way with each other, then both ordered an unprecedented second piece of pie for good measure, and slowly savored the carbs.

Mine was almost gone when my lunchbox cell phone rang. "'Scuse me," I said to Kat. "I need to take this." I lifted the receiver. "Hello?"

"Mrs. Callison?" a woman's voice asked.

"Yes."

"This is Dr. Richardson's office calling with your test results."

Every molecule in my body vibrated in anticipation. "Oh, good."

"Your test was positive. Congratulations."

Tears of joy spilled from my eyes. "Thank you. Thank you so much."

"Dr. Richardson would like to see you in four weeks for a sonogram. Will August fifteenth at ten be all right?"

I couldn't stop grinning. "Yes. Fine," I said without a thought of looking at my calendar. "Thank you."

"Please call us right away if you have any questions or problems," the nurse said.

"Of course. Thank you." I hung up in a haze of joy.

"You're pregnant," Kat said as if it was a great relief.

She hadn't even let me tell her, but I was too happy to get my nose out of joint. "Yeah. At long last." I started making plans for the nursery. Cheerful, sunny yellow, with white. That would do for a boy or a girl.

I wondered if Greg would want to know the sex.

"How far along are you?" she asked.

"Six weeks," I said, even though I couldn't be positive. Now that Greg was home, we'd resumed our five-times-a-week lovemaking schedule as if he'd never been gone.

I could see Kat's mathematical mind calculating. "That means you'll be due in mid-March," she announced.

"I guess so." I couldn't wait to see the sonogram.

"That's good," she said in a distracted tone. "You won't be big in the summer."

"I wonder when I'll start showing?" I thought aloud.

"Probably not till you're about five months," Kat said with the oddest look, halfway between tears and a smile. "At least, that's how it worked for everybody else we know, with their first."

A sob caught in her throat, and she bent her head into her arms on the table, shaking.

All eyes turned our way as I grasped her forearm. "Kat, please tell me what's wrong."

Before she could respond, her cell phone rang.

Kat swiped her eyes, her pale lashes clumped with tears, and fumbled with the receiver. "Hullo," she said, trying to compose herself. "Yes, it is."

In the silence that followed, she dissolved like a weary child up way past her bedtime. "Oh." Shaking and teary, she hung up, then dropped back down on her arms with gulping sobs. "Damn," she said, the hollow sound magnified by the plastic coating on the cloth. "Just damn."

Cancer? God, no. My heart raced like a sprinter's at the Olympics. "Kat, what is it? You have to tell me."

Eyes squeezed shut, she sat up, turning her face to heaven, and wailed, "I'm f——ing pregnant!"

Every woman in the place stopped talking and stared at us, some with outrage and some with sympathy.

Kat's voice dropped to a harsh, "The f——ing pills didn't work because I was taking antibiotics!" She glared at me. "Somebody should have told me the f——ing pills don't work when you take antibiotics!"

A murmur rose around us in the little dining room, but Kat was too upset to care, not to mention that she'd never cared what other people thought about her, anyway, and probably never would.

Too worried to be embarrassed, I got up and went around to

give her a sidelong hug. "Oh, honey, that's wonderful. You'll see. It'll be fun. We'll be pregnant together."

She stilled. "Maybe not."

Perplexed, I held on till I realized what she meant, then let go in shock. "Oh, no, honey. This baby is a part of you and Zach, a blessing from God. It already has all it needs to be the person it's going to be, and I know it's going to be wonderful, with you and Zach as parents. Surely you couldn't destroy that."

"Betsy, we can't talk about this," she snapped. "I know how you feel, but it's my body, my decision."

I couldn't keep from asking, "Why don't you want it?"

She turned hostile eyes my way. "For one thing, I love teaching. As for the rest, look at me. I'm a mess, with no idea what a normal family is supposed to look like. I can't possibly be a decent mother."

Oh, Kat. "You're a loving, genuine person. That's all the requirements you need to be a good mother." She wasn't convinced, so I added, "Look at me. I have a terrible mother, but I turned out okay."

The look she shot me said the verdict was still out on that one. "Neither one of us has any idea what a good mother looks like."

That stung, but I couldn't let her kill her unborn child. She'd regret it for the rest of her life. "Then give your child to somebody who does, but can't have their own. That would make a blessing out of this for everybody."

Kat stood. "I mean it, Betsy. Mind your own business on this one."

We should have been celebrating together, not arguing. "Kat, I love you, no matter what. I just want you to consider all the alternatives before you make a decision. Please promise me you'll talk to Zach and not do anything hasty."

Her expression went cold. "Of course I'll talk to Zach. But the decision's mine, not his. It's my body. My life."

Typical left-wing women's lib baloney. "And your baby's," I was compelled to add.

Furious, Kat snatched up her phone and her purse, and stalked out.

Damn. What should have been one of the happiest days of my life was shadowed by Kat's dilemma.

I prayed she would think things over and come to her senses, but she was as stubborn as she was independent.

Composing myself, I wiped my eyes, then picked up my cell phone and dialed Greg's office.

"Mr. Callison's office," his secretary cooed.

"This is Mrs. Callison," I told her. "I need to speak with my husband, please."

"I'll see if he's available," she said with a proprietary edge.

Available? I bristled as hold music filled my ear. I never called Greg at work.

His little bitch secretary returned. "He has a few minutes before his meeting," she said, as if she were his keeper. "I'll connect you."

Anxious, Greg skipped the amenities. "Is everything all right? Are you okay?"

"Better than okay. You're going to be a father in about seven and a half months."

A brief, stunned silence followed, then a pleased, "Honest to God?"

"Cross my heart and hope to die," I said with a grin.

"I'm going to be a father," Greg boasted. "Honey, that's fabulous. This is the best news ever. I hope it's a girl, just like you."

My chest swelled. "That's the nicest thing anybody ever said to me. I love you."

"I love you too."

I heard a door open in the background, then the little bitch's, "Time for your appointment in the conference room, Mr. Callison."

Greg's voice shifted away from the receiver. "Janie, guess what? I'm going to be a father," he bragged, God bless him. He came back on the line. "This calls for a celebration. Put on your best duds. We're going to Pano's and Paul's for dinner, the works, including champagne."

"You can have the champagne for both of us. No drinking for me till I hold this baby in my arms."

"Right, right," he said, his enthusiasm undiminished. "I'll see you at six."

"With bells on," I said. "Bye."

I hung up, paid the bill, and happily headed home. I got halfway there on the glow before thinking of Kat. *Please, God, let her have the courage to have this baby. I know she'll love it, if she does. Let her give it life. Even if it will mean bringing another Democrat into the world.*

Eleven

Kat had been avoiding me since we both found out we were pregnant, so all I could do was wear out my knees praying that God would convict her about having an abortion. Keeping my nose out of it wasn't easy, but I knew that badgering her would only make things worse.

Greg had continued to play tennis with Zach, but in the way of men, he said they never talked about anything personal, yet they both considered themselves best pals. What is it about time and sports that makes men think they're close, when they barely know what makes each other tick?

So Greg had no news from Zach to share about what was going on across the street. Kat looked as skinny as ever, which made me worry.

Then my doorbell rang at nine o'clock on the first October morning that held a welcome hint of fall.

Still in my robe, I looked into the peephole and saw Kat standing there with a box of Krispy Kreme doughnuts and a container of fresh vegetable soup.

Soup definitely meant something was up.

Hopeful, I opened the door with a smile. "Hi. Would you like some coffee to wash down a few of those doughnuts?"

"Only if you help me eat 'em," Kat said in good humor as she entered.

I shut the door and headed for the kitchen. "I think I could manage that." After all, I was eating for two.

Kat settled to the breakfast table like old times. "I owe you an apology," she said, her expression earnest.

I poured our coffee, then sat beside her, placing the mugs and spoons on the tablecloth. "No you don't. I'm just glad you're back, no matter what."

She smiled in gratitude. "That means a lot to me. I'm really sorry I didn't talk to you for so long."

My days had been really lonely with only Mama to talk to, or more accurately, to listen to as she complained. "You don't have to apologize for anything."

"No, I do." Her mouth flattened. "I was so freaked at first, and you were only trying to help. I had a lot to think through." She gazed into her coffee, unfocused. "I love my job." Teaching math at Oglethorpe. "And I was so scared that I'd be a terrible parent. Not like you. You'll be a great one, I know."

I cradled my warm cup. "I hope so, but as you reminded me, I'm no more qualified than you are."

Kat winced. "Sorry about that too."

"Don't be. It was the truth," I said without resentment. "But I'm reading every book I can find on the topic, so I plan to be forearmed when the time comes."

"That sounds like a good idea," Kat said, the unspoken hanging heavy between us.

Please, just cut to the chase. I could hardly stand the suspense.

She looked down, stirring sugar into her coffee. "Turns out, Zach was only saying he didn't want children to humor me. He got so excited when I told him about the baby, and for every argument I raised against having it, he came back with one for keeping it." One side of her mouth crooked up. "Even the fact that he works undercover."

Undercover?

My mouth dropped open. "Undercover what?"

"You've gotta swear you won't breathe a word of this, even to Greg," she warned.

"I swear," I said, without considering the consequences. "Undercover what?"

Kat peered into her coffee. "Back in seventy, Greg was replacing the plumbing at what turned out to be a huge drug dealer's place. The DEA approached him about working with them. At first, he said no. Then his best friend died of bad drugs cut with rat poison. Greg was so angry, he agreed to be an undercover agent. He was so fit and smart, he passed the agent's requirements without any problem." She finally looked at me. "He's been working with them ever since."

"So that's why the police chief said we didn't have to worry about y'all!" I blurted out.

Kat tucked her chin. "You had the police check us out?"

"Well," I fumbled. "Greg was really worried when y'all first moved in. He couldn't figure out how y'all could afford the house. Worried that you might be drug dealers," I said, "which is pretty ironic, considering what you *finally* just told me."

Kat chuckled. "That's rich. We bought the house when Zach came into his trust fund."

"What trust fund?" Our favorite hippies had a trust fund? "Ten years, and you never said a word about any of this," I scolded. "What else haven't you told me?"

Kat didn't get upset. She just smiled like the Mona Lisa, then told me, "Only that I'm having this baby. And keeping it."

My indignation evaporated. "Oh, Kat. You have no idea how happy that makes me."

Her green eyes sparkled. "Oh, I think I do."

She looked into her coffee. "I was so stubborn. It was my body, my career. But when it came down to the end of my first trimester yesterday, I had to go through with it or risk a second trimester termination." Her eyes welled. "Zach was so sweet. Before he went to work, he told me he'd love me just as much, no matter what I decided." She inhaled deeply, then blew it out with force. "After he left, I realized this child is Zach's too, and he wanted it. He's been so good to me, so good *for* me, that I couldn't deny him based on principle or my job. My decision had to be based on love."

Thank You, God!

"So when it came right down to it, I couldn't do it," she finished.

"Are you sorry?" I couldn't believe I was asking. I should have reinforced her decision.

"No. I'm at peace," she said with conviction. "Zach is so excited, and I can go back to teaching when the baby goes to school."

"You could go back to your job right away, if you want," I offered. "I'll keep the baby while you work."

Kat cast a skeptical glance my way that said, *And turn my child into a neurotically clean archconservative? No, thanks.* "That is so generous of you," she said warmly, "but if I'm going to do this, I'm going to do it right. The first few years of a child's life are so important. I want to be there for all of it. School will come soon enough."

Good for Kat! I agreed a hundred percent. "So we're gonna be pregnant together!" I got up and gave her a big hug. "I'm so excited. When's your due date?"

"March the third."

"You're kidding! Just two weeks before mine. How wild is that?" I sat back down, facing her. "What are your plans for the nursery?"

"We probably won't do one," she said. "I want the baby to sleep with us."

In the same bed? "What if you roll over on it, by accident?" I asked in horror.

She smiled. "We won't. People have slept with their babies for millennia. It's just since the Industrial Revolution in Western culture that the idea of separating a child from its mother came into

vogue. Except for royalty, which we definitely are not." She nodded. "I'll be nursing, of course."

In public, probably, Lord love her.

Not me. "I'm going with the bottle. That way, Greg and I can
take turns getting a good night's sleep."

Kat's face clouded. "But nursing is so important for babies' development and immune systems. You could still get a good night's
sleep. Greg could bring you the baby every other night, then put it
back to bed."

Which would still leave me awake at all hours every night.

I tested her with, "I'm using disposable diapers."

Kat recoiled slightly. "Cotton diapers for me, with no chlorine
and no phosphate detergents."

How did she expect to get them clean? Surely, she wouldn't
put germy diapers on her baby!

She must have read my face. "I'll boil them."

Of all things for her to cook up in that kitchen! Poopy diapers
on the stove. Gag. "Just make sure nobody thinks it's vegetable
soup," I teased.

Kat laughed.

I could see this was going to be just like everything else between us. "Maybe we can get somebody to use the two of us as a
case study on opposite parenting methods."

Kat laughed, back to her old self. "They oughta."

"Who are you using for a pediatrician?" I asked.

"I found a holistic MD up in Roswell. He can take care of all
of us."

At least he was an MD, a definite step in the right direction.

Kat reciprocated with, "What about you?"

"I'm using Dr. Denmark. I like her ideas about child-rearing; they're very practical. And her patients love her." I refrained from telling Kat that Dr. Denmark believed that babies came to live with their parents, not the other way around, so their schedules should accommodate their parents'.

"This is going to be fun," I told Kat. "How about we go shopping today? Spend some of that trust fund?"

"Great," Kat said. "We can start at the thrift shops, then go to consignments."

No musty, used things for my baby, but I humored Kat. "Great. Have another doughnut, and I'll get dressed." I got up and headed for the bedroom.

"Lunch is on me this time," Kat called after me.

"Lunch is on you forever," I called back, "Madam Trust Fund."

This was going to be so much fun.

"You're not supposed to tell anybody about that," she hollered back.

"I'm not gonna," I said, then closed the bathroom door to get ready.

Maybe I might just consider breast-feeding. It would be a whole lot simpler than washing bottles and making formula.

As it turned out, I did. Kat and I both had girls, just two days apart. Hers was late and mine was a little early.

We named ours Amelia Harcourt Callison, after Greg's late mother and dear departed grandmother.

Kat and Zach named theirs Sada Scopes Rutledge, after his maternal grandmother's first name, and Kat's maternal grandparents' last. And never was there a more loving, albeit misguided, set of parents than Zach and Kat. How Sada would end up after having no schedule whatsoever, running around naked all the time, and nursing till she was four, I couldn't say.

All I knew was that Amelia slept through the night after a month, took great naps, ate anything that was set before her, was potty-trained by two, and picked up all her toys after she was finished playing.

Twelve

April 1, 1985, one month after the babies were born. Eden Lake Court

Kat didn't argue when I put my foot down about subjecting Amelia to the dog hair all over her house, so we had our coffee klatches at mine, at whatever hour of the morning we could both manage to get up and start dressing. It wasn't easy with month-old babies, despite the overwhelming love and joy I got from being Amelia's mother. She slept more than Sada did, but I was exhausted from waking up to feed her, even though Greg brought her to me and put her down when she was done feeding every other night.

Mama had warned me that there'd come a time when I would turn my face toward heaven and plead to God, "What did I do, that I should never have another decent night's sleep?" and when I did, it was almost over.

Based on that, it should be over any time, now. But Amelia had her days and nights switched around, waking up every two hours in the night to feed.

That April Fools' Day, my phone rang at nine A.M., just as I finished cleaning up from the breakfast Greg had made himself—passive-aggressively dirtying up half the dishes in the kitchen because I'd been too tired to get up at five and do it for him.

Staring blankly out the window over the sink, I picked up the receiver and answered with a dull, " 'Lo?"

"Hey," Kat said just as dully. "Comin' over."

"See ya."

Ever since we'd come home from the hospital with our girls, our phone conversations were conducted in shorthand.

I glanced back at the window and caught a shocking reflection in the glass. Can we say Medusa, with dark circles big as teacups?

Too bad. No way was I getting up at five to put on a face for Greg anymore. I'd just have to take my chances.

Coffee.

I needed a jump start. I poured water into the Mr. Coffee to the twelve-cup mark and pressed the button to start it brewing, comforted by the promise of its pops and hisses. Then Amelia cried.

I glanced at the clock on my way to her nursery. Four hours, this time. If I could just get her to go four hours at night, we'd both fare a lot better.

On the way past the foyer, I detoured briefly to flip open the lock so Kat could get in, then I entered Amelia's dreamy pink-and-white princess room and scooped her out of her crib. "Well, hello," I crooned.

As always in the daytime, she woke up smiling, content with

my presence. "Are you a wet girl?" I said, kissing her hair and smelling that amazing baby-hair smell. Kat had been right: breast-fed babies definitely smelled sweeter than formula-fed ones. And it was certainly simpler and cheaper than fooling with bottles and formula.

Amelia's disposable overnight diaper squished against my forearm as I cradled her to me. "Do I need to change this girl? I think so, precious." I laid her on the changing table and got out a fresh diaper, disposable wipes with aloe, and A&D cream. "We're gonna get this baby changed, yesh we are." I flubbed her tummy, and she laughed, the purest, sweetest sound in the world. "Yesh we are. We are gonna change this girl. Yesh we are."

What is it about childbirth that compels perfectly sane, intelligent women to start talking like idiots—in falsetto? I knew I sounded ridiculous, but I couldn't help myself.

I heard the front door open. "'S me!" Kat called.

"Help yourself to coffee," I called back. "I'm changing Amelia."

Busy with the diaper and a fresh onesie, I didn't hear anything else till Kat came in behind me. I looked up to see her holding Sada in one arm—attached to one bare boob pulled out of the neck of Kat's peasant blouse.

In her free hand, Kat held my glass coffee carafe, filled with hot water.

"Damn," I said without realizing it came out. "Forgot to put in the coffee."

She turned, her garish gypsy skirt flaring above her wool socks and hippie sandals made from tire treads. "I'll do it. You finish with Amelia."

"Mmm." I headed to the closet and opened it to the array of gorgeous Johnson Brothers smocked dresses and adorable knit outfits the other wives from Arthur Andersen had given me at the baby shower they'd hosted at the PDC. (That's the Piedmont Driving Club, the most exclusive one in Atlanta.) Easter was only three weeks away, so I picked out a pink cotton dress with little white bunnies smocked across the front, and matching ruffled panties.

After struggling to get the neckhole over Amelia's large head without pulling off her ears, I finally managed to get her dressed, then brushed her hair and hit a lick at mine with her soft baby brush. Not that it did mine much good.

I hadn't been to the beauty shop since she was born. After taking off a week to help me with the baby when we came home, Greg had been working straight through, so he couldn't keep her for me, and I couldn't leave her with Kat because of the dog hair and cat hair and God knows what else was growing in her house. Not to mention the pot crop in her sunroom, the ultimate irony for a narc, but that wasn't my business.

What I needed was a reliable sitter. But all the good ones I knew about were already booked up by my friends.

Maybe an old-fashioned nursemaid. Whatever happened to nursemaids, anyway?

Weren't there agencies?

If Greg wasn't so anal about squirreling away every spare cent for our retirement, we could easily afford one. Even a single day a week to myself would do wonders.

I eased Amelia's hand into one puffed sleeve.

I needed help. Just enough to get some sleep.

I'd actually considered telling Greg he had to take another week off so I could leave him with Amelia and escape to the closest convent to hibernate for at least a week, with nothing but my Bible and a few good romance novels to keep me company. But I realized I'd never be able to express enough milk for Amelia (only hospitals had electric pumps for that), so it remained just a dream that I cherished from time to time.

Not that I'd ever tell anybody, especially Kat or Greg. The Department of Family and Children's Services would probably be on the doorstep the minute the words were out of my mouth.

I threaded her other hand through the other sleeve.

As I stood there in the nursery, Amelia looked up at me with such adoration that I immediately wondered what kind of heinously selfish woman would even think of leaving such a precious gift for even a day, much less a week.

Ah, yes, guilt: the inevitable flip side of the joys of motherhood.

"Coffee's ready!" Kat hollered.

Amelia started nuzzling at my breast, so I broke my own rule about nursing in front of anybody besides Greg and dropped the neckline of my nightgown to let her feed. But I did cover her with a lightweight seersucker receiving blanket, for modesty's sake. Not that Kat would care, but I did.

When I walked into the kitchen, Sada was still chowing down for any and all to see. Kat handed me my coffee. "I didn't put any poison in it." Her word for artificial sweetener. "You'll have to do that yourself, though why you insist on endangering yourself and your baby is beyond me."

Right. And what about the marijuana Sada was getting with her milk?

I'd quit drinking and smoking cigarettes the minute I'd found out I was pregnant, and so had Greg, but Kat still smelled of hemp. Instead of bringing it up, I held my peace and made a great production of adding three Sweet'n Lows to my cup. I savored a long sip, then smiled. "Aaah. Love that poison."

Cranky as I was, I couldn't resist waving a red flag with, "I think I'm going to start Amelia on some rice cereal at her ten o'clock feeding. Mama said it'd make her sleep better at night."

Horrified, Kat reared back, clutching Sada. "Need I remind you, your mother's crazy, and so is giving cereal to a month-old baby. It'll totally screw up her digestion, not to mention her immune system."

My, my. So how did all of us survive?

Kat was *so* brainwashed by all this supposedly natural hippie nonsense.

"She'll still be getting plenty of my milk," I told her, "and they have organic rice cereal at the health food store."

Kat was as cranky as I was, so she shot back with, "Even your precious überauthoritarian Dr. Denmark says it's best just to give breast milk for at least six months."

Hah. "I called Dr. Denmark," I gloated, "and told her I was so tired, all I want to do is lie down and cry all the time. So she said it would be fine to try the cereal. So there."

Kat rolled her eyes. "Lord help that child."

A huge, blubbering poot preceded a noxious odor from Sada's unbleached cloth diaper as a mustardy spot bloomed on the back of her little nightgown.

Gag. "Uh-oh. Bessie."

The poor child had terminal diaper rash (maybe from the pot), so Kat had stopped using rubber pants—yet another unsanitary choice among many.

And she thought *I* was horrible for using artificial diapers.

"Rats." Kat unplugged Sada, setting off a wail as she held the poor, scrawny little thing at arm's length—over my mahogany breakfast table! "I forgot to bring any diapers."

Quick as Wonder Woman, I whirled and ripped off a long swath of paper towels, then wrapped Sada's blooming bottom in them to prevent any leakage. "Guess you'll just have to make do with one of mine." Disposable. "And quick."

Kat made a face, but relented. "Guess I will."

"There are plenty on the changing table. And don't worry. I won't tell any of your eco-Nazi friends." I handed her a gallon-sized freezer bag—another convenience to which Kat took strong exception. "Please put the dirty one in here."

She just stood there like the true passive-aggressive she was, while another juicy blarp emanated from Sada's paper-towel cocoon. The more you try to hurry people like Kat or tell them what to do, the worse they balk. But I had to do something before Sada started leaking all over my spotless house. "*Please*, Kat."

"You and yer plastic bags and disposable diapers, stranglin' the ecology," Kat grumbled as she took it. "It's just baby poo, not nuclear waste. Everybody shits, for God's sake. People shouldn't be so uptight about it."

I motioned her toward the nursery. "I'm not uptight about

pooping. But I *am* uptight about pooping on my carpets or my furniture. I mean this, Kat. So kindly get a move on."

"I'm going," she said as she headed that way in slow motion.

I had no intention of trying to help her. A queasy shudder rippled through me at the mere thought of her wringing out that diaper in the toilet with the same hands that held her baby—and her fork. Yuk.

The bad news is, Kat went right back to cloth diapers after that one "lapse," and she continued to smell of hemp.

The good news is, my house escaped being christened by Sada poop. And Amelia *loved* her baby cereal mixed with mother's milk. I gave her some at ten that night, and she slept for six hours. So I gave her some more at her four A.M. feeding, and she slept for another six.

Glory hallelujah! Within a week, she was sleeping from ten at night till six in the morning, and I was beginning to get my sanity back.

Sada, on the other hand, continued to nurse at will and sleep with her parents. And the dogs. And the cats. With the rabbit she got for Easter looking on.

The Tuesday after Easter, 1985. Eden Lake Court

The second-worst day in Kat's life happened without warning. We had all been so involved with our new babies that we'd forgotten fate can change everything without warning.

Amelia was finally breathing deep for her afternoon nap when the doorbell rang and sent her howling. Annoyed, I scooped her up and went to see who it was. I opened the door to find Kat standing there, bawling, in her bare feet and usual drab, baggy earthmother dress, with Sada on her hip.

She thrust the baby at me, prompting Sada to start howling, too. "Here. Take her. I have to get to Grady."

Grady? The public hospital was way downtown. Only poor people went to Grady—or those with severe traumas. Kat started running toward her house. "Wait!" I called after her, babies screaming in stereo. "What happened?"

She only turned back long enough to say, "Zach's been shot!" Her features crumpled, voice breaking. "He might not make it. I have to get there." She turned and sprinted for home.

Dear God. What had happened?

Zach couldn't die. He couldn't.

I turned and took the wailing babies inside to the playpen, then called Greg at the office.

His officious little secretary answered, "Mr. Callison's office. How may I help you?"

"This is Betsy," I shouted over the babies. "I need to speak to my husband at once."

"I'm sorry," she oozed, clearly enjoying it. "But Mr. Callison is in a very important meeting. Shall I have you call him back when it's over?"

I flushed to the top of my head. "What you *shall* do is go into that meeting and get him," I ordered. "This is an emergency. Get him. Now!"

"One moment, please. I'll see if he can come."

"If he doesn't, he may regret it enough to get a new secretary," I threatened.

While I waited, phone glued to my ear, I nuked two emergency breast-milk bottles and gave them to the babies in the playpen, which finally stopped them crying.

My threat to Greg's secretary must have worked, because Greg came on the line, his voice muted. "This had better be important, because I'm in a partner's meeting."

"I wouldn't have interrupted you if it wasn't," I snapped. "Zach's been shot. Critically. Kat said he may not live. They're taking him to Grady."

Greg's iron self-control failed him for the first time I could remember, and he let out a shaken, "God, no," before he regained enough composure to say, "I'm heading for the hospital. Find a sitter for the kids. Kat will need you there."

"Okay." Good plan.

He didn't even say good-bye, just hung up.

Twenty minutes passed before I finally located a friend from church I could trust—director of our Sunday nursery—who said she'd come over and watch the children. I threw on clothes, then scribbled down instructions for the babies that would take them through the next day, if necessary. When she got there, I went over the instructions, then got in my Town & Country minivan and raced toward Grady, as fast as I could drive.

Of course, when I could have used a police escort, I never saw a cop.

By the time I'd parked and found my way to emergency, an hour and a half had passed since Kat had left. I asked the nurse at the ER desk where Kat was, and she directed me to a private conference room—not a good sign.

Several grim men in suits outside the door stood as I approached. Probably DEA.

"I'm Betsy Callison," I told them, and they relaxed, stepping clear of the door.

Hearing sobs inside the little conference room, I assumed the worst and let myself in quietly.

Greg was holding Kat, comforting her with soft shushes as he stroked her back. She was still barefoot, God bless her.

He caught my eye and nodded in relief that I was there to take over.

"He's still alive," he told Kat. "They didn't even think he'd make it to the hospital, and he's made it up to surgery. Zach's a fighter. It'll take more than four bullets to kill him, mark my words."

Four bullets!

I circled Kat's shoulders, surrounding her with caring. "Greg's right, honey. Zach wouldn't leave you and Sada."

Kat reared back to glare at me. "Good people die all the time! Or hadn't you noticed? And the ones who ought to die live on and on, just like the scumbag who tried to eliminate Zach!" All her anger and frustration came out, focused on a safe place: me. "The police have no leads," she went on. "All they know is, somebody was waiting when Zach showed up at his undercover job, then shot him and disappeared without leaving any evidence." Hatred burned in her green eyes. "The shooter's out there somewhere, and he knows who Zach is. What he is. Somebody betrayed him." She pulled free and paced the tiny room like a caged tiger. "His cover's been blown. If he lives, he probably won't even have a job anymore."

"Shhh, shhh, shhh, shhh." I pulled her to me despite her resistance, then put her into a chair and sat beside her, taking her cold hand in mine. "Forget about all that. Just focus on Zach, and his getting well. The DEA will take care of the man who did this. And find the leak." I wished I could believe what I was saying. "You know they will. Just focus on Zach now."

All cried out, Kat blinked her swollen eyes and sagged back into the chair, focusing unseeing on the middle distance. "You're right," she whispered, her words flat. "Think about Zach getting well."

Then her features contorted afresh, and the terror came back into her voice. "But what if he dies? I'll go crazy if he dies. I can't live without him."

"You can," I said sternly. "For Sada's sake, you can. But you're not going to have to." I sent God a bone-deep plea for mercy and healing. "Zach's going to live," I said with a conviction spawned by sheer force of will. "Believe it. I don't know how I know, but I know it," I lied.

Kat's eyes narrowed. "Where's Sada? And Amelia?"

"They're in good hands," I reassured her. "Melanie Scott, who keeps the nursery at church, is watching them at my house. She came prepared to stay all night and through tomorrow, so I can be here for you."

"She's good with babies?" Kat asked.

"Absolutely," I said. "Amelia adores her."

Kat receded in her chair. "Okay, then."

Greg knelt on one knee in front of her. "I'm praying that God will do a supernatural act of healing." Tears welled in his eyes. "Zach's the finest man I ever met, and there's a lot of good he can still do in this world, so God will heal him. He has to."

I was amazed to see such emotion from a man who never prayed besides the blessing at dinner, and then only when I asked him to.

The door opened abruptly, and a young African-American doctor walked in. "Mrs. Rutledge?"

Kat shot to her feet. "Close enough."

The doctor nodded. "The operating room asked me to let you know that things are going very well. They've removed Mr. Rutledge's spleen and resected part of his left lung, and he's stable now."

Kat crumpled to her knees, hands clasped as if in prayer. "Thank God. Thank God."

The doctor stepped closer to give her shoulder a reassuring squeeze. "They still have some other work to do, so he won't be out of surgery for at least an hour, but two of the bullets missed his vital organs completely. I'd say he's a very lucky man."

Kat rose up like the Phoenix, and just as fiery. "Lucky? What the hell are you talking about? He got shot! That doesn't make him lucky in my book."

The doctor backed toward the door. "Sorry. I misspoke." He glanced at me and Greg. "We'll let y'all know when Mr. Rutledge is out of surgery." Then he escaped, leaving us alone.

I went to Kat and took her shoulders in my hands, praying that I could get through the haze of anger that surrounded her. "This is amazing news. He's gonna be okay."

She crumpled in my arms, sobbing. "You're right. You're right. Thank God."

Greg made it a group hug. "Okay. Now I'm going to make arrangements for you and Sada to stay in one of the company condos we have near Perimeter Mall, strictly on the Q.T. That way, no one can find you till they catch this guy. Okay?"

The fact that she and Sada might be in danger, too, dawned in Kat's expression, followed by gratitude for Greg's protection. "Thank you. That would be good."

Greg looked to me. "Will y'all be okay till I get back?"

Kat and I both nodded.

"Okay," he said. "Is your house locked?"

"I don't know," Kat said, worried. "What if the man is there? I don't want you to get hurt."

Greg radiated calm and confidence. "I'll get some of Zach's DEA buddies to go with me. We'll collect the baby things and some clothes for you and Sada, then take them to the condo."

"Thank you so much," Kat told him, then looked to me. "I think you're married to Superman."

I looked at Greg with new appreciation. "So do I." As he started out, I told him, "There's a spare key to Kat's by the garage door at our house. It's labeled."

"Good." After he and two of the DEA agents had left, Kat and I settled side by side on the worn little vinyl sofa to wait for further word.

"When they told me Zach might be dying, I was suddenly sure I'd lose him, and it hit me like a ton of bricks why," she whispered softly after a protracted silence. "As punishment for what I did when I was fourteen."

What kind of craziness was this? I faced Kat squarely. "That's just the devil, taking advantage of the situation to whisper lies into your ear. God's not in the business of killing people for other people's mistakes."

"An eye for a eye, a life for a life. It's in the Bible," she said, tormented. "I killed my baby when I was fourteen."

I went still with shock. "You were pregnant at fourteen?" I asked gently.

Kat nodded. "Daddy told me Mama left us when I was twelve, but I found out later he threw her out because of her drinking. Then he started doing the same thing he'd thrown her out for. When I was fourteen, he passed out cold on the sofa, and his drinking buddy . . . took advantage of the situation. The next thing I knew, I was pregnant."

Dear God! Raped and pregnant at fourteen, by one of her father's friends. No wonder she didn't want to fix herself up, and wore such baggy clothes. It was camouflage. "Oh, Kat, honey. How horrible for you."

"I didn't say anything to Daddy till I was sure," she said, her eyes unfocused, moving back and forth as she relived that trauma. "When I told him, he said I had to get rid of it." She shook her head. "I should have run away. Gone to the Crittenden home and had it. But I didn't. I hated it because of its father and how it came to be, and I just wanted to go back to the way things had been before."

"Honey, you were just a child," I reassured her. "None of this was your fault."

She shook her head in denial. "I should have run away, but I didn't. I told myself it was for the best, so I let some backroom butcher erase what had happened. *Then* I ran away."

All this time, she'd been holding this awful secret. I thought of the way I'd pushed her not to have an abortion when she got pregnant, and my heart broke for her. "Oh, sweetie. It's okay."

She let out a deep sigh. "Now, I don't know what to believe."

"Does anybody else know about this?" I prodded gently.

"Only Zach." She managed a fragile smile. "He said it was okay, that he understood perfectly, so I put it away in a dark closet at the bottom of my mind, and moved on. But when he got shot . . ."

"That has nothing to do with what happened to you back then." I hugged her. "We knew there were risks to Zach's undercover work. That's what's behind this, not some twisted form of divine retribution."

She leaned her head on my shoulder. "I sure am glad that you're my friend."

"I love ya, girl. And your secret's safe with me. I'll take it to my grave."

"Thanks."

The door opened to reveal a nurse. "Mrs. Rutledge?"

Kat looked at me briefly before responding, "Yes."

"Mr. Rutledge has been transferred to intensive care. If you'll come with me, I'll show you to the waiting room. Once he's stable, you can see him briefly."

Relieved, Kat stood. "Thanks."

"See," I told Kat. "He's still hanging in there. He's gonna be okay."

We followed the nurse to the ICU waiting area, where I was able to commandeer a set of those hospital socks with the rubber treads on the bottom for Kat. It was like locking the barn door after the cow was out, but anything was better than Kat's walking barefoot in that germy place for one minute longer.

Several hours passed as we shared the waiting room with a varied assortment of worried families of all colors and income brackets. Then Greg returned with the condo key for Kat and some Varsity lunch for all three of us.

"The condo's all ready for you and Sada," he said as he handed us our red boxes and drinks. The rest of the waiting families inhaled the scent of fries, rings, and burgers with envy. "I talked to the sitter," Greg went on, "and she's agreed to stay with the girls as long as necessary. Two agents will take her and the babies to the condo, then stay there with her, just to be safe." Nothing like an executive to get things done in a hurry.

Greg patted my shoulder, his voice low when he confided, "I've talked to the agency and the doctors here too, and as soon as Zach's strong enough, we're going to transfer him to Northside under an assumed name. Meanwhile, there will be two agents guarding his room, one inside and one out, till he's well enough to be released."

Relief cleansed Kat's expression. "Thank you so much. I don't know what I'd have done without you."

What she and Zach would do after he got well hung heavy in the air between us, but no one brought it up.

"Zach's the only close friend I've ever had," Greg told her. "I know it just looks like we play tennis and watch ball games together, but I'd do anything to help him, and you and Sada. Y'all can count on me, no matter what."

I'd never been as proud of my husband as I was then, and I believed he would always be there for me and Amelia, too.

Greg went back to work after we'd eaten, but told us to call if anything came up. It was eleven P.M. before Kat and I finally got to go see Zach in intensive care. The agent outside his cubicle nodded with respect, as did the one who was sitting by his bed, but neither of them budged.

Zach's torso was so swollen and swaddled in bandages that he looked pregnant, and he was on a respirator, with tubes running everywhere.

"Oh, God." Kat turned into my shoulder, unable to face it.

"Don't look at the bad things," I told her. "Look at his heart rate, steady at eighty-five. And his blood pressure's at ninety over sixty. After losing all that blood, that's great."

Kat peeked at the monitors above his IVs, and eased a little.

"Now I'm going back to the waiting room, so you two can have some time alone." As I left, the agent stepped out of the cubicle to wait with his colleague in the hallway.

"We'll find who did this," he told me quietly. "Until then, nothing's going to happen to Zach." From the tone of his voice and the look on his and the other agent's face, I believed him.

Amazingly, Zach was able to be transferred up to Sandy Springs three days later, his face swaddled in bandages to conceal his identity. There, registered as Jason Smith, he was close enough for Kat to come and go several times a day. In an effort to conceal her identity, I took her shopping for some nonrevealing but tailored clothes and regular shoes, as a disguise. Then I plaited her unruly mane into a flattering French braid. Kat didn't like it, but for Zach's sake, she looked the part of a suburban housewife.

The first time he saw her incognito, Zach did a double take, then gave her a thumbs-up.

A week after Zach had checked into Northside, he was sitting up and having conversations.

I was home making supper when the phone rang at four.

"Betsy, it's Zach," he said in a stage whisper.

I didn't like the surreptitious tone in his voice.

Unconsciously mimicking him, I whispered back, "Is everything okay?"

"It will be, if you and Greg can be at the hospital at six," he murmured. "With Amelia."

Odd. "I'll get Greg to come home early, so we can be there," I promised. But the baby . . . "Are you sure it's okay to bring her? I didn't think they allow babies in the hospital."

"They've made an exception, just this once. There'll be an agent waiting in the lobby to escort y'all to my room."

What was he up to? But I didn't press, because he clearly didn't want to go into the details. "Okay. Whatever you say."

Zach let out a wicked chuckle, then said, "Bye," and hung up.

I called Greg at work and told him what Zach had asked.

"I have a meeting at five-thirty, but I can change it," he said. "I'll pick you up at twenty till six."

"We'll be ready."

When we walked into the hospital's main entrance, a smiling DEA agent escorted us up the elevator, then to Zach's room, making sure nobody was following us.

We walked in to find the room filled with white roses and gardenias, Kat's two favorite flowers, and Kat in an antique-white vintage wedding dress with Sada happily decked out in white on her hip. A robed minister beamed beside them.

"Now that everyone is here," the minister said, "shall we begin?"

Kat motioned me to her side. "C'mere, matron of honor."

I hurried to her side, delighted that they'd decided to make things legal.

"C'mere, best man," Zach said, patting the other side of the bed.

Greg let out a brief bark of laughter, then said, "It's about time." He stood beside his closest friend with pride and approval.

"I had to get shot to get the woman I love to finally say 'I do,'" Zach joked.

The service was short and sweet. Maybe it was divine intervention, but the babies stayed quiet and interested.

When it was done, the minister congratulated the newlyweds, then we all signed the marriage license, and it was done. Kat was officially Mrs. Zachary Rutledge III. Or was it IV?

Then two DEA agents rolled in carts that smelled divine. "Congratulations, Zach," the one who had escorted us said. "We had a running bet about you and Kat at work. I said she was too smart ever to marry you, so this is on me, prescreened and security cleared, from the Ritz. I watched them make it, myself." He removed the silver domes to reveal a gourmet feast and a gorgeous little white wedding cake with sugar gardenias and roses. "Enjoy."

Zach grinned. "Thanks, Bill."

Kat ran over and surprised the guy with a big kiss on the cheek.

Red with embarrassment, Bill retreated for the door. "If he ever does you wrong, just call me," he told Kat. "I'll straighten him out."

Kat laughed, happier than I had seen her in a long, long time. "He's straight enough for me, and then some."

As we demolished the food, accompanied by the minister and Zach's security detail, one at a time, we fell into a comfortable silence.

Once he'd eaten his fill, the minister rose. "I've got to confess," he said. "This is the best wedding I've conducted in a long time." He shook Zach's hand. "I look forward to seeing you and your family in church."

Zach flushed, shooting Kat a sidelong glance. "As soon as I can."

The minister looked at Kat. "Sometimes the worst black clouds can have a silver lining."

"I'll be there with him in church," Kat said, to my surprise. When she saw my reaction, she arched an eyebrow. "What? It's the least I can do. God answered my prayers. I figure I can come see Him at His house every once in a while."

One of the guards poked his head in the door. "I forgot to tell you, Zach, there's a little wedding gift from the department," he said. "We finally brought down the local arm of that Colombian cartel, thanks to the info you got us. The losers started singing the minute we had them in custody. So we arrested their hit man this morning, and the agency has put so much heat on the street, the contract on you is officially canceled."

Kat crumpled over her husband, with Sada in her arms. "Thank God! It's finally over."

Patting Kat, Zach eyed the agent with suspicion. "There's more. Spit it out."

The agent grinned. "You've been promoted to full-status agent, with a commendation."

Kat perked up immediately. "Zach! That's what you always wanted."

Mischief sparked the agent's expression as he said, "Welcome to the world of dark suits and clean-shaven faces and short haircuts." Then he popped back out.

Kat was dismayed. "Is he kidding?"

Zach shook his head. "Nope. I'm afraid your new husband is going preppy. No choice."

"But I like your beard," Kat protested. "It's so soft. I won't feel right kissing you without it."

Zach pulled her close. "I think I can take care of that."

Greg sobered. "You'll still be at risk."

Zach laughed. "After the work I've been doing, being a regular agent will be safe as a tricycle ride."

"I sure hope so."

Zach stroked his bride's back. "God kept me around to do this. I think I can count on Him to keep me safe from now on."

And God did, on the job, at least, but I'm getting ahead of myself.

I took Sada from Kat's arms. "Come on, sweetie. We'll take

you to Aunt Betsy's to play with Amelia, so your parents can have a little alone time."

Kat smiled in gratitude. "Thanks. I need as much time with him as I can get before they turn him into a stranger."

I waved good-bye, and Greg followed me out with Amelia.

"I hope Kat doesn't hate the way he looks, cleaned up," I confided when we were out of earshot.

"It'll be okay," Greg reassured me. "I'm sure he'll clean up fine."

Boy, did that turn out to be an understatement!

Thirteen

March 1989

The girls were four and Kat and I were both about three months pregnant with our second—planned this time—when Zach and Greg decided they were old enough to play T-ball. Never mind that they were girls. This was the South, where fathers from Texas to Virginia considered Little League a mandatory rite of passage, even for little girls.

Which was all well and good for tomboy Sada, who'd been hitting Zach's pitches in their front yard since she was three. But Amelia was a girly girl, without any sign of athletic ability, just like me. After much patience and practice, Greg had gotten her to hit a few times off the tee, but I worried how she would respond in competition.

Sada bounced back, no matter what. Amelia, though, was pensive and easily crushed. I had plenty of my own awful memories about how humiliated I'd been whenever I had to participate in games at recess; I didn't want that for my daughter. But Greg was adamant that she at least try, and there was no talking him out of it.

One of his pals from work—a very kind man, he assured me—was the coach of a girls' team, so against my better judgment, I gave in and went with Kat and the girls to get their uniforms. When we got to the athletic supply, Sada immediately disappeared into a carousel of Windbreakers, something she did easily, small and quick as she was.

Kat paid no attention, as usual, and I prayed there wasn't a back door to the place. Sada had been known to strike off on her own, but so far, we'd managed to find her every time, and Kat had merely chided her, then acted as if nothing had ever happened, which drove me crazy.

Standing there in the store, Amelia tightened her grip on my hand, studying all the unfamiliar gear and the faintly musty smell of the place. "Mama, where are our uniforms?"

"They're here, sweetie." I spotted a clerk at the register in the back. "That man can help us find them."

Kat, currently sporting the Cyndi Lauper look, eyed a pair of orange baseball leggings on her way back. "Ooo. Wouldn't this look cool with rolled-up camo pants and a big, orange sweater, and green basketball shoes?" Oblivious to the fact that Sada was nowhere to be seen, she carried the leggings to the register. "I'd like to git these. And a uniform for my daughter. She's on the Falcons T-ball team. Mike Williams is the coach."

The clerk, balding and slightly paunchy, nodded. "Sure. We'll fix you right up."

"Us, too, please," I said, joining Kat.

The clerk got out his T-ball notebook, then flipped through the pages. "Here it is. Falcons: orange shirts, white pants, and orange leggings."

Kat grinned, pointing to the leggings. "See? I told you I'm psychic," she said to me for the jillionth time.

Hardly. We both knew orange was her favorite color.

"I always wanted to play baseball," she mused, "but Daddy wouldn't let me." She brightened. "Maybe I'll git a uniform too. I always wondered what it'd feel like to wear a real uniform. It'd be great fer team spirit."

The clerk was delighted, but I put the kibosh on that idea. "I'm pretty sure only the coaches get to wear uniforms. It might confuse the kids if you did too." And embarrass Sada.

Kat deflated. "Hadn't thought of that."

The clerk shot me a brief, hostile look.

"Oh, I know," Kat said. "I could wear it at home on game days, to git Sada in the mood."

I gave up. It was her money.

The clerk beamed. "And what size would you and your daughter be needing?"

"I normally wear a four," Kat said, "but maybe we need to try a six. I'm expectin'." The girls' games only lasted six weeks. "I'm not sure what size fer my daughter. I get most of her stuff at thrift shops, and we just keep tryin' things on till we find somethin' that fits. Hang on."

I was prepared for what came next, but the clerk jumped half out of his skin when Kat put her baby and index fingers in her mouth and let out a whistle that could be heard two blocks over, her earsplitting method of summoning Sada, indoors and out.

Sada cheerfully materialized with two mismatched golf shoes. "Look, Mama."

Lord knew what sort of mess the child had left in the shoe department.

"Um-hm." Kat plucked the shoes from her and casually laid them on the counter. "Do you need to measure her?" she asked the clerk.

"That won't be necessary," he said. "I'm thinking she's a toddler three." He eyed Amelia. "Girl's five, right?"

Amelia was taller and heavier than her best friend, and very self-conscious about it. "That's right."

"They're in the stockroom." He handed Kat two forms, and me one. "If y'all could please fill these out for me, we'll have their last names put on the backs of their shirts. I'll have those uniforms for you in a jiffy." He headed through the dingy curtain behind the counter, calling over his shoulder, "You can try them on here, just to be sure."

Kat filled out Sada's form while I did Amelia's, but when she got to hers, she wrote a G for Gober, then hesitated.

She'd always insisted it was sexist to take the man's last name, but she frowned. "If I put Gober on mine, nobody will know Sada's my daughter. But there aren't enough spaces for Gober-Rutledge on either of ours."

God help the genealogists in generations to come.

I wasn't touching this one with a ten-foot pole. "I guess you'll have to pick."

"Maybe we could use first names." Rules had never bothered Kat before, so she wasn't about to start accepting them now. But part of my job as Sada's godmother was to spare her embarrassment. "Everybody else will have their last names. Would you want to risk embarrassing Sada by having the only first name on the team? Kids can be awfully mean to somebody who's different." We both knew the truth of that all too well.

"Hadn' thoughta that," she said, serious. Then she aimed the pen at me. "Not that there's anything wrong with bein' different."

"Not a thing," I agreed.

Kat hovered over the blank spaces. "Oh, what the hell." She wrote in "Rutledge" in firm caps, then shoved the forms onto the counter.

I eyed her askance. "You okay with that?"

She cocked a wry half-smile. "About as fine as you are about Amelia bein' on the team."

"Here they are, ladies," the clerk said as he emerged with two small and one larger uniforms. "Y'all be needin' cleats with any of these?"

Cleats? Please.

"Already got 'em," Kat said, then pierced the air to whistle up Sada, who'd disappeared yet again.

She emerged from behind the curtains and playfully swatted the clerk's ample bottom with both palms, which scared the bejeebers out of him. Then she laughed and ran to Kat, who was laughing too, instead of correcting her for slapping an adult, and a male at that. "C'mon, Mama." She dragged Kat's hand toward the three haphazard changing areas on the side wall. "Let's be twins."

After instructing me to hold the curtain closed tightly so no one could see, Amelia tried on her outfit in the dressing room beside them, then all three came out to show off. Their uniforms fit perfectly, with a little extra breathing room for Kat and the baby.

For the first time, Amelia seemed a little excited. She hugged Sada and singsonged, "We're on the same team. We're on the same team."

"I guess it's official," I said to Kat.

She gave me a sidelong hug. "Trust me, darlin', both of you are gonna come through this just fine."

Back home that night, Greg was so excited to see Amelia in her uniform that she proudly paraded for him, talking about practice without worry. But when we all got there the following afternoon, her optimism faded.

Awkward and self-conscious, she did her best to blend in.

The coach turned out to be a wonderful man, very supportive and encouraging, but I couldn't accept his reassurances, when any fool could see that Amelia was miserable.

During practice, Greg was right behind the chain-link fence, urging her on, but she kept looking back at him and missed the tossed pitches without even swinging. The coach came over and gently suggested that Amelia might do better if Greg sat with me. Sheepish, he agreed, but when he sat beside me, his body was taut with tension.

"This is T-ball. Why are they throwing pitches?" I asked under my breath.

Greg didn't look at me, his eyes glued on our daughter. "To get them used to having the ball come their way. And some of them can hit it. They get three pitches, then three tries to hit it off the tee."

"Whose idea was it to pitch in the first place?" I grumbled. "If you call it T-ball, it ought to be T-ball."

Greg ignored me, something he'd long done whenever I raised an issue we didn't agree on.

Amelia finally managed to get a piece of the ball on the tee with her last try, but it dribbled only a few feet in front of her.

Kat and Zach made a big deal out of it, applauding and cheering.

"That's okay," Greg called. "You'll do better the next time."

"Good try, honey," Kat hollered. "You'll do better the next time."

What is it about parents and kids' sports? Perfectly rational people forget every rule of good parenting and become obsessed with performance.

When it was Sada's turn at bat, she whaled the daylights out of the first pitch, sending it into the back fence.

Zach roared to his feet as the rest of the parents cheered. "That's the way to do it, baby! Slam the skin off that ball!"

Amelia clapped as hard of the rest of them, but when it came her turn at bat again, she shrank with dread.

Greg made a megaphone with his hands. "You can do it, 'Melia," he hollered. "Just keep your eye on the ball."

"Come on, baby," Zach called. "Remember how we practiced?"

Don't say that! Amelia hadn't connected with one of his practice pitches.

Responding to their voices, she immediately looked to the

bleachers and missed the pitch. My heart ached for her as I remembered being the last one picked for teams in school. It took
all my self-control to keep from running out onto that field, scoop-
ing her up, and taking her home. If it hadn't been for Greg, I
would have.

So what if she wasn't an athlete? Big deal.

"Eye on the ball, 'Melia," Greg ordered.

I elbowed him and hissed, "Shut up, please. You're distracting
her."

Amelia sent me a plaintive look that said, "Save me!"

I flared at Greg. "Why are we subjecting her to this, anyway?
She's just a baby. Who cares whether she can play baseball? Can't
you see, she's humiliated?"

"Maybe she needs to toughen up." He patted my arm in dismissal. "She'll get the hang of it," he said confidently. "Just you
wait and see."

"What if she doesn't?" I whispered. "She'll think she's let you
down, all over stupid baseball."

Greg kept his eyes on the field. "She'll get it. She just needs
practice."

As it turned out, practice didn't help.

No matter how hard I begged Greg to let her quit T-ball and
take ballet instead, which was what Amelia wanted, Greg wouldn't
budge, claiming she needed to learn good sportsmanship and how
to handle adversity.

At age four!

The man had lost his mind.

The day of their first official game, a cold front barreled in from Canada. By the time the kids gathered at six under the lights on the field, it was fifty degrees with a cold east wind, and Amelia shivered in her uniform despite the long shirts and pajama pants she wore underneath it. When I tried to bring her jacket, Greg grabbed me and pulled me back into my seat. "She'll be fine. Once she gets moving around, she'll be fine." This, from the man who wanted to put a sweater on her in July when she was a baby.

"It's freezing out there," I argued. "It's freezing right here, despite my fur coat." A full-length mink Greg had given me the Christmas before, when Kat had threatened to throw red paint on it.

Greg went icy and commanding. "I said, she'll be fine. End of discussion."

Crazy.

But he was my husband, the head of the household, so I choked back my maternal instincts and subsided to my seat.

The Falcons lost the toss, so things went okay for the first half of the inning. Amelia watched earnestly from left field as the other team scored five runs. Blessedly, none of the hits went in her direction. (Like me, whenever the ball came at her, she always shut her eyes and covered her face with the mitt.)

At the inning change, we all went down to the end of the dugout, and Greg gave her a pep talk through the chain link. Amelia tried to keep a brave face, but I could see she was on the ragged edge. Her freezing little fingers gripped the fence.

"Honey, it's going to be okay, no matter what," I reassured her. "You're perfect to me, just the way you are. Don't worry about all these other people. You're mine, and I'm proud of you."

She shot me another heartbreaking look.

The coach gave us a thumbs-up, then motioned us back to the bleachers. "Thanks, moms and dads. Time for us to huddle up."

So I sat in the bleachers, snuggled in my mink, and watched my shivering child await the worst moment of her young life.

One by one, our batters came, and all of them hit the ball. Then it was Amelia's turn.

Her shiny black helmet reflecting the lights, my precious darling walked toward the plate like it was a guillotine. Zach and Greg called instructions to her over the slight patter of applause and the daunted murmurs of the other parents.

Then Amelia turned and looked at all the people staring at her, and promptly disintegrated. Sheets of tears poured over her cheeks as her mouth trembled, soft sobs escaping, but she did her best to stay erect and face the ball.

Murmurs of sympathy and criticism buzzed from the other parents.

I rose to go rescue my daughter, but Greg tugged me back down. "She can do this," he insisted. "Do you want her to run away whenever she faces something difficult?"

"I want her not to be traumatized at four," I snapped, but he circled my shoulders to hold me in place.

"She'll be fine," he ground out as my own tears overflowed.

Kat and Zach looked away. "You can do it, sweetie," Zach called to Amelia.

The first pitch went by her as she woodenly pivoted in its general direction, then looked back to us like a lamb to the slaughter.

Dear Lord, please help her.

Trembling visibly, she turned back toward the pitcher, then repeated the empty swing as the second pitch went by, her mind on everyone watching her instead of the ball. She probably couldn't see it through her tears, but she stoutly remained in position.

Finally, the last pitch whizzed by, and they placed a ball on the tee. Amelia took another wooden swing, and the ball dribbled onto the ground not three feet from her as she dropped the bat and numbly walked toward first as if she was wearing full leg casts. The opponents' shortstop scooped up the ball and easily tossed it to first.

"Out," the opposing pitcher called.

That did it. Amelia started sobbing and ran into the dugout to cower in the corner.

I jumped up, and Greg tried to pull me back down by my coat, but nothing was going to keep me from my child. So I let him keep the coat and pulled free, then rushed to the dugout, where the coach had collected Amelia and was holding her in his arms, stroking her back as she sobbed. "It's okay, sweetie." Keeping her back to me, he raised a staying palm in my direction, then placed a silencing finger to his lips. "You did great for your very first time. Everybody has to start somewhere. Some of the people on the team had all last year to practice. It's okay. They had to start out just like you, and they love it now."

Her other teammates crowded around them, offering consoling touches and encouragement.

Chewing gum, one little girl stroked her leg. "Please stop crying, Amelia. I'll give you my bubble gum if you stop crying."

Not used!

To my relief, she proffered three pieces of wrapped gum. "See?"

Amelia actually stopped crying and studied the gum, something she'd never been allowed at home.

"It's fruit flavored," her little friend clarified. "Try one."

Her breath still catching in soft spasms, Amelia unwrapped the pink cylinder, then put it in her mouth and relaxed against her coach's shoulder, clearly enjoying the burst of sweetness.

The coach seized the opportunity to sit with her on the bench, still cradling her so she couldn't see me and react.

All my instincts cried out for me to take her away and never let her come back, but the other children were being so sweet to her, and . . .

I sensed Greg's presence before I felt him place my coat on my shoulders. "Come on, honey," he said gently. "Mike's got this under control. If she sees us, she'll just start crying again."

He was right.

I stepped back, then went behind the dugout, clutching my coat around me as Greg stroked my arms.

"I know, honey," he soothed. "I know."

Then, on the cold wind, I heard a familiar giggle and the sound of little-girl cheers and applause.

It was Amelia.

"Maybe this is why little girls have fathers," I said to my husband.

"Maybe it is." He kissed my hair, then led me back to the bleachers.

The minute Amelia was done, we took the kids to McDonald's, and she acted as if everything was hunky-dory, carousing in the indoor playscape with the rest of her teammates amid the infectious sound of little-girl laughter.

Then I took her home and gave her a long, hot bath, and put her to bed.

After she fell asleep, exhausted from her ordeal, I did my best to talk Greg into letting her quit, but he still wouldn't budge. "Hell, Betsy, we're not torturing the child. It's just T-ball."

"You are torturing her," I countered, "and I, above anybody, know how that feels. It was the same way with me when I was little. I hated for anybody to notice me, to criticize me. This is cruel."

He pulled me into his arms. "No it's not. Hard maybe, at first. I don't want her to be a quitter. It will not serve her well in life."

I stayed rigid in his embrace. "Please let her take ballet instead. That's what she wants."

"She's four years old," he said evenly. "How can she possibly know what she wants?"

But she did. I wanted to haul off and sock my husband for being so detached, and I might have, but what he said next stopped me.

"How about we tell Amelia she can take ballet if she finishes the season? How does that sound?"

It was a compromise, but at least she'd be earning something she really wanted. "Maybe. But I can't bear to see her so upset again. Do you think it would hurt her feelings if I wasn't there?"

Greg gave me a squeeze. "I don't think so. I'll be there, and Kat and Zach and Sada. As a matter of fact, Amelia might not get as upset. You two are so closely attuned, she was probably reacting to how upset you were too."

Much as I hated to admit it, he had a point.

As it turned out, the promise of ballet went a long way toward easing Amelia's stage fright—that, and my absence at the games. But Greg and Kat and Zach were always there to cheer her on— with plenty of bubble gum if she didn't cry.

Sada turned out to be the ringer for the team, and Amelia survived, though not unscarred. To this day, she doesn't like sports of any kind.

But in ballet, she was free and happy as a butterfly, and Greg's penance was having to pay for her lessons and sit through all those recitals.

Turns out, I was the one who learned the most from T-ball. I learned that sometimes empathy isn't the best thing, so little girls need their daddies too.

But if I had known what Greg was going to end up doing to both of us, I might have taken Amelia and headed for the hills, along with my unborn child.

Fourteen

Having two kids was like having one, times ten. My Emma turned out to be a wildwoman, into everything, all the time, from the minute she could inch her way to whatever it was she wasn't supposed to touch. And across the street, Little Zach was like his mother, on testosterone. Kat and I were so busy that it seemed like the next time I came up for air, time had telescoped, and there I was, getting dressed for Amelia's first day of kindergarten.

She and I had chosen a special outfit, just for the occasion: a pretty little floral jumper, a matching pink T, and Mary Janes.

When I'd asked Kat if she had anything special for Sada to wear, she'd said she didn't want to put so much emphasis on what people wore, so Sada would pick out whatever she wanted, and let it go at that. At least the child would be clothed, for a change.

At five, Sada still loved to escape and run naked at least once a week, which Kat considered a sign of a healthy body image.

At two, it was funny; at five, alarming, especially considering all the perverts that roamed the world. But get me off my soapbox on that one. I'd long since given up trying to argue with Kat over her parenting methods. All I knew was, Sada was clothed and well behaved on her days at my house.

"Hold still, sweetie," I told Amelia as I brushed her thick, dark hair up at the crown. "I want to make sure your ponytail is just perfect."

As always, Amelia did as I asked immediately.

"Look, Emma," she said to her little sister, who was happily ransacking Amelia's bottom dresser drawer. "See my outfit? I'm going to school, s-c-h-o-o-l." She stroked the grosgrain bow we'd gotten to pin at the base of her ponytail. "It's really kindergarten," she said gravely, "but I don't know how to spell that yet."

"Milla," Emma said, the closest she could get to "Amelia." Unimpressed, she dove deeper to throw out more clothes.

As always, Amelia indulged her little sister. "Mama, how do you spell 'kindergarden'?"

"That's a tricky one," I said as I finished her ponytail and clipped in the bow. "It sounds like kindergar*den*, but it's spelled kindergar*ten*. K-i-n-d-e-r-g-a-r-t-e-n. It comes from the German."

"Oh." She would remember it. Amelia had been reading since she was four.

Her little sister Emma was another matter. She had no interest in letters or numbers. The only time my one-year-old sat still was when she finally, finally fell asleep at night, exhausted from a day of constant motion and exploring. If a book had more than three words on a page, she wiggled out of my lap and took off. In self-defense, I'd emptied the whole house from the eyeballs down and put the medicine under lock and key. You have to pick your battles, and I had no intention of trying to hammer the curiosity out of her, but it sure was tiring.

Amelia inspected herself in the full-length mirror beside her closet. "Okay. I am ready to go to school."

I gave her a hug. "Just enjoy yourself and relax. I'm sure you'll have fun and meet lots of wonderful new friends."

She smoothed her skirt, still checking her image. "But I don't need any new friends. I have Sada."

"Of course you have Sada." Frankly, I was hoping they'd both branch out a little. "But you and Sada can make new friends too, and still be best buddies."

Amelia looked at me as if I were simple. "If you say so."

Translation: not on your life.

I loaded the baby and her car seat into the backety-back of my Grand Caravan, then strapped Amelia into hers behind me. Then we drove over to pick up Kat and Sada, who were late, of course. True to form, Sada had chosen a long-sleeved camo T-shirt, purple corduroy pants, and orange rain boots.

"Hey, 'Melia," she said, completely unselfconscious as she climbed into the car seat Kat had put in the middle seat.

"Hey, Bets." Kat heaved Little Zach and his car seat beside Emma, then secured it. Blowing her red bangs upward in exertion, she came up and sat beside me. "Can you believe it? D-day has arrived."

"Yep." I had no idea her combat metaphor would end up being prophetic.

When we got to school, I felt a lump in my chest when Kat and I teared up as our little girls waved good-bye, then walked hand in hand to their first day of school.

All the way home, Kat and I reminisced about their toddler years.

No sooner had I dropped Kat and Little Zach off, and gotten Emma down for her nap, than my phone rang.

My hello released a string of profanity from Kat that would put a sailor to shame.

"Whoa!" I guess even a Christian like Kat could relapse to her "old man," as Saint Paul put it, given sufficient provocation. The question was, what had set her off? "Calm down. What's the matter?"

"The freakin' principal just called and said my daughter had *molested* a little boy in her class! Have you ever heard anything so absurd in your life?" Uh-oh. "That woman talked like I was some kind of trash, said I had to git down there right away so they could decide whether or not to notify the *authorities*, fer God's sake." She snorted in derision. "Authorities, my ass. Kin you look after Little Zach?"

"Sure. Drop him by on your way out." Molested? This had to be some kind of awful misunderstanding. Sada was a free spirit, but the child didn't have a sinister molecule in her body.

"Thanks." Kat slammed down the receiver.

I'd barely hung up when the phone rang again. "Hello?"

"May I please speak with Mrs. Callison?" asked an exaggerated alto voice.

"This is she."

"Mrs. Callison," the affected voice drawled on, "this is Mrs. Bainbridge, the principal of Twelve Oaks Elementary School. Your daughter Amelia is a new student here?"

Obviously, or she wouldn't be calling. "Yes. That's correct."

A jolt of adrenaline shot through me. Had something happened to Amelia? "Is she all right? Has something happened to her?"

"Not to her," the principal said at an annoyingly deliberate pace, "but to her teacher." Why wouldn't she just get to the point? "There was an *in*-ci-dent with another student, and your daughter *bit* her teacher, Miss Wilkerson."

What? That was absurd. Amelia was the kindest child in creation. "Are you sure you have the right child, Amelia Callison?"

"Yes. We have the teeth marks to prove it," the woman said without a shred of humor.

"There must have been some provocation," I shot back. "My daughter has never bitten anybody in her life. What was that teacher doing?"

"Merely trying to discipline another student." I sensed some defensiveness in her at last.

I put two and two together. Sada must have been the other child. Amelia was fiercely loyal to her best friend.

The principal grew stern. "We do not tolerate physical violence of any kind, Mrs. Callison, *especially* against our teachers. According to our rules, your daughter must be suspended immediately for three days, during which there will be a thorough investigation of the in-ci-dent, as well as your household."

Our household? Of all the nerve! "You bet there'll be an investigation," I snapped. "That teacher must have done something awful to provoke my daughter to such behavior!" I struggled to regain my composure. Heart pounding, I managed a grim, "I will contact our attorney, then be there as soon as possible to get to the bottom of this." I slammed down the receiver without saying good-bye.

I called our lawyer, who was in court for the rest of the day, so I left an urgent message with his secretary. Then I called Greg's beeper and put in my cell phone number followed by 911, our signal for an emergency. I'd just hung up when the horn of Kat's ancient station wagon tooted in the driveway.

Still furious, I charged out of the front door and motioned her to move the car so I could get out the minivan. "Park it! Amelia's in the doghouse too."

Their first day—their first *hour*—of kindergarten, and the two of them were already in deep doo-doo.

"We'll have to take the babies and go to school together," I instructed.

Kat nodded, then pulled over behind Greg's empty space in the garage. When she got out with Little Zach, I saw she was wearing her best green church dress and the matching flats.

Incognito again, for Sada this time, not Zach.

By the time we finally got the babies in and hooked up, I was still so mad I could hardly speak.

"What happened with Amelia?" Kat asked as I backed out with a vengeance. "She's a model child."

"They say she bit her teacher," I snapped, "but I know it had to be provoked." I didn't mention that it probably had something to do with Sada, because I didn't have the facts.

At the corner of our street, I made sure nobody was coming, then ran the useless stop sign. "The nerve of those people, saying they were going to investigate our household."

"Same here," Kat fumed. "*Molested*. How the hell can a five-year-old little girl *molest* anybody?"

"Ridiculous," I told her. "Did you call your lawyer?"

"We don't have a lawyer," Kat said. "Did you call yours?"

"Yeah, but he was in court. Figures." I turned onto the street that led to the school. "Greg was out of pocket too," I told her, "but I left my number on his beeper with a 911."

"I couldn't get Zach either," Kat said. She peered out the window, indignant. "Good thing the both of us have each other."

"Yeah." But I wasn't sure what help it would be to have Kat on my side when it came to school authorities. Kat was against authority of any kind, except for God.

"Molested," she muttered. "Sada might whack somebody who crossed her, but she's hardly a sexual being, for God's sake."

Undisciplined, yes. Sexual, no.

We approached the school in tense silence, but when I pulled into a visitor's spot, Kat said, "You better go into that meeting with me, in case I start to lose it with that officious idiot of a principal." She pointed to me. "I need you fer a witness."

"With both our kids in trouble," I told her, "I doubt having each other as witnesses will do much good, but I'm there for you."

"Good. And you kin count on me," she said.

Ten minutes later, we sat holding our babies in half-sized chairs outside the principal's office.

The female equivalent of James Earl Jones finally opened the office door. She looked down at us over her ample, tightly controlled bustline. "Mrs. Rutledge?" she said in a deep, resonant alto.

Kat stood up. "That's me."

The woman frowned. "I'm Mrs. Bainbridge, the principal," she announced as if she was declaring herself queen. "Would you please step inside?"

Kat bowed up. "I'd like to bring my friend, Mrs. Callison, in with me, if you don't mind."

The principal arched a brow. "I'm afraid I do mind. These proceedings are meant to be confidential."

Kat advanced on the woman, motioning behind her back for me to follow. "My lawyer wasn't able to attend," she lied, "but he advised that I have a witness present. Mrs. Callison has agreed to act as one."

The principal rolled her eyes, but retreated to her desk. "Very well. Normally, our counselor would be present as well, but she's in testing." She motioned to two adult-sized chairs facing her desk. "Please be seated."

We eased down, both of us balancing cranky babies who should have been at home napping.

"Mrs. Rutledge," the principal began with authority, "are there any unusual practices in your home?"

"Everything in our home is perfectly wholesome and natural," Kat replied with a glare.

The principal sized her up. "Have you ever had any reason to suspect that your daughter might have been sexually molested?"

"What?" Kat asked, aghast. "Why on earth would you ask me such a question?"

"Sexual abuse and incest cut across all incomes and occupations," the principal stated. "Such questions are awkward, but necessary in *in*-ci-dents of this nature."

"And exactly what is the nature of this *in*-ci-dent?" Kat demanded. "You still haven't told me what happened."

The principal shot a disdainful glance at me, then leaned forward to reveal, "Your daughter went behind an easel with one of her male classmates and displayed her private parts to him. When he . . . laughed, half the class came to see what was going on, and your daughter paraded in front of them with her panties on her head."

For heaven's sake. So she dropped her pants! Big deal!

I clamped my lips to keep from smiling.

Kat stood in outrage. "That's *it*? A five-year-old little girl plays show-and-tell behind an easel, and you call this *molestation*, and insinuate there may be *incest* in my home?"

I shot to my feet, alarming Emma, who started crying. "This is preposterous!"

Little Zach started howling too.

The principal didn't back down. "Please sit down immediately," she ordered in a voice that brooked no contradiction. "Let us act like adults." When we sank to the edges of our seats, she went on. "We must ask these questions to protect our children." She glared at Kat. "It concerns me to see you make light of what your daughter did."

"It's perfectly normal for children to experiment in that way," Kat shot back. "Or haven't you read any books on child psychology?" She joggled to soothe Little Zach, who had subsided to a whimper. "The proper response to such behavior," Kat bit out, "is to quietly cover the child and explain that certain parts of the body are private." She narrowed her eyes. "What did your *Miss Wilkerson* do?"

The principal shifted in her seat. "Well, the entire in-ci-dent was so upsetting, she picked your daughter up and tried to cover her, but your daughter started screaming 'child abuse' at the top of her lungs, and saying that Miss Wilkerson was breaking her arm."

Mrs. Bainbridge looked to me. "That's when your daughter bit her, Mrs. Callison."

"I knew it was provoked," I said. "Amelia was trying to protect her friend."

Kat shook with controlled rage, her voice cold. "Where is my daughter?"

"In the clinic," the principal said. "There is some discoloration on her arm, but only because she struggled to get away when the teacher tried to control her."

Kat pulled open the door with a grim, "I am going to get my daughter and take her to have her arm examined. If there is any evidence of excessive force, you'll be hearing from my lawyer. And she will *not* be coming back here."

Uh-oh. She might live to regret that last.

"Perhaps that might be best for everyone," the principal clipped out.

I've never wanted to slap anybody so much in my life, but I had

Amelia to think about, so I didn't. "I'm taking Amelia home too. We'll discuss this again when my husband and our lawyer are present." I glided out behind Kat, then followed her to the infirmary.

The school nurse looked like ex-army. "Mrs. Rutledge?" she asked when we stormed in. I nodded, but Kat hurried to comfort Sada, who was still crying with an ice pack on her arm and a red-eyed Amelia by her side.

"See, Sada?" Amelia said. "I told you our mamas would come."

Kat managed to control herself as she gently started removing the towel and ice pack. "Hey, honey. It's okay, now. I'm here. How are you feeling?"

Sada shot a look of gratitude at the nurse. "She gave me some ice, but it still hurts down inside."

Kat's eyes welled when she saw the purple marks that circled Sada's forearm.

The nurse came over and whispered, "I'd have that X-rayed if I were you. Could be a spiral fracture, but you didn't hear it from me."

"Thank you," Kat told her. "You're the only one who's been decent in this whole situation."

"New teachers," she whispered after making sure nobody was nearby. "They tend to overreact."

I'll say.

"Come on, sweetie." I gave Amelia a kiss atop her head. "Let's all go to the emergency room with Sada, so they can make sure she's okay."

Amelia looked up at me with trepidation. "Mama, I'm sorry I

bit Miss Wilkerson, but she wouldn't stop hurting Sada. I begged her, but she wouldn't listen, so I had to."

"We'll talk about that later," I reassured her. "But everything's all right, now. Come on. Let's go."

Two hours later at Egleston Children's Hospital, the babies were wild with fatigue before the doctor finally came in to show Kat the X-rays. "The nurse called it." He pointed to the two X-rays on the light box. "See that thin, white line? A classic spiral fracture." He turned off the light. "We'll put her in an air splint, and you can see your orthopedist to have it casted. Six weeks, and she'll be good as new."

Worn out from wrangling the baby, Kat nodded. "Thank you, Doctor. We don't have an orthopedist. Could you recommend anybody in Sandy Springs?"

"I'll check on that and give you a name before you leave." He sobered. "You say this happened at school?"

I knew they probably had to report suspicious injuries, but this one was a slam dunk. "The teacher did it," I volunteered in outrage. "First day of school, and look what happens."

The doctor let out a low whistle. "I'll give you my name and information, in case you need to contact me in the future."

As in witness.

Kat thanked him again.

"I'll go get that splint," the doctor said. "Then you can take her to the orthopedist." He left us alone.

Amelia busied herself entertaining Zach and Emma. Meanwhile, Sada chanted idly as she inspected her bruised arm, "Child abuse, child abuse, child abuse, child abuse."

I couldn't help it. I burst out laughing.

Indignant, Kat straightened. "And what's so funny, might I ask?"

"One hour," I managed, overwhelmed by the twisted humor of the situation. "They're only in school for one hour, and we're talking lawsuit." I couldn't help myself. The tension and absurdity of the situation struck me as hysterical. "God help the teacher who gets them next," I told her. "And God help us. One hour of kindergarten."

Sada exploded with laughter, setting off Amelia and the babies, none of whom got it, but all of whom could use a good laugh as much as I could.

Kat tried not to laugh, but couldn't help it either. By the time the doctor got back, we were all weeping with hilarity.

"I'd like a shot of whatever y'all are having," he said, gently positioning Sada's arm into the cast.

"Hoo-hoo." Kat wiped her eyes. "Trust me, you don't want enny."

I blew my nose on a paper towel and wiped my eyes. "Katie bar the door," I warned her. "We've got twelve more years to go."

Kat sighed with a wry smile. "Guess it's Montessori for our Miss Sada."

I nodded. "A much better fit."

"Thank the good Lord for that trust fund," Kat said. "What about Amelia?"

Considering the girls' first day of school, I realized that both of them would probably be better off in separate schools. "I'm thinking D'Youville Academy." We didn't have a trust fund, but there was no way she was going back to that public school.

Amelia straightened, horrified. "But we don't want to go to different schools!"

Sada started crying. "Don't separate us! I swear," she hollered at the top of her lungs, "I'll never take off my panties again."

"And I won't bite the teacher," Amelia howled, joining in and setting off the babies.

The doctor glanced at the guilty parties in surprise, then shot us a look of sympathy. "Looks like you two ladies have got your hands full."

"You ain't just whistlin' Dixie," Kat said. She comforted Sada. "You'll still be best friends, every day when you get home from school." Sada's tears abated.

Kat stood. "Come on, let's get that arm fixed. Then I'm takin' everybody to Shoney's, my treat."

And we were off to the orthopedist.

We didn't sue. The teacher wrote a letter of apology, and Kat went to talk to her, coming home with the woman's solemn vow that she would never get physical with a student again. "After all," Kat said, "people make mistakes. Long as she learns from this one, I'm happy."

The girls carried on something fierce about being separated at first, but they gradually got used to it, and their new schools were definitely what the doctor ordered.

But they still managed to get into plenty of trouble after hours, sneaking off to cruise for boys at Lenox Square. Putting on heavy makeup in sixth grade after we dropped them off at school. Trying pot—out of Zach's secret stash. And cigarettes—out of Kat's.

The list of infractions was endless, but never dire—and never Amelia's idea.

By some miracle, though, they escaped juvenile detention and lived to graduate high school. In Sada's case, by the hair of her chinny-chin-chin. That's when Sada decided to live *la vida loca*. But I'm getting ahead of myself.

Fifteen

March 7, 2004

We'd all been reading about the whole Enron thing, but I was as shocked as anybody when I went to get the morning paper and opened it to see that Arthur Andersen had been indicted for fraud and tax evasion.

I stopped in the middle of the driveway and let out a strangled yelp.

Dear God. The goose that laid our golden egg was under arrest!

What if Greg lost his job? Ohmygod.

He was eligible to retire. If the company bellied up, would he lose his pension?

How would we manage? (I didn't know about his condo developments in the Caymans till long after that. Or the racehorses. Or the stocks.)

Visions of homelessness and destitution chased me back into the house to call Greg on his cell phone.

He answered with an annoyed, "I really don't have time to talk right now, Betsy."

"Greg, the paper—"

"This whole thing is politically motivated," he recited briskly, like a presidential press secretary facing reporters after the chief of staff got caught having sex with a hooker in the Oval Office. "The company is fine."

Fine, with its founder indicted for corporate fraud?

Even I didn't buy that.

My insecurities swelled as big, and as heavy, as Stone Mountain.

Greg had grown increasingly distant in the past few years, but I'd assumed that was normal. Relationships cycle, and he had a lot on his shoulders at work. The higher he went in the company, the closer to his vest he played it. And the longer hours he worked. After getting the top job in the Atlanta branch two years before, he'd begun to sleep over on the sofa in his corner office several times a week, but I hadn't complained. I'd actually felt sorry for him. And I'd believed him when he told me they had so much business he couldn't get it all done in a day.

When one gin and tonic turned to two or three whenever he finally did get home, I didn't comment, or say anything when he came to bed so snockered that sex was nothing but a dim memory. I just had his drink and supper ready when he did come home, massaged his shoulders while he was in his chair, and made sure he always found peace and refuge at our house. But I needed to know if our home was threatened.

"Greg, this is me, your wife, not a reporter," I pleaded. "Please talk to me. I deserve the truth. What does this mean for us?"

He covered the receiver, and I heard him bark muffled instructions to somebody. When he came back on, he practically shouted, "I told you, I'm too busy to talk now."

He'd told me before we married that he had a bad temper, but I'd never seen it. Till then, when I finally stuck up for myself. "Don't you dare hang up on me," I insisted. "I deserve the truth."

I looked at the headline again, and my blood ran cold. Indicted.

Could Greg be indicted too? His nickname at work was "the shark." He'd always been so ambitious, it wouldn't surprise me if he'd cut corners to get ahead.

"Talk to me!" I all but yelled back.

I heard a chair scrape back, then the sound of footsteps, followed by a door opening, then closing. His words slightly deadened by close quarters, Greg turned into somebody else and started yelling a string of profanity the likes of which I had never heard, punctuated by the sound of breaking glass, crashing metal, and papers flying.

Oh no, oh no, oh no! Mustn't make him mad, my inner child scolded.

When Greg ran out of breath from cussing, he panted hoarsely a few times, then tried to yell again, but his voice was broken by strain. "How will this affect us?" he accused. "Are you a moron? An idiot? How the hell do you expect me to know that? I'm up to my ass in Feds, here, trying to keep this office afloat! And now I've just trashed my storeroom, thanks to you!" He paused briefly, but I was too stunned by his transformation to say anything, so he added, "I could end up in jail, that's what could happen!"

Jail. Would I end up homeless and destitute, married to a jailbird?

He inhaled deeply, collecting himself. "Or I could get another job. Or keep running the Atlanta office." He was calmer, but his voice was still harsh. "Which I know you would prefer, since all you care about is having nice things, never mind what rules I had to break to get them."

That one sent a javelin straight through my heart, because it was true.

I never should have confronted him, with all that was going on. "I'm sorry," I said. Sorry, sorry, sorry. "I didn't mean to make you so angry. Of course you're under a terrible strain. Please forgive me."

"Don't ever ask me about this again," he said, and hung up on me.

It took me a while to regain my equilibrium, hampered by an inner voice that said I'd ruined everything.

I needed to talk to Kat, but decided not to tell her about Greg's lapse—after all, he was under all that pressure, and it was the only time he'd ever done it.

Such things should be private.

I dialed her number, and she answered with a cautious, subdued, "Hey."

"Have you seen the paper?"

"Yeah. Zach showed me before he went to work. So what does this mean for Greg?"

Ironic, that she could ask me, but I couldn't ask Greg without provoking the Hulk.

"I have no idea," I lied. "I'm hyperventilating, here. I called him, but he said he couldn't talk. All he told me was that this was all politically motivated, and the firm was fine, but it sounded like a sound bite from the PR department. He's under a huge amount of pressure." I sighed. "Sometimes I wonder if he'll ever tell me the truth."

After a pause, Kat said, "Well, sugar, good for you for finally waking up and smelling the coffee. I was beginning to wonder if you ever would."

My frustration found a safe target. "What do you mean by that?"

"I just mean that you never look past the surface with Greg, and it may come back to bite you in the ass."

"Thanks a lot for your support," I snapped.

"Oh, honey, you know you have that," Kat said, contrite. "I didn't mean to upset you when you're down. This is all gonna be okay. Greg's a whiz with money. He's helped me and Zach make some really good investments, so I know he's done well for y'all."

An excellent point, though I had no idea how much money we really had. That was Greg's department. All I knew was that he had three million dollars of life insurance, he'd made trusts and college funds for the girls, and I had an extra ten thousand dollars in my household account for unforeseen emergencies.

It occurred to me that I probably should get the particulars about our finances, but this was hardly the time to rock the boat.

Kat went on. "No matter what happens to the company, I'm sure y'all are well fixed."

"Thanks," I said, feeling better. "I needed to hear that."

"And I'm sure things at Andersen are a zoo right now, so that's why he couldn't talk to you."

Another good point.

"It'll probably get worse before it gets better," she cautioned, "but I'm sure y'all will be okay, regardless."

"Thanks," I said. "I think I can breathe again."

Rule number one for best friends: even when the bombs are dropping, say it's going to be okay.

Greg didn't come home that night. Or the next. But when he did, I made him welcome and fed him his favorite foods.

Ask me no questions, I'll tell you no lies.

I truly intended to find out where we stood financially—I mean, what if something happened to him? I'd need to know. But when I mustered up the courage to ask Greg, after his second gin and tonic, he frowned and said everything was all arranged, that the firm would handle everything, so I shouldn't worry. The girls and I would be well provided for.

I meant to talk to him about it again, but he was always so harried when he got home, the opportunity never came up. He did confirm what Kat had said: we were fine, financially, no matter what happened. He even went so far as to tell me he'd sold off most of his company stock years ago and invested in managed portfolios, but that was as much as he was willing to discuss. So I swatted down my fears and hoped for the best.

Even after Andersen was convicted, and the company was sold off by divisions, Greg got a golden parachute and continued to do consulting work. He hired his secretary from Andersen, which I thought was very kind, considering she'd lost her job. So life at 3278 Eden Lake Court remained the way it had been, with both of us pretending everything was perfect, even though we knew better.

The second Sunday in June, 2004

Hindsight's twenty-twenty, but I can honestly say that the day Kat and I got back from a long weekend at Royal Palms Spa Arizona, I was completely clueless about what I'd find—or didn't, to be more accurate.

Greg had been so sweet before we left. He'd actually begun to *see* me again, and I thought the last few years of distance between us had turned the corner back toward closeness. He'd told me I deserved a treat, then given me the plane tickets for Kat and me to go to the spa. When I told Kat, she said Greg had been planning this for weeks, which made me feel really special. So off we'd gone to take advantage of three days of pampering, though Kat still stubbornly refused to get a makeover.

I should have suspected that something was up, but as always, I took Greg at his word.

Zach picked us up at the airport, saying Greg was out of town. By the time we got to Eden Lake Court, I was ready for some rest.

Zach drove up my driveway, then left Kat in the car while he brought my things inside for me.

I turned, one hand grasping the edge of the front door. "Thanks, sweetie." Seeing him in the afternoon light, I realized he looked exhausted. "Are you okay? You look whipped."

He sighed heavily. "Frankly, I am. Kat keeps giving me vitamins, but I think it's just my age. We're not spring chickens anymore."

Zach was violently allergic to needles, and doctors. "Maybe you ought to see somebody," I suggested. He really did look awful. "It could be something really simple, blood pressure or anemia. One pill, and you're good as new."

"Start taking pills, and they'll just give you more," he grumbled, then left with, "Call if you need anything. And tell Greg, thanks again for including Kat."

I watched him head down the walk toward the car. "Maybe we ought to send you to a spa."

Zach shook his head with a wry grin.

I closed the door and locked it, then started for the bedroom with my carry-on before I saw the envelope on the table in the foyer. "Betsy," it said in Greg's impeccable handwriting.

Puzzled, I opened it and read:

Betsy—the last thing in the world I want is to hurt you, but the time has come for honesty. We both know our marriage has long been stale. It's my fault. I admit it. I put so much of myself into my work, I didn't have time for you.

The paper started to shake as the words sank in. I steadied it with both hands.

I never meant for this to happen. Melissa and I were just coworkers for so long. But when she came to work for me, everything changed. We'd been through so much together, spent so much time together, that we'd become halves of the same whole. And suddenly, there was love. Neither one of us planned it.

He was leaving me for his *secretary*? That officious little bitch? He couldn't be more original than that?

I dropped to my knees on the hard stone tiles, but didn't feel it. The last decade flashed past me, and I realized what a fool I'd been. Stupid, stupid, stupid! No wonder he'd left me. I was an idiot. It was right there in front of me all along, and I was too stupid to see it.

Gullible!

Kat was right! I should have wised up!

Nausea gripped me.

I didn't want to see what Greg had written next, but couldn't help myself, twisting the knife that had just slashed a hole in my soul.

I've filed for divorce, but I don't want you to worry. I'm giving you the house and a generous settlement, and a hundred thousand a year in alimony till you die or remarry. You'll also get my pension, if it's still there after all the economy's been through. I want to be fair about this.

He must be a lot richer than I'd ever imagined, offering to buy me off with that! God only knew what he'd squirreled away to keep it from me. After all, he'd probably been practicing fraud all along.

You've been a devoted wife, and don't deserve to suffer in any way for what I've done.

Don't deserve to suffer? The man had been cheating on me, abusing my trust, for years, and just abandoned me, but he didn't think I deserved to *suffer*?

Time suspended, and the earth stopped turning on its axis. I heard wheezing, but didn't realize it was coming from me.

For the sake of the girls, I'm hoping we can get through this as amicably as possible.

That *bastard*, using our daughters to try to keep me in line! Had he even considered what this was going to do to them, having their father desert their mother for another woman? What kind of example was that?

If you have any questions, please feel free to contact James Travis—

The sharkiest divorce lawyer in Buckhead! So much for being amicable.

He's handling this for me. As I said, I'm hoping we can get through this as quickly and painlessly as possible. Again, I am so sorry. Greg

Damn right, he was sorry.

All the frustration, fear, and anger I'd suppressed since I'd married him exploded inside me like an atomic bomb, rising, red and lethal, obliterating everything else.

For the first time since I was five, I had an asthma attack.

Phone!

I didn't dial 911, I dialed Kat.

When she answered, I wheezed out as loud as I could manage, "Who's the second-best divorce lawyer in Atlanta? Greg just hired James Travis so he could divorce me and marry his *secretary*!"

"Oh, Betsy," she comforted.

"I can't breathe." I burst into tears. "I want to kill him!" I gasped for air. "Never mind the lawyer. I want a hit man! Tell Zach I need a hit man."

"I'll be right over!" Kat said. "Don't do anything till I get there!"

The line went dead, and I stood there sobbing, gripping the cordless phone. Then I threw up. Fortunately, the garbage can was close by.

My breath coming in high, tight squeaks, I heard Kat's key in the door, then it burst open as she ran inside with a panicked, "Betsy? Where are you?"

"In here," I managed, starting to see stars.

She took one look at me and blanched. "Oh, Lord." She pulled the phone from my hand and dialed 911, then shoved me toward my room. "I need an ambulance at 3278 Eden Lake Court," she said to the dispatcher who answered. "Asthma attack. Hurry. She's about to pass out!" We went by one of Greg's clean socks in the middle of the carpet as she steered me into the bathroom. "I'm going to put her in the bathroom with steam till they get here," Kat told the dispatcher. "The front door's wide open. Tell them to come in."

Greg's closet in the master bath was open, and empty.

My chest tightened even harder.

"Stay with me," Kat ordered, urging me into the enormous shower Greg had insisted we put in when we'd added a new master suite and bath ten years before. She took me to the marble shelf in back. "Okay. Lie on your right side. Or is it the left?" Not waiting for an answer, she pulled off our shoes and set them out on the edge of the Jacuzzi, along with the phone, then closed us in and turned on the hot water. Thanks to the recirculator on our system, it came out scalding right away.

"Ouch!" I squeaked as a few stray drops hit me.

Kat adjusted the shower head away from us and added a little cold. "Sorry. Just stay on your side and try to breathe easily. The steam will help."

I nodded and closed my eyes.

I heard the glass door open and looked to see Kat race out for a couple of towels. Back inside, she rolled them into a makeshift pillow. "Here. Put this under your head." She studied me with barely concealed panic. "Let me know if the steam helps."

The air was thick with hot vapor, and I began to breathe just a little easier. "Better."

I heard an approaching siren, then the phone rang. "Don't answer," I said, but Kat just told me to sit tight and keep breathing long, slow breaths, then went for the phone.

"Callisons' residence," she said in her broad accent, accenting the last syllable. "Oh, hi, 'Melia." She shot me a worried glance. "She's kinda busy right now. Kin she call you back?"

"Fire department!" a male voice shouted from the foyer.

Kat stuck her head out of the bathroom door. "We're back here, in the bathroom!" Then she said into the phone, "No, honey, the bathroom idn't on fire. No, no, no. Yer mama just had a little asthma, so I called 911. Might as well git some use out of all that tax money, you know. But she's doin' okay." She pointed me out as the paramedics entered. "Don't you worry. The paramedics are here and she's gonna be just fine."

It wasn't until the two men came in and turned off the shower that I realized my good white linen slacks and silk shirt had gone transparent, showing my pink panties and matching bra, and what was under them. But I was so glad help had arrived, I didn't care.

"Hi, Mrs. Callison," one of them said as he dropped his bag, then bent to check my eyes and my carotid pulse. "Do you have any drug allergies?"

I shook my head no.

"Have you ever had an asthma attack before?"

Words wouldn't come out, so I raised five fingers.

"Five?"

I shook my head again, placing one hand at the height of a child and showing five fingers with the other.

"Oh. When you were five?"

I nodded, feeling really dizzy.

"Let's get you some oxygen, first."

He put a mask on me while his partner asked Kat, "What brought this on? Did she eat something she was allergic to?"

I tried to tell them, but nothing came out.

"No," Kat said for me. "She just had a shock." I heard Amelia's response to that all the way from where Kat was standing, which prompted Kat to respond, "Honey, I've gotta go. Yer mama's gonna be just fine, but I need to talk to the paramedics." She frowned in frustration. "Well, she cain't talk to you right now. She's got a little oxygen goin' there, which is a good thing. I'll call you back in a minnit."

Amelia wasn't letting her off that easy. Kat scowled. "Now, don't you go gittin' all upset, or you'll have a spell like yer mama." She shook her head. "All right, I won't hang up. Just hold on a second while I talk to these people."

Kat set the phone on the edge of the tub, then stuck her head into the shower as the paramedics took my pulse and blood pressure. Lowering her voice so Amelia couldn't hear, she told them what had happened—in way too much detail to suit me. I didn't want my shame bandied about at the firehouse.

I lifted the face mask and stopped her with a high-pitched, "Kat! Hush!"

"Ooo, sorry," she said in her regular voice, which echoed in the tiled space. "Yer husband just dumped you. I thought they needed to know how serious this is."

Amelia's voice squawked from the phone.

Perfect.

"I got upset," I forced out. "End of story." Now that the cat was out of the bag.

My chest got tighter, so I replaced the mask and tried to inhale, but couldn't do a very good job of it. Glaring at Kat, I pointed to the phone, and she went over to start damage control, thanks to her big mouth. Now Amelia knew, but I didn't have it in me to reassure her. I couldn't even reassure myself.

The paramedic looked at the readouts on his medical gizmo and frowned. "Try to relax, Mrs. Callison. Your oxygen levels are low, so I'm going to give you something to ease your breathing." I nodded as he rolled up my sleeve and swabbed my arm. "This will hold you till we get to the emergency room." He shot a look to his partner, who went for the stretcher.

Kat followed him with the phone, still trying to appease Amelia.

My groan came out like the sound of a mouse fart.

Devastated by Greg's loss and my own complicity, I lay back down on the bench and wished that I could die.

I didn't. Forty minutes later, I was sitting up in the emergency room, breathing some kind of mist from an inhaler for the second time. The asthma was gone, but the doctor wouldn't let me go till I finished the second treatment. When he finally came in to release me, he asked, "Do you need anything to help you sleep? Sometimes the steroids and adrenaline make it hard for people to sleep."

"I have some Ambien at home, for trips."

He put a reassuring hand on my shoulder. "I know this has been a really hard day, but don't take more than ten milligrams. We don't want anything to depress your respiration."

"Okay." I pushed back the sheet. Fortunately, my clothes had dried enough to conceal my underwear. But when I swung my feet over the edge, I looked at my bare toes in consternation.

Shoes. I had no shoes.

The doctor reached into a drawer and handed me one of those pairs of beige socks with white rubber herringbones on both sides. "Here. Take these. A hospital is not a safe place to go barefoot."

"Thanks." I put them on, then headed for the waiting room.

Kat dropped the tattered magazine she'd been reading and made a beeline for me. "You look a thousand percent better than you did when we came in here." She put her arm around me. "Come on. Let's get you home." We headed outside into the warm dusk. "It's time for this day to be over, so you can file it away and move on."

The last thing I wanted to do was talk about what had happened, but I asked anyway. "Did you get Amelia calmed down?"

Kat's mouth skewed down on the right. "Pretty much."

Meaning, no. "How much does she know?"

Kat sighed as she got to her hybrid Prius. "Well, she heard me tell the paramedics Greg had left you." She fished her car keys from her ragbag of a purse. "I'm really sorry about that."

"You're forgiven," I said dully. "She was going to find out, anyway, I guess." Frankly, I was glad I hadn't had to be the one to tell her. "Emma," I thought aloud.

"Don't worry about Emma. Amelia said she'd tell her." Kat opened the passenger door for me. "Amelia was pretty upset."

"Amelia gets 'pretty upset' when she runs out of orange juice." I slid into the seat and laid my head back against the headrest, closing my eyes. "Lord knows how *this* must feel. Poor baby."

"She'll get over it, and so will you." Kat closed my door, then walked around and got into the driver's seat. She started the engine. "Buckle up."

"Why? I'd rather throw myself out on the expressway at seventy miles an hour," I said as I obliged.

Between the asthma and the treatments, the paper-cut sharpness of Greg's desertion had subsided to a dull, relentless throb. Then a fresh stab of self-pity surfaced abruptly, bringing the threat of tears. "Oh, Kat. What am I going to do without him?"

Kat scowled, gripping the steering wheel. "I read the note. You're going to take what that cheatin', sorry-assed husband of yours offered you and have a great life, that's what you're gonna do."

I stared out the window at the lights that shone from the buildings and houses we passed in the darkness. I didn't want Greg back if he didn't want me. What I wanted was for things to be the way they had been in the beginning.

But that wasn't possible. The truth had shattered the illusion I'd created about Greg and my marriage, and all the king's horses and all the king's men couldn't put Humpty together again.

They say the biggest lies we ever tell are the ones we tell

ourselves, and I'd done it up brown. Looking back, I finally saw my life for what it was, and it wasn't anything to be proud of.

Do over, do over, do over, my inner child wailed.

But life doesn't work that way. I'd been the perfect wife, and what good had it done me? Greg had taken me for granted, then dumped me.

It wasn't supposed to happen like that.

Would it have changed anything if I'd been brilliant and dynamic and challenging?

Experience said no.

Men leave. My father had left, but he'd had reason; he couldn't stand Mama's hoarding and craziness. So I'd done my best to make sure Greg didn't have a reason to desert me, but he'd left me anyway.

I wondered how long it would be before Zach left Kat, but felt disloyal just thinking it.

Greg shouldn't get away with this so easily. "I think he's hidden a lot of money," I told Kat. "Georgia has no-fault divorce. Half of everything is legally mine."

Kat exhaled. "Oh, honey." By the light of the dashboard, her freckled face mirrored the resignation in her voice. "He probably has millions, but you and I both know Greg's too smart to hide it where anybody could find it." She took a left onto Hammond Drive. "Take what you can get. You'll be sitting pretty. You can go to college, if you want, or start a new business, or just sit on your ass and collect the checks. But you don't have to figure that out now." She turned in at our subdivision. "All you have to do now is go home, take a couple of sleeping pills, and go to sleep. I'll stay with you, in case you need anything."

"Thanks." I didn't want to be alone. "I've spent twice as much time at home without Greg than with him," I mused aloud. "So why does the house suddenly seem so empty?"

"Give it time, sweetie." She turned onto Eden Lake Court.

When Zach saw us, he got up from his chair on Kat's porch and headed over at a lope. He was waiting to let me out when Kat pulled up at my walk.

"I sure am glad you're okay." He opened the door and leaned in for a hug. "Come here, sugar. Let me carry you."

"I can walk," I grumbled, but he scooped me up into his strong arms anyway, with only a slight stagger as he gained his balance.

"Put me down. I'm fine, really."

"I know you can walk," he told me. "I just want to give you something to hold on to for a little bit."

That did it. I started crying again and curled against him. "Oh, Zach."

Halfway to the door, he staggered slightly again.

"Put me down," I said, still crying. "I mean it. I don't want to give you a hernia."

"Oh, hush," he said, holding on tight. "I lift three hundred at the weight room all the time."

It felt so good to have the reassurance of his arms around me, I gave in. "This is the worst day of my life, right up there with the one when my daddy left. How could I be so blind?" I said into his neck. "Greg must have been sleeping with her for years. All those 'nights at the office,' he was with her."

"You want me to have the son of a bitch arrested?" Zach asked grimly as Kat let us inside. "I can *have* him arrested. Put him in a lockup where they'll screw him over the way he screwed you. See how he likes *that*."

I smiled in spite of myself. "Oh, right. What if I said yes?"

Zach lowered me to my hospital sockies and looked me in the eye. "I would do it," he said, and I believed him, which helped a little.

"He's too smart to leave any evidence." I shook my head, thinking of their tennis-only friendship. "What would you charge him with? Felony foot fault?"

Zach hugged me to him, patting my back, and Kat joined in. "I've played my last game of tennis with Greg," he said. "This is a deal breaker."

It felt good to hear Zach's loyalty for me, but he was Greg's only real friend, and vice versa. Greg had ruined that too.

I pulled free. "You two have been friends for so many years."

"Greg's a fool," Zach said. "You're the best thing that ever happened to him. Mark my words, he'll come to his senses one day. Until he does, I don't want any part of him."

Kat patted his shoulder. "Good for you, honey. Good for you."

Suddenly I felt so tired I could hardly stand. "Thanks. On that note, I think I'll lie down."

Kat gave Zach a peck. "I'm gonna stay over, if that's okay with you." She dropped her voice, but I heard her murmur, "We can finish what we started when I get home."

Zach pinched her butt, then headed out. "Call me if you need me." He hollered in my direction, "And call me if you want him locked up. Any time, day or night."

"Thanks," I hollered after him, then waited till the door closed to start shucking off my clothes. I never wanted to see them again, especially those wretched socks.

Kat got my gown from its hook on the back of the bathroom door. "Here. I'll get you some of that eco-wretched bottled water from the kitchen." She took the disposable bottles personally, in spite of the fact that I recycled them.

I stripped to the skin, tossing my clothes into the trash can, then put on my gown and crawled into bed. The adrenaline had worn off, leaving me deflated, but I decided to take the Ambien, anyway. With any luck, I'd sleep through the next three months.

The pills were in the top drawer of my bedside table, right where I'd left them when I got home from taking the girls to Europe three years before.

Greg had stayed home. With *her*. And I'd thought he was being so sweet, sending us first class, for two weeks.

God, would everything be tarnished by this awful truth?

I poured two pills into my palm, then lay back. The smell of him was still there, on his pillow. I threw it across the room, narrowly missing Kat.

"That's good, honey. Git it out." She sat on the edge of the bed and proffered the water. "Here." Seeing the pill bottle and my closed hand, she narrowed her eyes. "How many of them did you git? Lemme see."

I sat up and showed her. "Two five-milligrams. Just what the doctor ordered." I threw them into my mouth, then chased them with a slug of cold, sweet water.

"Just checkin'," Kat said. "Yer not thinkin' about doin' anything *crazy*, are ya? 'Cause trust me, sweetie, this is gonna be hard enough on the girls without you doin' something crazy."

"I'm not going to do anything crazy." I lay back, closing my eyes. "I'm too tired and too miserable to do anything but sleep."

"Okay, then."

"Oh, Lord," I groaned out, freshly horrified. "Mama."

The thought of dealing with her reaction was more than I could stand.

"Don't you fret one minnit about yer mama. I'll call and tell her, first thing in the morning." Thank God. "We'll have a little 'come to Jesus' meetin' about her leavin' you alone fer a while. Where's yer cell phone?"

"In my purse."

"I'll answer it fer you till you git ready to deal with things." She started to get up.

I grabbed her forearm. "Thanks. I don't know how I could get through this without you."

"I'm here, as long as you need me." Kat stroked my hair with one hand, palming the pills with her other. "Yer gonna be okay, sweetie. Okay. Just give it time."

I pretended I didn't see her take the pills. "Thanks."

She turned off my bedside light, then went into the bathroom and closed the door. I heard her quietly cleaning up, then blessed oblivion overtook me.

Kat was right.

I took what I could get, and I survived. And she was with me all the way.

I don't remember how long it was before I first woke up without thinking about what had happened, but the day did come. Followed by a whole day without thinking about it. And best of all, the day when my dreams were finally free of the past.

Thanks to Kat, a year later I was whole and healthier than I had ever been.

Which was a good thing, because Kat needed me to get her through something far worse than what Greg had done to me. Zach was leaving her, but not for another woman.

Sixteen

March 14, 2005. Eden Lake Court

It started so gradually. A stumble. Dropping little things. A hesitation with his words. We lost Zach by such small degrees that he wouldn't admit there was a problem till his leg stopped working in the middle of the night.

He got up to go take a whizz and fell flat on his face, waking Kat and scaring her so bad, she called 911 before she called me.

The first thing I heard was the chug of the fire department ambulance in the street, which roused me in an instant. Looking up the hall, I saw the orange and white lights cycling through the sidelights in the foyer.

I grabbed my robe and threw it on as I ran to see what had happened. Immediately, I thought of Kat. We had other neighbors on the cul-de-sac, but they were private people we only saw at the annual homeowners' meetings.

It was an ambulance, and the paramedics were headed for Kat's front door. Oh, God.

I raced outside without disarming the alarm, so it started howling behind me just as I reached Kat's walkway, but I didn't care. Heart pounding, I followed the paramedics to find Kat holding Zach on their bedroom floor, surrounded by all four of their dogs and three cats, who set up a cacophony of barks and distressed meows when the paramedics descended.

In the corner, Kat's nasty parrot shrieked at intervals, its feathers flared in alarm.

"Hush," Kat hollered at the menagerie. She swatted their fat golden retriever. "Butterball, shut up." Their three-legged rescue Dalmatian growled at the paramedics, while the wiener dog and the shaggy little white mop of a whatzit yapped away. "Betsy, help. Lock these fools in the bathroom before they bite somebody."

Like me? Animals can sense when you're afraid of them, but Kat needed help, so I didn't hesitate. I took the Dalmatian's collar, but she growled at me, straining to remain at Kat's side, so Kat told her, "It's okay, girl. Go on. It's okay."

"Spot, go," Zach ordered, and the dog immediately obeyed. What was it about a man's voice?

"Okay, girl," I said, grabbing the Dalmatian's collar with a cheerful little summoning whistle. "Come on, baby. Would you like a treat?" The magic words. She stopped growling and jumped up on me, tail wagging and a huge, wet tongue across my lips. Sputtering dog spit, I pulled her back down and led her toward the bathroom, lying with conviction. "C'mon. Let's get a treat." Once inside, I almost choked on the stink of cat boxes but closed the door behind me, then let go of the dog. Backing up, I grabbed the doorknob and readied my escape. "You wanta play catch?" I threw a washcloth toward the Jacuzzi. "Catch!"

The distraction gave me time to escape.

The same method worked on the others, but the wiener dog bit my ankle when I tried to squeeze through a narrow opening of the door to get away. "No!" I scolded, hopping back to close the door.

I turned to see that the paramedics had Zach hooked up with all kinds of wires on his head and chest.

Panting slightly from wrestling the dogs out of the way, I asked Kat, "Do you want me to put the cats somewhere?"

One of them arched its back and hissed as I went by.

"No, the cats are okay," Kat said, which prompted the two paramedics to exchange brief glances that said they weren't.

"Maybe I'll just get them out of the way." I crept up on the closest cat—a white one with big black splotches that was lolling on the bed behind Kat—and gently took it into my arms. "There, kitty. That's a sweet kitty." It didn't seem to mind till I got to the second bathroom in the hall, then it shot from my arms, gaining traction with its claws. "Ow! Damn." Thing must have read my mind.

When I got back to the bedroom, it was just where I'd picked it up, with a "na-na-na-boo-boo" gleam in its green eyes.

"What's wrong with my husband?" Kat asked the paramedic. "Is it a stroke?"

"My leg won't work," Zach snapped with uncharacteristic annoyance. "That's what's wrong."

"We can't be sure just yet," the paramedic said in a soothing tone, then halted when a blast of gobbledygook blared from the microphone pinned to his shoulder. "Roger that," he said into the microphone, then turned back to Zach. "There are some abnormalities in your EEG, so the hospital has alerted a neurologist. They'll be ready for you when we get there."

I circled behind Kat to give her shoulders a brief hug, whispering in her ear, "It's going to be okay. He's going to be okay." Please, God, let it be true.

"'Scuse me, ma'am," the paramedic told me. "Could you please step back a bit? We need room to work on Mr. Rutledge."

Chastened, I backed away and started for the door.

"Don't go," Kat said, her eyes telegraphing panic that only I could recognize.

"I'll just run get some clothes on," I told her. And call the alarm company. "I'll be right back." I touched the second paramedic's arm. "Where are you taking him?"

He looked to Kat. "Ma'am, do you have a preference as to where we take y'all?"

Kat and Zach both said, "St. Joe's," which was right across the street from Northside Hospital.

"St. Joe's it is." He radioed the information to their dispatcher.

I ran outside to find lights on in all the surrounding houses, and the alarm blaring *whoop, whoop, whoop,* across the whole neighborhood.

Shoot!

By the subtle gas streetlights, I saw my neighbor from two

doors down walking up the sidewalk in his robe and slippers, a long gun carried casually in one arm, barrel down. Recognizing me, he called out, "Is everything okay, Betsy?"

"Sorry!" I called back as I raced to shut the siren off. "False alarm. So sorry! But thank you for coming to help."

He stopped, his posture communicating disappointment, then turned back toward home, grumbling all the way.

Breathless when I reached the control panel, I punched the code, and the racket fell blessedly silent. Then I called the alarm company and explained what had happened, giving my password: Amelia.

"I'm sorry, ma'am," the alarm person said, "but the Sandy Springs Police Department has already dispatched a patrol car to respond."

Thank goodness, they didn't charge for false alarms. "Thanks. Bye."

I threw on clothes as fast as I could and was on my way out when the police car came up the drive, its spotlight scanning the front of my house.

The patrolman got out and approached me, shining his flashlight in my face as I hurried toward him. "Ma'am, we received a break-in alert for this address," he said tersely, his right hand dropping to hover at his gun. "Is there an intruder inside?"

A logical assumption to make, with me fleeing the scene.

"No, no. No intruder. This is my house." I placed my hand on my heaving chest. I didn't have time for this. "Thank you so much for coming so quickly, but it's just a false alarm."

Across the street, the paramedics opened the door and started wheeling Zach out. Hurry, hurry. "My best friend's husband across the street had a medical emergency, and I was in such a hurry to go help that I forgot to disarm the alarm."

The policeman didn't seem convinced. "May I please see your driver's license or photo ID?" he asked, keeping the flashlight on me. I groped for my wallet, then opened it to my license and handed him the whole thing.

The officer stepped back as if I'd just proffered a bomb. "Please remove the license and hand it to me," he ordered.

Lord. But then again, it could have been a bomb, I guess. These days, who knew?

After struggling to liberate the license from its plastic sleeve, I pulled it out with a jerk that made him flinch, then handed it over. "Here. Could we please hurry?" I pointed to the stretcher. "They're taking my friend to the hospital, and I promised to go with them."

He turned to confirm what I'd said, then handed me back my license. "Your name matches the one for the call, so everything's squared away." He turned off his flashlight. "Would you like a police escort to the hospital?"

"Thank you so much, but that won't be necessary. We're just going over to St. Joe's."

The paramedics were closing up the ambulance.

He touched the brim of his cap. "Drive safely, ma'am. Hope everything works out okay."

Get out of my way! You're blocking my car! "Thank you so much." I hit the garage-door opener on my key chain.

Taking the hint, the patrol car zoomed back down the driveway, lights flashing, then shifted into forward and took off with a squeal of rubber.

I got behind the ambulance, turned on my flashers, and followed them to the hospital.

Talk about hurry up and wait. Kat kept me apprised, but they didn't have room for me in the cubicle, so I got a cup of coffee and a paper, then settled into a corner of the waiting room. The longer it took, the better it looked. Really sick people got treated right away, and Zach was taking hours and hours. Maybe it was just a pinched nerve. Halfway through the crossword puzzle, I realized it had been a year ago, almost to the date, when Kat had come with me to the ER when Greg left me. In a way, it seemed like just yesterday, but then again, it seemed like eons since I'd lived that other life in blissful ignorance.

Adjusting hadn't been easy, but reality was a far better place to be in the end, so I offered up a brief prayer of gratitude. Mama still hadn't gotten over it, but I had. Closing my eyes, I said another brief prayer for Zach.

Kat came out at five-thirty, on the verge of tears. She collapsed into the chair beside me, placing her face in her hands, elbows on her knees. "The weird thing is, the MRI of his brain was normal, so they did his spine, and that was normal. So were the Dopplers. So were the angiograms. No blood clots. No pinched nerves. No tumors, no strokes."

"Well, that's good news, isn't it?"

She shoved her fingers through the gray and amber curls at her scalp. "I guess so. But his deep reflexes aren't normal. And he's been having trouble swallowing."

That didn't sound good. "How long?"

She exhaled heavily. "Months. He never said a word to me. I guess this scared it out of him."

"Maybe it's something obscure, but minor," I told her. "Something they just have to find to fix."

Kat leaned back in the chair and closed her eyes. "They sure don't act like it's minor."

"What are they doing now?"

"An electromyography." Her mouth quivered. "They have to stick needles in his muscles and run current through them." A tear escaped the corner of her eye. "It's not supposed to hurt, except for the pricks, but Zach freaked out about the needles, so they had to sedate him."

Poor Zach. He could stand down the most heinous of criminals without a blink, but he really was phobic about needles. "He'll be all right," I said, for lack of anything better. "Maybe it won't take long." I shifted the subject. "What's the neurologist like?"

"Very nice, but he's from India," Kat said, "so it's kinda hard to understand him." A sad smile eased her face a bit. "He couldn't understand me fer beans. Zach had to translate."

"How long will the test take?"

"I didn't ask. I was so upset about Zach, I just had to leave, or I might have come out swingin' when they stuck him."

"Want me to go back and check?"

Relief washed over her expression. "Would ya? I wanta git some coffee and go to the bathroom."

I stood. "You do that, and take your time. The coffee's down that hall. Just follow the signs. Might be a good idea to get a bite, while you're there."

She rose with obvious effort. Sitting in those ER chairs was hard on the bones. "I don't wanta leave him fer too long."

"He's not going anywhere. Take a break. I'll send for you right away if anything comes up."

She gave me a brief hug. "Thanks." Then she was off.

The nurse told me where to find him, then let me back into the ER. As I approached, a short, brown-skinned doctor in a white coat stood in a murmured huddle with several other doctors, some of them in white jackets instead of coats. Interns?

Pretending that I was on my way somewhere beyond Zach's cubicle, I walked slowly past and heard "Freidrich's ataxia?" "No. That presents earlier." "Parkinson's?"

Please, not Parkinson's.

Dr. Longcoat shook his head and said in an Indian accent, "We'll have to follow up over time, but this looks like ALS to me."

My heart skipped three beats, halting me in my tracks. I turned so they couldn't see my reaction. Lou Gehrig's! Please, God, no.

Alerted to my presence, the medical huddle moved farther down the hall.

Doctors don't know everything. He said it *looks like* ALS. He wasn't positive.

Wishing I'd never heard it, I forced a calm mask over my alarm, then peeked in to see Zach trembling on the table, eyes shut tight, his fists gripping the sides of the narrow mattress as the technician removed the leads from his body. He'd sweated through the sheets, which covered his necessaries, but I didn't want to embarrass him, so I waited till the technician finished and replaced his gown, then covered him back up before I said a conspicuous, "Thanks so much for showing me where he is."

I pushed aside the curtain and dodged the departing technician and his equipment. When we were alone, I told Zach, "If you wanted attention, we could have stuck needles in you at home."

He smiled, grateful that I wasn't acting serious. "Hey. Good to see you."

I answered his unasked question. "I talked Kat into taking a little break. She's gone to the bathroom, then to the snack bar for some coffee. Can I get you some?"

Zach glanced toward the hall with a frown. "I don't think they'll let me."

"Won't let you what?" Dr. Longcoat asked as he came in, only a flicker of recognition betraying that I'd overheard him. He had a name embroidered on his coat that started with a *B*, but it was so long, I couldn't make it out.

"Have some coffee," Zach answered. "Betsy, this is the neurologist. Dr. B, this is my wife's and my best friend."

"We'll be releasing you shortly," Dr. Longcoat said. "You may have some coffee then."

"Good." Zach leveled a piercing gaze at the doctor. "So what's the story? Give it to me straight."

The doctor pulled a card from his pocket. "I'd like to review your test results and consult with some of my colleagues, before I speak of this." He handed the card to Zach. "Would it be convenient for you and your wife to see me at my office this afternoon at four? It's located here in the medical complex."

Zach's eyes narrowed in suspicion. "Why my wife? Why not just me?"

He was a detective, after all.

"You shouldn't be driving right now, and your wife told me she'd like to be present when we discuss your case."

Zach backed down, but only a little. "Okay. Four it is."

"Very well." The doctor bowed briefly. "Please excuse me, but I have another case."

Caught off guard, I bowed right back, then felt like an idiot, my ears flaming. "I'll go get Kat. I know she can't wait to get you home."

"It's bad news," he said, staring without focus at the ceiling. "I knew this was going to happen. I've known it all my life."

"Oh, come on, Zach," I said, covering what I knew. "No sense getting all worked up till you find out what's really the matter."

ALS had no cure. It was a long, agonizing death sentence.

Zach's focus shifted to me and sharpened. "You know something. I can see it."

Damn. "I'm going to get Kat," I covered, "so we can take you home, and y'all can get some sleep before you have to come back. Then I'm going to bed."

I hurried down the hall, wishing I could erase what I'd heard, but knowing I couldn't.

Kat was just coming back from the snack bar with coffee when I found her. "They're about to release Zach," I said. "Maybe we ought to hurry. I just realized we left your dogs locked up in the bathroom." I motioned toward home.

Kat waved her hand in dismissal. "No we didn't. I put them in the backyard."

This looks like ALS. "Okay, then." I sank abruptly into a chair. "I'll just wait, then."

Kat exhaled a long breath. "Why don't you go on and go home? No sense waiting for us. I'll call you when we get home."

I stood. "Or if you need anything before that."

Kat nodded.

"Okay, then. I'll go." Escape. She would tell me this afternoon, and what I know wouldn't come between us after that. I hugged her briefly. "Zach's waiting for you. Now that the test is over, he's fine."

"See you."

I cried all the way home, narrowly missing several fender benders in the morning traffic. Back in my bedroom, I closed all the shades and curled up in bed, sobbing.

This would kill Kat. She and Zach were halves of a whole.

Why did it have to happen to Zach? He was the best man I knew. He helped people every day.

I smashed the pillow in anger, but it didn't help. Zach was going to die a horrible death, and Kat would have to die it with him.

I cried till I didn't have any more tears. Then I took two sleeping pills, the first I'd taken since Greg left, and slept the day away.

My doorbell rang at six.

My eyes almost swollen shut, I threw on my robe and hurried to answer it, swiping at my wild bed hair. I looked through the

glass curtains on the sidelight and saw Kat standing there with a
heavy pot, her expression contorting.

I opened the door and took the pot, which clanked. "Come in,
honey."

She didn't even react to my appearance, just came inside and
waited till I closed the door, then fell to her knees, wailing, "Oh,
God! Oh, God! Oh, God! He's dyin'! Not just dyin'—dyin' long
and horrible!"

I stashed the pot on the credenza, then pulled her up into my
arms. "Oh, honey. What is it?"

"ALS," she spit out sharply, as if it were poison on her tongue.
"He can't drive anymore. He can't walk. He can't work." She sobbed.
"It's taken his work. He loves his work." Her voice dropped, and she
punctuated her words with her fist on my back. "It's taking everything he cares about, and killing him, one molecule at a time."

I swayed with her, not knowing what to say. There were no
words of comfort. They would be lies. I couldn't tell her it would
be all right. It was all wrong, permanently and horribly and pain-
fully. "It's so unfair," I said, crying with her. "So unfair."

I led Kat into the living room and eased her onto the sofa, then
sat beside her.

"The worst thing is," Kat sobbed, "I think I lost him the minute the doctor told us." She shook her head. "He just stared at me
with empty eyes. Wouldn't say a word." She pulled back to look at
me. "The doctor said it was a shock, and he'd come around. But
all the way home, he didn't speak."

"The doctor's right. It is a horrible shock. Zach needs time to
come to terms with it."

Kat reared back, angry. "Come to terms with it? And how do you propose for him to do that? He's acting catatonic, but I can see the wheels turning in his mind. Already, he's pulled away from me, and I know what he was thinking." She pointed to the pot she'd brought. "I had to take his guns. I put him to bed, then grabbed the one from the bedside table, then got the others and put them in there. So he couldn't get to them."

I went to the pot and opened it to find three magazine-loaded pistols and a stainless steel .38, all fully armed.

Poor guy. I couldn't blame him for wanting a fast way out.

A dull resignation settled in me. "I'll buy one of those electronic safes and store them in my closet." Where nobody else could get to them.

Kat's face contorted. "I don't know how to tell the kids." She turned swollen eyes my way, her heart breaking all over again, the words coming in gasps. "How . . . can . . . I . . . tell . . . my . . . *children?*"

Sobbing, she flopped onto her side on the sofa and brought her knees to her chest.

I hurried over and pulled a lap robe from the chair, then covered her and sat beside her, stroking her hair. "Shhh, shhh, shhh. I'll call and tell them. You told mine about their father. It'll be easier if I tell them. They can react without worrying about how it will affect you." I stroked and stroked. "You just worry about you and Zach," I soothed. "I'll take care of everything else."

Kat cried for another twenty minutes before her tears subsided at last. She sighed heavily, then sat up. "I have to go." Her expression crumpled, the words thick. "I can't leave him alone for long anymore. The doctor told me. He could choke."

She stood, gathering what was left of her composure to face the man she loved.

I walked with her to the door. "Call if you need anything. Anything. Any time of day or night. Do you have food?"

She shot a glance at the pot. "Tons of soup in the freezer. I can whirl it in the blender a bit, so it'll be easier for Zach to swallow." Her eyes welled, but she didn't let it overtake her.

"I'll call Zach and Sada." Kat nodded, then I asked, "Is it okay if I tell my girls?"

"That would be good," Kat said. "Zach has Courtney"—his girlfriend—"but Sada will need somebody to talk to."

"Okay." I opened the door to a sweet, cool March breeze. "I'll start cooking some stuff for y'all tomorrow, and bring it over. I'll make all Zach's favorites." Fortunately, he loved casseroles, which went down easy.

Kat nodded. I felt like I should say something more, but there wasn't anything else to say.

She paused, as if she felt the same, then turned to go, bleak as a prisoner heading for the chair. But she was strong. Strong enough to do what she had to, and I would be there to pick up the pieces when it was all over.

It took quite a few calls, but I finally managed to get Zach and Sada. Predictably, Zach responded with a long silence, then, "Where is he? How long does he have?"

"He's home. Your mama's looking after him." As for the

other . . . "I wish I could tell you how this will play out," I said gently, "but nobody really knows. Some people last for ten years"—I'd looked it up on the Internet—"some only two."

"Then he has two," Zach said with a conviction born of hope.

"Zach, honey, I don't know, and I don't think the doctors do either, at this point. They'll track his progress."

Another silence, frozen thick with everything unspeakable. "I—thanks," he choked out. "Is Mom—"

"Your mother's a strong woman," I told him, "but she's going to need you and Sada very much to get through this. Not to help out physically, necessarily, although it might come to that, but for support."

"Thanks."

"Honey, I'm so sorry. So very sorry. Call me for anything, okay?"

"Mmm-hmm." The line went dead.

Sada finally called me back just as the *Tonight* show was coming on. "Nine-one-one?" she said without even saying hello. "Five nine-one-ones? What happened?"

"Calm down, honey," I said. "Breathe. I need you to be calm when I talk to you."

"Something's happened to my parents," she said. "A car crash. Is that it?"

"No, honey." No sense beating around the bush. "Your daddy's sick." My voice betrayed me, breaking on the last.

Silence.

Dread raised Sada's alto voice to a childlike soprano. "It must be really, really bad. What is it, a heart attack?" Pause, then a whispered, "Cancer?"

I tried to be gentle, but the words I had to say were machetes. "He has ALS."

"ALS? What's ALS? Speak English."

"It used to be called Lou Gehrig's disease. It's a degenerative neurological condition. Your daddy's having trouble swallowing, and his leg doesn't work."

"So what are they going to do about it? What, surgery? Medicine?"

I didn't know if she was unaware of what ALS was, or in denial. "This is going to be a long, hard fight for both your daddy and your mama. Kat was really tired and upset, so I said I'd call you and Zach. Honey, is there anything I can do for you?"

I could almost hear her mind spinning. "Tell me the truth," she said with uncharacteristic calm.

"There is no cure or treatment," I told her quietly. "We'll make him comfortable. Don't worry about that. Your mama and I will take care of him."

"I'm coming home," she said with a maturity I'd never heard from her.

"Fine. Do you want me to get you a ticket?"

"Thanks, no. There are flights every hour from here to Atlanta."

The New York route took only a couple of hours. "It would probably be best if you waited till the middle of the day tomorrow. Give your mama a chance to get some rest and be with your daddy."

"That makes sense. I'll call when I get the particulars."

"Great. I'll probably be up all night."

Sada finally started to cry. "Me too."

"I love you, sweet girl."

"I love you too," she said, then hung up.

I called my girls, who comforted me as I knew they would comfort Sada.

Then I stayed up all night, trying to numb myself with old movies, but it didn't work.

Seventeen

One long, hard year later, almost to the day, I sat between Kat and Little Zach—who was now a grown man, and taller than his father had been—at the funeral home while droves of Big Zach's friends, neighbors, church friends, aging hippies, straight-arrow agents, and street people, alike, paid their respects at the casket where he lay like a perfect marble Grecian statue, his pale, handsome face arranged as it used to be, not drooping out of recognition as it was when he'd died. Kat had insisted on an open casket, so people wouldn't gossip and wonder what *really* happened to him, but Sada couldn't handle the whole body thing, so Emma had taken her to a movie.

Sitting there, I couldn't help wondering if my father was still alive out there somewhere, or dead and buried by those from his new life. Suddenly, I ached for him with such surprising sharpness that I forced my attention back to the hard work of the present.

After the mourners stood by Zach's body, they moved to murmur condolences to Kat and Little Zach. I listened in awe, feeling like an eavesdropper, as one after another shared the positive influence Zach had been on their lives.

Exhausted, Kat had been stoic since Zach stopped breathing three nights ago. She hadn't called anybody right away. Instead, she'd lain beside him and talked as if he were his old self, about all the things they'd discussed when he could still speak. About what they'd done together, good and bad, and the fun they'd had. About the kids, and their growing up. About how Zach would always be in her heart. About how she would show their grandchildren his picture and tell them his story. About how she would find love again, which Kat had insisted would never happen.

Then, when the faintest hint of dawn had shown in the east, she'd called hospice to tell them, and they came and got his body before the neighbors were up to see and comment.

It was a quiet, gentle leaving, his release, but that didn't make it any easier.

Kat had borne it all with dignity, but I knew the worst was yet to come, when everybody went back to their lives, and she would be alone.

A sudden hush fell on the room, and I looked up to see Greg signing the book by the door. I don't know why, but that made me very angry. I'd heard he had broken up with his secretary and moved back to town, but he had some nerve, showing up now.

For Kat's sake, though, I didn't react.

He crossed to sit by Amelia, who glared at him, then carried Madison out of the room. Unfazed, Sonny leaned over and shook Greg's hand, then introduced Macy to her grandfather.

Greg melted. He shot me a watery look, then turned his attention back to Macy, who climbed into his lap and barraged him with little-girl questions.

As the line to the casket lengthened, the space between us filled with people, so I didn't see Greg again till he got to the front. Visibly distraught, he looked down on the friend he'd lost, and started to cry.

At first, I thought he was just pretending, but when he looked at me again, his eyes were filled with a pain I'd never seen.

I looked away, feeling sorry for him, but not wanting to.

Greg wiped his eyes with his spotless handkerchief, then approached Kat. "I—" His eyes welled again. "God, Kat, I'm so sorry." He broke down and hugged her, his shoulders heaving. "So sorry."

Taken aback, Kat shot me a look of confusion as she patted his back. "Git a grip on yerself," she said quietly.

Chastened, Greg stood up, smoothing his tie, and nodded, then turned and left.

After the visitation, Amelia sat between the girls' car seats in back of their rented minivan and ranted about Greg's taking advantage of the situation to see her and the children. I leaned back from the front seat and tried to change the subject, but she ignored me.

Then Macy put her hand on Amelia's arm and asked, "Why do you hate my granddaddy? Did he kill somebody?"

Amelia's mouth snapped shut. "I don't hate him," she said. "I'm just mad at him."

Macy frowned. "Why?"

I lifted my eyebrows and stared at Amelia in challenge.

"I'll tell you someday, when you're older," my daughter deflected.

"Copout," Sonny said over his shoulder.

Macy thought a bit, then asked, "Do you want me to hate Granddaddy too? I will, if you want me to. He was pretty nice, but I could hate him."

Out of the mouths of babes.

"*I* don't hate Granddaddy," I offered.

"I *like* Granddaddy," Sonny said from the driver's seat. He looked at Amelia in the rearview mirror. "Zach was his best friend, honey. He had a right to be there."

Amelia leaned back. "So now you're taking up for him?"

"It's called forgiveness," Sonny told her. "You might want to try it."

Amelia stared past sleeping Madison.

"I'm not saying it'll be easy," he went on, God bless him. "But he deserves a second chance, for the girls' sake, as much as anything."

"Oh, all right." Amelia sighed. "If everybody's going to gang up on me, I'll give him a chance."

Sonny grinned. "Good. Because I told him he could come over after the funeral and take us out for ice cream."

Wait a minute! "Come over *where*?" I demanded, causing the baby to stir.

Sonny grinned at me. "To your house. That's where we're staying."

Eyes sparkling with mischief, Amelia rolled her lips inward, clearly enjoying having the tables turned.

Now that my house was finally mine, I liked it that way, and the last thing I wanted was for Greg to set foot into it. "I'm afraid that won't work," I said. "I'm helping Kat with the reception after the funeral, and I don't feel comfortable about Greg's being there when I'm not."

"Who's Greg?" Macy asked, picking up on my agitation.

"Okay," Sonny said. "We'll meet him outside. How about that?"

If I said no, I'd end up looking like the one who was holding a grudge. So I decided to go against my instincts and set a good example. "That's fine." I looked at Amelia. "You ought to go with them, sweetie." I shifted my attention to Macy. "Would you like Mama to go with you and Granddaddy tomorrow for ice cream?" Dirty pool, but she deserved it.

Macy started clapping and bouncing her feet up and down between the front and back seats, singsonging, "Ice cream with Granddaddy and Mama! Yay! Ice cream with Granddaddy and Mama."

Amelia placed her arm across Macy's legs to still her. "All right. All right. I'll go."

Macy leaned over and hugged her mother's arm. "Thank you, Mama. Thank you, thank you, thank you."

Amelia patted her. "I can't believe you just did that," she said to my smiling reflection in the rearview mirror.

I broke into a grin.

At least Greg had gotten our minds off our grief.

. . .

The next morning dawned cool and gray, suitably dreary for what we had to do. The funeral was at Zach and Kat's church, Mount Vernon Baptist. The large sanctuary was filled with flowers, and I was glad to see that the casket was closed, covered with a blanket of red roses. The ceremony was very nice, with a poignant message from the minister about the brevity and uncertainty of life, versus the reassurance and peace of reconciliation with God through Christ. He thanked God that we had been allowed to have Zach with us, and that Zach was now whole and free in heaven.

Then Sada got up and spoke about her dad. How she managed, I couldn't say, but she only faltered a few times. I was so proud of her, and I could see that Kat was too, even though she was silently crying the whole time.

Next, the director of Zach's division praised his service to the community, telling stories of Zach's generosity and bravery.

Last, Little Zach talked about the ways his father had shown him how a Christian man should be. The anecdotes were ones I'd never heard, and they almost undid me with their simple clarity and power.

Then Little Zach paused, looking pointedly at the other side of the pews, and I followed his line of sight to see Greg with his face in his hands.

Good. Maybe this would make Greg look at his life and change his ways.

We were over, but I didn't hate him anymore, and I sincerely hoped he could get his life together. After all, he'd provided well for us, and he *was* the girls' father.

Little Zach finished by challenging the men in the room to follow his father's example while they still had a chance to make things right. Then he sat down, and a Scottish pipe-and-drum band marched in from the back of the church, the sound of "Amazing Grace" filling the air to bursting.

That did it. Amelia and Emma and I leaned on each other and started to sob.

After the service, Emma took Sada back to Kat's, and I followed. Frankly, I couldn't handle seeing that coffin go into the ground any more than Sada could. Better I should get everything ready for the luncheon. So back on Eden Lake Court, the three of us distracted ourselves with work, helping the ladies from the church set out the food. By the time everybody started to arrive, I was ready to sit down with a cool glass of tea and rest a little.

I didn't see Greg come in. I just heard his voice from the front room, where Kat was sitting. I got up and went to see. Greg was sitting next to her, his forearms braced on his thighs, hands linked, in earnest conversation. Blending into the conversations all around them, they talked for a long time before he got up. I backed out of sight before he could see me.

I didn't ask Kat what he said. If she wanted to tell me, she would.

After everybody went home, I sent Kat to bed, then made sure the house was in good shape. Frankly, it was better than it had ever been. The church ladies had given it a real going-over while we had been at visitation, banishing the dogs and cats to the playroom downstairs, then cleaned the kitchen till it shined.

Scratches and whines came from under the basement door.

For the first time ever, I was glad for those animals. I let them back in, whispering, "Go see Kat. Go see Mama," as they escaped and made for her room.

They could comfort her in a way I couldn't.

I followed them to find Kat and Zach and Sada piled up in her bed, looking at photo albums—surrounded by licking, purring pets.

Kat looked up with a sad smile. "Thanks so much for everything."

"It was nothing," I said, and meant it. "I'm going home now. Greg's coming over to take the kids for ice cream."

Kat nodded. "I'm glad. He talked to me for a long time today. He really wants to get his life turned around."

Typical. His best friend just died, and he bends Kat's ear about himself. "For the girls' sake, I hope he does."

Greg's behavior would speak far louder than anything he said. If he'd reformed, we'd see it. If not, nothing lost, nothing gained.

Noting my skepticism, Kat added, "This really hit him hard, Betsy."

This was no time to discuss Greg's egotism, so I responded, "It hit us all hard." I turned to go. "Call if you need anything. I'm right across the street."

Kat hesitated briefly. "I think we could all do with a few days' rest." It was her way of letting me know she wanted some space, and time alone with her children.

"Sounds good to me." The real work would start when Little Zach and Sada went back to their lives, leaving Kat alone in that big house while the rest of the world went right on spinning. I'd be there for her then.

Little Zach . . . Now that his father was gone, we'd have to stop calling him that.

I got home to find that Greg and the kids had already left for ice cream, so I started making supper. I had just put a roast in the oven when I heard a car pull up, then the sound of Macy's laughter. I went to the door and opened it, only to find Greg standing there with a vanilla ice cream sundae from Bruster's in his hand, all hot fudge topping, with no cherries, just like I liked it. "Hi. I brought you a treat."

Macy raced past us as I accepted it. I stepped back to let Amelia and Sonny in.

Sonny clapped Greg's back. "Thanks for the ice cream, Granddaddy. See you tomorrow."

Tomorrow?

He bent to chase Macy. "C'mere, you! It's time for somebody to have a nap."

Carrying placid Madison, Amelia trailed her fingers across my shoulder as she passed. "We're going to breakfast, then the children's museum. You sleep in. You've earned it."

She shot a look at her father, then at me, and went into the guest room, closing the door behind her.

Left alone with Greg on my doorstep, I felt excruciatingly awkward, but some stubborn part of me kept me from asking him in.

"Is it okay if I come in?" he asked with a tentativeness I didn't recognize.

Since he'd given me the house, I decided it would be too rude to say no. "Just for a minute."

He stepped inside, then closed the door behind him. Glancing around, he said, "You know, I never appreciated this the way I should have." He looked at me with intensity. "I never appreciated *you* the way I should have."

Two years ago, I'd have killed to hear those words, but now, they just made me wonder what he was after.

He looked down at his feet. "Betsy, I'm so sorry for what happened."

Not what he *did*, what *happened*, like having an earthquake open up the ground and swallow him, instead of choosing to throw me away.

He ventured a glance at my face. "It didn't take long for me to realize what a horrible mistake it all was."

Translation: his secretary wouldn't wait on him hand and foot the way I had. I took perverse satisfaction in that.

His voice was hoarse when he said, "It's so lonely on my own."

I met his eyes with a confidence born in the ashes of what I'd lost, and for the first time, I saw him for the man he was, his strengths balanced by very human flaws, just like me. Just like everybody else in this crazy world.

Mistaking my acceptance for encouragement, he ventured, "Do you think there's a chance . . . Do you think you could ever forgive me?"

I shook my head, feeling pity for him. "I did that a long time ago, Greg, for my own survival. I couldn't have healed if I didn't."

He brightened. " 'Cause I'd like to see you, if that's okay. Start over. Give it another chance."

To my awe and amazement, I wasn't even tempted. It felt so wonderful.

In that moment of insight, I realized that I had helped make him the spoiled, self-centered man he was, but I wasn't stupid enough to sell myself back into his service. I truly felt sorry for the guy. "Greg, for the girls' sake, it would be nice for us to be on friendly terms. I'd like that. But I can't see you anymore."

I didn't even feel compelled to explain!

"I swear," he said, "I've changed."

"So have I." Thank God, thank God. "Greg, you deserve to be loved for who you are. I hope you find that. But I'm very happy on my own now, and I don't want to complicate things with a relationship—with anybody."

I could tell he was shocked. He'd probably thought I would fall into his arms and beg him to come home.

Men.

I could see the wheels turning in his brain. "Okay, friends, then," he said. "We could see each other as friends."

Translation: "I'll wear her down."

I took Greg's arm and steered him toward the door. "Time to go. I'll see you tomorrow when ya'll get back from the museum."

Greg hadn't gotten as far as he'd gotten by giving up. "Come with us. It's not a date. Just family time."

I opened the door and steered him toward the porch. "Go home. I'm exhausted. Or have you forgotten? We buried your best friend today."

"I haven't," he said. "And I don't have a home to go to, just a house, with nobody there."

The world's smallest violin played "Hearts and Flowers," but I couldn't blame him for trying. "Nice to see you. Bye."

To my horror, he spun around and took my face in his hands, drawing me hard against him the way Richard Gere grabbed Guinevere in *First Knight*, one of my favorite movies. Then he planted a foul, demanding kiss on me, his tongue trying to part my tightly closed lips.

Gross!

Instinct told me to knee him in the groin, but a deeper wisdom sent me absolutely inert, teeth locked behind compressed lips and arms rigid at my sides.

It took a few seconds for him to realize the siege hadn't worked. He let me go and stepped back. "Sorry. I . . . I just miss you so much, and I wanted to . . . sorry."

It was pretty funny, actually. "Had to try that, did you?" I asked, deadpan.

Greg smiled like a kid caught with his fingers in his mother's wallet. "I thought . . ."

I put my splayed hand on his chest and shoved him out the door. "Well, now that you know, go forth and find somebody to love. With your money, that shouldn't be hard. Good luck, and good night."

He stood there in dismay as I closed and locked the door, then armed the alarm. "Good night!" I repeated through the door.

And it had been a good one. A very good one. No more ghosts hovered on the corners of my heart or my house.

Greg would find somebody else to take care of him.

I just never in a million years imagined it would be Kat.

Eighteen

Three years ago. Eden Lake Court

A week after I got home from visiting Amelia in California, my phone scared me awake at one o'clock in the morning. Fearing the worst, I groped for the cordless receiver on my bedside table, then fumbled with the buttons in the dark.

I hit the red one instead of the green one, and the ringing stopped.

Rats. Who'd be calling me at this hour, and why?

I sat up and turned on the two-fifty bulb in my bedside lamp, blinding me as I squinted down at the bedside table and poked around for my reading glasses amid the cable remote, my night cream, the ceiling fan control, my lip balm, and my bedtime pill minder. I found them hiding under the TV listings from the paper. By the time I got my glasses on and looked to see who'd called, the phone rang again in my hand, jarring me so, I almost dropped it. This time I hit the green button and answered with an anxious, "Hello?"

"Why didn't you tell me he was getting married?" Mama's voice accused.

"Lord, Mama, you scared me half to death. It's one o'clock in the morning!"

"Well, it's only ten in L.A. where Amelia lives." Mama scolded. "She just called me and spilled the beans. So that sorry ex of yours has taken up with that hippie girl, right across the street, in your face. I'd scratch the bitch's eyes out. And his."

This was why I hadn't told her. I'd never hear the end of it. I didn't respond.

"According to Amelia, this has been going on for months," Mama accused. "Why didn't you tell me?"

"Mama, that's none of my business anymore. I've told you a hundred times, I'm over Greg. What he does and who he sees is none of my business."

"That's the biggest load of hogwash I've ever heard of in my life," Mama countered. "Why in God's good green earth would that woman want anything to do with him, in the first place? She has to know how many assets he hid from the courts during your divorce. The man's nothing but a liar and a cheat."

"No, Mama," I countered, amazed to find myself taking up for Greg. "He lied and he cheated, but that's not all he is. He was a wonderful husband to me for more than twenty years, and a great father to the girls. What he did when we broke up doesn't erase that."

"Blah, blah, blah," Mama responded. "You might be able to put that baloney over on the girls, but this is Mama. I don't buy it."

Fuming, I told her, "Greg made a big, fat, wretched mistake that ruined things between us, but that doesn't define him. I loved him once, so it makes sense that somebody else might love him too." I meant that, but it came out sounding hollow, even to me.

"That hippie girl has betrayed you," Mama accused for the jillionth time.

Mama had only met Kat twice, and briefly, decades ago when Kat had ridden with me on my food runs. Mama had been so rude both times that Kat had avoided her ever since, staying in the car whenever she'd accompanied me after that.

Mama's harangue went on. "She never has been worthy of your friendship. Havin' you arrested. Goin' around lookin' like some old washerwoman who just fell out of a hayloft."

"Mama, if you start in on Kat again," I warned, "I'm going to hang up and unplug the phone for three days. I mean it."

A disgruntled pause followed, then, "Well, if you ask me, it's adding insult to injury, them living there across the street in sin."

"Mama," I scolded.

"And that wedding. Of all the places in all the world, they're getting married *there*?" Mama let out a derisive snort. "I can't believe they're rubbing your nose in it that way."

That did it. Miserable, I hung up, then unplugged the phone and turned off the light. Flouncing back under the sheet, I tried to shoo away the hurt and anger that had bloomed inside me, but Mama had laid the situation out straight, and her resentment was contagious.

Maybe they were rubbing my nose in it, but seeing it that way would only make me miserable, and I had no intention of letting that happen.

After ten minutes of tossing and fretting, I got up and went to the bathroom, then took five milligrams of Ambien. On further consideration, I took another five milligrams, then drank a cold bottle of water from the white minifridge on the far side of the bed, and promptly fell asleep.

As I began to come back from the depths of oblivion the next morning, I dreamed that Kat and I were in her kitchen, both of us wearing the wedding rings Greg had bought us, arguing with him over some awful, elusive thing. In the safety of my dream, I finally felt the anger I hadn't allowed myself when he'd betrayed me. As Greg screamed at me, blaming me for everything he had done, I surrendered to my fury for a terrifying, exhilarating ride, and Kat was riding with me.

Then, without warning, Kat turned and stabbed Greg right in the stomach, releasing a fire hose of blood. Eyes and mouth open wide in surprise, Greg looked at the life spurting from him, then toppled like a fifty-foot pine. Shocked, yet eerily calm, I bent to find his pulse, but there was none. And the awful thing was, that made me happy.

Kat dropped the knife, then hugged me hard, repeating, "It's over. It's over. It's over." A tidal wave of relief brought me awake.

Then, immediately, guilt and practicality pounced on me.

Horrible, to wish such a thing on the father of my children. And stupid, to be glad Greg was dead.

Greg carried a shipload of life insurance, but he'd told Emma that Kat was the beneficiary now. So if he died, Kat would be sitting pretty, and I'd be left high and dry—since his pension had gone with the wind, along with Arthur Andersen—with just half his Social Security to keep up my house and sky-high taxes. Not a happy prospect.

Since the divorce, I'd supplemented my alimony by doing makeovers for business types and special occasions, but I could never live, even modestly, on what that brought in.

So I definitely didn't want Greg dead. I needed him alive and paying alimony.

Just not across the street.

Three years ago, the third Saturday in July. Eden Lake Court

The day of the wedding dawned clear, but as hot and muggy as the butterfly house at the botanical gardens. Emma was still sleeping when I went down to the mailbox at eight to get my paper before breakfast. Three steps into the humidity, I felt perspiration coat my whole body like a soggy blanket. The weatherman said it was the hottest decade in recorded history, and I believed it.

How had I managed, growing up in heat like this without air-conditioning?

I remembered taking off my nightgown as a child and standing in front of the roaring box fan in my window, the night air like an oven as it blew past me. Mama wouldn't run the attic fan, because it sucked up the bills and junk mail that were lying all over everything stacked in the hallway.

Just thinking about it gave me a hot flash.

Grateful that I didn't have to go back to that life, I hurried into the house and splashed cold water on my face, then wiped my arms and neck with a cool, damp paper towel. Outside, I heard the roar and jingle of a truck, and looked out the sidelight in the foyer to see a lawn crew pull up and start cutting my grass.

Guess Greg didn't want anybody thinking I wasn't well provided for.

Worked for me.

Happy to have it done, I made the coffee, then fixed my usual breakfast: three pieces of bacon microwaved inside thick paper towels till it was crisp and dry, and three scrambled eggs with just a little water and margarine. I'd been doing low-carb to get rid of the pounds I'd gained in L.A., and I was almost back down to a bearable weight of 150. With my height and big bones, I looked almost slim at that weight—if I dressed very carefully, which I always did, even when I was just home by myself.

The truth was, I was afraid not to. Sure as I let myself go, some rich, gorgeous, caring unattached male would turn up on my doorstep, and there I'd be, looking like the Wicked Witch of the West. Plus, image was my business. I had to look my best.

At the sound of air brakes out in the cul-de-sac, I left my half-eaten eggs and looked out to see an Aaron Rents truck pull into Kat's driveway and start unloading white-slipcovered gilt chairs for the wedding. And unloading. And unloading.

How many people had they asked to this thing, anyway?

Not that it mattered. I'd just be glad when it was all over and things settled down again.

Pouring my Eight O'clock coffee, I wondered idly where Kat and Greg were going for their honeymoon. Greg took me to Gatlinburg, Tennessee, but he'd probably take Kat somewhere expensive and exotic. Not that I cared. At least they'd be gone for a while.

A fleeting thought of arson flitted through my mind before guilt extinguished it.

I had just settled down to finish my eggs and bacon when my phone rang.

I looked at my watch. Eight-thirty.

Probably Mama.

Rats.

I considered not answering, but got up and went for the receiver anyway. It might not be Mama. Maybe it was Kat, telling me she'd come to her senses.

It wasn't Kat; it was Amelia, calling at the wee hours in L.A.

"Hey, honey," I answered in a worried tone. "Is everything okay?"

"Oh, Mama," she said, her nose stopped up from crying. "I just can't stand that Daddy's doing this to you."

Oh, for heaven's sake. "Sweetie, he's not doing this *to* me. He's doing it for himself. I'm glad he's turned his life back around. He has a right to be happy."

"Not after what he did to you," she said. Her tone dropped for a menacing, "I want him to suffer, the way he made you suffer."

I had to laugh. "Honey, you don't mean that. He's your father, and he loves you. And anyway, if I'm okay with this, why aren't you?"

"Because I know you're not, not really," she countered, "not down inside. You're a one-man woman, just like me."

I didn't want to tell her that I'd never felt the passion for her father that she felt for Sonny. "Sweetie, I am currently a *no*-man woman, which suits me absolutely fine. I wish I could convince you. Why won't you believe me?"

"Because I can't stand for you to be so alone now, that's why." She blew her nose, but it didn't help. "Why don't you come here and live with us?"

I heard a groggy, startled, "What? You said what?" from Sonny in the background, but Amelia ignored him.

"I mean it, Mama. You could sell the house and make a new start. Prices here are better than they've been in decades. You could have a fabulous condo. It would be fun."

Not for me.

I liked breathing, and I was too firmly rooted. "Sweetie, you know I can't leave your grandmother."

"Well . . ." Amelia paused to consider, then resumed with a bright but stopped-up, "I know. We could find her a little place out here and fix it up really cute, then give her a Mickey Finn and keep her knocked out till she wakes up in her new house. Fly her by air ambulance."

Amelia, Amelia. She just didn't get it.

"Honey, she can't leave her home or her things. It would destroy her. She's too sick to make an adjustment like that."

Chastened, Amelia said, "Well, maybe there's some treatment—"

"She won't take the meds, and I can't shove them down her

throat. Mama's crazy, but she's not incompetent. The kindest thing I can do is let her stay where she is and visit her and bring food, so she eats decently."

Amelia started to cry again. "There you go, looking after everybody but yourself. Mama, you have a right to be happy too. At least move to somewhere else in Atlanta."

I bristled. "I am not going to let this run me out of my home. I love this house. I have it just the way I want it, and I'm not going anywhere." Shades of Mama.

"Well, at least leave for the rest of the day, then. Promise me you won't be there when they . . . Just go to a movie. Or have lunch with one of your *real* friends, then go shopping. Pick out a new outfit, my treat. Just please don't stay there. That would be too tragic to endure."

For whom? But Amelia always had overdramatized. Still, she really was upset.

"I might go out for lunch and a movie," I conceded, "but I'm not promising anything. It's too hot to go anywhere."

"I'm glad it's hot," Amelia said. "I hope they all roast at Kat's, and everybody stays home."

"Amelia," I scolded, "that is most ungracious of you, and it pains me to hear you say such things."

"Then I won't say them. But you can't stop me from thinking them."

I couldn't stop *myself* from thinking them, but I kept that to myself.

Emma appeared at the door, yawning. "Who's that?"

Good. Let *her* deal with her sister. "It's Amelia." I proffered the phone. "Why don't you talk to her while I fix your break-fast?"

Emma brightened. "Great." She took the phone. "Hey, Mealy"—a nickname Amelia had always hated—"what are you doing up at this hour? It's like, five there, right?" She made a face as Amelia started in about the wedding. Unable to get a word in edgewise, Emma covered the mouthpiece and whispered, "Whole wheat bagels with low-fat strawberry cream cheese, please."

As if I didn't know. She'd been eating bagels since way before bagels were in. "Coming up." I left the dregs of my now-cold eggs and went to defrost some bagels.

I tried not to eavesdrop, but couldn't help it.

Listening to Amelia's tirade, Emma sighed in disapproval. "Amelia, why are you being hysterical about this? It's not gonna change anything. Daddy's a free agent, and so is Kat. So just get over it, okay?"

I could hear Amelia's outrage from where I was standing.

Emma scowled. "I am *not* being disloyal to Mama!" She pulled the phone away from her ear to ask, "Mama, do you think I'm being disloyal to you if I go to the wedding?"

I put the bagels into the toaster oven, then took the phone. "Emma is not being disloyal to me by going to the wedding. Amelia, honey, you've got to let go of this, or you'll make yourself sick. I'm fine."

"Mama," she said in a calmer tone, "please let me speak to Emma."

"Only if you promise not to let this come between you. That's the only thing that bothers me about this wedding. I don't want it to come between you and your sister."

Chastened, Amelia promised it wouldn't.

"All right then," I told her. I handed the phone back to Emma, who accepted her sister's apology, then told her to go back to bed, and hung up.

The toaster oven dinged, and I fixed the bagels, then served them to Emma with some orange juice.

"Thanks, Mama." She licked some cream cheese from one. "Man. What a drama queen." She took a bite, then paused, studying me as I sat across from her to drink my coffee. "You don't really think I'm betraying you by accepting this thing with Kat and Daddy, do you?"

"Don't talk with your mouth full," I chided.

Emma's expression clouded. "You didn't answer my question."

I shook my head. "How many times am I going to have to tell you girls I'm okay before you believe it?"

"Sorry." My younger daughter sent me a worried look. "It's just, well, Amelia said it's not natural for you to be so calm about all this."

Oh, good grief. Why can't a person be well adjusted? "Would you rather I shut myself away like Mama did?" I asked. "Or maybe you'd feel better if I go Jerry Springer during the ceremony. Would that be better?"

Emma laughed. "No. I think you've been great about this, Mama, really I do. I just don't want you to stuff it all inside. That could eat you up."

I lifted my coffee mug her way. "Don't worry, honey. I get it all out of my system in my dreams."

She cocked back with a grin. "Tell, tell."

"Never. Now eat your breakfast so you can go to the salon and get your hair done for the wedding." As usual, she'd put her thick, wavy brown mane into a hasty ponytail.

I reached into my purse and handed her the certificate I'd gotten before she came. "Here. Manicure and pedicure, my treat."

"Rad!" She accepted it with delight, then sobered. "I sure wish Amelia could be as sane as you are. All she wants to do anymore is rag on Kat and Daddy."

"She'll have to work this out with her daddy in her own time," I said, "but you are certainly entitled to tell her that subject is off limits."

"Good idea." Emma got up and gave me a hug. "Thanks, Mama. Not just for the manicure."

I savored the feel of her in my arms. "For what, then?"

"For being so surrealistically *good*."

She wouldn't think so if she could read my mind—or my dreams.

Emma nestled against my shoulder the way she had as a child. "I sure do miss you in Alaska."

"I miss you too." I gave her a brief squeeze, then pulled back to look at this plump, confident woman my little girl had become. "Any chance I can talk you into moving back home?"

She smiled, shaking her head no. "Down here, men look right through me because I'm not some blond flat-belly. But in Alaska, women are so scarce that I'm the belle of the ball." Pride radiated from her. "I get asked out all the time, and not just by the nerds. I'm talking *manly* men. Gotta tell ya, it's great."

"Try not to break too many hearts," I said as we released each other.

"I'll think about it."

Thirty minutes later, the house was spotless and Emma was off to the salon. I went into her room to lay out the slenderizing dress we'd picked out for her to wear, and I decided to give it a fresh press. Then I hung it in her closet and went back to my room to pile up in bed and watch back episodes of *What Not to Wear* I'd recorded on the DVR.

Usually, this was a real treat for me, but on that particular day, I felt restless after only two episodes. I got the cable remote and went through everything on the guide, but nothing appealed to me. On Saturdays, even cable left a lot to be desired if you weren't a kid or a sports fan. Nothing worth watching on the pay-per-view either.

Nonplussed, I turned off the set and got up to check the laundry. The hampers were empty, and so were all the trash cans in the house, leaving me without a single chore to pass the time.

Back in the bedroom, I decided that maybe I *should* have lunch and go shopping with somebody.

I got out my address book and started calling the girls I knew fairly well from church and charity work. The first two didn't answer, so I didn't leave a message. The next three I called were tied up for the day. After all, it was last-minute.

I made five more phone calls before I ran out of people I felt comfortable asking, which made me pretty grumpy.

So what if I didn't have many friends? I'd managed fine before Kat, and I would again.

Sulking a bit, I told myself I could always go somewhere nice by myself. La Grotta, or the Fish Market. But I wasn't in the mood to eat alone in public.

I got the paper and looked into the movies, but I wasn't into vampires or computer-enhanced action movies, or chick flicks that were supposed to be fun, but were really just so-so. And I hated going to movies alone, anyway.

Amelia. This was all her fault. If she'd just left me alone, I'd be perfectly fine, going through my day as usual.

At sixes and sevens, I decided to kill some time by calling Mama. (That'll tell you how desperate I was.) "Hey, Mama. How are you feeling today?"

"I'm fine, but I can't talk now," she said in an odd tone. "I'll have to call you back."

A click, then a dial tone. What was up with that?

Maybe a burglar had broken into her house and was holding her hostage. I hit redial.

After several rings, Mama answered with a breathless, "I *told* you, I can't talk now." I could have sworn the sound she made next was a stifled chortle.

"Are you okay? Is anybody threatening you?"

Another stifled chortle. "Not hardly. See you later."

An odd choice of words. Again, the dial tone.

I considered going over to find out what was up, but decided it would be wiser not to set such a precedent.

An inspiration came to me. I could bring her a cake, my famous devil's food with seven-minute icing. And while I was at it, I could bake one for Emma. And one for Kat, as a gesture of goodwill.

So I set about baking, and three hours later, the cakes were cooled, iced, and sitting on the kitchen table while I took a long, cool soak, then washed my hair. I'd just finished drying it when Emma came home.

"Mama?"

"I'm in the bathroom," I called from my dressing table, sponging a little bronzer on my pale cheeks.

I heard her approach, then looked in the mirror to see her framed in the doorway. She looked gorgeous. "Oh, honey, I *love* your hair. You let them cut it."

Emma swung the layered, shoulder-length curls. "Yep. It's still long enough to put up, but the layers in the front give it more volume."

I hugged her with pride. "It's beautiful, and so are you."

She slipped off her Crocs and wiggled her toes, now adorned with bright red polish. "You like it? I thought it would look good with the red flowers on my dress." She waggled her scarlet fingernails at me. "What do you think?"

"I think it's perfect, just like you." I put my arm around her shoulder. "Come on. It's time for you to get ready. Will you let me do your face?" Mine could wait.

Emma nodded. "Okay, but only if I have the right of refusal."

"Deal." We headed for her room.

Thirty minutes later, she emerged looking like a model, only subtler. Her long empire-style dress flattered her figure, and her floral platform sandals showed off her pedicure.

"You look mah-velous," I told her.

"You do too," she said.

She'd insisted on doing my makeup, and I looked pretty exotic.

Emma studied herself in the full-length mirror. "Mama, this is fabulous. No wonder people pay you. I look almost pretty."

"You *are* pretty," I told her with a mother's conviction.

Grinning, she shook her curls, looking like she believed it.

I glanced at the clock. "You'd better get going if you want to help Kat with the last-minute arrangements."

"Okay."

I got Kat's cake and handed it to Emma in the foyer as she left. "This is for the reception."

"Oooh, my favorite." Emma eyed it with lust.

"Be sure they keep it inside," I told her. "The heat'll ruin the icing."

"I will." Emma paused by the door. "I thought you were going to go out this afternoon."

Apparently, nobody was going to be satisfied if I didn't. "I am," I lied, "I just wanted to help you get ready first."

Emma gave me a peck. "Good. I'm glad you decided to get away."

I opened the door to the inferno. No way was I going out in that. The cake's icing would probably melt before Emma got it across the street. "Have fun. I'll leave the key under the door-mat."

Emma waved. "I doubt I'll be very late. Bye."

Once inside, I decided to do something I'd never done before in my life. I went for the white zinfandel and poured myself a huge gobletful, then cut myself a slab of fresh cake and had a party of one, long before the sun was over the yardarm. The wine was almost as sweet as the cake, and it went down smoothly. Feeling better when that was gone, I refilled my goblet and my plate. Twenty minutes and two thousand calories later, I got up for some iced water and wavered as I stood.

Whoo! All that sugar and alcohol in the middle of the day had gotten me way past high.

I guzzled a bottled spring water, then lurched back to the shady recesses of my room and promptly fell asleep.

I was worriedly working my way through some formless ordeal dream when a door slammed in my dream, and Emma and somebody else started hollering something I couldn't understand. As I focused harder, I realized the hollering wasn't imaginary, and I woke up.

I leaped to my feet, setting off a hand grenade in my skull. Covering my left eye to keep it from falling out, I staggered toward the light and sound and saw two figures in the foyer, backlit by the blazing sun.

"I cannot believe you disrupted the wedding and insulted Daddy and Kat in front of all those people!" Emma shouted. "You owe everybody there an apology, especially Kat!"

"I don't owe that hippie girl *squat*!"

Mama?

I blinked hard. Must still be dreaming!

I focused as my eyes adjusted to the brightness, and sure enough, there Mama stood, looking like Mrs. Gotrocks in a vintage Chanel suit and Italian heels, her hair pulled back into an elegant chignon.

"Mama?" I stopped breathing, and tiny stars danced around the edges of my vision. No more booze in the middle of the day. I was honest-to-God hallucinating.

"Emma," Mama barked out, "you'd better grab your mother before she passes out."

"Mama!" Emma hurried over and steadied me. "Are you okay?"

It sure *felt* real.

Stunned, I patted her arm, my eyes glued on a defiant Mama. "Is this really happening?"

Emma winced and drew back in disapproval. "Mama! You've been drinking."

"Just two glasses of wine," I defended, my stomach roiling at the mention, "with some cake."

My mother sidled toward the door. "Well, while you two are talking, I'll just slip out. The meter's running on my cab."

Emma abandoned me to block the way. "Oh, no you don't. You're not going anywhere till you apologize to Kat and Daddy for ruining their wedding."

"Mama," I said, "what did you do?"

"Turnabout's fair play," she said, straightening her cuffs. She jerked her chin upward. "They embarrassed you by having that travesty right across the street. I just decided to give them a taste of their own medicine."

Oh, Lord. "Thirty years, you haven't set foot out of that house, and you finally do it for *this*?"

"I did it for *you*." Mama leveled a clear gaze at me. "Nobody ever takes up for you, including me. I decided it was time."

Deciding didn't cure mental illness like my mother's. Something else was going on, here. I turned to my daughter. "Emma, please go over to Kat's and explain that I had no idea Mama was going to do something like this, and I deeply apologize on her behalf."

"Don't you do that," Mama warned her. "I do not apologize."

I motioned Emma to go anyway.

"Don't worry, Mama," she said. "I'll tell them. And I'll also tell them Nana is mentally ill." She shot a scowl at her grandmother, then departed with a slam of the door.

As soon as Mama and I were alone, I didn't mince words. "What's going on here? How did you manage to leave that house?"

Mama lifted a shoulder and both eyebrows, looking down. "Well, if you must know, I've been taking my meds and practicing going out for months."

"Why? How?"

"You're not the only one around here who has her secrets, you know."

What was she up to? "Okay, Mama. Let's hear it."

"I have a boyfriend," she gloated.

What?

Maybe she'd finally lost touch with reality completely. "Oh, really. Who?"

"Claude Brenner, from next door. His wife died a year ago.

Somebody told him I was a collector, so he came over to see what I had." She straightened the hydrangeas in the vase on the foyer table. "Brought me some roses from his garden. I fed him supper, and one thing led to another, and we've been seeing each other ever since."

Was she hallucinating? I talked to Mama every day, and she'd never even hinted at anything like this.

"That's great, Mama," I said, still suspicious. "What does he look like?"

"Tall and lanky, just like I like 'em." She looked twenty years younger when she said it. "He thinks I'm pretty. And he's been helping me find the real treasures in all the things I've been saving."

If this guy actually existed, I couldn't help wondering if he was taking advantage of her. "Mama, did you give him any of your collectibles?" Some were actually valuable.

"Heavens, no," Mama said. "He's got a houseful of his own. We just started clearing out the spare room, so we could put the good things in there."

Clearing out? I hadn't seen any evidence of clearing out. But then again, I hadn't looked in the spare room for ages.

After all my years of trying to get her to clean up, to take her meds, to reach out to life, some guy comes along and she does it, just like that?

Blindsided, I tried to think of what to say. "I think that's great, Mama." Another packrat, lonesome and available, right next door? That was too weird to be believed. "How long has he been visiting you?"

"It's not visiting," she corrected. "We're dating, with a capital *D*."

Sex? Was she saying they were having *sex*? I flashed on a recent article about rampant STDs in senior communities. "Mama, you're not . . . I mean, are you two . . . you're not *sleeping* together, are you?"

"Lord, no," she said. "There's no way I'd let him stay over after we have sex. I need my rest. And my privacy."

I almost swallowed my tongue, at a total loss for words. The idea of my mother with some old man . . . Wash my eyes out with soap. "But Mama, you've always been so strict about sex outside of marriage."

"Well, yes, I have," she said, tapping her forefinger across her lips. "Seeing as how there is no degree of sin with God, I don't imagine that what we're doing is any worse than you not telling me about Greg and that hippie girl for months. A lie of omission is still a lie, and the Lord loves the truth and hates a lie." She certainly didn't sound repentant. "Claude and I will have to work this out with the Lord, but any way you slice it, it's our business, not anybody else's."

"Then why did you tell *me*?" I grumbled, still trying to assess what had happened.

"Because I didn't want to keep something that important from you." Her expression begged for me to understand.

"What am I supposed to do with it?"

Her eyes shuttered with disappointment. "You might say, 'Thanks for telling me, Mama. I hope you're happy.'"

She was right. Crazy as this all was, I really did want her to be happy. "Thanks for telling me, Mama. I hope you're happy."

"That's more like it."

Mama, Mama, Mama. "Well, don't tell the girls," I said. "About the sex part, I mean." Nothing like setting a bad example.

"Of course I won't," Mama snapped, "and you'd better not either."

"I won't."

"All right then," she said.

This was insane. "I hope you're using protection," I couldn't resist saying.

Mama stiffened. "Oh, please. Claude's the cleanest man I ever met, and neither one of us was ever *with* anybody but who we married." She pulled a spotless handkerchief from her clutch and dabbed at her neck. "I can't think of any STD with an incubation period of fifty years."

At least they'd discussed the subject. "He may have told you he wasn't with anybody else, but men lie about these things, you know. What if he's lying?"

"He's not."

I couldn't believe we were having this conversation. "I still think you ought to have safe sex."

"Safe sex is a myth, and you know it," Mama said. "Condoms fail all the time. How do you think your father and I got you?"

"Mama!"

She patted my arm. "Now don't get all in a huff. *I* was thrilled."

Typically, she'd diverted the conversation from what we needed to address. "Mama, it's crazy not to use protection these days. Please promise me you will."

She bristled. "The way we're doing it is safe enough to suit me, end of story." She tucked her clutch under her elbow. "Now, if you'll excuse me, my cab is waiting."

"Let it wait," I told her with a warning forefinger. "You're not going anywhere till you apologize to Kat and her guests."

Mama glared at me, her mouth a flat line. "You can't make me."

Aaargh! My eyes narrowed. "If you don't apologize, I'll have you committed."

Mama gasped. "You wouldn't."

"Oh, yes I would." Would I?

Her façade broke. "I don't have time to go to the hospital. Claude's taking me to Branson on Sunday. Why do you think I've been taking my meds and working my way out of that house?"

For a trip to Branson, with *Claude*? My lips rolled inward as I extended my palms, fingers clawed, in frustration. "You're apologizing to Kat if I have to drag you!"

"You wouldn't."

"Oh, yeah?" Oblivious to my bed-head and wrinkled clothes, I grabbed Mama by the elbow and opened the door, then pushed her out ahead of me. "You are going to apologize, or I will never speak to you again. I mean it, Mama."

She jerked loose. "All right. All right. Have it your way."

Across the street, guests huddled and looked our way.

"I'll apologize," she repeated. "I already told them you had no idea I was coming."

I crossed my arms over my chest. "Well, tell them again."

Mama marched down the driveway past my neatly manicured lawn, then headed for Kat's. But when she passed the waiting cab, she shot back on the far side and jumped in, then told him, "Gun it!"

I was halfway down the driveway, screaming, "Come back here!" when they rocketed past and took the corner on two wheels.

"Mama!" Furious, I stomped my bare foot on the concrete so hard I almost sprained my ankle, then limped back to the house.

Emma rushed over and came inside. "Mama, are you okay?"

"Your grandmother lied to me. She said she was going to apologize."

Emma covered her mouth to hide the smile that threatened to escape. "Nana's a wildwoman. What happened?"

"She's a wildwoman, all right." I headed for some hair of the dog that bit me and some Advil. "The good news is, she's finally taking her meds."

"I knew *something* must have happened." Emma grabbed a plate and served herself a slab of cake. "Is that why she got so aggressive?"

"She's always been aggressive," I said. "The meds just got her out of the house." I waved a fresh wineglass Emma's way. "Drink? I think this definitely calls for a drink."

"Me too." She took a bite of cake and savored it with joy. "Mmmm. And some carbs."

I poured the wine, then put the glasses on the table and sat.

"Want some cake?" Emma asked.

"Nooo," I told her, queasy at the prospect.

Emma lifted her wine for a toast. "Helluva day."

I tapped my glass to hers. "Amen, sister."

I exhaled heavily, then took a long, cool sip of sweetness. Hair of the dog.

"I met a really nice guy at the wedding," Emma told me. "Bill Carlsson. He's some computer whiz at Tech. Made a million before he was twenty-five. And he's cute."

I did my best to focus on what she was saying, but my mind kept spinning about Mama and Claude, and how she'd ruined Kat's wedding. "That's nice, sweetie."

"Bill said he's coming to Fairbanks to supervise some kind of massive research installation."

Going with Claude to Branson. "That's nice."

"I told him he could stay with me," she said with a slight frown.

"Um-hmm." Greg would never believe I hadn't put Mama up to what she did. Still, it sure would have been great to see the look on his face when she showed up. I smiled, just thinking about it.

"I told Bill we could have nonstop sex for a week, then run naked down Main Street."

Finally, I came to and realized what Emma had been saying. "You said *what?*"

"At last. You were ignoring me," Emma scolded.

"Sorry. I was thinking about what your grandmother did. It's probably all over Sandy Springs by now." I sighed. "Nobody will ever believe I didn't have anything to do with it. Especially your daddy."

"Actually, it was pretty rich." Emma let out a wry chuckle. "None of us recognized her till she started in on Kat and said who she was. Daddy looked like she was a ghost, for real. Then Nana started insulting Kat and Daddy, calling them every name in the book. We were all so shocked, nobody moved. But when Nana started pulling the flowers out of Kat's hair, that was the last straw. Zach and I dragged her away before she hurt anybody. That's when we brought her over here. Zach had to carry her, kicking and screaming, till he set her down inside and split."

Pulling flowers out of Kat's hair? Mama was lucky Kat didn't call the police. But then again, Kat owed me one on that score.

"Has Nana gotten Alzheimer's?" Emma asked.

"Could be," I told Emma honestly. "She's doing a lot of things she hasn't done." Still, just because somebody was old didn't mean they couldn't plain old act up without being crazy.

Mama had found herself a man—or vice versa—somebody she cared about enough to break out of the prison she'd made for herself. I should be happy.

If only she hadn't used her new freedom to humiliate us all.

I patted Emma's hand. "Shouldn't you be getting back to that cute boy at the reception?"

"His name is Bill." Emma blushed, then finished her cake. "Maybe not. I hate to leave you here alone."

I laughed, standing. "Don't worry about me. Who knows? Mama might drop by later for a visit." If she wasn't busy fornicating with Claude.

"You're sure you're okay?"

No, but I wasn't about to ruin Emma's chance to bring something good from this day's insanity. "I am fine. I'm going to have another glass of wine, then go to sleep. We'll deal with Mama tomorrow."

"I'm not sure she can be dealt with," Emma said, then gave me a peck.

"Oh, I think I know somebody who can handle her." Maybe Claude would cooperate if I offered him some homemade devil's food cake with seven-minute icing.

Nineteen

The day after my best friend married my husband

The morning after Mama's surprise apparition at the wedding, my landline and cell phone started ringing off the hook and didn't stop. (The more subtle gossipmongers sent me e-mails with lunch invitations. Where were they yesterday, was what I wanted to know.) The grapevine was working at light speed.

All the women who'd ever set eyes on me in Sandy Springs called to get the gory details, pretending they just wanted "to catch up." A few who knew me fairly well even had the nerve to ask straight-out about what happened. To those, I explained that I hadn't seen anything personally, and that my mother was "confused" and hadn't given me any warning she planned to go to the wedding.

I could tell right away that they didn't believe me. Worse, they were clearly annoyed that I wouldn't dish the dirt.

Not wanting to burn any bridges now that I was on my own, I mustered up a cheeriness I didn't feel and told the callers I had to leave for a dentist's appointment (I forgot it was Sunday), but suggested we do lunch sometime soon. Predictably, they blew me off.

But the calls kept coming, so by eleven that morning, I finally gave up and shut off or unplugged every method of communication in my house.

Oddly, it was the lack of noise that brought a fuzzy Emma from her old room. Smeared mascara ringed her eyes like a raccoon, and her new haircut stuck out every which way as she shuffled into the kitchen and wrapped me in a silent hug that reminded me how much I'd missed human touch since she'd moved away.

Holding on to each other, we gently swayed till she let out a huge yawn, then arched her back and pulled away. "Coffee," she croaked with morning-after breath.

I poured her a mug. "Have fun last night?"

She brightened, still squinting against the morning light that flooded in from the sunroom. "*Oh*, yes."

I handed her the coffee. "The rich, cute, smart nerd from the wedding?"

Emma curled up in her chair, heels on the seat, with a secret smile. "Not a nerd, as it turns out. A total stud. Rocked my world."

I made a face. "Uh-oh. Maybe I don't need to hear about this." Mama's escapades had set me back far enough.

"Down, girl," Emma said. "He's a perfect gentleman. Didn't even try to kiss me till we got to the door at two."

While her mother lay in a drunken stupor.

"But when he kissed me, it was . . ." She blushed, her eyes losing focus. "*Whew* . . . incredible." Her features eased in wonder. "He's so sweet and old-fashioned. And intelligent. And funny. And *hot*." She took another sip of her coffee. "I know better than to believe in love at first kiss, but last night made me understand why some people have sex on the first date."

I closed my eyes, stuck my fingers in my ears, and started chanting, "Na, na, na, na, na, na, na!"

Emma laughed and pulled my finger from one ear. "Oh, quit that. We just kissed. And kissed." She went dreamy. "And kissed."

I'd never seen her act this way about anybody. "And?"

"And . . ." She grinned. "Do we have any more whole wheat bagels and strawberry cream cheese?"

"You know we do. Don't change the subject." I got up to make them for her. "Come on. Let's have it."

She exhaled briefly, then said, "Well, actually, he proposed. And proposed. And proposed."

I stopped in mid-schmear. "You're kidding, right?"

Emma shook her head again. "Nope. And I don't think he was kidding either." She frowned. "At least, he said he was serious." Her mouth went askew. "Of course, we'd both had a few."

Seeing the concern on my face, she added, "He had a limo, with a driver, so don't get upset. The man's way too smart to drink and drive."

"Good." I handed her the bagels and sat beside her with my coffee. "So, what now?"

She shook her head again with that same dazed, can-this-be-real expression. "I don't know. We'll see what happens in the harsh light of day."

A chattering buzz erupted in the huge, slouchy purse she'd dropped by the door. Emma leaped five feet to retrieve it before it quit ringing. "Hello?"

In an instant, she went radiant, crazy hair and smeared mascara and all. "Hi." She collapsed back into her chair, pulling her knee to her chest.

"I don't know." Emma cocked her head. "I'll have to ask my mother." She tucked the cell phone against her shoulder for an amazed, "Bill wants to know if I'll marry him."

I almost choked on my coffee, but I managed to get it down. "Tell him yes," I said, which seriously took her aback, till I added, "In two years, and not a day sooner."

Emma grinned. "Mama says it's okay," she told Bill, "but not for two years."

She laughed at his response, then settled to listen with a look of pure adoration. "Well, okay, then," she finally said. "How about twelve?" She nodded. "Okay. See you soon. Bye."

She pushed the disconnect button, staring briefly at the screen before she lifted her eyes to me in amazement. "Well, looks like we have a date."

"The Cheesecake Factory is a great place for a second date," I said. "Lots of noise and energy. And sugar."

"No, I mean a wedding date," Emma corrected. "I am officially engaged, and the wedding's two years from today."

Back up, Jack. "But you two just met each other." This time, my objections were sincere. "You live in Alaska. What about all those hunky men up there? What about being special up there? And your job?"

She rolled her lips inward and shrugged. "Suddenly, all those men don't look so good. And Bill thinks I'm special right here."

Wait a minute. "Honey, I was only kidding about accepting his proposal."

Emma smiled. "Well, I wasn't. This could work."

Just when I thought things couldn't get any crazier.

"Sweetie, please promise me you won't do anything till you two really get to know each other." Like Mama had promised to apologize? "You just met this man. For all you know, he could have been brought up by ax murderers. Family is very important, you know."

"Ah, family." There was that mischievous look again. "You mean, like my agoraphobic hoarder of a grandmother?" Emma said calmly. "Who went totally Jerry Springer at my father's wedding to your best friend, then had to be dragged away, kicking and screaming?"

Ouch.

"Bill's got a fabulous family," Emma went on. "His father's a minister, and his mother's a teacher, and he has two sisters and a brother—all decent, productive people." She patted my arm. "So you don't have to worry on that account."

I sank to a chair. "I think I need some water."

Emma got me a cold spring water from the fridge, then set it in front of me and hugged me from behind. "Don't worry, Mama," she said beside my ear. "I'm a big girl. I can take care of myself. If things don't work out between Bill and me, then so be it. But at least I was willing to give it a chance." She kissed the top of my head and let go. "I think I'll stick around for a few weeks, if that's okay with you."

"I'd love that, but your job—"

"I have tons of vacation built up," Emma mused. "Think I'll take a month or so. Who knows? Maybe Bill really is Mr. Right."

Whistling, she retreated to get ready for her date.

Alone in the kitchen, I suddenly felt as if everybody in the world was paired up but me. Kat had my ex-husband, may God have mercy on her soul. Amelia had Sonny. Mama had *Claude*. And now Emma had Bill.

For the first time in a long time, I felt deeply and grievously lonely.

Not in the spiritual sense. I had a strong, active Christian faith. But God couldn't put His arms around me and shelter me with warmth when my mother publicly humiliated the whole family. And God couldn't stroke my hair and tell me it was going to be all right when I woke from a bad dream, or found myself living one for real.

Then I scolded myself for sitting on the pity pot.

I was whole and healthy and had a wonderful home and two healthy, loving daughters and grandchildren, and enough alimony to live comfortably. I had work I loved that helped other people achieve their best. So I was blessed beyond ninety-nine and nine-tenths of the world.

Even when that blessing included Greg, right across the street, and Mama shagging somebody named Claude who was probably only looking for some hot food and an easy lay. And Emma was engaged to a man she just met yesterday.

Hallelujah, amen.

What next?

Twenty

Trying to move on with my life while living across the street from my ex and my wife-in-law was like trying to climb out of a pit with my feet stuck in bowling balls. I wanted to lay the past to rest, truly I did. But how could I, when every time I saw Greg's car parked in Kat's driveway, I was reminded that he had come between me and my best friend?

Lord knows what lies he'd told Kat to make her stop speaking to me. Probably that I'd put Mama up to crashing their wedding, which Kat would have known wasn't true, had she been in her right mind.

Not that it mattered. The truth would come out eventually, and Kat would finally realize what she'd gotten, God bless her.

As for Greg's claim that he'd "gotten right with God," the fact that he continued to sabotage my relationship with Kat told me he was only using his so-called conversion as an excuse to keep Kat all to himself. My heart ached when I thought of what it would to do to her when she found out he was the same manipulative, lying cheater he'd always been.

If only he really had turned his life around. That would be so wonderful, not just for Kat, but for the girls. But my mama didn't raise no fool, so I remained skeptical and focused on minding my own little red wagon.

All by myself, for the first time in my life.

Emma had gone back to Alaska and was seriously dating Bill the rich computer whiz. Amelia and my grandbabies were healthy and busy with their lives and work. I couldn't even count on Mama for a distraction, because her meds had worked so well on her trip to Branson with Claude that they'd decided to tour the American West, then go to Amelia's for Thanksgiving. Mama sent postcards, but never bothered to call. As much as I had once resented her interference in my life, living without it left a huge, ironic void.

Ever since my father left us, I'd prayed somebody would rescue me from taking care of Mama, but now that it had happened, I was strangely resistant. Maybe it was the devil you know. Or maybe it was the fact that once Mama was squared away, I had no more excuses for not dealing with my own issues.

I was responsible for no one but me.

So I cranked up my makeover business and did more charity and church work, despite the fact that my married women friends now regarded me with subtle suspicion, as if divorce was contagious. Or worse, as if I might go after *their* husbands.

Now, that was a laugh.

Men their ages wanted younger women, and the *last* thing I wanted was another man to take care of.

When I mentioned the chill from my married friends to a divorced acquaintance who worked with me at the thrift shop, she invited me to a twelve-step divorce recovery group. I was so bored and lonely that I took her up on it, and I'm glad I did. Over the next few months, I went to three meetings a week and learned that there were lots of other women who'd been through what I had. I heard my own story over and over, which freed me from thinking my situation was unique. Far better women than I had been dumped too.

After working my steps and going to meetings, I finally had the tools and the courage to examine my marriage realistically and see how my fear of losing my home and security had caused me to enable Greg's selfishness and duplicity. Thanks to my support group, I didn't feel guilty about it, just relieved to see the truth at last and recognize its causes. Best of all, I finally realized that I wasn't responsible for anybody's happiness but my own. Not my girls'. Not Mama's. Not Greg's. And not Kat's.

So I took responsibility for my life and started over, in earnest, and things got better.

I began having lunch and going to movies and outings with some of the women in my support group, and for the first time in my life, I didn't feel like I had to hide who I really was. We kept each other's confidences from our meetings as a sacred trust, and were bonded by our common ordeal.

Not that it was all roses and revelations. The little girl in me often wished I didn't have to take responsibility for getting what I wanted all the time, but when she did, I just gave her a metaphysical hug and told her it was going to be all right. And I still missed Kat like I would my two front teeth, but the ache grew smaller. So did the awful feeling I felt when passing their house.

I spent Thanksgiving in L.A. with Amelia's family, Mama and Claude, and Emma and Bill, which turned out to be a surprisingly fun experience. Emma and Bill were clearly smitten. The grandbabies were even more precious than ever. And Mama and Claude acted like randy teenagers—which amused Amelia and Emma greatly—then announced they were wintering in southern Arizona.

In the past, I'd have argued that they couldn't just leave their houses unattended for all those months, but thanks to my twelve-step program, I wished them well. Still, my old self couldn't resist suggesting they have somebody turn off their utilities back home and winterize their plumbing. Claude's chest inflated with pride when he said he'd already done it, which earned him an adoring look from Mama.

So much for taking care of Mama.

Afterward, it was hard, going back to Sandy Springs alone. So I consoled myself by booking a flight to Fairbanks to spend Christmas with Emma.

Once I got there, I ended up seeing more of Bill than my daughter, thanks to his more flexible schedule, which was great. I liked him immensely. But when January fifth rolled around, I was ready to leave the bone-chilling cold and head back home.

All spring long, I prayed that Bill and Emma would just go

ahead and elope. But for the only time in her life, Emma did exactly as I'd asked and waited two years before meeting Claude and Mama in Las Vegas for a double ceremony, which, I can tell you, was quite an event, complete with an Elvis impersonator. After the wedding, Claude and Mama headed for New England in the brand-new RV Bill gave them for a wedding present, and Emma—my crazy, unconventional, stubborn, talented Emma—moved into a penthouse at Park Place on Peachtree and started working for her master's at Georgia State while her new husband designed electric cars at Georgia Tech.

Coming back to my house after their double wedding, I found it sterile and empty, so I made a life-changing decision and bought a ficus tree and three potted plants to warm things up, microbes be damned. And I broadened my friendships on a much healthier basis.

All in all, life was good.

Before I knew it, three years had passed since Kat became my wife-in-law, and I was more content than I could ever remember—content enough to wish that Kat and Greg really could be happy.

But one Sunday afternoon on a particularly gorgeous day in May, my phone rang.

"Elizabeth?" asked a vaguely familiar female voice. "This is Anna Ordman from Service League."

Oh, her—the cattiest woman I'd ever met.

Instantly, my defenses went up.

"Did I catch you at a bad time?" she oozed out.

"Well, I have to leave in a few minutes," I lied, "but we can talk till then."

"I was just wondering if you'd heard anything lately about your *ex*," she said with alacrity.

"I don't really think about my ex much anymore," I told her firmly. "Much less care what he's doing."

I could sense her annoyance that I didn't want to play along. "Well, do you care about *Kat* anymore?" she challenged.

I had a bad feeling about this, but concern for Kat kept me from ending the call. "What about Kat? Is she okay?"

"She might be for now, but that's going to change," Anna teased.

Bitch. She was enjoying this *way* too much.

"Why?" I demanded.

"Because your ex is cheating on her," she gloated, "just the way he cheated on you."

I felt as if somebody had thrown me against a wall. All the air went out of me.

No!

"Are you there?" Anna asked.

I breathed in, then let out a heavy sigh. "I'm here." Damn, damn, damn.

"Is this just gossip?" I asked. "Because I know better than to trust the grapevine, and so should you." She *was* the Buckhead grapevine.

Anna let out a huff. "What do you want, pictures?" she snapped. "I happen to have it from several very reliable sources that he's been seen going to the Ritz for afternoon delights with a blonde half his age, who dragged him by his tie into the elevator, whispering hot nothings for all to hear. Word is, she's a Falcons cheerleader."

A groan escaped me, along with, "Oh, God. Poor Kat."

I could *kill* Greg Callison!

"I must say," Anna told me smugly, "you're being very charitable about this, considering what Kat did to you."

"Kat didn't do anything to me," I defended. "She was lonely and vulnerable, and Greg took advantage of that. For her sake, I'm devastated. Assuming this is true."

"Oh, it's true, all right."

"Did you see them?" I challenged.

"No, but several other people did," she snapped.

That was the trouble with rich-bitch housewives like Anna. They didn't have enough to do, so they spent their time gossiping about everybody else.

"Then it's simply hearsay," I told her, even though I knew better.

"You want proof?" Anna retorted. "I'll get you proof."

Idiot woman.

Oh Kat, oh Kat, oh Kat.

I hated this. Hated it.

When I didn't say anything, Anna tried to rattle my cage again. "I heard you still considered Kat a friend," she said. "That's why I called. Though, personally, I think it serves her right, but I thought you might want to warn her. God knows where that cheerleader's been. Kat could get AIDS."

Three years of twelve-step work told me it was time to put a stop to this. "My ex's behavior, good or bad, is none of my business anymore. Neither is Kat's marriage. She and Greg will have to work this out, but I'd appreciate your putting a lid on this, if you can."

"Oh, right," Anna scoffed. "You can't put the fire ants back in the mound after somebody stomps it. This thing is out, and Kat's going to hear it from somebody. If you really consider her a friend, you should be the one to tell her. Wouldn't you have wanted her to tell you about his secretary, if she knew?"

She had me there. If this was true—which I knew it was, as much as I wished it otherwise—Kat deserved to know. She really could get AIDS.

It occurred to me that Greg might be HIV positive, himself, which spun my brain around like Linda Blair's head in *The Exorcist*.

But this wasn't my business. It was Kat's.

"I'm sorry, Anna," I said, "but I really have to go." Dangerous as it was to confront her, I mustered up my courage to finish with, "I really don't want to hear any more about this. As I said, it's not my business."

"We'll see if you still feel that way when I get proof," Anna retorted, then hung up on me.

Furious, I blocked her number on my phones, then collapsed into a chair at the breakfast table and planted my elbows, head in hands.

Just when I was finally feeling whole and happy and content with my life as it was.

"They drag you back in," I imitated Al Pachino from *The Godfather*, gripping the hair at my temples.

Damn, damn, damn.

All of the pain and betrayal that I'd worked so hard to leave behind caught up with me and attacked like a screaming tiger, as bitter and wounding as it had ever been.

So I went to a support group meeting every night for the next week and worked on detaching from the whole, sordid mess. But I knew that this would end up in my lap, in spite of everything, and it did.

My doorbell rang at two in the afternoon ten days after Anna called me.

Fresh from a shower and change after working in my garden, I looked through the sidelight curtains to see her standing there, dressed and jeweled to the nines, with a large tote and a look of smug satisfaction on her face.

I seriously considered sprinting back to my bedroom and hiding till she went away.

She rang the bell again three times. "I know you're there," she shouted, her strident voice amplified by the porch ceiling. "I saw your car in the garage."

That didn't mean I was under any obligation to answer the door. But I knew she wouldn't give up.

Just damn.

I opened the door with a scowl. "Hello, Anna. What do you want?" No way was I going to ask her in.

She pulled a large manila envelope from her thousand-dollar designer tote and shoved it toward me. "Proof," she said in triumph. "With pictures." She straightened, with a lofty, "Do you want to give this to her, or shall I?"

Hell.

I knew I should steer clear of this, but I couldn't leave Kat in Anna's talons. Anna would enjoy watching Kat suffer.

I took the envelope. "You leave me with no choice."

If only I had sent her, and that envelope, away. I'd give anything for a do-over, but only hindsight is twenty-twenty.

Anna granted me a smug smile. "Come on. Confess. Doesn't this give you just the teeniest sense of satisfaction?"

"It makes me want to throw up," I said honestly, then closed the door in her face.

Anna laughed, then went back to her red Jaguar and left.

I threw the envelope on the hall credenza as if it had been poisoned.

It *was* poison.

Part of me said I should throw it away without looking at it and let Kat and Greg deal with this in their own way. But another part of me worried that she might really get some social disease before she finally wised up. And Anna was right in saying that somebody would tell Kat if I didn't.

For three days, I struggled with what to do. Meanwhile, my phone rang off the hook. Anna had definitely stomped the fire ant mound, and every stinging female in Sandy Springs was out to spread venom and offer me advice.

I finally quit answering and let the message center screen my calls.

But when my phone rang at five A.M. on Monday morning, I answered on reflex, alarmed. "Hello?"

"Hey, Mama." It was Emma.

I flopped back into bed with relief. "Sweetie, you scared me, calling at this hour. Is everything okay?"

"No, and you know it." Only a mother's ear could detect the fact that she'd been drinking. "I woke up early and checked my e-mail. I got one from a friend that says Daddy's cheating on Kat, and you have proof."

"Damned Internet," I muttered.

"Is it true?"

"So Anna Ormand says, but she's the worst gossip in Atlanta," I said. "I told her it wasn't my business."

"What about the proof?" Emma challenged.

"Anna says so, but I haven't opened the envelope she gave me," I told her, wretched that Emma had been dragged into this.

"Well, open it," she ordered. "I'll wait."

"Honey, I don't know if I should. The last thing I want is to end up in the middle of this. It's not my business."

"If you still care about Kat, it is your business," she said. "She deserves to know, and so do I. I want the truth, Mama."

Wakened at the crack of dawn, I was supposed to make a decision like this?

"Why don't you call me later when I can think?" I deflected. "We can talk about this then. I'm still half asleep."

"No, Mama. I need to know now if Daddy's done this." Her voice faltered. "Please," she pleaded, "I need to know."

My twelve-step program told me to stay out of it, but my mother's heart understood Emma's request.

Looking at the envelope's contents wouldn't necessarily commit me to telling Kat. Maybe the proof wasn't really proof at all. "All right. Hang on. I'll get it."

Emma responded with a teary, "Thank you."

I turned on my bedside table lamp, punched the wireless switch that lighted my way to the foyer, then retrieved the envelope. I returned to sit on my bed and unlock the clasp in the circle of light from the lamp. Pulling the contents out with one hand, I retrieved the phone with the other. "I'm back."

"Good," Emma said. "What's inside?"

Right on top was a faintly grainy photo of Greg in the Ritz restaurant, nuzzling a sluttily dressed blonde who looked younger than Emma. More photos of him with the same girl, getting out of his car, going into various local hotels. More tasteless snuggling in restaurants. Then several copies of his bills for expensive suites in town, with check-in and checkout on the same afternoons. How had Anna gotten hold of *those*? Greg hadn't even tried to cover his tracks, charging them to his American Express.

The evidence merely confirmed what I'd known deep inside, but that didn't make it any easier to take.

"Mama?" Emma prodded.

"Looks like it's true."

A long silence passed, then she sniffed, collecting herself. "Mama, you have to be the one to tell Kat. I talked to her yesterday. She's so clueless, and so sweet. Better it comes from you than somebody else. Please."

I'd known since Anna's call that I'd have to be the one, but I hated it, hated it, hated it.

"Okay," I relented, against my better judgment. "I'll tell her."

"Today, Mama, please. The clock is ticking."

Nausea rose in me at the thought, but Emma had a point. I sighed heavily. "All right. Today."

"I hate Daddy for doing this," she said with a malice I'd never heard from her before. "And for what he did to you. I wish he was dead."

"Honey, you don't mean that," I said. "He's done some bad things, but he's still your father."

"Amelia was right about him. Why didn't I see it?" Hate poisoned her voice.

"Sweetie, I know you're terribly disappointed in your daddy, but give yourself some time to think about this," I advised. "No matter what he's done, he's still your father, and he loves you."

"He doesn't know what love means." Emma's words were bitter with disillusionment. "I'm divorcing him. He's not my father anymore."

"Honey, don't say things like that. You'll regret them later."

"Why are you defending him?" she accused, her anger shifting to a safe target—me.

"I'm not defending what he did, to me or to Kat, but I choose not to live with anger and bitterness. They only harm me." How could I convince her? "Thanks to my support group, your daddy can't hurt me anymore," I lied, for my child's sake, then finished with a truth. "I've moved on, and I'm happy now. Kat will get through this too."

"I don't know," Emma said. "She's not as strong as you, Mama. She never has been. That's why she married Daddy. She couldn't be alone."

Insightful, but not necessarily productive.

"She'll get through this, I promise."

"Only if you're there to help her," Emma said.

"Lucky thing I'll be there, then."

"Thank you, Mama. I know you didn't want to do this, but thank you."

"Do me a favor in return, all right?" I asked.

"What?"

"Try to forgive your father. It's the only way to heal."

Emma snorted in derision.

"I'm not asking you to condone what he's done," I went on. "Just to see him as he is and accept it without resentment. It won't be easy, but it will come in time, and I promise, you won't be sorry."

"I'll try," she said without conviction. "But only because you asked me to."

I closed my eyes, drained. "Good night, sweetie. I love you."

Emma started crying openly. "I love you too." I started to disconnect, when she added, "Call me when it's done. Any hour. I want to know."

"I'll call," I promised, but didn't commit to doing it right afterward. I would need time to recover.

"Thanks, Mama." She hung up.

Feeling the weight of the world, I stuffed the evidence back into the envelope, then returned it to the foyer. After a cup of hot cocoa and a sleeping pill, I watched bad TV, wide-eyed, till the sun came up, then finally fell into a few hours of fitful sleep tormented by nightmares involving Greg.

When I woke up, hungover from the pill and cotton-mouthed with death breath, it was almost noon.

Time to face the dragon.

I took a long, cool shower, then dressed and made up, slowly and deliberately. By the time I was ready, it was nearly one. Like a death-row inmate taking his last walk, I forced myself outside with the envelope in my hand.

Bad idea, but so were my alternatives.

Crossing the cul-de-sac, I felt as if somebody was watching me and scanned the neighborhood, but saw nothing out of the ordinary. Probably just paranoia about Anna. With her track record, she could be in the bushes with a video camera, eager to put this on YouTube.

I walked up to Kat's front door and rang the bell, setting off the dogs, then knocked.

"Hang on," she hollered over the barking. "Let me put these beasts away, and I'll be right there."

I tucked the envelope under my elbow. Dread sent my heart hammering in the eternity that followed till Kat opened the door.

Seeing me, her welcoming expression fell to one of suspicion. "What do you want?"

I pushed past her, the envelope burning a hole in my side. "This is the last thing in the world I want to do," I said, "but we need to talk."

Twenty-one

Upset though I was, I couldn't help noticing that Kat's garage-sale decor had been replaced with tasteful new furniture, and the place was clean as a whistle. Greg had made his mark, though I couldn't help wondering how Kat had felt about it.

She eyed me with suspicion. "I didn't ask you in," she said tersely.

"I didn't want to come," I answered, heading for the breakfast table in her renovated kitchen, the first time I'd ever seen it clear of clutter. "But I didn't have a choice."

Gone were all her smarmy collectibles and layers of ancient artwork from her kids, replaced by a sleek new kitchen that would do a professional cook proud. Ironic, for a woman who only made vegetable soup.

I sat down and laid the envelope on the table. No sense beating around the bush. "I have some bad news for you, Kat. I didn't want to be the one who brought it to you, but everyone's convinced me it will be better coming from me than someone else."

"Who's everyone?" she asked sharply, her accent broadening as it always did when she was afraid. "And whut business is it of theirs?" Compulsively, Kat got out her chopping block and chef's knife, placing them on the island between the table and the door to the garage.

"None," I said. "But they were right about one thing. You deserve to know the truth, and I care about you. I always have, no matter what Greg's told you, so I'm here."

On automatic pilot, Kat got celery and onions from the hydrator, then started peeling the Vidalias for vegetable soup.

I waited for her to speak, wishing it was the next day when this would all be behind both of us.

When she started chopping the onion, tears came to her eyes, but she doggedly chopped and chopped. Swiping the tears away with the back of her wrist, she said without looking at me, "It must be somethin' pretty awful, to git you over here after not speaking for three years."

"It wasn't my choice that we didn't speak," I reminded her. "It was yours."

"Yeah, well, after what Greg said you'd told everybody about me," she said bitterly, her eyes still on her task, "I figured it was for the best."

"Kat," I said, "look at me."

She glanced my way.

"No, I mean, really look at me. I want you to see me when I say this."

Grudgingly, she stopped the knife and did as I asked.

"May God strike me dead on the spot," I told her, "if I've *ever* said anything bad about you to *anybody*."

Kat's eyes narrowed.

"I don't know why Greg felt he had to drive a wedge between us. Well, maybe I do," I corrected. "He probably didn't want me telling you the details of what he'd done to me. Not that I would have. But he lied when he told you I'd run you down, to anybody."

I could see she wanted to believe me, but couldn't let herself. Without comment, she got out the big soup pot and slammed it onto her new commercial gas range.

"Why he told you all that garbage doesn't matter," I went on. "It only matters that you believe I'm your friend and always have been."

"Yeah, right." Kat went to the new pull-out pantry beside her stainless steel refrigerator and started grabbing cans of organic tomatoes and vegetables. "After I married your ex? And your *mother* ruined the ceremony."

"Everybody wanted me to be mad at you for marrying Greg, but I wasn't," I explained. "You didn't break up my marriage." How could I convince her? "I know how lonely you were after Zach died. You'd stripped away everything to take care of him, then when he was gone, everybody went back to their lives, leaving you alone with your grief and all that nurturing, with no place to put it."

Kat stilled, genuine tears welling in her eyes.

"I know how charming Greg can be," I went on. "How could I blame you for believing him? But I swear, I never did or said anything negative when y'all got married. I genuinely hoped he'd really changed, and y'all could be happy."

Kat snorted, then snatched a long-handled spoon from the utensil holder and pointed it at me. "Oh, right. Like you didn't know your mother was going to come ruin my wedding." She started opening cans with the electric opener. "I'm not saying you put her up to it," she said over the grinding appliance. "I know what a bitch your mother can be. But you might at least have warned me."

Oh, come on! "Damn, Kat! Mama hadn't been out of the house in forty years! How the hell was I supposed to know she'd started sleeping with her next-door neighbor and taking her meds so he could take her to Branson?"

Kat's expression shifted to one of surprised amusement, her lips folding inward. "Emma didn't tell me that when she came back over."

"She didn't know," I told her. "All she knew was that Mama showed up and embarrassed the hell out of all of us. I didn't know, myself, till she and Zach dragged Mama to my house, where Mama spilled the beans after Emma left." I had to make Kat believe me. "I made Mama swear to go apologize to you and your guests, but she acted like a brat and ran away."

I could see Kat was softening.

"Why do you think I was yelling at her to come back and apologize?" I asked.

Kat dumped a can of tomatoes into the pot. "Greg said you were just doing it for show, to keep up your Goody Two-shoes reputation. I was so mad, I believed him." She bent her head without looking at me. "I'm sorry."

"I believed him about a lot of things for a long time," I said softly, "so I can hardly blame you for doing the same thing. But there comes a time when you have to face the truth, as painful as it may be. For your own survival, if nothing else."

Leaving the celery unchopped, Kat kept opening cans, the grind of the can opener filling the silence between us.

She would ask for the bad news in her own time, so I waited, grateful that at least part of the bad feeling between us had been cleared.

Compulsively, she opened can after can and package after package, till the pantry and freezer were empty of every form of tomato, mushroom, bean, dried bean, okra, and corn.

Kat lit the burner beneath the pot. Then she came and sat facing me at the table, her expression that of a weary, disappointed child. "Okay. Let's have it. What's in the envelope?"

Tears surprised me as I pushed it across to her. "I swear, this wasn't my idea," I said, struggling to regain my composure. "Anna Ormand did it, after I refused to talk to her—or anybody else—about the gossip. But you know Sandy Springs. Once something makes it to the ALTA grapevine, it might as well be on the cover of the AJC." I sighed. "Anna threatened to give it to you herself if I didn't, so here it is. I hate it, but here it is."

I wiped the tears from my cheeks. "I thought you had a right to know. If you hate me for it, I'll understand, but it was either me or somebody else who doesn't love you like I do."

Kat stared at the envelope as if it were a snake, then opened it with her usual lack of evasion and pulled out the contents.

I held my breath, then realized that the contents were facedown.

Kat turned them over and gasped, paling till her freckles stood out in alarming relief. "Oh, my God."

She shoved the photos away from her and jumped out of her seat, physically distancing herself from the evidence in a bent, defensive posture, as if she'd been struck in the stomach by a cannonball. "Oh, my God, my God, my God."

Her wounded glance fixed on me, the green of her eyes darkened to almost black. "You tried to warn me, but I wouldn't listen. How could I have been so stupid? I knew something wasn't right, but I couldn't let myself face it, and now . . ."

I got up and tried to hug her, but she warded me off like a wounded animal. "I should have known you'd never do the things he said you had, but he was so convincing. And I was so lonely by myself, with the kids gone back to their lives, that I truly wanted to die." Her face crumpled. "I even thought about taking some of Zach's leftover medicine and ending it, but then Greg came around and made me feel so special."

Both of us were crying. I pulled her into my arms and patted her back. "I know," I comforted, "I know. This is not your fault. It's his. You didn't do anything wrong. He did."

"I *did* do something wrong," she said harshly, rearing back to face me with bitter regret. "I believed what he told me about you, even though I knew better. I let him drive a wedge between us, just so he could cover his ass."

Her paleness shifted alarmingly to redness, and she jerked free. "The bastard!" She started throwing the empty vegetable cans across the kitchen, scattering their juices everywhere. "I was so stupid. All those lies about turning his life around. I swallowed them hook, line, and sinker." The dregs in a big tomato can sent red juice across the pristine white cabinets and new stainless hardware. "Lies. It was all lies." Kat started cussing like only a backwoods Kentuckian could, wreaking destruction in the kitchen till all the cans were flung.

She was making so much noise, neither of us heard anything till Greg opened the garage door and halted at the sight of the mayhem.

What was he doing home at that hour?

"What the hell is going on here?" He glared at me. "What kind of mischief are you up to?"

"Nothing like the mischief you've been up to, you lying bastard!" Kat shouted, throwing the spattered photos at him.

At the sight of the photos and bills, Greg's face went dark red with fury.

No repentance. No regret. Just anger.

Distraught, Kat started chopping the celery as if it were his balls.

My ex-husband zeroed in on me. "You bitch! You just couldn't stand for us to be happy, could you?"

The man's arrogance was breathtaking.

"Me? What about you, whoring around on Kat for all of Buckhead to see? I didn't take these pictures, but Kat has a right to know what a sorry-assed louse she married."

Sobbing now, Kat kept mincing and mincing away between us, unable to face the conflict directly.

"What did you do, have me followed, you white-trash, compulsive bitch?" Greg demanded. "Just couldn't let me go, could you?"

The hubris was staggering.

"Don't talk to her that way!" Kat hollered, still intent on her task.

I couldn't believe my eyes when Greg grabbed a long knife from the block on the island and lunged toward me. "Bitch! I'll teach you to ruin other people's lives!"

The whole thing happened like it was in slow motion. Just as he launched himself for me, Kat turned, knife in hand, and said, "Cut it out!"

Greg ran straight into her knife, impaling himself to the hilt, front and center, blood spurting everywhere.

Oh, my God! Oh, my God! Just like my dream!

Kat screamed and let go, covering her face with her bloodied hands.

Greg looked down in surprise and let out a strange, strangled sound, then went to his knees. Before I could stop him, he fell forward, driving the knife even deeper.

Frozen, I looked down on him with an overwhelming sense of detachment, as if it wasn't really happening, and I was watching it on TV instead of in real life. But the smell of blood brought me back to reality.

"Oh, God! Oh, God! Oh, God!" Kat knelt beside him and turned him over, her knees in a rapidly spreading pool of blood. "Call 911!"

I snatched up the phone and dialed.

Greg's eyes were wide open, and he wasn't breathing.

Kat started to pull the knife out, but I stopped her. "No! Don't pull it out. It will only make things worse! Do CPR!"

A recording came over the receiver. "You have reached 911 emergency. Please hold, and emergency personnel will answer your call as soon as possible."

Dear Lord! They put me on *hold?*

"Oh, my God! Oh, my God! Oh, my God!" Kat repeated as she straightened Greg's neck, then tilted his head back to open an airway and started CPR. With every chest compression, the pool of blood got larger.

He was dead. I could tell.

How could somebody die that fast from a single cut?

Internally cursing the delay with 911, I pressed my fingers to his carotid artery, but felt nothing. He stared at nothing, with no signs of life, the surprise rigidly etched on his face.

Kat kept up the chest compressions, but I pulled her away. "He's gone, Kat. The more you push, the more blood comes out. You have to stop."

She fought free of me and resumed the CPR. "He can't be dead," she said breathlessly after forcing air into his lungs. "He can't!"

"Nine-one-one emergency," a live voice finally said into my ear. "What is your emergency?"

"There's been a horrible accident," I said. "We need an ambulance right away at 3232 Eden Lake Court." I tried to gather my wits. "Someone was stabbed by accident, and he's not breathing. We tried CPR, but every time we compress his chest, more blood comes out."

"Then stop the chest compressions," the operator told me.

"Stop the chest compressions," I ordered Kat, who promptly collapsed, sobbing, over the man she'd just killed.

"Help is on the way," the operator said. "Try to remain calm and stay on the line with me."

Inanely, I nodded, as if she could see me.

"Is the victim breathing?" she asked me.

"No." The word came out hoarse. "And his eyes are wide open." Dear Lord. I'd wished Greg dead a thousand times, but I hadn't really meant it. *Please God, You know I didn't mean it.*

Kat pulled Greg up against her and started rocking, holding the corpse of her illusions along with him, an eerie moan escaping her as shock set in.

"Just try to stay calm," the operator told me. "Who else is with you there?"

"His wife. It was a horrible accident." Blood was everywhere now, filling the space between the island and the cabinets. I didn't know a person could lose so much blood.

"Help is on the way," the operator soothed. "Dispatch places them at less than ten minutes out. Just try to hang on."

"Ten minutes might as well be ten years," I ranted.

"I know it feels that way," she said, "but your friend needs for you to be calm."

My friend. Did she mean Kat or Greg? "My *friend* is his wife, and she's devastated." I'd never seen Kat so pale, and her eyes were glazed and she rocked and mourned. "I think she's in shock."

"If she seems faint, have her lie down and elevate her feet."

"She's holding her husband on the floor," I said as the sound of distant sirens finally reached my ears. "I don't think she'll let go."

"Then let her be," the operator said. "But if she passes out, just lay her gently on the floor until she comes to."

In the blood?

This couldn't really be happening.

For all her feistiness, Kat was the gentlest soul on earth. She couldn't have killed Greg, but there he lay, dead as a carp.

Rattled, I hung up the phone and went to kneel beside her, circling her shoulders. "It's gonna be okay," I comforted, knowing it wouldn't. "It's gonna be okay."

Kat came to herself, her expression furious. "How can you say that? He's dead, and nobody's gonna believe it was an accident. Half of Sandy Springs and Buckhead knew you were coming here today, and why." She rocked him again. "Nobody will ever believe it was an accident!"

I pressed my forehead into her hair. "Yes they will, because I'll tell them what happened. You had no intention of hurting Greg. They'll have to believe me."

"Right," she said bitterly. "His ex, the woman he cheated on too. They'll probably think we were in it together."

I shook Kat. "Shut up! I don't want to hear another word out of you. When the ambulance gets here, let me do all the talking. That's an order. This is going to be okay, but you have to let me do the talking."

Kat crumpled against me, her expression as dead as Greg's. A harsh laugh escaped her. "Okay." She closed her eyes and pulled Greg tighter to her. "It's gonna be okay, honey. It's gonna be okay."

The sirens were upon us, but when I went to the front door to let them in, I saw it wasn't the ambulance, but the police.

Damn.

Think. Get this straight. I only had one chance to get it right.

Anything you say can and will be used against you.

Bracing myself, I opened the door as the officer got out and hurried toward me.

"Thank God you're here, Officer. It was a horrible accident. I'm afraid he might be dead."

The officer spoke a code into his shoulder mike, then strode past me.

I could hear another siren approaching, but knew the ambulance was too late.

Thank heavens, I had the wherewithal to keep my mouth shut, and I prayed Kat would do the same.

The cop entered the kitchen, then halted, taking in the bloody scene: the photos of Greg and his hussy scattered on the island and the floor; Kat hugging Greg in the blood; the minced celery on her chopping block; the bubbling pot of soup on the stove.

The policeman stepped gingerly into the blood, then bent to feel for Greg's carotid pulse, but didn't find one. Standing back up, he backed out of the blood and got his tablet and pen, then asked, "What happened here?"

I answered before Kat could. "Some friends brought me evidence that my ex-husband, here, was cheating on my best friend, who is currently my wife-in-law, so I brought the evidence over to show her. She always makes soup when she's upset, so she started chopping things up for the soup. Then Greg came home unexpectedly and started screaming at me for telling her. He got so mad, he grabbed a knife and tried to kill me, but Kat turned around with her knife still in her hand, and he ran right into it. It was a horrible accident. She never meant to hurt him."

"Just the facts, ma'am," he said, conjuring *Dragnet*.

I looked him dead in the eye. "That's exactly what happened."

In the assessing silence that followed, I heard the fire department ambulance career into the cul-de-sac with siren blaring, then brake and roar into the driveway. Doors outside slammed, and equipment jangled as they rushed up the stairs and into the open front door.

"Back here," the cop hollered.

The EMTs hurried past him to assess Greg.

"Ma'am," the female EMT told Kat gently, "I need for you to step back so we can do our work, please."

I circled the island to draw Kat to her feet from behind. "Come on, honey. Let them do their work." Kat lurched erect, then promptly passed out. I barely managed to keep her from falling. "Help. Need some help here."

The second paramedic and the cop hurried over to help me lay her down beyond the blood, then the paramedic started working on her. "She's in shock. Please step away, ma'am," he told me.

Helpless, I did as he asked, the full impact of what had just happened finally hitting me like a Hummer at ninety miles an hour.

I felt the policeman take my arm as if it were someone else's. "Maybe you ought to sit down, ma'am."

Nodding, I sank to the breakfast table chair he brought up behind me.

Light-headed, I bent my head into my hands and leaned forward.

This was really happening. Greg was really dead, and it was all my fault. I never should have gotten involved. If I hadn't brought those pictures over, he'd still be alive.

The father of my children was dead on the floor, and it was all my fault.

God, how was I going to tell the girls?

Twenty-two

Things went downhill from there. When the paramedics' heart monitor and remote EEG showed no activity, they said Greg was gone, which sent Kat into fresh waves of sobbing.

Before they could transport his body to the hospital to be officially declared dead, a Sandy Springs detective arrived, along with the forensics team, and they started taking samples and pictures. When Kat asked to go with Greg's body, the detective gently insisted we wait in the living room. So I wrapped her in a beach towel to cover the blood then sat beside her on the sofa, hugging her as she moaned her grief and remorse.

When the stretcher went by with the body, I shielded Kat's vision and started talking loudly in an effort to distract her, but she went so still I knew she'd noticed. Half an hour later, a female forensics officer came in and told me the doctor at the hospital had declared Greg officially dead, which was hardly news to anybody. Kat heard her, but didn't react.

Almost an hour passed before the detective came in and asked us what happened. I repeated what I'd said to the first policeman, and Kat confirmed it, but the detective regarded us with frank suspicion.

"I saw it happen," I told him. "It was a horrible accident. But if Kat hadn't stopped him, God knows what he'd have done to me with that knife."

He stood, his expression unreadable as he closed his notebook. "We'll need official statements from both of you ladies. It shouldn't take too long. We'll transport you to the station."

The station? As in, "you're under arrest"?

I tried to keep the panic from my voice. "Please, can it wait till tomorrow? You can see, she's beside herself. Please let me get her out of here and cleaned up. I just live across the street. I swear, we won't go anywhere else."

The detective frowned.

I finally had the wherewithal to remember. "Kat is the widow of Zach Rutledge, a distinguished DEA agent. Please, could you just cut her a little slack, for Zach's sake, if nothing else?"

"Zach," Kat moaned, closing her eyes. "Oh, Zach."

The thin blue line worked in her favor. "Okay," the detective said. "We can take your statements tomorrow." He handed me his card. "If you think of anything you forgot to tell us, please give me a call." He looked to Kat. "We'll need those clothes as evidence before y'all leave. I'll have a female officer help collect them."

I nodded, holding on to his card. I could fit into one of Greg's shirts and sweatpants. "Thank you so much, Officer," I said.

Disaster averted—at least for the moment. I'd find Kat a lawyer once we got to my house.

I turned my attention back to her. "Come on, honey. Let's get out of these clothes."

Still without focus, she followed obediently. Her skin was cold as ice as I steered her toward the stairs.

"Mandy," the detective summoned, and the female police officer followed us with two large plastic evidence bags, through the master and into the bathroom.

Oblivious to our presence, Kat stripped out of her bloodied things, insensible of her nakedness as she jerked off her blood-soaked pants and panties in front of both of us, then wrenched off her blood-spattered peasant top and bra. The policewoman bagged everything, then looked to me.

"Just a sec." I went into the master closet, closed the door, then stripped down to the skin. When I went over to Greg's clothes, I caught the scent of him, and it almost sent me over the edge. But I got a grip on myself for Kat's sake, and put on a dark business shirt and navy sweats.

When I emerged proffering my clothes, Kat was wearing some of her baggy old clothes and Birkenstock sandals.

The policewoman bagged my clothes, then pointed to my shoes. "We'll need those, too."

I handed them over.

I circled Kat's shoulders with my arm. "Come on. We'll get you to my house and you can get clean, without all these people around." I gathered some gowns and underwear for her to sleep in.

Still blood-spattered on her face and icy hands, she moved like the living dead. I tried not to think of what was going through her mind, focusing instead on the tangible things we had to do.

Slowly, we headed for the front door. "Before you know it," I murmured, "a month will have passed, and this will all be behind you."

Her vision cleared for an instant, tears welling in gratitude, then she sank back into her stupor.

When we reached the veranda, I looked outside to see that the neighbors had gathered, murmuring in speculation, on the sidewalk, and there were two news vans setting up their cameras.

Damn. We'd have to hustle to get to my house before the cameras were up and running.

"Come on, honey. We need to get to my house. Don't pay any attention to the people out there. Just step it up, so we can make it to my house."

Kat recoiled, registering the whole debacle, but I pulled her onto the porch with me. "Come on. You can do it. Just get to my house, and everything will be okay."

Her body obeyed, despite the fear and revulsion on her face.

The neighbors buzzed louder when they saw the blood on her face and hands, but we managed to get past the camera crews unrecorded, thank God.

Once safely inside my house, I ran Kat a hot bath in my spa tub, laid out her summer gown and underpants on the vanity, then sat outside with the door ajar to wait till she finished bathing. "Do you need anything?" I called over the running water.

"No." She turned off the taps. "I can do it."

I heard her sigh with relief as she sloshed into the welcome warmth. Then silence.

"Are you okay?" I called to her, worried that she might do something foolish, either consciously or unconsciously.

"No," she said harshly. "I'll never be okay again."

"Yes you will," I said, leaning my head back against the wall. "It's just going to take time, and it might get worse before it gets better, but you are going to be okay. I swear it on my life."

I heard her scrub the washcloth against the soap, then start rubbing harshly at her fragile skin as if she could wash away what happened along with the blood.

Then she turned on the hand shower to wash her hair, rinsing and rinsing and rinsing, followed by another protracted silence.

"Kat?"

"I'm not going to drown myself," she said, her voice wooden. "Though the thought occurred to me. But I couldn't do that to my kids."

The kids. God help me, I had to call them, and soon, before this got onto the grapevine. With the Internet these days, gossip made it round the world in an instant.

I heard Kat open the drain, then get out of the tub, and I sighed with relief.

It took her forever to dry off and dress, but as long as I could hear her, I knew she was okay. Finally, she emerged in her gown, her hair twisted up in a towel.

I stood. "Come on. Let's get you to bed."

Blank and docile, she followed me into the guest room and climbed into the bed that had been Amelia's.

I got some water, then gave her a mild sleeping pill I had left over from a trip. "Here, take this. The paramedic said you need sleep."

She took it, then lay back and closed her eyes, pale as death, herself.

I closed the blinds and curtains, leaving the room in cozy dusk. "You'll feel better when you wake up."

"God, I hope so," she whispered, then turned onto her side, facing away from me.

I waited till I was sure she was asleep to close the door and go into the kitchen to make the dreaded calls.

The cordless phone felt like lead in my hand as I looked up Little Zach's cell number in my directory, then dialed.

He answered right away. "Well, hey, Miss Betsy," he answered with his usual good nature.

"Oh, Zach," I managed. "I don't know how to tell you this, but there's been a terrible accident at your mother's, and Greg is dead."

"Mom. Is Mom okay?" he shot back.

"She's devastated, but she'll be all right. I finally got her cleaned up and into bed at my house. She's sleeping now."

"What happened?"

I told him as clearly and briefly as I could.

When I got to the stabbing, he groaned into the receiver. "Oh, God, no. Poor Mama."

"I wish I'd never gone over there," I said bitterly.

"You were being a friend," Zach countered. "You couldn't have known this would happen. Nobody could. Like you say, it was an accident."

"It was."

"Did the police come?"

"Yes." I told him what had followed. When I was done, he said grimly, "I'll be there on the next flight."

"Come here, not to your house," I warned him. "It's a horrible mess over there, and I don't want you to have that image burned into your brain for the rest of your life."

I flashed on the blood and chaos, prompting a stab of nausea. "I'll go over and clean things up as soon as the police are done."

"No," Zach said. "You've been through enough already. Stay there and look after Mom. There are special cleaners for situations like this. I'll call the police and find out who they recommend. With luck, I can get somebody to come over right away and take care of it."

I gave him the numbers on the card the policeman had given me.

"Just take care of Mom till I can get there." He sounded so much like his father.

"I will."

"And don't let her talk to anybody without a lawyer. An old friend of mine does criminal defense. I'll call him and have him contact you."

Thank God. "Good. I'm worried. I don't think the detective believed us."

"So much for innocent until proven guilty," Zach said. "And never mind the eyewitness." He let out a sharp breath. "I'll call some of Dad's friends and see if they have any connections with the Fulton County DA. Maybe we can make this go away."

I hadn't realized how heavily this all weighed on me till "Little" Zach shouldered some of its weight. "We just need to make them see the truth."

"They will," he said with a conviction I didn't share.

"I never should have gone over there."

"This is not your fault," he repeated. "It's Greg's."

True, but that was cold comfort.

"I'll call when my plane lands." He hung up.

It was a relief to know that Kat's son was on the case, but I still felt queasy about calling the others. I looked up Sada's number and dialed. When she didn't answer, I hung up, only to have the phone ring immediately with her name on the caller ID.

I clicked onto the call. "Sada, it's Betsy. I'm afraid I have some terrible news." I took a deep breath, then told her. As I began to explain, she peppered me with irate questions about why I'd gone over there in the first place, then accused me point-blank of being responsible.

It was one thing to feel guilty, but another entirely to have Sada blame me, point-blank, for what had happened.

"Sada, if it were possible, I'd go back and never leave my house this morning, but that can't happen. What's done is done. Your mother needs your help now, not blaming and accusations. This is the hardest thing she'll ever have to go through, besides losing one of you. Please try to find it in yourself to support her and stay calm."

"I will," Sada snapped, "but I still think this is your fault."

"Come to my house when you get here," I instructed. "Zach's having the mess cleaned up at your house, but till then, your mother's better off over here."

"We'll see about that," Sada bit out, then hung up on me.

I closed my eyes, sick inside, but I still had to make the hardest call of all. Amelia would understand, but Emma . . . Emma was her father's pet, and vice versa. This would destroy her.

I hit the speed dial for her home phone, and it rang four times before she answered with a cheery "Hullo?"

"Emma, honey, it's Mama. I'm afraid I have some terrible news for you. Your daddy's dead."

"Daddy?" she shrieked. "No! I just talked to him last night. He can't be dead!"

I heard Bill ask, "What's happened?"

Emma dropped the phone onto the covers, then I heard a muffled, "My daddy's dead!" followed by wrenching sobs.

Bill comforted her, then picked up the phone. "Hello?"

Thank God for Bill. "Bill, this is Betsy. I'm so sorry, but there was a terrible accident at Kat's, and Greg is dead."

Blessedly, he didn't ask for any details. "We'll be right there," he said over the sound of Emma's sobs.

"There's no need to rush," I told him. "Kat's here, sedated. There will have to be an autopsy before we can plan the funeral. Kat's staying with me till things are worked out."

"Under the circumstances, I don't think Emma will want to see Kat for a while," he said. "We'll call you later, after she's had some time to absorb this."

"God bless you, Bill, and thanks for helping Emma through this. She loves you so much."

"I love her too. And you. Call if you need us."

"Okay."

I disconnected the call, then laid my head on my arms and sobbed myself dry and swollen. Then I blew my nose with a paper towel and called Amelia.

She answered on the first ring. "Hey, Mama. What's up?"

I surprised myself by starting to cry all over again. "Oh, Amelia," I moaned out, the words thickened by my stopped-up nose. "It's awful. There was a horrible accident at Kat's, and your daddy's dead, and it's all my fault. I never should have gone over there. If I hadn't, nothing would have happened."

Her usual dramatics conspicuously absent, Amelia told me firmly, "Calm down, Mama, and tell me exactly what happened."

I did. When I finished, she said grimly, "It's not your fault, Mama, and it isn't Kat's. Daddy brought this on himself. If he hadn't cheated in the first place, you'd never have gone over there. And if he hadn't tried to stab *you*, he'd still be alive."

My heart twisted to hear the coldness in her voice when she spoke of her dead father.

"I just wish I could go back and live this day over differently," I told her.

"You were only trying to help Kat, Mama. That's all you've ever done."

Now that it was all out, I barely had the breath to speak, totally deflated.

"Do you want me to call Emma and tell her?" Amelia offered.

"I already did. She took it really hard, but was with Bill, thank goodness." Shame welled up in me afresh. "I didn't tell her what happened, just that Greg was dead. I told Bill the rest."

"Let me talk to her," Amelia said. "She'll listen to me. And I'll call Nana, and make sure she doesn't bug you."

Mama would probably do a jivin' devil-dance for joy.

Grateful to have Amelia's help, I nodded. "Thanks, honey. I really appreciate that."

"We'll be there tomorrow," she said. "But for now, I want you to take a hot bath, yourself, then get some sleep too. Promise you will."

"I will." The prospect of oblivion was distinctly appealing. Assuming I didn't have nightmares about what happened.

As if she'd read my mind, she said, "Take a sleeping pill, so you won't dream."

"Okay."

"I love you, Mama. It's gonna be okay."

No it wasn't. Not for a long, long time. "Call me when you find out about your flights. And don't all fly together."

Disaster hung heavy enough over my head. I didn't want to tempt fate any further.

"Okay," she said. "Now get some sleep."

I hung up and took my daughter's advice. I hadn't been in bed more than a few minutes before a dark curtain descended, blotting everything out. I slept like the dead till I heard someone at the bedroom door and opened my eyes to see Kat, silhouetted by the strong western sun from the foyer, her tousled hair aflame, and her thin body outlined inside her summer gown.

"Tell me this is all a horrible dream," she said, her voice hoarse.

I patted the plissé coverlet beside me. "C'mere."

She came to the far side of the bed and sank down with her

bent back to me. "I can't get it out of my head. I keep reliving it, over and over, wishing it would come out different, but it won't."

"What's done is done, Kat. We can't change it. But you didn't do anything wrong."

She turned to glare at me. "I killed my husband. That's wrong, any way you slice it. The last time I looked, infidelity wasn't a capital offense."

"It was an accident," I said, the words rote. "You never meant to hurt him."

"Then why do I feel like a murderer?"

I sat up in alarm. "Don't say that, Kat, not to anybody. They might get the wrong idea. I know you feel that way, but feelings aren't facts. There's a world of difference between murdering some-body and accidentally killing them. You didn't do anything wrong."

"But I was so angry," she said through fresh tears. "I wished he was dead, and then he was, and I did it."

"Don't say that. I mean it." I frowned, at a loss as to how to con-vince her. "I never should have butted in. If I hadn't brought you that envelope, none of this would have happened." My memory suddenly triggered. "It's just like my dream. We were in your kitchen fighting, the three of us, and then he was dead."

Kat scowled. "You dreamed about this?"

"God help me, I did, and I was glad he was dead."

"Don't say that, not to anybody," she quoted me. "They might get the wrong idea."

I flopped back against the pillows, staring at the slow-rotating ceiling fan. "Helluva mess we've gotten into, ain't it?"

Kat reclined. "Damn straight."

We lay there on opposite sides of the king-sized bed, pressed down by the weight of what had happened. Long seconds passed before she ventured, "How long do you think it'll be before the police arrest me?"

I bristled, rearing up to say, "They're not going to arrest you, period. They have no case."

"I stabbed him in the stomach," Kat said. "With an eyewitness. That sounds like a case to me."

"An eyewitness who saw that it was an accident," I said. "I told them what happened, and the evidence bears it out. Greg's prints are on the other knife, and he wasn't holding it like he was going to slice food. He was holding it like a weapon. And all the soup stuff you'd been chopping was there. The evidence bears it out."

"I sure hope so," Kat said numbly. " 'Cause I cain't feature goin' to prison."

"You are not going to prison," I fumed. I picked up the TV remote and punched on the Ellen DeGeneres show, wishing some of her lightheartedness could penetrate the darkness that surrounded us. "Here. Stop that foolish talk and watch Ellen. Look. There's Dennis Quaid. Now, there's a man who got better looking when he got older."

Kat ignored the TV. "Are the police still at my house?"

"I don't know. Let me look." Groggy, I got up and went to see that everyone had left except a forensic cleaner's truck.

I returned and flopped into bed. "The police are gone, and the cleaners are there. Zach called them. You can go home as soon as they're done, if you want."

"I never want to set foot in that house again," Kat said.

"Nobody's going to make you," I promised. "You can stay here as long as you want."

"Thanks." She paused. "You called Little Zach?"

"And Sada. And the girls." A long sigh escaped me. "Emma took it hardest."

Kat covered her face with her hands. "Oh, God, Emma. She's going to hate me for this forever!"

"Not as much as Sada hates me for butting in and causing the whole thing, to start with," I said dryly.

We lay there in silence with Ellen's incongruous banter filling the room.

"I wish it was me, dead," Kat said softly, "instead of Greg."

Bull hockey. "I don't. Greg caused this whole thing. Even Amelia said so."

Kat faltered. "What are we gonna do?"

This wasn't getting us anywhere.

I stood. "First, we are going to eat a whole half gallon of Breyer's chocolate. Then we're getting drunk, then going back to bed. Tomorrow, we'll go give our statements. *With* a lawyer." I realized Little Zach's friend hadn't called. "Zach knows one who can help us. We'll figure out the rest after the kids get here."

Kat stood, looking more like her old self than she had since the stabbing. "Sounds like a plan to me."

When the going gets tough, the tough go for carbs.

Over ice cream, we started talking about the funeral, and Kat decided she wanted to have Greg cremated, if that was okay with the girls, which suited me fine, since it was lots cheaper. Under the circumstances, we both agreed that a private funeral would be best. No sense parading our tragedy in front of every curious acquaintance in Sandy Springs.

By the time we went to bed, we were snockered, but the final arrangements were made.

Then the next morning, the sun came up on our day of reckoning.

Twenty-three

The next day was a blur of phone calls and sad but necessary activities. Zach's lawyer friend, Scott Brown (who, it turned out, specialized in DUIs and domestic cases, not murder), met us outside the police station and accompanied us inside to give our official statements, which were the same as our unofficial statements the day before. Scott's presence was reassuring, but the fact that our stories didn't vary only made the detective more suspicious. After he'd grilled us for the third time, Scott reminded him that the truth is the truth, then escorted us out.

Once we were outside, he said he'd find someone who could defend Kat if they arrested her. "How much money do you have on hand?" he asked Kat.

"Plenty," I answered for her. "Greg had gobs of insurance."

The young lawyer pulled a face, glancing around to make sure nobody overheard me. "I wouldn't go mentioning that to just anybody," he said. He looked to Kat. "Do you have any other funds on hand? Because the insurance company isn't going to pay as long as there's a chance this might go to trial."

Kat blanched. "I have about five thousand in my household account, altogether. But that'll only keep me fer a few months. Greg took care of everything else."

Scott frowned. "A good trial lawyer's going to expect more than that on retainer."

Kat shook her head. "I got an IRA from Zach's years with the DEA, but I'd only git fifty cents on the dollar, time I paid the penalties."

"Don't worry about the money," I told Kat. "I saved up about thirty thousand over the years. It's yours if you need it."

"Betsy, no," Kat said. "You'll need that money to live on. With Greg gone, there's no more alimony. You're up the creek. I couldn't take your savings."

"You'll take it, and that's that," I said, then turned to Scott. "Find her a good trial lawyer. We'll get the money."

He nodded, then gave us his cards and left.

Back at my house, we Googled budget funerals and came up with several prospective providers in Atlanta, most of them on the south side of town. Since the service itself was going to be private, at Kat's church, it didn't matter where the funeral parlor was.

By the time we made lunch, Sada arrived (needing sixty dollars for her cab), followed shortly by Little Zach.

I greeted them, then melted into the background, letting them console their mother.

Little Zach tried to coax Kat into going home. He'd checked things out on his way in, and the place was spotless, even the soup debris cleared away. But Kat resisted till he said it was his home too, and Greg shouldn't be able to deprive him and Sada of that.

Shaken, Kat agreed at last to go.

I watched the three of them cross the cul-de-sac. *Please, God, take away all the awfulness from that house and fill it with Your peace.*

I closed the door with a sigh, then got busy changing beds and getting ready for my girls. When the house was ready, I started cooking enough pot roast and mashed potatoes and pole beans for both our families, plus four apple pies. (If you make one, you might as well make four.)

Emma called at six. "Hey, Mama," she said, subdued. "Is Kat still there?"

My eyes welled at the sadness in her voice. "Hey, precious girl. Kat's gone home. Y'all come right over. I'm fixing supper for everybody."

"Kat too?" she asked, wary.

"Kat too," I said gently. "Emma precious, I was there. She never meant to hurt your daddy."

"I . . ." She faltered. "I'm just not sure I could . . ."

Why was I taking up for Kat? Emma needed my support, not justifications. "Honey, just come home. Nobody's going to make you do anything you don't feel up to, I promise." I could send food across the street, if necessary.

"Thanks, Mama. I really appreciate it." Emma sniffled. "See you there."

Thirty minutes later, I'd just put the pies in the oven when the front door opened and Emma walked in, looking small and fragile as she stood silent next to her tall and steady husband.

Her father's death had turned her from a girl into a woman, which caught me by surprise.

"Hello, Mrs. Callison," Bill said.

"Please call me Betsy," I asked for the umpteenth time, giving him a brief hug.

"Betsy," he corrected, visibly uncomfortable with the familiarity.

I turned to my daughter. "Hey, sweet girl. You look worn out." I pulled her to me, and she started crying.

The only comfort I could offer was to hold her and let her cry. There were no words that wouldn't sound trite or self-serving, so I just let her sob in my arms till she was spent. Meanwhile, Bill disappeared into the living room, leaving us in privacy.

When at last Emma pulled away, I guided her to a chair, then got her some cold water and tissues before going back to my cooking. I knew she'd talk when she was ready.

I didn't have to wait long.

Emma blew her nose hugely, then asked, "Has Kat said anything about the funeral?"

"She has some ideas, but she wants to do what you and Amelia want."

Emma looked out over the garden. "I never thought about it, really." She paused, then asked, "How long will it be before they . . . before his . . ."

"Thanks to Big Zach's connections, they're going to do the autopsy right away," I said, "so we can make arrangements."

"Good." She stared back out at my flowers and vegetables in the yard.

"What are your feelings about cremation?" I asked her gently.

"Ecologically sound," Emma said with a maturity I hadn't seen before.

"I know it makes sense," I prodded. "But how would you feel about having your father cremated?"

Emma frowned, considering. At length, she answered. "It feels okay. As okay as it can when it's Daddy we're talking about."

She looked down, staring at her hands as if she were seeing them for the first time, and I wondered what she was thinking.

"Kat would like to have a private ceremony at their church," I said, "if that's okay with you and Amelia. Under the circumstances, I think it would be easier on us all if we kept things small, don't you?"

Emma's chin went up, a defensive spark in her eye. "Daddy really was a Christian, Mama. I know he committed some big sins, but he believed in the cross. He wasn't just faking it for Kat's sake. We talked about it." She turned an anguished expression my way that begged me to agree. "The cross part, not the sins. But nobody's perfect. He messed up, but he was a believer."

"Of course," I soothed with what I hoped was believable conviction. "He's in heaven, beyond the shortcomings and disappointments of this life, now." I truly hoped he was, but I wasn't sure if I felt that way out of nobility of spirit, or guilt because I'd triggered the whole mess.

Emma searched my expression. "Christians have the same choices as unsaved people," she said as if she was quoting. "And they can make just as many bad choices, but that doesn't mean they're going to hell."

I certainly wasn't going to argue with her. "Nobody's perfect, honey."

"Right. Nobody but Jesus. Not even you."

That stung. I stopped stringing the pole beans with the potato peeler. "Do you think I think I'm perfect?"

"No. That's not what I'm saying," Emma hastened to say. "It's just that Daddy . . ."

I resumed peeling down the sides of the long, lumpy beans. "Honey, I loved your daddy very much for a long time, and we were very happy." I was, at least. "That's what I'll remember about him, not the rest."

Emma nodded. "That's good. That's what I'll remember too," she said as if she was trying to convince herself. "All the good things, and not the bad."

A lengthening silence stretched between us, broken at last when the phone rang, causing us both to jump.

Emma got up as I picked up the receiver. "I'm going to see about Bill," she told me as she left.

I nodded, then answered, "Hello?"

"Hey, Mama. It's me," Amelia said. "We're here."

My heart swelled. I loved both my daughters, but Amelia was so much less complicated than Emma, and she never judged me. "Oh, honey, I'm so glad y'all had a safe flight. What about Sonny?"

"His flight got in thirty minutes before ours. As soon as we rent a car, we're on our way." She sounded calm, almost cheerful, which was what I'd expected. Amelia had buried her father emotionally a long time ago.

"Everything's ready for y'all here," I told her. "And Emma and Bill are here too."

"Good. How is she?" Amelia asked.

I dropped my voice to a whisper. "As well as can be expected," I said. "But I know she'll be better when y'all get here."

"The kids will be a good distraction," Amelia said.

"For all of us."

Forty minutes later, Sonny and Amelia's rented minivan rolled into the driveway, and I was able to put the past day's events from my mind as we all gathered in the family room that opened onto the kitchen. My grandbabies were as adorable as ever, and Emma brightened immediately when her sister came in and wrapped her in a brief, reassuring hug.

Sonny offered to get a hotel room, but Emma and I convinced him to stay with us.

In deference to Sada, I sent Amelia across the street with the food. When she got back, we all sat down and pretended that love, not death, had brought us together.

There's nothing like a couple of grandbabies and a good meal to make things right.

The next morning at breakfast, Emma announced she was going across the street to talk to Kat. I was proud of her, and said so. Amelia offered to go along, but Emma turned her down and went alone. She came home at peace that what had happened really was an accident, but annoyed that Sada still blamed me.

"Don't worry," Amelia told her. "I'll talk sense into Sada."

The next few days flew by. The autopsy report confirmed that Greg had died from a single stab wound to his abdominal aorta, with the blade flat to his waist. Ironically, Kat's knife had severed the one structure guaranteed to kill him on the spot.

Nobody said anything about the possibility that the police might charge Kat with murder, but it hung over us all like the big, dirty cloud of pollution that hovered over Atlanta.

To keep myself from worrying, I dove into helping Kat plan the memorial service and the reception her church ladies were giving afterward at her house.

Then, in what seemed like a blink, the service was behind us, and our children went back to their lives. My house was empty again, as was Kat's.

For the next few weeks, we ate breakfast together every day, then worked on settling Greg's estate.

Still, no word came from the police, but I was afraid to get my hopes up, for fear the hammer would fall.

Little Zach continued to work behind the scenes to get his mother cleared outright, so she could collect the insurance, but the insurance company stalled and stalled. So Kat and I kept taking care of business, till it was all attended to, and we were left at sixes and sevens, going through the routine of our days. It was good to have my best friend back, but our reunion was shadowed by the threat of a murder charge.

Kat never talked about what Greg had done, or how he'd died and what that might mean for her, so I didn't either. I just tried to make her laugh and cheer her up. We went to funny movies and chick flicks and yard sales and consignment shops and all the free art exhibits and museums in town, tiptoeing around the sleeping dragon in the middle of our lives.

Another month had passed when I went to bed early and found myself even more bored and lonely than usual, so I phoned Kat. "Hey."

"Hey," she answered.

"How are you?"

"Lonely."

"Me too."

She sighed. "The house feels . . . wrong without Zach and Sada."

I remembered how loneliness had prompted her to marry Greg in the first place. God forbid she make a similar mistake. A distraction was in order. "We need to take a trip," I proposed. "Together. Somewhere foreign and sunny."

"Cain't," she said. "The police won't let me leave the country. And anyway, I'm broke, remember?"

"You won't be broke for long," I told her. "The insurance company will have to pay off eventually, and you'll be set. What's the policy? Three million?" For once, Greg's ego had come in handy.

"Actually, if I'm cleared, it's six million," Kat said. "Double for accidental death, which is why they're so sideways about payin' me. I'll probably be stuck here, old and gray, before I see a cent of that money."

She could be right, but I wasn't about to tell her that. "Okay, so we can't leave the country," I said. "Or spend a lot of money. But we can still go somewhere." An inspiration struck me. "Be ready tomorrow morning at ten. I'm taking you up to the Dillard House, my treat, for lunch. And we'll stop back by Jaemore Farms on the way home for fried dried peach pies."

Her tone brightened. "Ooo, yum. Good idea. See you then."

I was just about ready the next morning when the phone rang, showing Kat's caller ID. I hoped she wasn't calling to cancel. My stomach was set for country cooking and fried pies. "Hey."

"Scott called," she said, breathless.

Oh, Lord. "And?"

"We're off the hook!"

What? "What do you mean?"

"The DA refused to prosecute!" Her words came out rapid-fire. "You were right about Greg's prints on that knife. It showed he was holding it as a weapon. And mine showed I was holding my knife sideways, not as a weapon, just like the autopsy said." She started to cry with relief. "They ruled it an accidental death. The DA told my lawyer there was no way they could prove it wasn't, thanks to your testimony."

I felt as if someone had suddenly pumped oxygen into my airless universe. "Thank God. Thank God."

Tears of joy slurred Kat's words. "I have some legal stuff to do about Greg's estate." She paused, then added, "I almost forgot: thanks to your Bill's connections in the DA's office, the prosecutor is holding a press conference to announce that the forensics and eyewitness account—that's you—prove Greg's death was accidental, which officially clears me."

"Kat, that's fabulous." They never did that. God bless our Bill!

"Sit tight," Kat instructed. "I have some legal stuff to do about the insurance. I don't know how long it will take, but we might still be able to go to Dillard." She laughed semihysterically through her tears.

"Oh, Kat, we can both finally breathe again. It's really over." A revelation hit me. "If it's accidental, you get twice the insurance!"

Kat didn't share my elation. Abruptly, she fell silent. When she spoke again, her voice was shaky. "I'd give every cent of that six million dollars if it could bring him back." She drew a shuddering breath. "I loved him, Betsy, even after I found out what he'd done. I know it's crazy, but I still loved him."

Stricken, I said, "Oh, sweetie. You loved him a whole lot better than I ever did, and wherever he is, I'm sure he knows how much you cared."

She brightened a little. "Oh, well, I have to go to the lawyer's. I'll call when I'm done. Bye."

I immediately called Emma and left a message that it was all over. Then I called Amelia, and we talked for almost an hour, shifting from what had happened to what was going on at her house in L.A. When we finally ran out of things to talk about, I hung up, then took my floral scissors and went out and deadheaded all my double-knockout roses, a mindless chore that provided a perfect way to kill an hour while I waited for Kat to come home.

When I got back inside from doing that, there was no message from her, so I looked across the street and saw that her car was still gone.

My stomach rumbled, annoyed that we weren't going to indulge in a pig-out lunch at the Dillard House.

I had to eat something. A healthy salad later, she still wasn't back.

I turned on HGTV and watched *Sell This House*, *Holmes on Homes*, and *Curb Appeal*.

It was two before my doorbell rang, and I hurried to find Kat standing there, her hand behind her back, grinning like an ancient debutante after her fifth face-lift. "Hey!"

Thank goodness, she'd gotten out of her funk. "Hey, yourself. Come in, O innocent one."

She kept her hand out of sight, taking a seat at the breakfast table. Then she pulled out a silk-flower lei and threw it at my head.

It caught half on, half off my face. "What's this?"

"It's a lei," she said with a grin.

I played along. "I know it's a lei."

"It goes with this." She brought out her hidden surprise and pushed a packet bearing Atlanta's most exclusive travel agent's logo across the table. I opened it to find first-class airfare to Hawaii, departing in three days, plus another ticket for a balcony stateroom on a three-week, round-trip cruise to Bali from there that included a week, carte blanche, at the most famous spa on Bali!

"Damn, Kat," I breathed out in amazement. "This must have set you back thousands."

She waggled her own tickets. "Tens of thousands, but I can afford it. And that's not the best part."

"What could be better than this?"

She giggled like a girl. "It's a Cougar cruise." Palms together, she pressed the sides of her hands to her lips. "Tons of gorgeous escorts to dance and do massages and eat with us and take us to see the sights."

I waggled my lei at her. "And maybe get leis."

Kat laughed at the double entendre, then lifted her eyes toward heaven for a heartfelt, "Thank you, Greg."

I laughed with her, feeling nineteen again. "Hallelujah and amen! But I think you're aiming that in the wrong direction."

I looked at the tickets. "This is going to ruin me for my life of poverty when I get back."

"Don't worry about that for now," she said, her eyes sparkling in her plain, unmadeup face. "For now, I want you to worry about doing a total makeover for me. I want face, hair, clothes, everything."

I almost jumped out of my skin. "Hallelujah! At long last!" I could hardly wait to get my hands on her. "When?"

"Tomorrow?" she said. "Cash on the barrelhead. Give me the works."

I'd have to call Adrien at my favorite salon for the cut and color. Nothing drastic, just bring back her natural shade, then cut off all those thinning ends. "Just you wait," I promised. "You are gonna knock 'em dead."

Kat tucked her chin with a mock scowl. "Do me a favor. Don't mention knocking 'em dead, okay?"

Oops. "Sorry."

Arms wide, Kat gripped the side of the table. "Okay, then. Where do we go first?"

"How about shopping?" This was going to be *fun*! "Am I gonna pick a great wardrobe for you."

Kat stood up. "Now that I'm not going to prison, I am ready to be *gorgeous*!"

I grinned, my mind spinning with possibilities. "You will be."

Kat picked up her purse and headed for the door. "But for now, I'm going to go home to get a good night's sleep, now that the electric chair isn't hovering above my bed anymore. We can go shopping tomorrow at ten, okay?"

"Ten's perfect." I accompanied her out, then went back to the kitchen to call the salon and the personal shopper at Saks and Macy's and Nordstrom. When that was done, I called my girls to tell them about the cruise and Kat's exoneration.

They were thrilled, especially Emma when I told her how Bill had helped, and how proud and grateful we were.

I waited to call Mama last.

"Hey, Mama," I said. "How are you?"

"I'm great. Won twenty dollars in the slots," she said cheerily. "What's up?"

"The police cleared Kat, and she got double indemnity from the insurance company, since they ruled Greg's death an accident."

Mama actually laughed. "Well, good for her."

I recognized the voice, but not the graciousness.

Pleased that she hadn't said something negative, I told her about Kat's hiring me as her accomplice and taking me on the cruise.

There was a pregnant pause. "Y'all aren't leaving anytime soon, are you?"

"Three days," I said, wondering why she cared. "We'll just have time to shop and pack."

"Can you put it off a little?" Mama asked.

I tensed, wondering why she was trying to come between me and what I wanted, yet again. "Why, Mama?"

"Well," she said calmly, "I've been working on a special surprise for you for quite a while now, and it's finally ready."

Something more important than a cruise to paradise? I tried to keep the suspicion out of my voice, but heard it anyway when I asked, "What kind of a surprise?"

"Well, it wouldn't be a surprise if I told you, would it?" she snapped. "Just trust me. You'll want to be there."

"Well," I said, "I'm afraid it'll have to wait till we get back."

"Oh, all right," she said, clearly not happy. "Just try not to hate me when you get it," she said cryptically. "I gotta go. Talk to you later." She hung up.

Mystified, I stared at the phone, then hung up and went to assess my wardrobe for the cruise.

Twenty-four

The day Kat bloomed

I'd always known Kat would turn out beautiful if I could just get my hands on her. My only regret was that Zach couldn't be there to see it.

The next morning when she came for her makeover before we went shopping, I kept Kat's back to the mirror in the dining room while I used a sponge wedge and moisturizing concealer to cover the dark circles she'd had since the Greg thing. I applied an alabaster mineral-powder foundation to even out—but not erase—her freckles. Then I moistened a sponge wedge with distilled water and used it to apply a subtle glow of mango stain on her cheeks. Some mango lip stain brought her perfectly shaped, but washed-out, lips into focus. Then I rimmed her eyes with a warm brown liner, then used a soft brush to add depth to her outer lids and brow arch with a subtle, smoky brown shadow. The same shadow, lightly applied to her brows, made them visible, but not overpowering.

Then I did her inner lids with a brightening shadow, blending it in where it met the brown.

Presto. The girl had eyes! But they needed the finishing touch to really set them off. "Okay," I told her, bracing myself for a struggle. "Time for some mascara."

Kat tucked her chin like a kid facing a spoonful of tomato aspic. "Do I have to?"

"If you want to be beautiful, yes," I said. I opened the dark brown mascara, then coaxed, "Just keep your neck straight and look down, so I can do the tops of the lashes. Once we get that done, you can look up, so I can do the bottoms." From her tense posture, I knew this wasn't going to be easy. "Ready?"

How could somebody get this old in America without ever wearing mascara?

Kat straightened her neck and looked down, but every time I got near her lashes, she started blinking furiously. I backed off, and the blinking stopped. I moved in, and it cranked up again, fast as a hummingbird's wings. "Try to relax," I told her.

"I'm tryin'," she said, her cracker accent deepened by the stress, "but it's a protective reflex to tense up. Things aren't supposed to git so close to yer eyes."

"Why don't you try closing your eyelids all the way?" I suggested. "I can still do the tops that way."

"Okay," she said with obvious reservation.

I tried to swoop in quickly, but as soon as I got close, her lashes started fluttering.

"Kat," I scolded. "Just keep them closed."

She glared at me with those green eyes—even greener now, thanks to my efforts—and snapped, "I cain't. I can feel you comin' with that poky-lookin' thing, and it just happens. I have no control."

"This is why teenagers need to learn to put on makeup," I muttered. "Sit tight," I ordered. "And do not look at yourself in the mirror. I want you to wait for the full effect."

"Where're you goin'?" she asked.

I pointed my finger at her. "To get you some holy spirits."

Kat straightened. "Since when did you become a Pentecostal?"

"Not 'Spirit,'" I corrected on my way into the kitchen, "'spirits,' plural, as in 'communion wine.'" Uncut, a few sweet sips of that stuff should do the trick. It had to be ninety proof.

I headed for the pantry.

"But it's only ten in the morning," Kat protested from the dining room.

"Just consider it necessary anesthesia for a cosmetic procedure," I told her as I got out the wine and poured a generous slosh into a brandy snifter. "This is really nice for sipping." I poured myself a taste in another snifter, just to make sure it was as strong as I remembered. Wowser, was it ever. I couldn't feel my lips.

I went back into the dining room and handed Kat her snifter, with a cheerful, "Drink up."

Kat eyed the wine with suspicion. "I don't think it's wise to get snockered before I go shopping for a new wardrobe, then get my hair cut by a total stranger."

"Not to worry," I told her. "Adrien's the best with cut and color in Atlanta. He'll make your hair look better than it ever has, in a way that suits you. As for the wardrobe, all you have to do is try things on. I'll be there to help you pick out what looks best on you."

Kat frowned, one eyebrow cocked. "Okay. I'll trust you, but you've gotta *swear* you won't make me look like a Republican."

"How about Libertarian," I suggested, evoking a brief chuckle.

"Good one," she said, "but khaki. I don't do khaki."

"Okay. No khaki." Not a good color for her, anyway. "And no tennis outfits or dark suits." I noted she hadn't tried the wine. "Come on, drink. We need to get this show on the road."

She did, and her eyes widened. "Wow. Sweet. And strong. I like it."

"Good." I patted her shoulder. "Let me know when you start to feel it."

"Okeydokey." Kat kept on sipping.

Young. She looked so much younger than I did, which stung a little, but I was proud that I'd been the one to bring out her beauty. She could pass for a coed. Gorgeous, gorgeous, gorgeous.

And tipsy. Kat let loose with, "Whew, thass *really* strong. I cain't feel my nipples."

I laughed. Perfect timing. "Okay, then," I said, "let's try the mascara again."

This time, Kat didn't spasm, so I managed to get the medium brown mascara on her thick, pale gold lashes in a few strokes. For the first time since I'd met her, Kat's lashes were visible, setting off her eyes without looking harsh or made-up. Her green eyes sparkled and looked enormous, and her face had a healthy glow.

"Okay, almost ready," I said.

Kat responded with a huge yawn.

"Just let me French-braid your hair for the meantime."

Before I could finish with her hair, Kat started nodding and sank lower in the chair, but I skooched her back up till I was done. I secured her braid, then pulled the towel from around her shoulders with a flourish and announced, "Kat, stand up, turn around, and meet the new you."

"Okay, but I'd better not look like some Stepford wife," she muttered thickly, "or a hooker." Wavering slightly, she rose to face the mirror. When she saw herself, her expression went slack with amazement. "That can't be me! She looks like a movie star."

"It is you," I said. "Now get your purse and let's go grab some protein at the Waffle House, to sober you up before we go shopping. We're behind schedule."

Kat couldn't tear herself away from her reflection. She moved closer, her hand touching the mirror. "I look beautiful," she said in awe. "Really, actually beautiful." When she recovered herself, she grabbed me and planted a huge kiss on my forehead. "Thank you, thank you, thank you! If I'da known this was how I'd turn out, I'da let you do this years ago."

That's what I'd been telling her, but I spared her the "I told you so." Instead, I said, "Well, I'm really glad you finally trusted me. Trust me a little more, and we'll get the rest of this makeover done today." I looked into the mirror and used the towel to remove the perfect mango kiss-mark from my forehead. "You're gonna knock 'em dead on that cruise."

Kat snorted. "Not me. *We*."

I stood beside her to assess our reflections, then laughed. Kat looked thirty years younger than I did. "Whatever. Now get into my car, so we can get to Waffle House, then complete the transformation."

True to form, Waffle House offered quick service with Kat's coffee, three eggs over medium, double order of bacon, raisin toast, and hash browns. Fifteen minutes and fifteen thousand calories later, we headed for the Lenox-Phipps shopping district in Buckhead. (None of those pricey designer boutiques between East Andrews and Paces Ferry.)

First, I took her to Nordstrom, where her personal shopper measured Kat's petite frame every which way. (I'd promised the woman a huge tip, so she was really sucking up to Kat.)

"We're looking for cruise wear," I told her. "Nothing too trendy"—translation: no "maternity" tops or balloon minidresses—"or loud prints. Just good, classic lines that show off her figure discreetly, in colors that work with her eyes and hair. We'll jazz them up with a few . . ." How could I describe it? Aha. " 'Free spirit' accessories."

"But no Republican matron stuff," Kat chimed in.

"I know exactly what you're looking for," the shopper said. "I can pull it all together by three. And I'll have alterations here to do whatever needs doing, available day after tomorrow."

I frowned. "We're flying out day after tomorrow. But we're willing to pay extra to get it done by tomorrow."

The woman didn't miss a beat, dollar signs sparkling in her eyes. "I can call in some extra seamstresses, so we'll have the alterations finished by close of business tomorrow."

I tell you, money does the trick. "Perfect."

Kat leaned close and whispered, "Lord knows what they'll charge me fer those seamstresses."

"Trust me, it'll be worth it to have your clothes fit right." I sent the shopper to work while we went to Saks, Macy's and Neiman's and repeated the process. Then we headed to the salon, where Adrien put some rich, believable red lowlights into Kat's hair, then did a deep conditioning treatment. Last, he gave her a blunt cut about six inches below her shoulders, then styled it smooth and wavy with a huge curling iron. The result was shiny, glamorous, and beautiful.

Proud of the results, Adrien unplugged the huge curling iron, then handed it to Kat, along with a big bag full of enormous self-clinging rollers. "These are for you. A bon voyage gift."

Good. I'd sent him so much business, he was overdue a lagniappe.

Staring at her newly gorgeous hair in the mirror, Kat had another session with her reflection, then kissed Adrien and paid the bill, including a hundred-dollar tip!

Then we had to hurry to see what the personal shoppers had found for Kat. Back at Nordstrom, the clothes were all hanging in a huge bridal dressing room, along with a minibuffet, complete with champagne and two glasses. "Ooooh. Very nice things. Let's see how they look on you."

"Okay," she said, but frowned at the outfit I was putting together.

I took her arm and whispered so the shopper and the alterations lady couldn't hear, "I know it's going to feel awkward wearing more form-fitting clothes, but I promise, you'll look like a lady, not a tart. You'll feel safer, more confident, once you've gotten used to your new look."

Kat exhaled heavily. "All right. Bring it on."

I loved many of the clothes the shopper had picked out, but Kat balked at a lot of them. Meanwhile, the seamstress hovered, pinning the clothes so Kat could see what they'd look like, tailored to her petite frame.

I was beginning to worry if we could get this done in a day, so I shifted tactics. "You need to rest a minute," I told Kat. "Come eat something." I got her some chicken salad and smoked salmon on toast with sour cream, then poured a flute of champagne and set it on the little table between the two upholstered chairs.

Kat started eating, then washed it down with champagne—just enough to take the edge off her stubbornness, so we could come to a compromise and buy a lot of what she needed for the cruise.

Then we moved on to the other stores.

By nine o'clock that night when everything closed, we'd decided on a very nice wardrobe for home and cruise.

"Are you gonna do my makeup tomorrow?" she asked as we merged onto I-400 north.

"Sure. But I want you to start learning to do it for yourself," I answered, navigating the heavy traffic.

Kat shook her head. "I don't know if I'm ever gonna be able to put that poky mascara brush so near my eyes."

I chuckled. "Well, you can't get smashed every day just for that. Trust me, it'll be a lot easier when you do it yourself."

"I'll try," she said, "but I cain't guarantee anything." She yawned, long and wide. "What're we doin' tomorrow?"

"Going to Ulta to get you your own makeup," I said, "then picking up the clothes and packing. No time to waste; we have too much to do."

"Works for me," Kat said.

We didn't get a lot of sleep in the next two days, but despite the usual travel glitches, we made it to our flight on time, passports in hand, and boarded our seats in first class. Greg had always been too cheap to fly any of us first class, so I really enjoyed getting the royal treatment and having all that leg room.

Once we were airborne, Kat and I talked about what we were going to have done at the Bali spa, but neither of us brought up what we planned to do with the escorts on the cruise, which suited me fine. Assuming they were willing to offer extracurricular activities, which was assuming a lot.

I'd been happily single and celibate for a long time, and I didn't want to end up a headline on the *National Enquirer*: SIXTY-YEAR-OLD WOMAN CONCEIVES ON COUGAR CRUISE AND GIVES BIRTH TO TRIPLETS. Or worse still: SIXTY-YEAR-OLD WOMAN CONCEIVES TRIPLETS AND GETS FATAL SEXUAL DISEASE ON COUGAR CRUISE. FATHER JUMPS SHIP. So I planned to bask in the escorts' attention, but leave it at that.

As for Kat, I didn't know and didn't want to. Some things are best kept discreet.

Once we settled into our flight, Kat and I were both so worn out from getting ready that we slept most of the way to L.A., then ate in the secure area while we waited for our flight to Hawaii.

Once we were settled in the ministateroom on the megajet, we both conked out a fourth of the way to Hawaii and didn't wake up till the flight attendant announced we were approaching Honolulu.

Stiff, cranky, and jet-lagged, Kat and I spoke in monosyllables till we collected our stuff, then waited to disembark. Her mascara smeared, Kat looked like a raccoon with its finger stuck in an outlet, so I took her straw hat and sunglasses from her carry-on, then handed them to her, with, "Put these on till we can find a place to clean you up."

Kat jammed the hat on her head, then glared at me as she put on the sunglasses. "There. Do I look socially acceptable enough to be seen in your presence?"

"Whoa." I retreated, palms up. "I am doing this for you, not me. I just want you to look your best when you go aboard."

Kat sniffed. "Well, okay."

The flight attendant came to our door. "Thank you for flying Jumbo Airlines," she said. "You may now exit the aircraft."

We took the stairway to the tarmac, where we were greeted by hula girls who gave us real, live leis. The air was perfect, clear and about seventy-eight, with a soft sea breeze. I breathed it in deeply and felt revived, but still crabby.

"Mrs. Callison?" a ground attendant said as she pulled an electric cart up beside us.

"Yes," Kat and I both responded at the same time, then laughed.

The attendant's cheeks colored. "If you'll hop on, I can take you ladies to meet your cruise's representative." She checked her clipboard. "That's Ultimate Cruises?"

"Yes," we answered in unison, again. Love that VIP treatment.

The attendant smiled as we got onto the cart. "You're going to love it. It's my very favorite cruise line in the world. Only three hundred passengers, but five-star, all the way."

She drove us inside then down the corridors, then through the security doors to the greeting area, where a tall, dark, and handsome man in a black uniform and cap was holding up a sign with the ship's name, then ours.

"Aloha, ladies," the driver greeted in a smoky accent I couldn't place. "Please follow me." He took us to the limousine parked at the curb, its windows open to the breeze, and a silver wine bucket chilling champagne between the two facing rear seats. The driver handled our luggage, then took us to the ship, where we were welcomed like long-lost relatives.

I worried that our ship was so much smaller than the megaliners moored beside it, but when the handsome steward opened the doors to our suite, all that went out the window.

"Kat, look!" A gorgeous living room offered a huge flat-screen TV across from a soft leather sectional, and a small dining table sat in front of the glass doors to the balcony. On either side of that, two spacious master suites provided every convenience we could possibly want, including huge soaker tubs.

"Wow," Kat said as we looked into her bathroom. "Like they say, you git what you pay for."

I couldn't wait to eat something wonderful, then try out my big, soft bed. "I'm gonna order in, then take a nap," I told Kat. "I'm still jet-lagged."

Kat rubbed her hands together. "Not me. I'm gonna scrub up,

then do my face and hair, then check out this little floating paradise."

"Have fun." I waved her off, dialing room service. "Hello?" I decided to test them. "I'd like to order a broiled lobster tail and some grilled asparagus. And some iced, decaffienated green tea with agave nectar."

He didn't bat an eyelash. "Very good, madam. May I suggest a nice rosé with that?"

"No, thanks. Just the decaf green tea and agave."

"We'll have that up in . . . thirty minutes."

Just enough time for me to take a long, hot soak to rehydrate myself after that long flight.

While I was doing that, I heard the luggage arrive. There was a quiet lull, then the steward asked through the bathroom door, "Mrs. Callison, would you like for us to unpack for you?"

Man, this was the life. "Yes, thank you." Then I went back to soaking and washed my hair. Guilty, I wondered how I was ever going to be grateful when I went back to my ordinary life on Eden Lake Court.

As it turned out, I discovered one very important thing very quickly on that cruise: I do *not* do nothing well.

Three days into the cruise, Kat came into my bathroom while I was getting ready for dinner. Standing behind my right shoulder, she frowned at our reflections in the mirror. "What's the matter?" she asked. "You don't seem happy."

"I'm happy," I said, not sounding convincing even to myself. How could I explain without hurting her feelings? I looked up at her image. "This is all fabulous, a dream. But I'm so used to working . . ." I shifted my gaze to the cosmetics I used to disguise my shortcomings. "I want to slow down and relax, really I do, but I don't know how." I turned to face her. "I really appreciate your bringing me, but I don't know how to do this."

Kat brightened. "You want work? I'll give you work." She pointed at me. "Stay there. I'll be right back."

What was she up to?

When she got back, she was carrying a dark blue velvet draw-string bag with my name embroidered on the front in gold. "I was gonna wait till we finished the cruise, but now works better."

She faced me squarely. "What would you say to being my partner?"

Taken aback, I hastened to clarify, "What exactly do you mean by partner? 'Cause if you've decided to switch to women after Greg, I sure wouldn't blame you, but I'm not—"

Kat burst out laughing. "Lord no. I don't want you to sleep with me. I just want you to help me keep up with all this money stuff, and my house, and all. And go with me on trips, because you're my best friend."

Boy, was that a relief. "Honey, I'd be happy to help you with that for nothing."

Kat grasped my upper arm, handing me the velvet bag. "You cain't live on nothin', so I intend to pay you, and pay you well. Yer worth every penny." She nodded at the bag. "Go on. Open it."

I did, and found a business checkbook with my name on it, D.B.A. Krazy Kat, with a balance of $100,000.

Smug, Kat pointed to it. "I am now a limited-liability corpora-tion, and you are CEO. This is your operatin' account. Use it to set up an office where Greg's used to be. Get all the equipment we need. If you need more money, just let me know. I already got a good CPA. You can pick our assistant."

"But Kat," I worried aloud, "what if we don't work well together? We're so different. I don't want this to come between us."

"It won't," she said, "I trust you completely, and I need yer organization skills and yer honesty to help me keep track of all my money, so I won't git scammed by some Birdie (!) Madoff. To keep my money insured, I've got accounts from Lawrenceville to Switzerland."

She definitely needed someone to look after her interests. But still . . . "What if I make a mistake," I said, "or do something you don't like?"

"We'll cross that bridge when we git to it," Kat said. "We'll talk it out. If you want to quit, there's a golden parachute, and we can go back to bein' just friends, but I sure hope that doesn't happen."

"I just—"

Kat's eyes narrowed. "Are you sayin' you *don't* want to work with me?"

"No, no," I backpedaled. "I'd love to work for you. I'm just afraid you wouldn't like it—or me—if I did."

"That's hogwash. You are officially hired." Kat reached into the bag and pulled out a folded printout from an online bank famous for their high-yield savings accounts. "Job pays in advance, three hundred thousand a year."

Stunned, I opened the printout and saw the notation of the initial deposit in just that amount, at five percent interest.

"Now let's go to dinner," Kat said. "I'm starvin'."

I started to put on my pink linen blazer, but she stopped me. "Now that you are my CEO, I think you need to dress up a little more. We're eatin' with the captain tonight, so I'd like to see you in somethin' sparkly."

I'd created a monster!

She went to my closet and came back with an elegant tuxedo jacket demurely studded with fake diamonds beside the lapels and on the cuffs. I'd bought it years ago at the Icing in St. Louis. "Now, this is more like it." Kat handed it to me, then produced a necklace box. "Here. You can borrow this." She watched me open it to reveal a necklace of diamond teardrops that would do a rani proud.

Holy crow! Had she lost her mind and gone Elizabeth Taylor on me?

"And don't look at me like that," she warned. "Those are real zircons, and necklaces like this are all the rage. I looked last night at supper."

Whew.

Maybe the other passengers were wearing zircons too. You never know.

"Okay, boss."

"I am not yer boss," Kat corrected. "We're business partners."

"Okay, partner." I changed into a black silk camisole that matched my slacks, then put on the necklace and jacket. "You're right," I told her with amazement. "It doesn't look tacky."

We were the belles of the ball that night. And for the rest of the trip to Bali, I kept myself busy making plans for the new office and thinking up trips to take.

One week later, on the Pacific, a hundred miles west of Hawaii

After being spa'd to smithereens in Bali, we were finally on our way back to Hawaii, but I had gotten spoiled, so I treated myself to a massage every day.

"Mmmm." Stretched out on the massage table on my stomach, every muscle in my body let go into blissful relaxation—except for the ones at the base of my skull. "Could you please do the neck-head joint?" I asked the Nordic Adonis with magic fingers.

"Uf course, madam." He started working the pressure point immediately.

"Oh, that feels *sooooo* good," I murmured.

His hands shifted to caress my fanny. "I could make madam feel even better," he singsonged in his Scandinavian accent. He kissed my shoulder, his hand sliding down my fanny where no man but Greg had gone before.

Grabbing the sheet, I whirled into a sitting position. "No. Thank you, no."

He peered at me, perplexed. "You do not like me?"

Flustered, I felt myself turning red from my toes to my temples. "You're very nice. And very sexy. I'm just not—"

He leaned back, a light dawning in his face. "Oh. You don't want man. You want—"

"No, no, no, no," I sputtered like Woody Allen in one of his first movies that were still funny. "I just want a massage. Nothing more."

He leaned in to whisper, "You not nun, are you?" He straightened with a sympathetic smile. "I do nuns. Plenty. Never tell."

Like a nun could afford this. I don't think so.

"No," I told him. "I'm not a nun. I just want a massage. No sex."

How crazy had the world gotten, that nobody could understand celibacy anymore, much less respect it?

Then it occurred to me why he suddenly was so aggressive. We were about to get off the ship, and he'd lose his chance to get a tip for "extras." "Before we leave," I promised, "I'll give you a nice tip."

Lord, I was paying *not* to have sex.

The masseur brightened. "Okay. Massage, no sex, big tip," he said cheerfully just as Kat walked into my room.

"What?" she asked in amazement.

I closed my eyes and let my head drop back. "I was really hoping to avoid this conversation."

"Could you please leave us now?" Kat asked him.

The masseur leered at her. "You want massage *wit* sex?" he asked her. "I free now."

Kat burst out laughing. "No, no massage with sex. No sex." She waved him away. "Now, go."

He picked up his gear. "You change mind, just call for Bjrn-stjerne."

No wonder I couldn't ever remember his name.

I watched him leave, then apologized to Kat. "Sorry you had to hear that."

Kat shook her head. "Don't worry. I'll let you in on a little secret." She glanced into the living room to make sure we were alone. "I didn't do it with anybody either."

"What?" I teased. "Wildwoman Kat?"

She sniffed out a short breath. "We both know that's pure nonsense. I tried free love before I met Zach, and it just felt like I was giving away important pieces of me for nothing. Once I knew what life was like with him, I could never make love to anybody I didn't care about and trust with both my body and my heart. I like the male attention here, but for these men, sex is just a job. Thanks to Zach, I know how amazing and spiritual it can be."

"You're lucky," I told her. "I never had that kind of sex with Greg. I loved him platonically, so our love life was hardly spectacular."

"You were good to him for a long time," Kat said. "Better than he deserved. Try to think about that, instead."

"You loved him better than I ever did," I confessed.

She gave me a sidelong squeeze. Talking about it was healing, somehow, but we didn't bring him up again.

The ship's horn sounded, and the intercom came on. "Ladies and gentlemen, we will be docking in Hawaii tomorrow morning. Our stewards are ready to assist you with your packing. Please let them know, and they are at your service."

All good things come to an end. Then the day came that I had dreaded. After two days in the air, we arrived at the Atlanta airport, and it was over. The cold felt sharp when we hurried out to our limo, and Atlanta was as noisy and polluted as it always had been, but now, I noticed it more.

By the time we pulled into my driveway on Eden Lake Court, it was afternoon. I kissed Kat good-bye in the limo, then showed the driver into the house with my bags. I tipped him forty dollars, closed the door on the stale air of my cold, empty house, and watched as he took Kat home.

Bed. I needed a long soak, then my own bed.

I was adjusting the taps when the phone rang. I hurried into the bedroom to pick up. "Hello?"

"Hey." It was Kat. "It feels really weird in this house all by myself, without the animals, even." We hadn't picked them up from the Pet Ritz. She inhaled a juicy sniff. "I got used to havin' you right across the cabin."

I could hear the letdown in her voice. "I'm just right across the street," I said. "You want to spend the night in Amelia's room?"

"Nah. I've gotta get used to it sometime."

"Well, just call if you change your mind."

"Okay. Bye." She hung up.

I had just taken off all my clothes and was adding bath salts when the phone rang again. Again, I hurried to answer in case it was Kat.

It wasn't. "Where've you been?" Mama scolded. "I was getting worried when I didn't hear from you when y'all landed."

"Mama, I just walked in the door, and I need to take a bath and soak, because long flights really dehydrate you."

She paused, then asked, "How long will that take?"

Why did she care? "I don't know. An hour?" When she didn't respond, I prodded, "Why do you need to know?"

"I've got that surprise for you, all ready for tonight."

The last thing I wanted was to unwrap some package before I'd even finished unpacking my suitcases, but there was a strange intensity in Mama's tone. "I'll finish and get dressed by five," I relented. So much for bed.

"I'll tell them six, just to be safe," Mama said. "Enjoy your soak, sweetie. I love you."

She sounded so normal, it scared me. "Mama, where are you?"

"In Phoenix with Claude," she answered.

"Is everything okay?"

She sighed, then said, "It's about to be, I hope. Just remember, your mama loves you."

"I love you too." I went back to my bath, soaked till all the hot water was gone, then put on a comfortable jogging suit and lay down on the bed to wait for the surprise to be delivered.

It was almost dark when the doorbell rang. I flipped on the porch light and looked out to see a tall, thin, white-haired man standing with his back to the door, his posture bent by the heavy weight of the large cardboard box in his hands.

I opened the door. "Yes?"

He turned, his face vaguely familiar as he studied me intently. "Elizabeth Callison?"

I nodded.

Where had I seen him before? Somewhere, but he'd looked different . . .

His eyes welled. "Betsy-girl, you sure did grow up, didn't you?"

What? What did he say?

His mouth tried not to crumple, but a tear escaped his familiar blue eyes as he choked out, "It's me, Daddy. Surprise."

I stood there frozen, stunned. *This* was Mama's surprise?

Daddy got a grip on himself. "Do you mind if I come inside? This is pretty heavy."

"Of course. Where are my manners? Come in." I led him toward the kitchen. "Please let me fix you something to drink."

"Nice place you got here," he said, standing there with the heavy box.

Nothing like your mother's hung unspoken between us.

"Thanks." What do you say to the prodigal father? "I'm afraid I took the opposite approach to Mama's. I'm crazy clean."

"Works for me," he said with a shy grin.

I moved a chair away from the kitchen table to give him easy access to the table. "Here."

He deposited the box, then sank into a chair. "Whew. Feels good to put that down."

I wanted to hug him, but felt awkward about it, so instead, I stepped over to inspect the box. It wasn't taped shut. "What's in it?" I prodded.

Daddy smiled and opened it up for me to see. "Take a look."

I stepped closer and saw that it was full of letters and snapshots, some of them brown with age. Hundreds, maybe thousands, of letters, neatly stacked. And they were all addressed to me in Daddy's slanty penmanship, with the addresses scratched through and "Return to Sender" written in Mama's handwriting.

All the air went out of me.

Return to sender? Mama wouldn't set foot out of the house for anything—but that. She'd gone to the mailbox to keep my father from me. *Return to sender.* And kept it from me all these years.

I felt like I'd been blindsided by a commuter train.

Daddy looked down. "I wrote you every day for six years, till they started coming back stamped 'No such person at this address.' So I wrote your mama, but I got the same thing." He glanced at me and sighed. "I should have made sure, but I was working twelve-hour days to pay your child support to the courts and save up enough to try for custody again. So I put it off till I got back Stateside, which kept getting delayed by another contract, and another. Sorry. Guess I let you down."

Overwhelming love and sympathy for my father battled a sucking vortex of hurt and betrayal aimed at my mother, and I baptized the evidence of Daddy's love with big, slow-falling tears that smeared the ink on the envelopes.

"Oh, Daddy," I whispered, "you have nothing to apologize for." My mother did, but she could apologize till eternity, and it wouldn't be enough.

"Betsy, look at me." Daddy met my reluctant gaze with a steady one of his own. "Don't go letting your mama spoil this." He could still see right through me, just as he always could. "We should be celebrating. If it wasn't for her, I wouldn't be here."

"If it wasn't for her," I said, the words shaking with bitterness, "I'd never have lost you."

"Don't think about that now," Daddy said with a calm I envied. "Think about me." He pulled an envelope from the box. "Here. Start with this."

I opened it as if it was a sacred thing, which it was. The date inside was November 23, 1962.

Precious Betsy,
We have two days off for Thanksgiving, but nobody around here
has any turkeys, so I am eating fire-roasted mutton with mashed
chickpeas and olive oil—with my fingers—in a Bedouin tent

made from handwoven fabric. The Bedouins weave their tents supertight and thick to keep out the wind and sand for generations. Beautiful handmade rugs cover the ground in deep reds and blues and caramel, and these, too, were made to last. They are the only color in this brown, desert place.

Though the Bedouins don't put down roots in houses like Americans do, they bring their heritage and traditions with them, in their close-knit families. Just like I bring you with me, in my heart, wherever I go even here, half a world away.

Though I haven't been able to contact you, I am still thankful that you are my daughter, and I think about you every day, wondering what you're doing and what you look like now. I pray that you won't forget me, and that I'll find you again someday, and you can read these letters.

Love,

Daddy

Poor Daddy.

And Mama. How could I ever face her again, now that I knew the full extent of the evil she'd done to both of us?

I boo-hooed.

"Aw, honey." Daddy got up and put his arm around my shoulders, drawing me into the chair beside his. "I didn't mean to make you cry."

His peace spread into me through the comfort of his sheltering arm, and I laughed through my tears. "These are good tears," I lied, "not bad ones."

Daddy wasn't fooled. He kissed the top of my head the way he used to when I was little. "Don't worry about me, sweetie. I've forgiven your mama. It wasn't easy, but she was sick, and terrified of being left alone. She did the best she could."

I'd believed that, too, before I found out the truth of what she'd done.

Daddy went on. "Now, thanks to Claude, she's back on track, taking her meds and doing the right thing."

For how long?

"She told me Claude took her with him to Al-Anon meetings," Daddy said, "and it helped her so much that she worked her way through the steps to the one where she makes amends for past wrongs. That's when she paid somebody to find me, then called to apologize for lyin' to you and the judge, and sendin' back all my letters." He tightened his embrace. "That's why I'm here. She's making amends to both of us."

Would he still be so gracious if he knew it all? "When you were packing to leave, Mama told me you had another family, one that wasn't crazy, so I let you go and hoped you were happy."

Daddy let out a low whistle, but maintained his composure. "There was never another family. And precious few women at work. I was so angry with your mama, and so obsessed with getting you back, that I ended up running off the few half-decent girls I met."

Was there no end to the lies Mama had told me? But I could spend all night bumping into that, and it wouldn't do a bit of good.

Daddy was back, and I meant to make the most of it. "I'm *so* glad you're here. How long can you stay?"

Daddy cocked his head. "Well, that depends."

Good. He didn't have a deadline. "Where are you staying?"

He shifted, uncomfortable. "Well, I haven't actually found a place yet. By the time I got through security and rented the car at the airport, then got stuck in traffic, I barely made it here on time."

I didn't hesitate. "Then you can stay here, as long as you want."

My father was back!

"Don't get up, Daddy. I'll fix us some supper." What did I have in the freezer? "Do you still like butter peas?"

He grinned, relaxing at last. "Love 'em."

My daddy was back! I had a million questions, but before I could ask them, the phone rang, and I flinched, fearing it was Mama, but it was only Kat. "Hey."

"Hey. Are you okay? I just saw that car parked in your drive-way, and I—"

"I'm fine. As a matter of fact, I'm fabulous. Thanks to Mama, which is an irony of galactic proportions, I am sitting here with my long-lost father."

After a startled pause, Kat exploded with, "Ohmygosh! What's he like? What does he do? Where does he live?"

I covered the mouthpiece of the phone and told Daddy, "My best friend Kat, who lives across the street, wants to know where you live and what you do."

Daddy exhaled heavily, his mouth flat, then confessed, "I used to manage a car factory, but the company went bust, taking our pensions with it, so now I am involuntarily unemployed."

Ouch.

"What's he saying?" Kat demanded.

"I'll tell you later."

Daddy didn't skip a beat. "So I lost my house," he went on, matter-of-fact. "Then the condo I was renting went into foreclosure. That's when your mother found me. Worked out perfect. So I packed up and came here."

"Betsy!" Kat scolded. "Tell me what he's saying."

For the first time in forever, I hung up on her. "Oh, Daddy. I'm so sorry you went through all that."

Then the most brilliant idea in the universe struck me. "It gets really lonely here by myself," I told him. "Would you be willing to try living here? I'll be traveling with Kat a good bit, and you could look after our houses while we're gone." A man had his pride.

Shame tightened his expression. "Darlin', that's a real generous offer, but you don't even know me. I couldn't just horn in on your life like that."

"Oh, yeah?" I challenged. "Who says? You know nothing about me either. Like how I butted in when I found out my ex was cheating on my best friend across the street, and she accidentally killed him, and it was all my fault? Got anything to top that?"

Daddy's eyes widened. "What was that again?"

"Infidelity, manipulation, and murder, to put it in a nutshell. But don't worry," I told him. "The DA dropped the charges, so Kat got double the insurance. Enough to hire me as her personal companion. Or accomplice, more accurately."

"And I thought *my* life was colorful," Daddy said wryly.

It might have been colorful, but he was still my beloved father, and that was all I needed to know. "Trust me, there's lots more where that came from. But if you move in, we'll have plenty of time to talk about all that. And about your two beautiful granddaughters, and your amazing great-granddaughter and grandson."

Daddy brightened. "Okay," he said, "but I have to warn you: I never lie, which can get awkward."

I closed my eyes with a grateful sigh. "Truth. What a relief *that* will be."

"You've got to promise you'll tell me the truth, too, if I ever do anything you don't like," he qualified.

"Done!" I stuck out my hand to shake, and he took it in affirmation.

We were hugging when Kat burst in—she has a key—wearing her new fur coat over flannel pajamas and big, fuzzy blue slippers, her hair like Medusa. "Don't tell me this is all over but the huggin'," she demanded. "'Cause if it is, I want an instant replay."

I laughed. "Daddy, this is my best friend, Mrs. Greg Callison, aka Kat-with-a-K, from across the street. She knows no boundaries when it comes to our friendship."

"It's about time you came back," she scolded Daddy as she shook his hand. "Betsy thought you were *dead*." She motioned to me. "And this is *my* best friend, Mrs. Greg Callison the first, who hung up on me just when things were getting good over here." She turned back to Daddy. "So fess up. What did I miss?"

Daddy winked at her, then came back with a sassy, "Betsy can tell you *her* secrets if she wants, little girl, but I'll hang on to mine."

Kat was captivated. "Well, aren't you the daddy?"

"Daddy just retired," I told Kat, "and I asked him to move in with me."

Kat sized him up. "You're not gonna try to come between us, are you?"

Daddy laughed, then told me, "I like her. She's a straight shooter."

"And a Democrat," I retorted.

Kat refused to be deflected. She folded her arms and stared at Daddy. "You didn't answer my question."

Daddy's eyes crinkled with smile lines. "I will *never* try to come between you."

I started to change the subject, but Kat raised a staying palm my way and asked Daddy, "Do you use drugs or alcohol, and how much?"

"Kat!" I glared at her, even though I was dying to know the answer.

"Just lookin' after you," she told me, then confronted Daddy yet again. "Well, do you?"

Daddy faced her squarely. "Clean and sober since 1991. I find life a lot better when I'm not under the influence."

It was true, I could see it.

"Good," Kat said. "That just leaves one more question."

Daddy and I braced ourselves.

Kat suddenly seemed very young, and very fragile. "I could use a father too. Do you think you could adopt me?"

Daddy pulled her to his side with one arm, and me with his other. "Works for me, as long as it's okay with Betsy."

"It's very okay with Betsy," I said without hesitation. The Daddy I knew had room in his heart for all of us.

Kat let out a long, relieved sigh, wiping her eyes free of tears, then pulled away and headed for the front door. "On that note, I'm goin' to go home to sleep for three days, and I don't want to hear a peep from either of you."

"Bye," Daddy and I said in unison.

When the door slammed, he motioned to a chair at the table. "You must be whipped. Sit down, and let me do the cooking."

My eyes widened. He cooked?

Of course he cooked. He'd fed me and Mama all those years, and it was good.

Thanks be to God. I got my daddy back, and he could *cook!* "That would be great."

While he was concocting something that smelled wonderful and singing country gold in the kitchen, I went to my little office and e-mailed Mama, thanking her for giving me back my father, and assuring her that I forgave her for what her illness drove her to do. (Okay, so the forgiveness part wasn't true yet, but I was working on it, so one day it would be.)

Mama e-mailed back with humble thanks, swearing that she would never, ever stop taking her meds again, a promise I prayed she could keep.

"Supper's ready," Daddy called, and I thanked God and my mama for bringing him home. And for the fact that I am now, officially, the highest-paid, happiest professional accomplice a best friend ever had. It doesn't get any better than that.

Turn the page for a sneak peek at
Haywood Smith's new novel

Out of Warranty

Available January 2013

One

Cassie

A fresh stab of loneliness sharded through me as I looked into my ten-times magnifying makeup mirror-of-the-awful-truth, trying to erase the ravages of grief with concealer for yet another day.

Old. I looked old and haggard.

I closed my eyes. *God, thank you for this day and my life, just as it is,* I prayed as a sacrifice of obedience, wondering how long it would be till I could mean it. *Help me, please. I can't do this without you.* That, I meant with all my heart. *I know your love should fill the hole Tom left in my heart, but it doesn't. I'm sorry, but it doesn't.* As always, I sensed God's consoling arms about me, but it wasn't enough.

Focus on today, I told myself as I did every morning, focus on gratitude, the blessings you have, not what you've lost, and you'll get through this. Think of Haley and Tommy, and Paige and precious Ethan and little Catherine. And Mama.

And the house: it was paid for, even though the taxes were ridiculous. And I had what was left of Tom's life insurance, and my widow's health benefits, even though they cost a fortune and didn't cover squat. Still, that was a lot more than some people had these days. And I had new knees and new hips and plates and screws that worked just fine. I needed to focus on that.

Instead, I focused on that honkin' huge zit beside my nose in the mirror.

There's just something so *wrong* about having zits and arthritis at the same time. I broke out the workout makeup, waterproof and thick enough to cover a doorknob, converting the zit to a mere lump that I hoped would be taken for a mole.

Thirty minutes later—dressed, made up, and coiffed—I braved the muggy July heat and left Juliette to do her business in the backyard while I went to the mailbox before heading to my appointment with the new ENT/allergist. In the mail I found a Chico's flyer, catalogues from Vermont Country Store and Harriet Carter, my bank statement, a notice from the Fulton County tax assessor's office, and an explanation of benefits from Green Shield Heath Insurance (or the antichrist, as I thought of them).

Always one to face the music without delay, I opened the bank statement first. Though I knew things had been a lot more expensive lately than I'd planned, I wasn't prepared for the closing balance.

Shoot a monkey!

Half a million dollars of life insurance had seemed like a lot till

I'd paid off all my medical bills, plus the refi and equity line we'd done in 2005, and the kids' student loans. I'd also bought a dependable hybrid minivan to last me the rest of my life, which I now suspected would be cruelly long. (Mama was eighty-nine and strong as an ox, in much better shape physically and mentally than I was. It would be just my luck to inherit her longevity along with Daddy's bad bones.)

I looked at the closing balance again and shook my head in mute denial. I was down to only two hundred thousand and facing more medical bills, plus property taxes out the wazoo, thanks to my location in what was now considered Buckhead.

Speaking of taxes, I switched to the letter from the assessor's office, hoping they'd reduced the value of my house to reflect the depressed market. Then I opened it and discovered that they'd reassessed the house, all right: they'd upped it by fifty thousand!

Based on what? Nothing but foreclosures and short sales had sold in our neighborhood for almost a year!

Shoot, shoot, shoot! My blood pressure shot up, making my pulse pound like an anvil in the July heat.

I would have contested the increase, but I didn't have the moxie, and Tom had always fought our battles for us.

Tucking the bank statement and reassessment under my arm, I wheezed as I walked back up the gentle slope of our short driveway. One more letter left to open.

I ripped the end off the explanation of benefits. For thirteen hundred dollars a month, plus a two-thousand annual deductible and out-of-pocket, my Green Shield PPO should at least cover sixty percent of the four thousand dollars plus I'd spent on tests and IV treatments at the holistic intern's. Never mind that all I'd gotten for my money was some validation and a referral to the ENT/allergist I was seeing that day.

I unfolded the EOB, scanning from the doctor's out-of-network fees to the zero fee adjustment, to the zero payout. Patient responsibility: $4,267.53.

What was with *that*? I'd already met my out-of-pocket for the year!

I looked at the code numbers beside the lab fees and treatment charges, then the key printed at the bottom. Disallowed: not standard medical practice. Disallowed: not standard medical practice. Disallowed. Disallowed. Disallowed. Followed by the fatal: nonnegotiable.

The antichrist had shafted me completely, not even applying any of it to my deductibles or payout ceiling!

I got so mad, I almost hyperventilated.

Criminal. The insurance company was criminal. And they knew I couldn't go elsewhere for coverage. Nobody would have me. I'd spent well over fifteen thousand just on coverage in the year since Tom had died, and that didn't even include dental or optometrist. And this was what all that money had bought me?

Afraid I might stroke out, I shepherded Juliette back into the blessed cool inside the house. I dumped the mail, then put her away in my bedroom.

Blasted crumby coverage, but what was I supposed to do? I couldn't go uninsured, and it was 2012, so I didn't dare opt for Obama's high-risk pool because of all the court challenges.

"I'll be back later," I called to Juliette through the door. Not that she cared. She slept all day on her pink bed stuffed with cedar chips.

Some company.

On the way out, I grabbed my purse and keys from their hiding place in the bread drawer. I activated the security system alarm, then headed for Dr. Patel's.

At least he was in network. The antichrist would *have* to pay at least seventy percent.

That's what I thought, anyway, before I heard the dreaded, "usual & customary treatment" loophole.

Fifteen minutes later, I drove up to yet another expensive parking lot entrance at yet another medical complex in Buckhead, so weak and depressed I could hardly sit up.

Rolling down the window to take my stub, I was smacked with a flood of heat and humidity that wilted me even further. Though I snatched the parking stub the nanosecond it appeared, the wretched machine scolded me with a loud, grating buzz anyway. Blasted machines. They'd leeched the humanity out of everything.

All the parking places within a thousand feet of the building were filled, and the lot sizzled in the sun.

I coughed heavily, rattling loose some of the "psychosomatic" gunk (according to the doctors at Emory, who had run a jillion tests, then referred me to a psychologist) in my lungs.

For some bizarre reason, the handicapped spaces were at the far side of the lot. Gasping, I pulled into one (with four joint replacements, you get a handicapped pass, and you need it), sicker than I'd ever been, and lonely to the bone.

Cursed Green Shield.

I got out of my car into the hazy heat, then trudged to the atrium lobby, arriving breathless and light-headed. The elevators—of course—were on the far side of the atrium. Whoever designed this place must never have been sick and alone.

When the elevator doors finally opened, I stepped inside and pressed three as a young mother with a stroller whipped in beside me.

I looked at the child in the stroller. "What a cutie." I studied her big, black eyes and was rewarded with a deeply dimpled smile. "What floor?" I asked her mother.

"Five, please," her mother said with a grateful nod.

"How old is she?" I guessed nine months.

"Nine months," the mother said proudly, bending to stroke her daughter's fuzzy halo.

Bingo. "I have a three-year-old grandson and a ten-month-old granddaughter."

"That's nice," the mother said, clearly not interested.

Embarrassed by her dismissal, I realized I was officially one of those old ladies who bothered perfect strangers in the elevator. Shoot.

At the third floor, I waved to the baby as I got off, then headed for the main corridor. But a familiar bladder sensation caused me to back up and detour to the ladies' room. After four bladder tacks, the last of which was failing, I agreed with George Burns: "Never pass up a chance to pee." The rest of the quote was X-rated, but I agreed with most of it, too, except the sex part.

The last thing in the world on my mind was sex.

After finishing and washing my hands, I braved a series of hallways that seemed to be numbered at random, in search of my doctor's office.

The Web site had provided directions to the address, but it should have given me a map of the maze inside. Hopelessly confused, I halted briefly, lost.

Maybe it was a sign that I shouldn't go to this new guy. Save my money, go back to bed and not get up.

Then I started coughing again. Breathless by the time the spell ended, I steadied myself against the wall, seeing stars.

Maybe I should go to the doctor, after all, even though he might end up bleeding me for tests and start-up fees, pun intended. If somebody didn't help me, I was going to croak, no two ways about it. For all I'd said I wanted to die since the funeral, when it came down to it, I wasn't ready. I couldn't leave my son and daughter orphaned, and I loved my grandchildren to distraction. And what good would the money I had left do me if I croaked from my "psychosomatic" condition?

I decided to take the chance on Dr. Patel. So I'd end up in the poorhouse a few days sooner. At least I would have tried.

I turned down yet another hallway and discovered I'd been going in a circle.

Shoot!

Then I spotted a sign pointing toward a snack bar and set out to get directions, mustering up the last of my energy to put on a happy face for the world one more time.

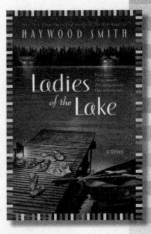